D0192791

SPECIAL MESSAGE TO READERS

THE ULVERSCROFT FOUNDATION
(registered UK charity number 264873)
was established in 1972 to provide funds for
research, diagnosis and treatment of eye diseases.
Examples of major projects funded by
the Ulverscroft Foundation are:-

- The Children's Eye Unit at Moorfields Eye Hospital, London
- The Ulverscroft Children's Eye Unit at Great Ormond Street Hospital for Sick Children
- Funding research into eye diseases and treatment at the Department of Ophthalmology, University of Leicester
- The Ulverscroft Vision Research Group, Institute of Child Health
- Twin operating theatres at the Western Ophthalmic Hospital, London
- The Chair of Ophthalmology at the Royal Australian College of Ophthalmologists

You can help further the work of the Foundation
by making a donation or leaving a legacy.
Every contribution is gratefully received. If you
would like to help support the Foundation or
require further information, please contact:

THE ULVERSCROFT FOUNDATION
The Green, Bradgate Road, Anstey
Leicester LE7 7FU, England
Tel: (0116) 236 4325

website: www.foundation.ulverscroft.com

Saskia Sarginson grew up in Suffolk, in the middle of a forest. She was awarded a distinction in her MA in Creative Writing at Royal Holloway after a BA in English Literature from Cambridge University and a BA in Fashion Design & Communications. Before becoming a full-time author, Saskia's writing experience included being a health and beauty editor on women's magazines, a ghost writer for the BBC and HarperCollins, and copy-writing and script-editing. She has four children and lives in London.

WITHOUT YOU

Suffolk, 1984: When seventeen-year-old Eva goes missing at sea, everyone presumes that she has drowned. Her parents' relationship is falling apart, undermined by guilt and grief. But her younger sister, Faith, refuses to consider a life without Eva; she's determined to find her sister and bring her home alive. Close to the shore looms the shape of an island — out of bounds, mysterious and dotted with windowless concrete huts. What nobody knows is that inside one of the huts Eva is being held captive. That she is fighting to survive — and return home.

Books by Saskia Sarginson
Published by Ulverscroft:

THE TWINS

SASKIA SARGINSON

WITHOUT YOU

Complete and Unabridged

CHARNWOOD
Leicester

First published in Great Britain in 2014 by
Piatkus
An imprint of
Little, Brown Book Group
London

First Charnwood Edition
published 2015
by arrangement with
Little, Brown Book Group
An Hachette UK Company
London

A catalogue record for this book is available
from the British Library.

ISBN 978–1–4448–2638–8

Published by
F. A. Thorpe (Publishing)
Anstey, Leicestershire

Set by Words & Graphics Ltd.
Anstey, Leicestershire
Printed and bound in Great Britain by
T. J. International Ltd., Padstow, Cornwall

This book is printed on acid-free paper

For Hannah, Olivia, Sam and Gabriel

PROLOGUE

It was April when I drowned, a month after my seventeenth birthday. We were out at sea when the sky darkened to black and a storm blew up out of nowhere. We worked fast to get the sails down and start the engine. At the tiller, Dad tried to hold the boat steady. The engine strained against huge waves, as we wallowed and rolled. There was a creak of fibreglass, and water washing over the deck. We'd never been out in anything as big. I should have been afraid. Except I didn't believe that I was going to die. It wasn't just that I had faith in Dad's sailing; I was angry with him, and my rage made me feel superhuman.

When the wave hit sideways I saw it from the corner of my eye: a wall of water towering over us. As it crashed down, the boom must have swung around and caught the back of my head, because I felt a blow against my skull, and I was falling, slipping across the tilting deck and over the side. I saw Dad reaching out, his hand opening in slow motion. Water closed over my head and there was nothing except darkness and cold.

It's odd, because I have no memory of waking, just of existing at a distance, hovering far above the ground. Moonlight spun around me. The universe was rich in stars, a great sweep of planets, and I floated with them. Below me I could see the white spume of breakers rolling onto a shore, a helicopter circling out at sea, and the lights of the village shining through the dark. I noticed a form lying on the pebbly beach: something thrown up by the waves. I couldn't make out what it was: a coiled wet rug perhaps, or a large fish. Looking again, I made out the curve of a hip, an arm thrown back, hair spread like seaweed. A girl, curled on her side, motionless.

An upright figure toiled into view: a solid shadow moving towards the dead girl, his feet rolling and crunching over the uneven camber. He jerked to a stop when he saw her, then lurched into a run, dropping to crouch beside her. I watched all this without any real interest. I felt detached and calm, with a lovely floaty sensation in my stomach, like the flicker of butterfly wings.

The man moved the girl's head and her neck fell back limply so that I saw her face and I was staring into my own features, darkened and smudged by the night, but definitely belonging to me. A distant voice in my head wondered at how strange it was to be up here and yet, at the same time, able to observe the details of my gaping mouth, teeth showing between slack lips, and my wet pointed eyelashes. I had a bruise on my cheek. I thought I looked peaceful. Empty.

I watched as the man hunkered over my body. He threw his head back and shouted something into the sky. He looked ridiculous, desperate. Then he put his hand on my chin, tilting it up and his fingers slipped into my mouth, stretching it wider. I wanted to leave the two humans there: the dead one and the live one. But it was as if I'd become heavier. I'd dropped down through layers of night sky, closer to the man. I noticed the curly depths of his greasy hair, an unravelling elbow in the wool of his jumper. Underneath the man's bent shoulders, I saw the girl's chest shudder, the rise and fall of her ribcage. My ribcage. He pulled me back with his breath. It hurt. With a shock I became aware of the clumsy alignment of bone and cartilage under my skin, the density of flesh. I was disappearing out of lightness, sucked back into myself, squashed into the crushing weight of my body.

I woke with him above me, his mouth covering my own. Rough, hot lips. My lungs burning inside my chest. His heat inside me. I struggled to gasp fresh air, raising myself onto my elbow; then I was retching and gagging. He sat back to let me be sick on the pebbles, salt in my throat, as an ocean flooded out of me. I was so cold. His hands were on my shoulders, fingers clenched tight against my wet jumper. He leant close, and I smelt musty clothes, unwashed skin. He whispered in my ear, 'Thank God I found you.' I struggled to understand. I was shivering so much I could hardly hear for the chattering of my teeth, but I thought he said, 'She sent you. You're mine.'

PART ONE

LOST

1

There are boys fishing for crabs off the quay. I stop dead in the sunshine, blinking and uncertain. Then it's OK because it's nobody I know. Just townie kids here for the summer holidays. They're squatting next to buckets, poking at crabs they've caught on lines baited with bacon rind, strangers with pale skin and funny accents.

It's low tide, so I sit on the end of the quay, swinging my legs over the edge. There's only a couple of feet of water around the slimy wooden base, clumps of brown bladderwrack tangling under the surface. Even if I was stupid enough to fall in, I'd be able to stand up, my toes squelching in the mud. It's already hot. The sky is clear, and there's a breeze strong enough to set masts clanking. Seagulls hover overhead, alien eyes swivelling for scraps of bacon fat, wings bright against the sun.

Ted, the quay master, walks by with a coil of rope over his shoulder and ruffles my hair with his thick hand. 'Not crabbing today, Faith, eh?' he says in a normal, friendly voice, but the look he gives me is like all the other adults' — full of pity for the little girl with the drowned sister. I concentrate on watching a plump boy hauling up his line, hand over careful hand, leaning over to

3

see if he's caught anything. There is a barnacled crab at the end, hanging onto the bacon with pincer claws. Just as the boy is about to reach out and grab it, the crab falls with a splash. Crabs that have been caught before know exactly when to let go, escaping with shreds caught in their cunning jaws. I watch the boy's face, how his mouth droops and his cheeks redden. He scowls at me.

I shut my eyes with a snap and turn away, telling myself to ignore him: sticks and stones. I begin to hum under my breath. *Hello Dolly, you're still glowin', you're still crowin', you're still goin' strong . . .*

The boats on the river flit past on gusts of wind. Red, white and brown sails flapping. It used to be Dad and Eva out there. You could hear him shouting from the shore. Mum said it was embarrassing. Dad has always had a temper. In a boat he was worse. Eva ignored him or shouted back, standing up to her knees in the river, Dad struggling with the ropes — 'Keep her steady, damn it!' But then they'd go off and by the time they came back, wind-blown and red-cheeked, they were smiley and pleased with themselves, talking about how they went past the island and out to sea.

Dad hasn't lost his temper since the accident. He can't remember what happened the day that he and Eva sailed into the storm. The boat capsized and Dad lost consciousness. He was fished out of the water by the coastguard but they never found my sister. The doctor says Dad's put up barriers in his mind and I know

4

that Mum is angry with him for keeping the barriers there when there are so many questions to answer. Eva's lifejacket was found floating in the waves. Mum keeps asking why he let Eva sail without it and Dad swears that she must have been wearing it. Dad has sold the boats, says he'll never sail again. I don't mind. I'm not a sailor. Capsizing was the worst. But they were Eva's boats too.

Still humming, I shade my eyes to stare at the island. It lies beyond the mouth of the river, about half a mile offshore. A long time ago it was connected to a spit of land that runs along the other side of the river. But tides and waves have worn the spit away. Without the boats, without my sister, there's no way I can go back there. It's private, out of bounds. When Eva and I landed we had to do it in secret. The island squats on the horizon, the pagodas sticking up like weird chimneys. I screw up my eyes against the glare and think about the last time I was there with her.

The boat flew over the water's surface, spray kicking up under the prow. Stars rose from the glittering river to break against my gaze. The sail strained, fat with wind. Eva, sitting at the tiller behind me, was already ducking her head ready for the swing of the boom.

'Hey Shrimp, going about!' she yelled and I released the jib. The dinghy turned and slowed inside the choppy waves. Then with a snap, the wind caught the sail again. I yanked as hard as I could, my fingers tight around wet rope and we were flying across the water towards the island. I wasn't frightened in a boat with Eva. She's a good sailor.

We sailed onto the gravelly beach. The boat made a crunching noise, stones grating against the hull, scraping the paint. Eva winced. Dad would be furious. We left the boat half-hidden, pulled up on the shingle, with a big stone over the anchor to keep her safe.

'Race you to the other side!' Eva called. It wasn't a fair race. She's seven years older than me and her legs are twice as long as mine. I followed her, slipping on mud, splashing through shallow rivulets and puddles. I was glad to be on land again, relieved by the feel of earth under my feet. The island slopes up from the shore, becoming stony and dry. Gorse bushes cling, withered and stunted, to the pebbly, windswept crest. And then the land falls away and there is nothing but the grey North Sea, seagulls wheeling and crying as if they're flying over the edge of the world.

Stripping off her shirt and jeans, Eva threw herself into the waves in her knickers and bra. I sat on the steep bank of pebbles, watching. I can't swim properly. I can manage a doggy-paddle if I have to, swimming with my head clear of the water, mouth open to gasp air. I'm frightened by the waves. Whenever I wade into the sea, they push me over and drag me across sharp stones, splashing salt into my eyes, knocking the breath out of my lungs. I come out covered in bruises. I hate getting wet as much as I hate being cold.

'You've got to stop being a wimp!' Eva

shouted. 'There's nothing to be frightened of. Just let yourself float. Let the waves do the work for you.'

She couldn't understand what it was like to be afraid of the currents or unseen fish slipping past her legs, or a wave taking her out to sea. When I was a baby, they put a lifejacket on me and tied a rope around my waist, letting me bob up and down at the end of the tether, believing that I'd learn to swim like Eva had. But I didn't. I screamed and cried until Mum or Dad hauled me onto dry land, blotting the wet from my face, frowning at me anxiously.

I shivered, watching Eva swim back and forth, battling through the big brown waves. Her arms gleamed as they powered up and over her head, pulling her along. She only swam for a little while. It was too cold, even for her. When she was swimming, her movements were exact and elegant, but it's impossible to walk on shingle barefoot with any dignity and it made me laugh the way she staggered out, hobbling and wincing over the stones, limbs jerking like a rag-doll. To pay me back she flicked water from her dark hair at me as she knelt down, panting, her clothes in her arms. I could feel her energy, bright as the drops of moisture on her skin. Eva seems more alive than other people.

She lay back on her elbows. It was just the two of us on the long deserted beach, as if we were the only ones left on a planet made of shingle, sea and sky.

'What a mess,' Eva was saying, gazing at the rubbish that had been thrown overboard: plastic bottles, yoghurt pots, corks and bits of rope and odd shoes caught up in twists of seaweed and driftwood at the tide-line. 'Honestly — sometimes I wonder why we love it so much.'

I followed her gaze. Sometimes really disgusting things like Tampax or nappies got washed up on the beach. But I couldn't see anything revolting. She'd taken a cigarette out of her jacket pocket and lit it with difficulty, cupping her hands around the match and turning her head away from the wind. Her fingers were pink-tipped and puckered by seawater. Inhaling deeply, she sighed. 'Maybe 'cos it belongs to us.'

The island didn't belong to us. It belonged to the Ministry of Defence. It still does. We were trespassing. Half the island is fenced off by trailing wire and ruined by derelict huts, crumbling roads, rolls of razor wire and the concrete pagodas. People say they were laboratories, used for atomic-weapon research. The project's been abandoned and the buildings lie empty and forbidden. I don't like them, especially the pagodas. It feels as though things inside watch you, although there are no windows. Blank walls stare. Eva's smoke made my nose itch. I turned my head away. She would be in trouble if Mum and Dad knew.

'Actually, nobody should own this place,' she continued, 'not even us. It's too wild to belong to anyone, isn't it?'

I lay on my front on the stones, turning my head to look at her. She wasn't bothering to dry herself or get dressed, even though her lips were violet with cold and her skin prickled with goose bumps. Her knickers had 'Monday' appliquéd onto them. She had all the days of the week, wearing them at the wrong times. Her attention seemed to be on the slow movement of the cigarette to her lips, and the lazy drift of smoke out of her half-open mouth. She was practising her technique.

'Watch out for the oil.' Eva nodded to a sticky patch oozing over the stones as she stubbed the cigarette out on a bit of driftwood. I moved my hand. My warts looked worse in the sunlight. I got my first one when I was five. A lump that grew on my knee after I'd grazed the skin. More came, like mushrooms sprouting overnight on my knees and hands. I hate them.

She pulled on her clothes and we started to make our way across to the far tip of the island, to where the seals basked. There was a dead fox near the gorse bushes and I squatted to examine the way his fur had come away in chunks, exposing rotting flesh. You could see the white of his bones pushing through, like the wreck of a ship surfacing. There were living things writhing inside him. They'd already eaten his eyes. Soon it would be picked clean. I wondered if I came back in a couple of weeks whether I could persuade Eva to let me take his skull home.

'God!' Eva turned away, putting her hands over her face. 'It stinks!'

Better to swallow this dead-fox smell, I thought, than nicotine fumes. Eva had changed. Her new interest in boys and cigarettes and parties blotted out other parts of her, making her behave like an idiot. She pretended she was afraid of spiders and dead foxes.

'Guess what?' she asked as we walked through the samphire towards the point. 'I've met someone.'

I was silent. The gulls were swooping low over the river and the tide was going out, boats turning the other way on their moorings.

'He's . . . different,' she continued. 'He's really cool. Cooler than any of the boys around here.' She examined her nails and glanced at me sideways so that I was flattered that she wanted to confide in me.

I scratched around in my head for the right question. 'Where did you meet him?'

She grinned. 'A club. In Ipswich. Mum and Dad thought I was staying with Lucy. He's from London. He's even lived in America. He's a musician. He's into gothic stuff.' She flushed and nodded as if this was important information. 'He's called Marco. I'm not going to tell Mum and Dad about him. They won't like him, just because he's older than me, and he's got a tattoo and dyes his hair black. His parents moved to Ipswich, but he hates it here; he's planning to go back to London.'

Thinking about him seemed to put her into a trance. She tipped her head back, squinting into the sky. 'The way he makes me feel . . . I don't know. It's like being drunk without drinking,' she said in a low voice. 'It makes me feel like anything could happen. Anything at all.' She grabbed my hands and began to dance the polka, 'One, two, hop and turn,' across the stones; and I was caught up in the whirling movement,

10

stumbling and turning with our hair flying out behind us. Her fingers gripped hard. The sky and the beach blurred into a Catherine Wheel of blues and greens. And we were in the centre of it — the bright, turning centre. My stomach lurched as we danced faster, my head reeling with dizziness. Breathless, we broke apart, falling back onto the shingle. 'Maybe I'm in love,' she said.

We lay panting, spread-eagled, gazing at shreds of cloud floating past, and the wheeling birds making shapes against the sun. I wondered what Eva and I would look like from up there, through a seagull's eyes, imagining us as fixed dots inside the hard shine of its stare. Eva clambered back onto her feet when the beach stopped spinning, hauling me up. A few moments later we'd reached the point, and I could see fat bodies on the mud. 'Seals,' I mouthed, pointing, and she winked.

Eva stopped. Her hair, dry now from the wind, blew in curls across her face. She looked serious. 'Promise on your life that you won't tell Mum and Dad about Marco.'

She spat into her hand, a splatter of slimy bubbles, and put it out for me to shake. We locked fingers and I felt the wet of her spit.

Dropping onto all fours, we crawled quietly through the bushy green, sharp pebbles biting into palms and knees. The wind was blowing towards us so we were able to get close enough to the seals to see their noses framed by whiskers like oversized cats. Their eyes looked as though they were filled with tears.

'Selkies,' Eva murmured.

'Do you think all of them are, or just some?'

'Ah, well, we can't know that,' she whispered. 'It's only at night that the seals shed their skins and become human.'

I'd heard this story lots of times. But I never tired of it.

'And then they become women,' her voice was dreamy, 'slipping out of their seal form, and dancing on the beach all night with their webbed toes. If one of them falls in love with a mortal, some handsome fisherman maybe, then she'll give up her seal shape and live as a woman.' Eva smiled at me. 'But her husband will have to hide her seal skin, or the sea will call her back.'

'We should come at night,' I suggested, excited by the idea, 'sail over to see them.'

'Are you brave enough?' She tilted her chin. 'We'd have to be careful not to be caught by the selkies, or by them . . . ' She jerked her head in the direction of the windowless concrete pagodas. 'God knows what crawls out of those places.'

I shivered in the sun. Eva's eyes were liquorice dark, just as I imagined a selkie's would be. Her fingers brushed against mine and she took my hand and squeezed it. She didn't mind my warts. Her head touched mine and I smelt nicotine in her hair and the tang of the sea.

* * *

I miss her.

I miss her even though she'd do her big-sister act of slamming doors in my face and telling me to piss off. Once she locked me in the cupboard on the landing for an hour. But Eva's bedroom feels lonely without her, without her clashing perfumes, tantrums and dance routines, Police and Culture Club turned up too loud on the radio.

She's been gone for three months.

A few days before the accident, I walked in to find her kneeling by her dressing table, hands clasped tightly in prayer. She'd closed her eyes. *Anything*, I heard her beg, *I'll do anything if you let me not have a spot this weekend.*

I snorted, clasping my hand over my mouth. Eva threw a hairbrush at my head. It missed. She's rubbish at over-arm.

'I don't think God cares if you get a spot,' I said, picking up the hairbrush. 'Hasn't he got wars and starving babies to worry about?'

'Warts?' she exclaimed, eyes round.

'No . . . ' I began to explain, but she'd already forgotten me.

Mum says one day I'll wake up and my warts will be gone. Until that happens, I keep my sleeves pulled down. I thought Eva might lose interest in her mirror and speak to me. I'd lingered in her doorway, the frayed cuffs clasped between my fingers, loose threads tickling my skin. But she only gave me an impatient glance.

I don't know why Eva kept checking her reflection. It stayed the same. She has a wide mouth in a square jaw and sloping cheekbones, slanted as a cat's. She glows a kind of dark gold, her skin shiny as polished amber. My complexion is thin and white as a piece of paper.

At first Mum wouldn't even pick up the tangle

13

of dirty clothes lying on Eva's bedroom floor, although later they ended up clean and ironed and folded in Eva's drawers. I go in there and stroke her ornaments, her china rabbits and the desert rose; sometimes I try on her string of water pearls. They gleam in my hands, and they seem to hold the warmth of Eva's skin. If I crumple her clothes into a ball and push my nose into the folds, I can still smell her. Once when I pulled her nightdress from under her pillow, I found one of her dark hairs stuck to the fabric.

I hate it when people talk about her because they use a special hushed voice, as if they're in church. They say she *was* this; she *did* that. But she didn't drown, I tell them. They shake their heads, and give me worried smiles, glancing away, embarrassed.

She's not dead. Not like Granny Gale, cold in a box under the churchyard. I miss Granny too. She used to live in a caravan in our garden. Missing her is a low ache inside my bones. The thing is, she was very old and she wasn't afraid to die. She told me that she'd been blessed to find love at her age, 'After more than forty years of being alone, imagine that,' she said. 'But nothing lasts for ever, darling. The curtain always comes down when the show's over.' Eva is too young to die. She's only seventeen and she's lost inside deep water, far from the surface, far from human voices. Missing Eva is a sharp pain that makes my heart beat too fast.

There are creatures in the sea: ancient things, beyond imagination and knowledge, unseen by people. When they looked up through the waves

14

and saw Eva's black curls and golden skin with no spots, they must have fallen in love, like a selkie catching sight of a fisherman. Everyone fancies my sister. The boys that hung around at the village bus stop called after her, letting out long whistles, and scratching her name onto the wood of the shelter with their penknives. Robert Smith followed her home from school. He hung around behind the hundred-year-old oak across the road, peering up at her window. I looked under the tree after he'd gone and there was a mess of fag ends and a hard pink ball of chewed gum. 'Pervert,' she said when I told her he was there. But she was laughing.

'Don't let it go to your head,' Granny Gale warned when Eva got five Valentine's cards. I didn't get any, except the one that Mum sent. She put it through the letterbox but she forgot to put a stamp on it, so I knew it was from her. Dad told Eva that she was too young for boyfriends. They argued about how many evenings she was allowed out a week and what time she could get back. 'It's like living in a prison!' she'd yell. And Dad kept telling her that if she worked hard at school she'd give herself choices, would make her world bigger. 'You've got the rest of your life for boys,' he said.

Dad's nickname for Eva was 'Duchess'. It was supposed to be a joke, because of her airs and graces; but Eva had a way of walking, as if there was a pile of books balanced on her head, and a habit of tossing her hair when she was annoyed, that made you imagine her in a long, swishy dress with servants scurrying behind.

15

The coastguard worked for thirty hours before calling off the search. There was a helicopter and boats. A month afterwards, Mum and Dad held a memorial service for her. The church was packed — people standing in the graveyard sobbing, trying to sing hymns with shaky voices. *O Christ! Whose voice the waters heard, and hushed their raging at thy Word.* The vicar talking about Eva from the pulpit: the tragedy of her short life. Other people getting up to read poems and tell stories about her, stopping to blow their noses, wiping their eyes. They didn't seem to be talking about my sister. It was as if she'd been too good to be true — like a saint. I stood in the pew at the front between Mum and Dad, unable to sing, the closed hymn book clutched in my hands, white flowers glowing in the dim light, shedding their sickly scent.

Eva, if you can hear me, I hope that you aren't cold and lonely. You must miss Mum and Dad, your Topshop jeans and your old teddy. I want you to know that I haven't given up on you. And I'm sorry for using your lipstick and drawing with it so that the end squished down into a stub. I love you, Eva. I will find a way to bring you back.

2

He didn't tell me his name for a long time. But one morning he said that it was Billy. It sounds soft and harmless in my mouth, a lilting whisper, two syllables like a bird-call. I told him my name at the beginning, because I remembered hearing somewhere that it's important to become a real person, to make your kidnapper see you as human. But he keeps calling me 'girl'.

Coughing up my guts on the beach, lungs on fire, I couldn't see who crouched over me. I was confused and weak and he was just a blurry outline, dark against dark. He hoisted me into his arms, carrying me like a baby. He was panting, struggling to hold me, his feet working inside the crunch of pebbles. I was jolted, my head bumping against his shoulder as he scrambled up a steep, crumbling slope. There was the slide and clatter of stones under us. And then more walking — this time on a flat surface. We entered a building, so black that it seemed as though I'd been blindfolded. He laid me down on the ground: fabric at my chin, a scratchy blanket itching me, rough against my face. I smelt musty air, and I remember thinking that I should ask where Dad was, and if he was all right, but I didn't have the strength.

When I woke in the dim wash of early morning, I thought I could hear the sea. I looked around, turning my neck gingerly to take in the windowless peeling walls. My head felt heavy, bruised. The waves seemed to be inside my skull, pounding against my brain. I stared, puzzled, at frayed and severed wires hanging loose and a grid of corroded pipes under the vaulted roof. It was some kind of derelict shelter. I felt a tick of fear. I knew that I should be at home or even in hospital and that this wasn't right. My breathing came fast and shallow. I moved parched lips and swollen tongue, trying to find words to ask for help, to find out where I was, to call for Dad.

A faceless creature loomed. His palm sealed my mouth, the pressure of his fingers stopping my scream. I stared into a pair of grey eyes, expressionless as stones. The rest of his face was wrapped in a blue woollen scarf. I shrank inwards, as if I could hide inside my skin, shrivelling inside damp clothes. 'Awake then?' The voice sounded low, muffled by folds of fabric. 'You thirsty?'

It was then that I realised my wrists were tied.

He doesn't bother with the scarf anymore. He doesn't need to. His hair obliterates most of his face. He has a thick, brown beard and moustache and matted, shaggy hair that falls into his eyes. I hate it when he gets close and I smell the unwashed stink. It makes me want to gag.

'Time to go in the hole.' He nods towards the crater in the floor. 'I've got to get provisions.'

'No.' My toes clench with resistance, my heart beating fast. 'I won't run away.' I've taken on the pleading tone that I despise. 'Please don't leave me down there . . . '

'Nah,' he shakes his head, a sly smile as if he's

18

amused, 'you've tried it too many times. Come here.'

He has rope in his hands, a thick coil. I've backed into a corner. A broken metal rod sticking out of the wall pokes my back. There is no point trying to fight him, trying to struggle. Under the beard and the filthy clothes, he's young and strong, taller than me. Maybe even as tall as Dad. He carries a knife at his belt. He told me that he used to be a soldier; he's been trained to kill people. He has killed people. When I tried to slip past him before, he got my arm behind my back and the blade against my neck in one slick movement, pressing the sharp point into my skin, so that I felt my blood pulsing against it.

I wait in the corner. I've got nowhere to go. He's too fast for me. 'Please.' I try to sound reasonable, but my voice is a hoarse whisper. 'Please, Billy.'

He jolts when he hears his name. With a quick mutter, head down, he grabs my wrists. He secures the rope around my waist and then his own. Bracing himself, he nods to me, telling me that I should step backwards off the edge, so that he can lower me into the pit. Billy says that it was used for storing atom bombs. We are in one of the concrete pagodas on the island. Once I'd worked it out, I could see that the high vaulted roof with the glassless gaps between pillars, the odd metal casings and derelict equipment all made sense.

Whenever Faith and I came to the island, it never occurred to us to go inside them. There are warning notices next to the lines of barbed wire

19

telling people to keep out — to stay away from the unexploded landmines hidden under the pebbles in that half of the island. And I knew what the interior of the pagodas had been used for, so I suppose I'd thought the air would be tainted, poisoned by the fumes from bomb experiments.

My feet slip against the concrete wall; the rope digs into my waist. I hold onto the hairy, coarse twist of it tightly with both hands. It's about a ten-foot drop below me. Bruising my knees, scrabbling for control, I abseil slowly into the dank hole. As soon as I'm standing on the bottom, Billy indicates that I untie the rope so that he can pull it up. He throws down a plastic bottle of water.

I am rigid with a familiar fear. The tall, steep sides are scratched and pockmarked. They hold darkening shadows, heavy with stale air. There is nothing down here except rusting tin cans, bottle tops and broken glass, bits of screwed-up paper and a three-legged chair that the army must have left behind. Far above me I can hear Billy moving about, and then his footsteps as he leaves. He calls back, 'Won't be long. Don't go anywhere.'

They are new, these unexpected flashes of humour. They're cruel, I suppose, sarcastic, but it's an improvement. The first time he left me here he didn't say anything. I'd struggled against him when I realised that he'd wanted to put me in the crater. He'd bruised my arms forcing me in. I'd stumbled, swinging from the rope onto the bottom of the pit, scraping my cheek against

20

the rough sides. Staring up at him, I'd been certain that he was going to pull out a gun. I'd closed my eyes. Numb. Cold. There was nowhere to run. Nowhere to hide. Against my shuttered lids I'd seen flash after flash of snatched memory, a lifetime passing in the gabble of a speeded-up film. When I'd opened my eyes, he'd gone. I realised then that he could kill me without pulling a trigger. All he has to do is leave me here.

Even now that I know I won't be in the pit for more than a couple of hours, it's still unbearable. It smells of old urine and metal. Claustrophobia presses in, and it feels as though the narrow space is shrinking, the walls leaning in closer, squeezing the life out of me. Panic that something will happen to him and I'll be left here for ever scrabbles inside. Nothing will make it go away. I feel sick with anxiety. The helplessness of it carves out a hollow in my stomach. I crouch on rubbish, my back resting against the wall and close my eyes. I can hear the faint wash of the sea, looping cries of seagulls as they fly above the flat roof of the pagoda. Sometimes a bird will get in by mistake and flutter about in confusion, dropping acrid splatters of green and white.

The walls are straight, the pockmarks only big enough to slip a fingertip inside. I tried to scrape out toeholds with the jagged edge of a tin can that first time he left me and sliced my thumb by mistake, blood oozing in bright threads around my wrist. Another time I screamed until my voice cracked and broke, my throat stripped sore, so that I spoke in a husky whisper for days afterwards. 'There's no one to hear you,' he'd said, standing at the brink of the hole, hands on hips. 'Scream all you like.' Now I wait quietly, listening. But there are only the sea birds and the sound of wind and water. I remember that just after he found me there was a rush of helicopter blades above the pagoda and the sound of distant voices. I think they were searching for me, for my body on the shore. I know they've given up because those sounds haven't come back.

Against the dirty wall I see pictures of Dad and Mum and Faith. I tell myself that Dad is alive. That he didn't drown in the accident. He had his lifejacket on and he's a good swimmer. A very good swimmer. I have to believe he's OK. He's alive and at home, looking after Mum and Faith. Thinking of the three of them together makes me feel stronger, but I'm afraid of forgetting what they look like so I keep sketching their faces in my mind. I wish I had a pencil and paper. Instead, I pretend, frowning over details of exactly where a mole is placed, the shifting colour of an iris, the way hair falls across a forehead. I imagine scenes in my head, replaying Faith dancing around the kitchen table, her skinny limbs suddenly fluid; Mum curled in a chair, engrossed in a book; Dad pulling the sails down, wind in his hair. I think of Silver, his fur soft under my fingers, his doggy nose pressed into the palm of my hand.

And then there is food: food that I haven't smelt or tasted since I've been here. The food I used to leave at the side of my plate, turn my nose up at when I thought I needed to lose a bit of weight. I think about it all the time. My mouth watering at the idea of roast chicken, the flesh aromatic with butter, skin crispy and golden; imagining my favourite chocolate ice-cream, ice particles glinting inside creamy scoops. I wish for slices of brown bread spread with strawberry jam. Glasses of orange juice freshly squeezed, pips floating inside liquid the colour of the sun.

Billy said that I was sent to him. Before he came here, after he'd stopped being a soldier, a voice told him to come to the island. He'd had a dream about a girl. He would save her life and then he must keep her until a purpose was made clear.

What purpose? I'd been too afraid to ask. It sounds mad to me. Insane. I don't believe him. There must be a different reason for him taking me. But he hasn't mentioned money. When I told him at the beginning, 'My parents aren't rich, they can't pay a ransom,' he'd laughed. A short, rasping laugh. If he notices that I'm crying, he looks puzzled. Once he dropped a hand onto my shoulder. 'I saved you,' he said, as if that explained everything.

He is often angry. The second day here, I tried to make a run for it, and he grabbed me round the neck, throwing me backwards so that I banged my coccyx, bruised my leg. Mostly he turns his fury on himself: he hits his head against the wall and pulls at his tangle of hair, yanking clumps out, tufts sticking between his fingers like brown grass. When he is sick of me he binds my

23

ankles and wrists tightly, tells me to *shut it*. He made me sleep like that in the beginning; he still does sometimes if I've annoyed him and then the blood pools in my hands and feet, turning them blue and senseless. He has nightmares. Lying awake, I listen to him across the room. He screams and shouts words that I can't make sense of. My heart leaps, scared that he'll wake up and hurt me. He hasn't really hurt me though. Not yet.

★　★　★

He leans over the edge of the pit, leering down, and I'm glad to see him, relieved that he hasn't been arrested or knocked over by a car, or taken by the sudden notion not to come back. He holds the body of a rabbit by its ears. It swings above me, legs loose and dangling. 'Got her from the trap on my way over.'

Out of the pit, I shake and flex sore fingers, prodding at my waist where the rope has cut in, wincing at my bruised skin. He ignores me. He thinks I'm making a point. He squats on the dirty floor, pleased with himself, the returning hunter. He has refilled the plastic containers with fresh water, and has brought back two courgettes and some carrots. He must get across to the mainland to acquire these things, so he has to have a boat hidden somewhere. I think about where he could have left it. Finding his boat is my best bet, the surest way of escaping. Swimming might be possible, but the currents are strong. I've never swum that far. Anyway, we keep to the side of the island that looks out across the open ocean, staying away from the side that is in sight of land. And he ties my hands when we're out of the pagoda, watching me all the time.

The carrots are in a brown paper bag. I bet he hasn't paid for them. My guess is that he's stealing food from the tables locals set out to sell their garden produce. Or he could dig things out of fields: there's often potatoes and carrots left on the ground after harvesting — food ready for the taking. The dead rabbit lies in the dust, rodent teeth pushing between its lips. Filmy, dull eyes stare.

'Hungry?' He squats before me, takes the knife from his belt and, with a thrust and a tug, he opens the soft rabbit belly. A slithering of twisted flesh spills between his fingers, releasing the metallic smell of guts and bowels. I grimace. He shakes his head at me, amused at my squeamishness, as he pulls out the dark, dripping heart. If Faith were here she wouldn't look away; she'd be craning to get closer, itching to examine the ropy mess in his hands.

'I'll light a fire, after dark.' He is busy, ripping back the skin, turning the creature inside out. A naked milky thing emerges, blue-veined. I see the shocking contours of limbs and torso, the neck and shoulders, and I think of a child, the dead body of a child.

'I got you these . . . ' He kicks a pile of fabric towards me. There is a pair of boys' jeans, slightly damp and smelling of detergent. I imagine him taking them from a washing line, quick fingers pulling them from the pegs, a furtive dash to the gate. And there is a navy jumper, thick and oily. I don't ask where it came from. I clutch them to me gratefully. The nights are cold in the early hours, when the mist rolls in from the sea and the pagoda slips from black to grey.

3

Clara opens her eyes and frowns. This is how every morning begins. With one word in her head: 'No.' Sometimes she says it aloud. Her days are no longer a gift, but a shock of reality. Her daughter is dead. Every object in the bedroom, dim and implacable behind the drawn curtains, insists that it is true. The alarm clock begins to jangle. It's seven o'clock and she must get up. Her other daughter is alive and must have breakfast, have her homework diary signed, her shoes polished. Faith needs her mother to love her.

It's not the loving that Clara is finding difficult. It is the actions that love requires her to make. Her limbs are heavy, useless; her heart is a stone crushing her insides so that she can't pull air into her lungs. From her pillow she can hear the muffled voice of a man, the modulated tones of Radio Four. Max is listening to the news in the bathroom as he does every morning. She finds it strange that old habits continue to carry them through each day, the things they do, never-ending tasks and rituals performed over and over again. She can't listen to the news, isn't interested in politics, doesn't want to hear of other tragedies. The world is full of conflict: Arthur Scargill's battle with Thatcher, the Sikh militants' battle for the Golden Temple in Punjab. She saw the headlines announcing the introduction of GCSEs to replace O-levels and knows she must take an interest for Faith.

Behind the blare of the radio, she can hear Max moving around, the gurgle of water in pipes, a sudden splashing and the sound of a door closing. She must get out of bed and into her clothes before he comes in. She doesn't like him to see her naked anymore.

Clara struggles with a tangle of jeans. She's taken to wearing the same clothes for days on end. As she pushes her arms through the sleeves of her shirt she is aware of birds singing in the garden: ecstatic music. She imagines for a moment what it must be like to be a thrush, the air spinning with summer warmth, alive with pollen and the vibration of insects. Not to be herself. Then she remembers that baby birds fall out of nests at this time of year. She's seen the parents fluttering helplessly above their tiny offspring, a cat slinking low through petunias and lupins.

Max puts his head around the door. He's doing up his tie. He must have dressed in the bathroom. It occurs to her that her husband feels as uncomfortable naked as she does. It's part of the shutting down of anything natural between them, like open grief. There is too much anger in her, too much guilt in Max for them to risk anything but their new politeness. 'Want me to start doing Faith's breakfast?' He's breathing deeply as if he's been running.

'No, I'm nearly there.' She sits to tug on some socks.

He looks at her, rubs at his bottom lip with his

thumb. 'You don't have to get up . . . I can manage.'

'Don't be silly.' Clara pushes her hair behind her ears. 'Of course I'm not going back to bed.'

For several weeks after Eva went missing, Clara had hung onto the possibility that she was alive. That somehow she'd been picked up by another boat or had been washed up miles away and not made it home yet. But with every passing day it became more unlikely. Eva had disappeared into the mouth of the sea, swallowed whole by a weight of water. When Clara finally allowed herself to understand that, she'd gone to bed and stayed there. She'd taken an old T-shirt of Eva's with her and buried her face in the worn folds, breathing in traces of Eva's skin, the scent of her hair, a smudged imprint of lip gloss still caught on the neckline.

One morning she'd heard Max and Faith talking outside her door. Faith had lost her PE skirt. Max had no idea where it was. And Clara knew that it was hanging up in the airing cupboard and that she must get out of bed, fetch the skirt and put it in Faith's satchel. It was time to get up, to face the world, to be a mother to the child that was left.

'I'm sorry.' She'd pulled Faith into her shoulder, kissed the unruly hair as she handed her daughter the skirt. 'I'm going to do better now. Promise.'

'It's all right, Mum.' Faith had rubbed Clara's back with consoling palms as if she was the adult and her mother the child. 'I understand.'

Clara had felt ashamed. She'd finished with

29

staying in bed. Every day was a struggle. But she was determined not to let Faith down again. Faith, her miracle child, the one she never thought she'd have. A quiet baby, Faith had slept soundly at night, been content to sit on her bottom until she was nearly fifteen months. Despite her thin limbs, Faith had been surprisingly hardy, rarely falling ill. As a toddler, she'd squatted on her haunches to examine insects and flowers, happily playing in mud puddles, humming. It was too easy, because Faith didn't ask for attention, to forget that she needed it as much as her noisy sister. 'Eva's the squeaky wheel,' Max's mother liked to say.

The kitchen is full of steam, Max waving his hands through billowing white. 'Bloody kettle,' he says. 'Electrics must have gone.'

There is a heap of unironed clothes in a basket on the floor. Silver scratches at the door, wanting to be let out. Faith is peering into the fridge. 'Is there any cheese?' she asks. 'I've got to make a packed lunch.'

'I forgot to get any,' Clara bites her lip, 'sorry.' She turns the door handle, the dog pushing past her knees into the garden. Eva's dog. She watches the animal padding across the lawn, tail swinging. There's an unopened letter on the hall table from the vet. Clara suspects that it's time the dog had its boosters. The list of things to do starts to rotate inside her head, flipping round and round. A familiar stabbing begins at her temples.

Faith is putting an apple and buttered bread into a container, at the same time as cramming a

30

biscuit into her mouth. It's time for her to leave for school. Clara has failed to remember the packed lunch, failed to feed her child.

'That's not breakfast.' Clara blinks through the ache that shimmers across her vision. 'Let me get you some cereal.'

She reaches for a plate, and as she turns to pick up the cornflake packet Max is there at her elbow, stretching across her. 'Don't worry, I'll do it . . . ' he's saying, and she's about to protest when Max's long arm knocks the milk to the floor: glass smashes, milk exploding, rushing across the flagstones. Gleaming puddles form around their feet. She bends to pick up a large piece of broken bottle and gasps. A shard of glass protrudes from her finger. A small blue dagger. She pulls it out. Red pulses from the throbbing tip. Drops run down her hand, staining her clothes, splattering onto the floor. The milk curdles pink.

'God, Clara!' Max is close. 'That looks deep. Hold your hand up.'

She feels his fingers around her wrist, warm and strong. She wants him to hold her like that, not to go away. His touch has always made her feel safe. She keeps still and stiff. Closes her eyes. 'Run and get a plaster,' she hears him telling Faith.

She pulls her wrist away. 'Don't fuss. I'm all right.' The room tips and spins. She sucks in air, concentrates on clearing the wavering mist, pushing away the blur so that the clarity of everyday objects can centre her.

'You're not all right.' He takes hold of her

31

wrist again and walks her over to the sink, turns on the cold tap. She watches the flaps of her flesh spring apart under the sluice of water, the spiralling of red inside the clear gush. It nips with a sharpness that is almost a relief. The pain in her finger drawing away the dark, deep pain in her heart.

Faith has come back, handing the tin of plasters to her father with an air of importance. 'Get your satchel, Faith,' he tells her as he holds Clara's hand under the tap. 'I'll drive you to school, or you'll be late.'

When Faith has gone, Max leans in closer, wraps a plaster around her finger. 'You need help, Clara,' he says quietly. 'We should get an au pair. This is a huge house. You have too much to do.'

She turns away, looking into the garden. A blackbird pecks at the lawn with an orange beak. She can hear the low whine of the dog wanting to come in again.

'It would be the most sensible thing.' He looks at her. 'Even if it's just for the summer holidays. We talked about it before. I thought you agreed. Let me call an agency. I'm worried about you. Please.'

Clara gives a small shake of her head. 'I don't know if I can have someone else in the house.' Her voice cracks. 'A stranger. And the money . . . it's an extra expense we don't need.'

'Clara, look at me.'

Slowly she raises her eyes and sees that he has cut himself shaving and there are bits of tissue stuck to his face: dots of scarlet bloom in the middle of the white. 'We're both bleeding,' she murmurs.

'It would be good for Faith,' he says steadily, 'company for her.'

'All right.' Clara stands up. 'I'll think about it.' She looks at the mess on the floor, the uneaten cornflakes in the bowl. She must pick up the glass before she lets the dog in. Silver is barking outside, a frustrated yelping. He's hungry. She doesn't know where to start — the milk or the glass? Mop or broom?

She glances at the clock. 'Where's Faith? You both have to go.'

It's my fault, she thinks. I'm useless. Selfish. She has the desire to slap herself hard. Wake up, she tells herself, fiercely. She grabs the broom and begins to sweep the gritty mess into a pile, bubbles of liquid around her feet. Faith is neglected; Max is unhappy. She doesn't know what to do about any of it. Perhaps Max is right. Getting some paid help is the first step.

She hears the sound of the car engine starting outside and drops the broom with a clatter, runs to the front door. Faith is fastening her seatbelt. At the wheel, Max turns his head, surprise on his face. 'I'll call an agency,' she calls out. 'I'll do it today.'

Faith looks up at her mother, putting her hand on the passenger window, her fingertips white against the glass. Clara stretches out her own hand, spreading her fingers to mirror her daughter's, fingertips touching fingertips. But what she feels is the cold glass between them. 'Goodbye, darling. Have a good day,' she mouths as the car begins to move.

Clara forces her muscles to pull her lips apart, to make the shape of a smile. She waves as cheerfully as she can, her finger throbbing; the plaster sticky with seeping blood.

4

You can go anywhere in your mind. Closing my eyes I'm back in my bedroom where I tug open the chest of drawers, rooting through fabrics: here is the green Lurex skirt that I found in a jumble sale, my soft yellow T-shirt with FIORUCCI picked out in pink letters. I find the black dress cut off one shoulder, and untangle a pair of white fishnet tights to wear as gloves, a length of black fabric to twist in my hair. I will look like Madonna with my armful of bangles and a lipstick sneer.

I imagine Marco's gaze on me as I walk into a club. Music pumps from a sound system, something by Joy Division or The Cure. There are flashes of strobe in the darkness. A smoke machine fills the air with mist. 'You look incredible,' he says, with his lips brushing my neck, white skin glowing. I can put any words I like into Marco's mouth. But he really did tell me that I looked incredible, and I remember the lurch of my heart as he said it.

I concentrate on holding my daydream behind the tight press of my shut lids. I want to keep it there. But already it's fading, Marco's face slipping away, my sense of home dissolving. I can hear Billy moving about at the other side of the room. Reluctantly, I open my eyes. The pagoda pulls into focus around me. This is reality: these scratched, windowless walls, my filthy clothes

35

and an old blanket on the floor. It's the dim fading light and shadows hugging corners and crevices. I rub my face, pressing into the planes and hollows of my skull, needing to hold myself together. I want to go home, the real one, not the place in my imagination. I want it so badly that it creates a pain, sharp as curse cramps.

Squinting into the oblongs of sky visible in the gaps between wall and roof, I guess that it must be late evening. That means there's a whole night to get through. Even though it's summer, the floor is always cold, and the chill of it seeps through my blanket. However I position myself there's a draught on my back that makes me shiver. Inside darkness I strain to hear the sound of Billy. I listen for his breathing and his mutters and sudden shouts. If I can't sleep, the hours stretch and open up into a void of waiting, waiting for the light to come; but if I can sleep, really sleep, then it's a kind of escape.

My stomach rumbles — we've run out of food — all I've eaten today is a handful of wild sea peas. There was nothing in the traps this morning and no fishing today; it must be a Saturday or Sunday because there were sailing boats in sight of the shore, and Billy said it was too risky to fish. He gives me my quota of fresh water every morning and I have to make it last, sip by sip. I can't stop thinking about the contents of our kitchen cupboards at home. Even if supper had been overcooked or soggy, I took it for granted that there would always be packets of cereal and tins of biscuits to snack on, a loaf of bread to carve into.

Billy stands over me. He nudges me with the toe of his boot, a casual prod at my thigh. From this angle I can see the bones of his cheeks protruding, the sinews in his arms. Despite the disguise of his beard and layers of baggy clothes, I can tell he's lost weight since we've been here. I suppose I have too. I've got used to feeling hungry. But I can't stand the feeling of dirt on my skin. I itch under a layer of salt and grime.

'Get up, girl,' he says, holding a length of rope up. 'Boats have gone. We're going fishing.'

The sky is already dark, clouds obscuring the stars, so that we fumble our way without moonlight. We follow the concrete road, past empty huts, stepping over barbed wire. Tramping up the incline, we circle the gorse bushes and walk on across a crunching expanse of shingle. Waves surge onto the steep shore, pulling back over stones with a sigh and a rattle. It's hard to walk with my hands tied behind my back, following Billy, who doesn't slow for me. He picks a spot by the water and stops, squatting on his haunches with an 'omph' as he drops his rod, bucket and bundle of wood. I kneel beside him, blinking, my eyes getting used to the inky blindfold, picking out different shades of grey. Gradually the unfathomable night becomes a limpid blue. The dark sea shifts, silvery-skinned and restless, stretching out towards the horizon.

It is odd to think that Faith and I sat on this same stretch of beach in daylight, our boat pulled up on the other side of the island. I wonder what Faith is doing now. She's afraid of the water. She could never take a boat out on her own, so she won't come here, thank God, because what if she came to the island and Billy took her as well? She is safe at home humming some old dance tune she learnt from Granny and Jack, collecting bits of bone and flint, helping Dad make cakes in the steamy kitchen, flour on her fingers.

Billy said he threw my lifejacket out to sea so that it would be found floating alone. It would look as though I'd never worn it, or that it hadn't been done up properly and I'd slipped out of it. You wouldn't have survived without a lifejacket, he says. Not a chance. People get lost at sea. Bodies are never recovered.

Nobody is looking for me. Not anymore. I think of the last things I said to Dad, mean things. I told him that I hated him. When I was four he taught me to ride my bike without stabilisers, running next to me along the lane, shouting encouragement. He made me a sledge, hauled me behind him with the rope over his shoulder. He built snowmen with me. Helped me with my homework. Made me birthday cakes. Sat with me when I had nightmares. But he didn't tell me the truth. He lied. Mum lied. The thought makes me feel weak, bloodless, as if a vampire has emptied my veins.

Billy baits the hook with ragworm and casts off, sending the line far out into the night. The float lands invisibly. We sit in silence together, waiting. The rope itches the skin on my wrists. My shoulders have begun to ache. I search the horizon for a sign of a boat. There is one ship, silhouetted between sky and sea. Even if someone trains a pair of binoculars in this direction and picks out our small shapes, they will think nothing of it: two anonymous fishermen on a beach. Time passes, and my arms have gone numb, pins and needles tingling my fingers. I shift on the cold pebbles, trying to get comfortable. If I had an object to hide between the stones, something that was particular to me, perhaps someone would find it and understand that it's a clue. But no one comes, and Billy took away my silver earrings and watch. Even the clothes that I'm wearing don't belong to my old life.

The clouds have rolled back, exposing brighter patches of sky. There are so many stars. They seem bigger here, brighter. The Milky Way makes a wide swathe of paler light. Billy isn't looking at the stars; he's hunched into his jacket, smoking. The bitter scent brushes my face, stinging my eyes, making me crave a drag. I haven't had a cigarette since I got here. I know he wouldn't give me one. He ekes out his tobacco, almost counting the strands each time he rolls up. He stares at the waves as though he's willing a fish to bite. He must be as hungry as me. I close my eyes and rest my forehead on my knees. We sit together, side by side without talking, like an old married couple.

I want to hear Marco's voice. I want to feel him slip his hand into mine. What would he look like without his black hair dye and eyeliner? I don't know what colour his real hair is. His eyes are hazel, warm and golden, not like Billy's fishy grey gaze. I think it's brave of Marco to wear make-up, especially in Suffolk. He told me that as soon as his course at the Civic College ends, he'll go back to London and focus on his music. There's a band that's interested in him. I wish I could go with him. If we got married, we could have a gothic wedding, and I'd wear long, trailing black skirts with purple lace and backcomb my hair and stick plum roses in it.

There is a picture of Mum and Dad on their wedding day in the living room at home. It was in the sixties and Mum wears a white mini-dress with big fabric daisies around the hem. She's carrying real daisies and smiling up at Dad. They look so happy. But when I remember what happened to me the night before the storm hit, then suddenly the photograph that I'd grown up with doesn't mean the same thing anymore and everything is muddled and wrong.

Billy is reeling in the line with quick movements. A grunt of triumph escapes as he leans back to swing a fish in, unhooking it. It's small-ish, silver-bellied, with a speckled back. 'Hardly more than a codling,' Billy complains. It flails on the stones: eyes shiny, tail flapping. We stare at it for a second before Billy takes a large stone and brings it down on the head. Once I would have been repulsed. My mouth is already watering.

When it's dark, Billy will risk lighting a fire. Firewood is scarce — there are only a couple of stunted trees — so we collect driftwood and store it inside the pagoda to dry. He tips out the kindling, arranges it on a scooped-out space and leans down to blow on the spark. Flames catch and crackle. He unties me with a look that says, *don't think of it*, gives me the gutted fish on a stick, gesturing to hold it inside the heat. My fingers grow hot. The cooking smell makes my stomach clench in anticipation. I stare at the fish, watching as flesh bubbles and weeps. The golden circles around the eyes dim; bright scales scorch and char as skin shrivels across flesh.

He hands me a portion of steaming pink flakes, dropping them into my palm. I burn my tongue, filling my mouth with tender fish. I hardly pause to pull out a sharp bone, threading it between my teeth, before I continue chewing and swallowing. Billy is eating greedily too, crouched over the fire stuffing bits of fish into his mouth with both hands. If he was to choke on a bone, I could run. It might give me enough time to get to the other side of the island and find the boat.

Billy turns and stares at me as if he knows what I'm thinking. His eyes narrow into slivers of light. Grease slicks his lips; bits of fish are caught in the rough scrub of his beard. I think of Marco's smooth chin, how his inky hair always felt clean between my fingers. I drop my gaze but I can't pause in cramming fish into my mouth. The relief of food makes me want to cry. Tiny burning embers rise into the sky. They flare gold above our heads and disappear, dying in the wind.

'D' you know about the German invasion in the Second World War? The one that happened here?' he asks suddenly.

Startled, I shake my head. 'What, on the island, you mean?'

41

He nods. 'But the English army knew they were coming, see.' He taps his nose. 'They'd prepared a surprise for Jerry.' He gestures towards the land behind us, jerking a thumb towards the unseen water. 'The sea was set on fire — petrol on the surface — burnt the lot of them to death when they tried to cross it. The sky was ablaze. Must have been a lot of screaming.'

His voice is matter-of-fact. He lifts up the remains of the charred fish to inspect it for further scraps of flesh. The fire throws strange shadows across his face, widening his nostrils, casting bleak caverns under his eyes.

'There were burnt corpses washing up on the shore for weeks afterwards.' He gnaws at the head, uses his thumb and finger to gouge out a blackened eye, puts it in his mouth and swallows. 'Ministry kept it hush-hush. Churchill thought it would be bad for morale.' He licks his lips. 'But my granddad told me about it. Locals all knew because some of them were paid in fags to get rid of the evidence.'

I burp, putting my hand in front of my mouth, the habit of politeness still there. 'Really?' My mind is racing. It's the first time he's given me any hint about where he comes from. He doesn't have a Suffolk accent; but I'm not good at judging how people talk. With his drawn-out vowels, I'd thought maybe he was from the North somewhere. And there's something else that I can't place, a kind of nasal twang. I hadn't realised that he was local. Gradually I'm gleaning information about him and it feels important.

'The military is full of lies, full of cover-ups. You don't know the half of it.' He jabs a finger towards me, his mouth pulled down.

I stay silent, afraid of making him worse.

'That German stuff was child's play compared to what goes on now.' He glares at me. 'Under everyone's noses.' His left eye is twitching. A quick spasm of nerves flickering under his skin.

I shake my head tentatively.

'Bastards. All of them.' He stands up abruptly. His chest is heaving and he clenches his fists. 'Cover the fire. Make sure nothing is left.'

Eyes down, I hurry to gather stones, using my feet and hands to shovel shingle across glowing embers. The stones clatter as I rearrange them. They sound cheerful, as if I'm playing a game. I make the most of using my arms, swinging them freely, easing out any last feelings of cramp. Billy hides the remains of the fish. He's already pulling the rope from his pocket as he inspects my work, pushing at stones with his foot until he is satisfied. He grabs my wrists, wrapping the rope around them, his breath coming fast and hard.

Far under the surface, buried beneath the blackened wood of our fire and the fish skeleton, are bones of German soldiers. I think of how their families waited at home in Germany for news of their son or brother or husband, years going by, and never finding out what happened to them, the lost bones falling apart, drifting among stones, unclaimed and anonymous.

5

I swing my legs as I eat my boiled egg, the hard wooden edge of the chair banging against my shinbone. Mum boiled the egg for too long and the yolk is rubbery. There's nothing to dip my soldiers in. Sophie the new au pair arrived this afternoon. Dad went to pick her up from Ipswich. She arrived holding a glass thing that Dad said was a coffee maker. Mum took her straight up to her room before I could get a proper look at her.

Mum leans against the sink. She folds her arms. 'She seems OK,' she tells Dad. 'She liked her room. But I'm still wondering if we're doing the right thing.'

He sighs and runs his fingers through his hair, leaving it sticking up straight. 'We agreed, Clara, we talked about it,' he says quietly. 'I don't want you to be ill again.'

'That was a long time ago.' Mum makes a funny noise in her throat. 'Oh, never mind.' She turns her back on him. 'I'm sure it will be fine. Just ignore me.'

I catch all of this without moving my head, carving out rubbery orange with a teaspoon, dusting it with salt. Neither of them asked me if I'd like an au pair. I'm too old to need someone to look after me, to fuss over me and tell me what to do. Mum only works four days a week, and on those days I can let myself in after school, make myself something to eat. I'm quite capable. Before she went away, Eva used to make us toast and chocolate milk, standing in the kitchen in her socks, with her school tie undone.

'Come on, Clara, just think,' Dad says, forcing a smile into his voice, 'you'll have more time to read and you can let someone else burn the food.'

It's his idea of a joke. Funny. Ha ha. Mum doesn't laugh. She just keeps her back turned, picking up her cup of tea.

He watches me pour out a mound of salt. I put the egg in my mouth and chew, looking at him. 'That's a lot of salt.' Dad frowns. I scrape out the remains in the shell hat, load them with white crystals and pop that in too. I swallow the bitterness quickly.

I watch him, waiting to see what he will do. In the days before the accident he would have given me a lecture about how salt was bad for you. Maybe he would have shouted and he would definitely have taken the salt off the table. I wish he would shout at me now. Then I'd know he could see me. I keep being invisible. Like a ghost. Mum drinks her tea standing at the kitchen sink, staring into the garden. Dad hunches his shoulders and takes a wincing sip of coffee.

I wonder if he ever thinks about another summer day, years ago, when we'd been a normal family sitting down to breakfast: two parents and two children and no au pair. Eva and I had been eating boiled eggs then too, and squabbling. I remember Mum leaning across

45

Dad to reach for the butter, bending to kiss the back of his neck. That was the moment Eva had screamed, throwing down her spoon with a clatter, her hands over her mouth.

'It's got something in it, oh God.' She'd been pushing her chair back from the table. 'It's a baby . . . '

'Let me see!' I crowded forwards, peering at Eva's egg.

'Oh God, oh God! I'm going to be sick!' Eva was standing up, shaking her hands. Her eyes like goggles.

I managed to catch a glimpse of wet feathers curled inside shell, the small hook of a claw, before Dad removed it. The tiny creature had been cooked in its own gooey white. Then Dad tipped the whole lot, egg and chick, into the bin among carrot peelings and empty tins. The lid flipped shut as he wiped his hands on his trousers.

'It's over,' he said, pulling Eva onto his lap. She allowed herself to be held even though she must have been about fifteen. She hid her face in his shoulder. He wiped her tears away, his face puckered, eyes glistening, and a sudden fear that maybe he loved Eva more than me pushed itself into my head.

She sighed and wriggled further into him, her head hard against his chin. 'It was horrible — did we cook it alive?'

'No.' Mum was reassuring and brisk. 'It would have been dead already.'

'I'm never going to eat egg again,' Eva whispered.

46

Dad stroked her hair with clumsy fingers, planted a kiss on her forehead. I was itching to scrabble about in the bin, wanting to find the chick and take it to my room, to keep with my box of treasures. I already had the delicate hollow of a bird's skull, a dead beetle with the iridescent shine still on it, a collection of stones with holes worn through by the sea, a fallow deer's antlers and a handful of fossilised shark's teeth found in the mud.

'Please! I'll keep it in a matchbox,' I begged.

'It'll rot and start smelling to high heaven,' Mum exclaimed. 'Don't be so silly, Faith.'

Eva pinched me as we cleared the table, piling plates into the sink, back to her normal self. 'What is it with you and bones?'

I stuck my tongue out at her.

★   ★   ★

Sophie wanders into the kitchen yawning. I glance at her in snatches so that she won't think I'm staring, noticing her blue eye make-up and how the light catches in her hair. We all smile politely, using simple words, talking as if we are bad actors. Dad looks awkward. He shuffles his feet and says something to her in French. She answers in English. 'Excuse me,' he tells her, speaking extra loudly, 'I have some work to do.' When he leaves the room Mum offers Sophie a cup of tea, but Sophie says she only drinks coffee. Looking flustered, Mum sits down at the scratched pine table and explains about what housework needs doing and looking after me,

47

and which days she spends at the library. She's a librarian there and she works from Monday to Thursday.

'You have a big house,' Sophie remarks, staring at the flagged floor and high ceiling. Mum makes a sort of agreeing sound. 'It must be ... ' Sophie frowns, as if searching for a word, 'much money to keep it warm.'

I think about how we wait until November before the heating goes on, and even then it's only for a couple of hours. The clanking radiators never give out proper warmth. Instead we have a smoky fire in the living room. Eva and I usually go around with hot-water bottles strapped to our stomachs, gloves and hats layered on indoors. I don't think Sophie will last a winter here.

I can tell that Mum is uncomfortable because she shifts in her chair and clears her throat, tucking bits of hair behind her ears. We've never had anyone to help in the house before. She says she doesn't agree with employing people to do her dirty work, although when she was a little girl in Egypt she had a nanny and lots of servants. She's written a list out for Sophie and the biro has leaked, staining Mum's fingers blue. Mum explains that Eva's room needs to be cleaned, but that nothing should be moved in there. She pauses. I bite my lip, willing her not to cry. Sophie crosses her legs and nods with serious dips of her chin. Her face is a mask. I can't tell what she feels or thinks. She has a habit of examining her nails, as if they have something interesting on them.

Mum glances at me and says why don't I take

48

Sophie to see the castle? I frown and shake my head quickly behind Sophie's back. But Mum presses her hand to her forehead, smudging inky prints. She half-closes her eyes as if she has a pain, muttering that maybe seeing the village would help Sophie to get her bearings, and I know that I don't have a choice.

★ ★ ★

The castle is at the top of a steep hill on the edge of the village. It is famous for being a twelfth-century keep. Sophie drags her feet beside me as we walk up to the market square. I point at the battlements appearing over the treetops and she looks unimpressed.

'Whereabouts do you live in France?' I ask.

'Paris.'

I think of the Eiffel Tower. I've seen pictures of it. A strange, half-finished building with black metal ribs showing, and a point on top like a needle threading the sky. It must be taller even than the castle. I've never been to Paris, but I know that it's the capital city.

'Why did you want to be an au pair?'

'*Je me suis échappée* . . . ' She shrugs when she sees my puzzled face, and says carefully, 'To go away from my home.'

'Oh,' I frown, 'don't you like Paris, then?'

She glances at me, eyebrows raised. '*Paris, c'est la meilleure ville.*'

I frown, not understanding, and she waves her hands impatiently. 'The best city. The best in the world.'

49

We've come to the entrance to the castle. It looms above us in the sunshine. Sophie regards it without expression.

'So why did you want to come here?' I gesture around me, taking in the scrubby grass and the old cannon at the foot of the hill.

She puts her hands in her pockets. 'It was the first job the agency . . . offered to me.' She sniffs. 'You ask many questions.'

I open my mouth and close it again. There are lots more things I want to find out. She gives me an unexpected smile, and suddenly I can see how pretty and young she really is. I wonder if we could actually be friends. She isn't much older than Eva. She points to the castle. 'So, you will show me it?'

Inside the first chamber, she leans forward to peer out of the slit window at the sunlit view outside. She's chewing gum, her mouth open and slack. A smell comes off her: heavy sweet flowers. Lilies, like the ones at Eva's memorial service.

'Want to go to the top?' I ask, my feet on the circular step. 'It's really high.'

She has peppermint on her breath. She shrugs again, which I take to be a 'yes'.

I run up the narrow winding staircase, my feet hitting worn stone with a slapping sound. Thousands of feet over the centuries have climbed these same steps. Ladies with gowns trailing behind them and soldiers weighed down with chainmail. On the flat roof you can see across the village and over the marshes out towards the river and the sea beyond. Hands on hips, I stand and look at the long shape of the island. I have a different view of it from my bedroom window. Sophie is breathing heavily when she appears at the doorway. She leans against the battlement walls and pushes brown hair out of her eyes. A big seagull skims above our heads and she lets out a yelp, spitting out something in French.

Merde! I repeat in my head, trying to remember, because I bet it's a swear word.

Down at the foot of the hill I see Robert Smith from the village and a couple of the other boys. He's on his moped and the others are on bikes. They've stopped to have a smoke and chat. They stand in a group, shoulders slumped and hands cupped around their rollies. Sophie has seen them too. 'I will go down,' she tells me. 'You must play around here . . . ' She gestures at the grounds. 'But don't go away.'

I remain on the roof, touching the ancient grey stone of the battlements, feeling the rub of grain beneath my fingers, limestone with tiny fossils packed inside. I scratch at the surface with my nail, wondering how deep I'd have to sink my hand in to come up with a handful of ancient fish bones or a swirl of ammonite. Looking over the wall at the sweep of castle grounds I notice how untidy the grass is. When Eva disappeared it was green velvet. The summer has turned it scrubby yellows and browns, speckled with daisies. So much time has gone already.

Sophie is making her way down the narrow steps cut into the hill. From this angle, her bobbing head looks too big over her pin legs, like a toy in a car window. She's approaching Robert and his friends. They take her in with sneaky glances. She swings her hair and puts a bold hand on her waist. I can see her asking something and then she leans forward to take a cigarette from one of them. The wind carries the flutter of her laughter.

I drop down below the battlements. I don't want any of that lot to see me. They ignore me if I meet them in the street or on the river wall, looking the other way, spitting or whistling. Mum says they're embarrassed. They don't know what to say about Eva now that she has gone. A man climbs out onto the roof and nods in my direction. He has long bushy sideburns and green-tinted glasses. He's studying a guidebook.

I wonder what the man with sideburns is reading about. Perhaps he's learning about how different the coast was in the 1100s. Every year chunks of land fall into the sea. The coast is crumbling away, shored up by sea walls and defences. Strangers are surprised when they follow roads that go nowhere, stopping in mid-air. There are houses built too close to the sea that have slid down into the water, bricks and beds and washing lines scattering behind. Further up the coast, whole villages have been lost to the sea, church bells ringing under water.

The tourist is leaning on the battlements gazing out to sea. He looks wistful, or perhaps bored. I'm sure he'd be interested in the story of the Wild Man, how he was caught in fishing nets just after the castle was built, but Mum made me promise never to talk to strangers. So I won't tell about the morning that fishermen hauled in their nets, muscles hard inside sun-scorched arms, and discovered something strange.

The net would have been heavy, the fishermen smiling at such a big catch. They heaved it onto the boat, small fish slithering free and large ones struggling inside. I like to imagine their surprise, when they saw caught in the middle, limbs entangled, not a fish, but a naked man with webbed feet. He was covered in dark hair. His pale skin had a blue sheen like someone kept away from sunlight, dark eyes staring. When they kicked him, wrestling him out of the nets, he opened his mouth and made strange guttural sounds, speaking a language none of them had heard before, blunted as if he was missing his tongue.

In the guidebook it says that he was marched to the castle, put in an iron cage and beaten to make him talk. They kept him for six months. He never spoke a word they could understand. In the end, he escaped back to the river. The last that was seen of him was his dark head in the distance bobbing out to sea. Dad points out carvings of Wild Men on the font in the church. He says there are lots of other ones carved into baptismal fonts in churches across the area. It's in the guidebook, so it's real history.

'Perhaps there was a Wild Woman waiting,' Granny said, 'a lonely mermaid, pining away for him, swimming close to the shore and looking at the castle, unable to climb the hill to find him.'

A couple of years ago, coming back from a sailing trip, I saw something in the water. At first

I thought it was a seal. But the texture wasn't right: long hair tangled around a man's half-submerged head. I'd leant over the side, and looked into his hairy face before he sank under the surface. I told Eva, but she said he'd have to be hundreds of years old and how did that make sense? But the Wild Man isn't properly human, and if other creatures, like tortoises, can live for hundreds of years, then he could too. I try to remember his features, but they merge into a blur.

The tourist with the sideburns gives me a quick smile before he leaves the roof, dipping his head to avoid banging it on the low lintel. I wait for a moment, to give him time to get to the ground. The thick walls of the castle hold a chill even in the summer. Inside the narrow curving staircase my skin prickles with cold. Eva and I used to roll down the steep hill surrounding the castle, turning over and over in the long grasses, the sky flashing in and out of our vision, ending at the bottom in a heap, dizzy and wanting to do it again. Eva would sit up, grinning, grass seeds peppering her dark hair. I know without asking that Sophie won't want to roll down the hill. She's still with the boys, perched on the moped, smoking and talking.

There isn't much to do on my own in the grounds. Long shadows fall across my back. The sun is lower, the afternoon ticking away. The land around the escarpment is worn thin and dry, faded to a brownish shade. Bare patches show like scabs. The allotments next to the grounds are different, full of curling leaves and

54

healthy green plants. The small gardens have been lovingly watered and protected from the sun. Granny Gale had an allotment. Last summer, she had a party there.

★   ★   ★

'Look.' Eva broke into a run across the castle grounds. 'Fairy lights!'

Tea lights flickered around Granny's allotment. Small flames inside glass, bright sparks of yellow with blue hearts. The lush tendrils of bean plants and sweet peas were alive with flickering shadows. The allotment smelt of green things pushing through earth, damp soil and drifting scents of flowers. Gnats gathered in wispy clouds, hovering without sound.

I thought there'd be other people at the party. Everyone at the allotments knew each other, borrowing tools, united in their complaints about the man who did no gardening, only sat in a deckchair drinking wine on sunny days. 'Waste of an allotment,' they shook their heads as they leant over fences to comment, 'ground frosts early this year,' or 'badgers been at the courgettes again.' But there was only one other person, a white-haired man stepping out of the shed, holding out a hand to shake. I didn't recognise him. His fingers were crooked, knuckles swollen purple. In his grasp, my fingers disappeared. His skin felt warm and rough.

'This is Jack,' Granny said. 'Jack Train. He's taken over Nancy's allotment. Jack, meet my lovely granddaughters.'

Lilting strains of strings and piano floated up from Jack's paint-splattered transistor. 'Cheek to Cheek' and 'Face the Music and Dance'. We sat on the bench outside Granny's shed and listened, drinking sweet tea out of a flask and munching on slices of sticky lemon cake. Granny made the best cakes and luckily she'd taught Dad. Mum's baking efforts always sank in the middle or came out of the tin fossilised.

The old couple got up and danced. 'I've got you under my skin,' Granny Gale sang in her flat, reedy tones. They turned and stepped, dancing along the gravel paths around the vegetable beds, both of them with straight backs and smiling faces. Jack had a good voice, deep and honeyed.

'Sang in the choir when I was a lad,' he told us. 'Dance with me?' Jack held out his arms to me.

I shook my head. 'Don't know how.'

'Time to start, then.' He held me as if he were a proper dancer from the television — one of those men in tailcoats on *Come Dancing*, shoulders back and spine straight. He showed me some steps. 'A foxtrot,' he said. The candles flickered and moths fluttered, wings brushing the halos of light. Beyond us the sky had turned purple, the rest of the allotments a jumble of black shapes. I should have been wearing a puffy net skirt covered with sequins.

My feet scraped over the gravel, stumbling. Jack held me up, and kept on dancing. Slow, slow, quick, quick, slow. I stared at the ground and he stopped to raise my chin with his hand.

My feet began to follow his and I felt the pattern of the dance, how we moved to the music. He turned me under his arm.

'Like flying, isn't it?' His hand felt leathery, and I smelt tobacco and mildew on his clothes.

Eva wouldn't dance. She said it wasn't her kind of music. I liked it. It made me feel safe, and happy. You could hear the lyrics too. Jack had taken Granny in his arms again. Granny floated like a scarf over Jack's chest. He held her as if she was made of something delicate that could tear.

'Aren't you too old to have a boyfriend?' I asked Granny, and Eva kicked my ankle.

'You're never too old to fall in love.' Jack laughed and the laugh turned into a cough, rumbling inside his chest like an old car. He didn't have a Suffolk accent. He said he was from Yorkshire originally. Said it had taken him a time to get used to the lack of hills. 'Twenty years before it felt like home,' he added.

'His allotment is next to mine,' Granny explained. 'He asked if he could borrow a trowel.'

'And I told you what pretty sweet peas you had!' Jack reminded her.

They laughed and leaned towards each other. Jack swept a short grey curl away from Granny's forehead with a blunt finger.

Eva rolled her eyes at me. 'It's unsavoury,' she hissed.

'And what about you?' Granny saw everything. 'Any love in your life, Eva? Any of those young men taken your fancy?'

Eva scowled and dug the toe of her shoe into the gravel of the path. 'Maybe.'

'You don't have to tell me if you don't want to,' Granny said. 'I'm only teasing.'

I could see that Eva was longing to tell about Marco and his goth clothes and all the music he listened to and the places he'd been. I knew that she'd got bored of telling me. I watched her struggle for a moment. But she resisted. She shook her head and looked away, tearing off a long strip of bean plant instead and chewing at the pods.

★ ★ ★

Jack had a stroke and went into hospital a week after Granny died. When Mum told me about the stroke I remembered Jack's finger on Granny's cheek, the sweep of it across her thin skin. But that's not what Mum meant. She said that he'd had a blood clot, and it had stopped blood from getting into his brain. Someone else has taken over Granny's allotment. They've hung silver milk bottle tops along the tops of fruit canes. Granny would approve. I wish I could talk to her about Eva and the Wild Man. Because she'd understand that it's him that's taken her. And that he must be keeping her on the island.

'I told you not to go anywhere!' Sophie is beside me, panting. She looks hot. She puts out her hand and touches my bare arm.

I step away from her. 'I've been here all the time!'

'I couldn't find you.' She tilts her head to one side, begins to walk away. 'I was worried. Come along. Come home now.'

6

Max sits on an upright chair, an unread, out-of-date Sunday magazine drooping across his lap. He breathes through his mouth, sipping stuffy air, filtering it through his teeth as if he could stop himself swallowing the bugs and germs he imagines floating around him like dust motes. He hates doctors' waiting rooms.

'Max Gale?' The receptionist leans across the desk, smiling at him. 'Doctor will see you now.'

As he gets to his feet, turning to leave the magazine on a low table, he knocks into an empty pram. It judders, rolling forward, and he puts a hand on the silver handle to still it. People glance up and he feels their interest following him, their looks of sympathy or mistrust, or just plain curiosity. Since the accident the whole village knows the story. The tragedy is already a kind of local myth: the father found alive with his sinking boat, his daughter lost to the waves.

John McGee has treated their whole family since they moved to the village. He and his wife have been to supper. Their daughter was a school friend of Eva's. Max used to like the familiarity of it; now it feels oppressive. He longs for anonymity.

'How are things?' John leans over to inspect Max's scalp. The hair is newly grown back, softer textured, the skin knitted in a lumpy line across the back of his head. Max feels fingers prodding lightly. 'Healed up nicely,' John says. 'Any more luck with memories?'

'No.' Max places his hands carefully on his knees. His hands and feet are too big. He never knows what to do with them. 'Nothing.'

'Give it some more time.' John settles at his desk. 'You don't have amnesia, but the brain is a complicated beast. Has its own ways of protecting us against trauma.'

'Yes, I suppose so. It's just . . . frustrating.'

John tilts his head quizzically. He's a small, portly man and Max has a sudden image of a robin in the garden, alert eyes like black beads. 'How are you sleeping? Would you like me to prescribe something?'

Max moves his hands, tightening his fingers around the large bones of his knees. 'That's not a problem.'

'And what about Clara?'

'She's not.' Max rubs his temple. 'Not sleeping. At first she couldn't get out of bed and now she's restless all night and then up at the crack of dawn every day. I'm worried about her.'

'Of course you are.' John looks away, down at his note pad. 'Tell her to come and see me. Just for a chat if she wants.'

As Max shuts the door of the surgery he is struck by the certainty that he must take Clara and Faith away from here. They can't stay in Holt House, can't stay in the village. They'll never be free of the accident if they remain. He worries about Faith. She seems lost in an imaginary world much of the time. She's found an answer to the tragedy of her sister's death.

She's invented a mythical creature, her own Wild Man, that's kidnapped Eva and is holding her captive on the island. He'd mentioned it to John, who reassured him that it wasn't an unusual reaction from a girl with an imagination like Faith's. 'It's her own form of protection,' John explained, 'as memory loss is yours.'

Since Eva's drowning the dynamics of their family have changed. Passion and energy have been extinguished. The centre has been cut out. Faith is in denial, and he and Clara are failing to deal with it. A courteous, strained formality has seeped into the spaces between them, and it's solidified, trapping them in a glassy, airless place. He needs to find a way to shift things, to break out of the suffocating lethargy they're stuck in, bring them all together again. Moving will help. He is certain of it. But equally certain that Clara won't want to sell up. She'll see it as running away or being disloyal. Max walks quickly through the village, hands in his pockets, rehearsing things that he can say to convince her. He misses his mother. Grace would have had her own ideas about whether they should leave or stay. Sometimes he finds himself trying to second-guess her, hears her voice in his head.

Suffolk, 1963

Meeting Clara had been entirely due to his mother. Grace always went to the theatre for her birthday. And, despite the difficult travelling conditions in what was turning out to be one of the longest, hardest winters on record, Max managed to get back to Ipswich to take her to a Friday-night performance at the Regent Theatre.

The darkened theatre was half-empty. Outside the streets were caked in fresh snow. It was almost February and there was no sign of a thaw. The audience must have had an average age of about sixty. The programme in his hand said *The Importance Of Being Earnest*. He'd never heard of the small touring repertory outfit. Max sighed. He'd tried to persuade his mother to come up to London and see a real show — Me *and My Girl* was on in the West End — but she'd laughed at the idea. 'Waste of good money. The plays at the Regent are always worth seeing.' Back in his flat in Hammersmith, he had a stack of work to do. And now he was worrying that, with fresh snowfall since he'd got to Suffolk, he might not be able to get back at all. Snow had been banked up by the road in drifts several feet high as he'd driven his mother slowly into town, her ancient Austin 7 sliding around corners.

Lady Bracknell turned out to be a crowd-pleaser: a solid, middle-aged woman who played her part with just the right amount of exasperation and snobbishness. Sweet wrappers rustled. There were bursts of laughter. But it was when Jack was proposing to Gwendolyn Fairfax that Max leant forward in his seat, heart beating faster. The actress playing Gwendolyn was slender, her skin and hair almost the same shade. The colour reminded him of something: caramels he decided, those creamy toffees he'd stolen from his mother's handbag when he was little, his hand rustling inside a white paper bag, mouth already watering.

The actress stood awkwardly, as if she'd wandered onto the stage by mistake, reciting her lines with pauses in the wrong places. At one point it seemed as though she'd completely forgotten her words and he heard a desperate prompting whisper coming from the wing. The elderly audience was split between tittering and sighing. He held his breath. There was a tense moment of silence and Gwendolyn or, he checked the programme feverishly, Clara Allen, stared furiously out into the footlights. He looked at her scowling face and his heart contracted.

The prompt came again, this time clearly audible to the audience. Gwendolyn/Clara had taken her cue and recited her words in a breathless rush as she pushed past the actor playing Jack, tossing her hair, before she disappeared off-stage.

'I have to meet her,' Max thought, glancing around to find the nearest door that would take him backstage.

His mother turned and glared at him. 'What on earth is the matter with you? You're jumping around as if you've got ants in your pants.'

He waited until the final curtain fell and the smattering of applause died down and people began to shuffle slowly along the aisles, buttoning up coats and pulling on hats. 'Just give me a moment,' he whispered to his mother. 'I'll see you in the foyer.'

He'd been expecting bouncers and disapproving officials to block his way as he stalked the narrow corridors. But there was nobody to stop him pushing open the dressing-room door to find her sitting with her back to him in front of a huge mirror. She'd been rubbing cold cream over her face. The girl who played Cecily sat on the table next to her wearing a dressing gown, swinging her legs and smoking. They both stopped talking and stared. Looking at him in the mirror's reflection, Clara's eyes were huge inside her mask of glutinous white.

A crackling transistor radio was playing the Beatles' 'Please Please Me'. Max swallowed and cleared his throat. 'Clara Allen?'

'Yes?' She turned her luminous, sticky face towards him and frowned.

★ ★ ★

He'd persuaded her to have coffee with him the next day and risked icy roads to get back into town. They met in the Ponderosa Café just round the corner from her boarding house. She'd been walking with a book held open before her nose when he spotted her across the road. 'Don't you bump into things?' he'd asked. And she smiled as if he'd said something ridiculous.

She was smaller and more fragile sitting opposite him in the morning light than she'd appeared on stage. She seemed tired, with dark smudges under her lashes. It had made him want to take care of her. He sat back, taking deep breaths, telling himself to *relax*. She won't run away, he reasoned silently, not if I don't frighten her off. Although the way she perched on the

64

edge of her chair suggested otherwise.

They had slices of fruit cake and strong tea out of green china cups. She nibbled at sections of her cake, eating it almost crumb by crumb.

'By the way,' she said, 'please don't bother to try and find positive things to say about my performance. I know I'm terrible.' She looked at him, chin lifted. 'Acting isn't my thing at all.'

'Then why do you do it?' he asked hesitatingly. 'Do you like it?'

'Like it?' She laughed. 'You can't be in this business for a wishy-washy thing like 'liking'. No, I don't *like* it. I love it. I mean, what's not to love: waiting and waiting for the phone to ring; auditions where they give you three minutes before calling 'next'; boarding houses with dripping taps and lumpy mattresses?'

She looked up at him with one eyebrow raised.

He smiled. 'OK. I'm confused. Explain it again.'

'I love it because,' she spoke slowly as if he was a little hard of hearing, 'I can pretend to be someone else.'

'Don't you like being you?'

'Not really.' She shrugged and then flushed as she added, 'Joking apart, one of the best things about acting is the sense of camaraderie. When you're in a performance together, you're a kind of family. For a while, anyway. And I do love that.'

He told her that he was doing articles, but how he secretly worried that he wasn't tough enough or sharp enough to be a good solicitor. 'Really, I just want to be a sailor,' and she began to relax, eventually curling her feet up underneath her. She nodded and smiled in all the right places. 'I'd like to see it,' she said, when he described the Suffolk coast with its marshes and wild pebbly beaches.

'I spent my early years in Egypt,' she told him when he asked. 'I left it when I was ten.' She blinked and looked away. 'After that it was boarding school and holidays with an elderly aunt and uncle in Wiltshire.' Her lips lifted in a half-smile. 'I didn't really belong in any of those places. I never did go back to Egypt. Strange, but that's the place I think of as home.' He noticed how narrow her hands were, how her watch slipped around her wrist. And he had the urge to circle that small bone with his own fingers.

The next day he took her to the Gondolier espresso coffee bar. It was dark, cramped, the air heavy with cigarette smoke, a juke box playing 'Return To Sender' over and over again. They drank bitter coffee from glass cups, adding spoonfuls of demerara sugar. He stirred too hard and spilt his. Clara blotted the mess with tissues, without a fuss, even though there were coffee splatters on her cream cuffs. They sat close, their knees pressing together under the table. 'It's sad; I think I'm better at understanding plays than performing them,' she said, cradling the cup in her hands. 'When I read the text, I feel I know the characters I play. Sometimes I really love them. And then the words come out of my mouth and it's so disappointing. It's as though I'm letting them down.' She was wearing a shift dress with over-sized buttons down the back. He thought about how they would feel as he fed them through the buttonholes, the satisfying curve between his fingers, and how he'd like to lean forward to kiss the skin over the top of her spine where necklaces fastened. He longed to bury his face in her hair, smelling what kind of soap she used, what kind of shampoo, discovering her true scent underneath.

'Maybe you just haven't discovered the right role yet,' he said. 'You know, the one that will define you. Like,' he struggled to think, 'like Judy Garland in *The Wizard of Oz*.'

'Hmmm,' she said, her eyebrow raised, 'I'm not sure that's the kind of role I had in mind, much as I love Judy. Sadly,' she smiled, 'you can't get by as an actress only playing one part.'

She was leaving for Birmingham the next day and he had to get back to London. Outside on the frozen pavement, they stood revealed in the cold daylight. The end of her nose was pink, her cheeks chapped. A seagull wheeled above them, white feathers almost invisible in the pale air. He bent down and found her lips, and she kissed him back, urgently, with a hunger that he hadn't expected.

7

Joanna Price is not my friend. But Mum thinks she is. So Joanna has been invited for the day. She arrives with her mother and I watch them walk up the garden path from behind my bedroom curtain. Both of them have pale red hair and small, watchful eyes. Mrs Price is fat as a Russian doll, her face blending into her round body with no pause for a neck. She wears a dress with scarlet flowers bursting over it. Joanna has very short shorts in pink that hardly cover her bottom and a yellow top with lace around the neck. The clashing colours make me screw up my eyes.

'Hard to keep them occupied in the holidays, isn't it?' Joanna's mother is asking mine. 'These summer holidays, they just seem to go on and on. Joanna is ever so pleased to come over, aren't you, Jo?'

The three of them are standing in the hall, and Joanna turns to watch me walk down the stairs. I step slowly, clinging to the banister. She glares when I offer her a 'Hi.' Silver is growling and barking from the kitchen. He hates strangers. His hackles will be up, his ears back. I wish Mum would let him out. He wouldn't bite them but I'd like to see their faces.

'Good guard dog, isn't he?' Joanna's mother nods towards the kitchen nervously.

'Sorry about the row.' Mum smiles. 'Actually,

it's all just a front. He wouldn't hurt a fly.'

I raise my eyebrows. He eats flies. Snaps them up and holds them in his mouth. You can hear the wings vibrate behind his teeth. Silver was Eva's dog, a big, loping lurcher. She rescued him from travellers. For weeks after the accident, Silver waited in Eva's room. He settled on the floor by her bed like a sphinx, still and watchful. Silver had refused to eat at first, but gradually, Mum had tempted him into the kitchen and the food she left out disappeared.

★ ★ ★

Joanna wanders around my bedroom picking things up. 'Don't you have any Barbies?' she asks. 'I've got the new Peaches and Cream Barbie. She comes with extra shoes and a hairbrush.'

I decide that I won't show her my collection of treasures. It remains hidden under my bed in its cardboard box; the bird's skull and crab's claw are safe from her poking. I shrug. 'Mum won't let me have Barbies.'

Joanna looks at me pityingly. I don't tell her that I'm not allowed Trolls either. The other kids at school have whole families of them that they keep in their desks, sneaking them onto their laps in lessons to comb long green or orange hair, swapping them at break-time.

Joanna is staring at the poster of the human skeleton on my wall. Dad brought it back for me from the Natural History museum. She curls her lip. 'Doesn't that give you nightmares?' She chews her nail and stares. 'What about music?

Do you have any records?'

'Um,' I flip through the small pile of singles on the floor, 'Ella Fitzgerald?' I offer.

'Ella who?' She scowls. 'What about Sheena Easton or Bananarama?'

I shake my head, letting Ella slide back onto the floor.

'You don't have anything to do here,' she complains. 'It's boring at your house. I didn't want to come.'

'We could go down to the river,' I suggest, glancing out at the sunshine and the water shining on the horizon.

Mum tells me to take Sophie with us. When I knock on her bedroom door and put my head round, she lowers the magazine she's reading and frowns. I don't want her to come with us anyway. 'Just going out for a bit,' I say and she ignores me and goes back to her magazine.

Joanna has followed me along the landing. 'How many bedrooms have you got?'

'Six.'

'If you've got so much money, why is everything so scruffy and old?'

I look at her blankly. I'd never thought about it. It was just home.

'What have you got a nanny for?' she asks as we wander the track down to the marshes. Joanna has a pair of white leather scalloped sandals on. My brown sandals seem boyish and babyish in comparison. They have scuffed toes.

'She's not a nanny. She's an au pair.' But I can see from Joanna's expression that this doesn't make it any better.

We've reached the marshes where soft sedge plumes give way to mud banks dense with samphire, speckled with purple sea lavender. Narrow creeks wind inland, carving out tiny islands, opening out into pools of glistening mud. Wader birds pick their way across the surface, sketching tracks behind them like a code. Oystercatchers and sandpipers poke long beaks into the black. Squinting, I count three yachts moving slowly on the river: a Mirror and two Wayfarers. There isn't much wind today. Their sails billow and droop.

Joanna points to the river and beyond that, the sea. 'I wonder if your sister's skeleton is floating around somewhere, or if it's broken apart into different bones by now?' She could be discussing the weather. She snatches a look at me from below her lashes. 'Or maybe something ate the whole of her. There are sharks in the Channel. My uncle is a fisherman and he told me. Big 'uns.' She holds her hands wide. 'Get caught in the nets sometimes.'

I collapse onto my bottom because my legs have gone weak. Tufts of samphire make a spongy cushion. The mud on the path is cracked and dry; it splits into star shapes. I lower my head, so that my hair covers my face, leaning over to scratch a finger against the stars. Joanna lowers herself beside me, checking that she won't get mess on her pink shorts.

'My mum reckons that your dad pushed her in,' she continues. 'They was always rowing, weren't they, your dad and Eva? Everyone could hear them yelling blue murder.'

'He didn't push her in. The boat capsized.' My fingernail is black-rimmed. Dried earth packed in tightly between flesh and nail. It feels itchy. I have carved a letter in the surface.

'But your sister was a one, wasn't she? Enough to wind anybody up.' Joanna angles her head to look at me. 'Trouble with a capital T, my mum says.'

I kick off my sandals and step into the pool of wet mud. It gives beneath me slowly, slippery against my skin. There are the squiggled heaps of casings left behind by ragworms and razor shells. I wriggle my toes. The mud slurps and pops, pushing up through the gaps between my toes like folds of plush velvet. Beneath the greeny-brown surface is the oily black underneath. I taste the smell of fish guts and hidden things.

'She's not dead,' I say.

'Course she is. She's been gone months.' Her nostrils flare. Joanna's nose is tiny and short, like a Barbie doll's. It doesn't look right inside the round moon of her face.

'No.' I shake my head. 'She's been taken by selkies. Or the Wild Man.'

'You're nuts.' Joanna laughs. 'That's just a load of rubbish. Fairy tales.'

I look out over the mud flats and the sea wall towards the shape of the island. 'She's over there on the island,' I whisper.

'What?' Joanna's mouth is open in a gaping smile. Her eyes narrow. 'What did you say, Nutter?'

'Coming in?' I look at her. 'It feels lovely and cool.'

72

'No chance.' She grimaces. 'It smells.'

I grab her plump wrist and pull. She falls with surprising ease, toppling from her perch on the bank. For a second, she is an unresisting lump. Then, as her knees hit the slime, she screeches and starts to struggle, fighting me, scrabbling for a hold.

'Look what you done!' She slips on the mud, black smeared over her white legs and pink shorts.

Skidding at my feet, she kicks out sharply, catching my ankle, and I topple over, landing on top of her, pinning her down. She gets a hand free and swings it up, catching me under the chin. It hurts. A jolt to my teeth. I think I can taste blood. I am filled with a clear, ringing sense of rightness. It almost feels like joy as I grab her flailing wrist and push it down, down into the sucking mud. She's trapped. I have both of her hands prisoners. I'm sitting astride her, and she is writhing and screaming under me. There are splatters and streaks of black all over her. I am covered too. Her hair is spread out in tangles. Browny mud looks green against the red of her hair.

'You cow!' She's yelling. 'Wait till I tell on you!'

Her mouth is a slobbery pinkness, opening and closing. I grab a handful of mud and ram it in to take away the noise. She snorts and chokes. I watch her eyes crinkle and close, her face going pinker and pinker. Her plump body bucks violently under me, as if electric shocks are shooting through her spine, and I fall to the side.

73

She's rolled over, coughing and coughing.

She crawls across the slick surface, bedraggled, like a strange mud monster. I can't see even a tiny patch of pink on her shorts. In fact I can't see her shorts, only the wrinkles of them and the line where they meet the swelling rise of her plump thigh. She crouches over on the bank, spitting and retching. Dark spittle hangs from her chin. All around us are the tracks of our fight — gouges of deeper darkness in the muddy surface.

She's stumbling away. I can hear her breathless voice calling out between sobs, 'You're mental you are . . . warty hands . . . I'm gonna tell my mum on you . . . '

It's fading away: the heaviness of her footfalls and the screech of her voice. The air calms and settles, obliterating traces of Joanna. I lie back on the bank, wet and sticky. The sun is hot, drying the mud into a tightening embrace on my skin. I can hear all the proper things now: wash of waves, seabirds calling and the flap of distant sails. Underneath that there is the pulse of the sea, pull and push of water over shingle, the flit and swish of fins moving through deeper reaches of the ocean, movement of bigger creatures, stealthy webbed feet and fingers pushing through water and reeds.

I sit up. There is nobody here. I take deep gulps, letting the air soothe me like a glass of milk. The tracks of our fight are fading as the mud takes back its form, softening and sinking into a smooth, flat surface. Soon our struggle will be gone. Flies gather over the mud pool. A dragonfly skims the tops of the reeds, wings glinting green gold.

Lying down again, I roll onto my tummy in the samphire. I think I'm there for a long time. The mud is hard on my skin, less an embrace, more a brittle armour. Insects hum and whirr. I continue to scratch out letters inside the crusty surface of the path. EVA I spell out, over and over again, her name becoming a pattern. Lying with the sun on my back I sing *Love is the sweetest thing — what else on earth can bring such happiness to everything . . . love is the oldest yet the youngest thing*, humming when I forget the words and imagining Granny's voice singing with me. That's better. Another song. I suck my bottom lip, thinking, and begin *I wish that little girl could see . . . why was I so careless of that basket of mine!* I picture a girl with swinging plaits in a gingham dress, hands on her hips, her lost basket set down under an apple tree.

I know that I could be friends with a girl like that. I can see her in an orchard, sunlight dappling her dress, waiting patiently for me to find her.

Mum surprises me. She comes silently through the long grasses. She is breathing hard, so I know that she has been running. I thought she'd be very angry. But she drops down beside me and pulls me close. I can feel her swallowing, the slide of saliva in her throat. She makes a gulping sound and kisses my forehead. 'I was worried.' Her voice is tight.

I clench my fingers into balls and lie stiffly in

her lap. I would like to cry, but it's as if someone has sewn up my throat.

'Come on,' she says in her matter-of-fact Mummy voice. 'You're filthy. I'm going to put you in a bath.'

I stand up, my legs feeling odd and shaky, and put my hand in hers. It is good not to think, to be led away by her, to be a baby again. I want to get smaller and smaller, like Alice in Wonderland. I want to shrink into an acorn-sized baby that my mother will hold inside the warm, dark hollow of her mouth.

★ ★ ★

I'm naked in the bath, the room fuzzy with heat, mirror misted with steam. Mum gets up to open the window. 'Like a sauna in here,' she says. My limbs are pink and glistening, sticking out of grey water. Mum has soaped and scrubbed me, her sleeves rolled up. 'I've never known such tenacious mud,' she says. I don't know what 'tenacious' means. I'm too tired to ask and I'm too busy enjoying having Mum looking after me, having all her attention. It feels warm and comforting, like the bathwater swishing around me.

Mum says the first she knew of it was Mrs Price banging on the front door and Silver barking like a lunatic. Mrs Price had been raging on about me, and saying she'd send us the bill for Joanna's ruined clothes. But all Mum could think of was me, alone by the river, because I couldn't swim properly.

'What was it about?' she asks.

'Joanna was rude. She said mean things about Dad.' I bite my lip. 'And Eva.'

Mum frowns. 'What did she say?' She sighs and leans closer over the rim of the bath. 'Never mind. It doesn't matter. This is a small village, darling. People will talk. They have nothing better to do.' She pushes some hair from my eye. 'You must try and ignore them. They are in the wrong for saying those things. But you put yourself more in the wrong when you react.'

Her mouth twists and she turns her head away. I remember our bathtimes when we were little. Mum knelt beside me as she is kneeling now, soapy froth on her hands. Eva and I often shared a bath, Eva crouching by the taps, splashing me when Mum's attention wandered. I see Eva's thin brown fingers stretched out, holding bright bath toys, rubber ducks and plastic cars, one after the other, laughing as I reached for them.

'Do you want to try swimming lessons again?' Mum asks, swilling her hand through the dirty water. 'We could sign you up for a course in the pool in town.'

'Don't want to.'

'But you have to learn sometime.' She touches my shoulder.

'We don't sail anymore,' I argue.

'No,' Mum agrees slowly, 'but the water will always be there, Faith.'

'Don't make me.' I look at her and glance away.

I was five when we capsized. The boat pitched over, all of us falling into darkness, green bubbling everywhere as I opened my eyes into gritty swirls of water. I couldn't see the others. I was alone, sealed off from the outside world. A shape emerged out of the gloom beneath me, a figure with arms and legs. It reached for me. Fingers closing on my skin, a tug on my ankle. Water was in my eyes and my mouth and up my nose. It was salty and sharp and blinding. I flapped my arms till I broke the surface, gasping, and saw sails on the water, white and dead as a broken bird. Dad and Mum were shouting. Sounds burst into my ears: slap of waves, screaming of gulls, a motorboat's roar. Dad grabbed at my orange lifejacket, hauling me in.

★ ★ ★

'Come on then.' Mum is holding a towel open. 'Better get out.'

She wraps me up like a captive, rubbing at me through the fabric. My arms are pinioned to my sides. She leans close and smells my hair, kisses my ear with a wet explosion. 'You know, you are very precious to me,' she says quietly. 'I know it's hard without Eva. But I love you; Daddy loves you.' Her voice is wobbling and she stops and takes a deep breath. 'We all miss her. We have to be kind to each other.' She holds me very tightly for a moment, crushing my bones.

'But Mum, I don't think she's dead,' I whisper into her neck.

I feel her flinch. She pulls back, holding me at arm's length so she can look at me seriously. 'I know you want her to be alive. We all do.'

'No. It's more than wanting. I feel it.'

Her eyes widen; she moves her mouth as if she's searching for words. Then she says, 'You think the Wild Man took her, don't you?'

I nod.

'I know you've grown up with the story of him; but it is just a story, Faith.' Her fingers squeeze my arms. 'It's not real. He's not real.'

'I saw him once . . . ' I begin, but my voice trails into silence because she's arranged her face into a mask. And even though Mum is so close that I can see the pores around her nose and the shine on her forehead, I feel as though she's far away. I shiver.

'We just have to take it day by day,' she's sighing. 'We're going to get through this together, me and you and Daddy. Time will take some of the pain away. You'll see.' She turns the corners of her mouth up. 'There, all dry.' She releases me, giving me a small push on the back. 'Go and get dressed.'

8

He's shouting. It's too dark to see anything clearly. His voice is raw, urgent.

I peer into the blackness, making out the shape of him as he lurches to his feet. He's a dark silhouette looming, a staggering shadow in the furthest corner. He strikes out, a fist stabbing the air. He moves suddenly, jabs another blow into an invisible enemy. A scream lacerates the night. The sound makes me cold and I cower inside my blankets, heart thumping. Please don't notice me. Please don't touch me. I keep absolutely still, eyes squeezed shut, listening. Then he moans and I can hear the rustle and scrape of him getting down onto his knees. I pray for him to go back to sleep. There is silence. But it takes me a long time to stop shaking, my heart flipping like a caught fish.

★ ★ ★

I wake to the sound of crashing waves, remnants of a dream trailing with me: the whisper of male voices. I lose the meaning of their words as I wake properly, blinking in the early-morning light, yawning. Automatically I stare at the walls, tracing shapes of copper piping, my dull gaze running over metal shutters and the numbers engraved onto the wall in black paint. It's what I do to pass the time. I must know every detail of this place by now.

The voices haven't gone. They make a low muttering. I am shocked into a different stillness, all of me alert and listening as I understand that these are real voices, not dream ones. I strain to hear their words, mixed in with seabirds' cries and wave wash. I am sitting up now, heart thumping. I'm not alone on the island with Billy — there are other people here — people who can help me.

Quickly I glance over at Billy, checking that he's asleep. He's curled up at the other side of the room with his back to me, motionless. With any luck he is exhausted and sleeping deeply. As usual, my ankles are tightly bound with rope. But he's left my hands free. I sit up carefully, keeping one eye on him, as my fingers push at the coarse knot, pulling at the dense twist. My broken fingernails scrape against it. It is too tight. I must go faster. My fingers tremble and fumble. I can still hear the murmur of voices in the distance. I'm not imagining it. There are people nearby. Their faces will turn to me as I cry out, my feet crunching through shingle towards them. Billy stirs and I freeze. One more tug and the rope slackens, giving me a space to slip my fingers inside so that I can push it off.

I don't know where the key to the padlock is. It could be in his coat, which is draped over him, or inside his trouser pocket. My only hope is that it's in the coat. My mouth is dry as I get to my feet, the rustle of my clothes, even the flexing of my muscles, seems audible and magnified. I edge along the wall towards him, keeping my eyes on his inert form. My heart is pounding in my chest as I squat next to the curve of his back. The coat has slipped half off, and most of the fabric hangs down, trailing onto the floor. Slowly I reach out a hand and slide it inside the first pocket I can find. My fingers touch metal. I breathe out. He murmurs, smacking his lips, and I keep my hand still in the pocket, watching his shoulder, the pale point of his ear. Then I've got the key in my grasp, and I'm on my feet, treading stealthily, quickly, towards the door.

A bird lands far up in the open space at the top of the pagoda. Its wings flap. A feather falls, spiralling through dust motes. My insides tighten. I reach the door, insert the key and try to turn it, but it won't move. Billy stirs, stretching his hand behind him to scratch his leg with lazy fingers. Without turning over, he pulls at the coat, repositioning it over him. I wait for him to stop before I try again, wriggling the key as carefully as my trembling fingers allow, finding the bite. It clicks open and I slide the metal arc out of the top of the padlock. The door is heavy. It opens grudgingly. Sunlight slants into the room behind me, and I hear Billy mutter. I fumble my way down the narrow corridor towards the wire doors hanging off their hinges.

My limbs burst into action, legs carrying me into the dazzle of the day. Arms pumping, I'm sprinting away from the pagoda, cutting across the shingle, past the sign that says 'Danger — Unexploded Ordinance,' stumbling towards the cracked and broken strip of road. My foot catches in a pothole and twists, sharp pain shooting through my ankle. I stagger, biting the inside of my lip. But I keep running. I can see the men. A small group with fishing rods sticking up, they are diminishing black shapes against the light. They are heading for the beach, and they are far away. I won't let myself believe that they are already too far. I have to reach them.

Adrenaline kills the pain, forcing my legs to keep working, and I make it onto the concrete road, following the straight line of it in a blundering run towards the barbed-wire fence. A rabbit dashes out from under my feet, ears back. I falter, catching my breath, and push myself on, arms working, panting past the empty huts, windows gaping behind shards of glass. My feet slide across the crumbling surface, small stones skidding beneath me. I can feel my ankle now — a howling pain. There are footsteps behind me, the sound of breathing. I hurl myself forward, opening my mouth. A sound comes out of me, a noise I don't recognise, like an animal.

His body thuds against me, a heavy weight, jolting me off my feet. I hit the ground, hands flailing uselessly. My chin cracks against the road, my chest landing hard, pushing the breath out of my body. He's panting as he drops onto my spine. His fingers find my mouth and wrap around it. I struggle to inhale through my nose. My chest is exploding.

He rolls me over, squatting over me, his hand across my mouth.

'Not a sound,' he says, 'not a bloody sound.'

I keep still, nodding. He releases my mouth

and I suck deep lungfuls of air. He glances up towards the horizon.

'They're out of sight,' he says. 'Get up.'

Perhaps they'll find the remains of our fire. But even if they do, they'll only think it was other maverick trespassers, fishermen, someone like themselves. I'm crying. I don't want him to see. Rage and fear and disappointment cancel out the pain in my ankle and chin. I hate him. He has me by the arm, tight fingers squeezing above my elbow. We walk back to the pagoda slowly; I'm limping, pain in my foot when I put any weight on it. He gives a frustrated sigh and grabs me round the waist, throws me over his shoulder in a fireman's lift.

Hanging down, my head bounces against his back, his jumper in my face. Up close, the dank, mushroomy stink of the wool is suffocating. I twist my neck so that I can see behind us. The world has turned upside-down: scrubby gorse bushes and the huts hang into a bowl of sky and cloud. Everything jolts and shudders with his movement. There are no fishermen. They will be down by the sea, hidden out of sight below the bank of shingle, busy with their hooks and floats, opening flasks of sweet tea and talking about football scores and what bait to use for mackerel and cod. My tears trickle in snail tracks across my forehead into my filthy hair.

In the pagoda he sits me down on the only chair and holds my chin so that he can contemplate the damage. It stings. He wipes his thumb across it and I see a streak of blood. He picks up a bottle of drinking water and wets a bit of his grubby sleeve, dabs at my chin. I wince. 'Hold still,' he tells me. He is so close that I see grime shadowing his skin, crusted scales flaking from his lips. 'You want to get blown up, do you?' Hair flops in a matted tangle into his eyes. His thin face bristles. His beard has got longer, making him look like a character in a film about a castaway, or Jesus. 'I've seen it happen to people,' he says. 'Seen what's left afterwards. And it's not much, I can tell you that.'

I avert my eyes, closing myself off from him. 'You shouldn't have done that,' he says. 'You shouldn't have run again. You made me hurt you. I told you before I didn't want to hurt you.'

His breath is rank and warm. I can taste it on my tongue. I hold my breath, shutting my eyes. Then I feel his finger, brushing at my tears, smudging the wet away with firm stokes as if it's paint on canvas. I open my eyes and we look at each other. 'Let me go,' I whisper.

There is a moment in which I think I can hear his heart beating.

'Don't walk on the shingle.' He looks at me without blinking. 'Not this side of the barbed wire. I'll get some water for your ankle when the coast's clear.' He glances at the door. 'Till then I'll bind it up.'

He squats down and tears a blanket into strips to wrap my throbbing ankle. He is precise and methodical. I guess that he's done this before.

'You won't be running anywhere for a while.' I catch a twitch of movement under his beard, the faint hint of a smile.

'Bastard,' I say quietly, but there is no fight left in me. I am overwhelmed with hopelessness. I want Dad to come. I don't understand how they can have forgotten me. Why doesn't anyone come?

9

Eva is swimming up from the depths. I'm looking down, searching flickering water, as her blurred face comes streaming out of darkness. She's fixed me with a stare, her mouth trailing bubbles. Fingers claw the water. She can't break the surface. She's begging with her eyes, sinking backwards, hair and clothes tangling around her, floating up like seaweed. She is drowning. I can't help her. I'm afraid. I can't swim.

I wake with a sob to the hard thrumming of rain on glass. First day that it's rained this holiday. My curtains are slightly parted. Through them I see a dark sky with fast-moving clouds, the rain almost invisible, falling in silvered arrows. Branches of the acacia tree flutter. The window is open a crack, letting an earthy scent drift up from the garden.

Mum is in the kitchen putting papers into her handbag. She's getting ready to go to work in the library in town. She leaves after breakfast with Dad. Granny's old Austin is temperamental, but when it works Mum uses that. Once, Dad promised Eva he'd give her driving lessons in it. Mum hesitates at the front door, looks at me, bites her lip.

'What will you do today?' she asks.

I feel just like I used to when she left me at nursery school. I want to clamp myself round her legs like I did then, hold tight to her knees.

Instead I hunch my shoulders, saying nothing. Mum blinks. She suggests in her cheerful voice, 'Why don't you and Sophie make potato cut-outs or papier mâché bowls?' I won't look up. I'm not going to pretend to be enthusiastic. 'There's plenty of old newspapers next to the fireplace,' she continues, 'and I think there's glue in the kitchen drawer.' She gestures to the stove. 'Or you could make fudge . . . ' Her voice trails away. It was what Eva and I did on rainy days: the smell of hot butter and melting sugar. Burning our tongues when we licked the sticky liquid off the spoon.

After Mum and Dad leave, Sophie switches the radio on to a channel with pop music and turns it up. Silver lies in his basket by the radiator, nose on splayed paws. Sophie clatters the breakfast things into the washing-up bowl and starts to swish a brush around, placing soapy dishes and cups on the draining board. She hums along to Cyndi Lauper's 'Time After Time'. The song makes me think of Eva in her bedroom, singing into her hairbrush. As I take Dad's empty coffee cup over to Sophie, I notice a bruise below her ear, green against the pale of her neck. When she sees me looking she tosses her head so that curtains of hair slide forward.

'What is this . . . potato prints?' She leans up against the kitchen surface, pulling her sleeves down with wet hands.

'Potato prints are patterns made by cutting shapes into potatoes,' I explain, 'and then you dip them in paint and press them onto paper.'

She sighs. 'You want do this?'

'Not really.'

'You want to make . . . fudge?' She raises one eyebrow.

'No,' I say quickly. 'I want to go down to the quay for a bit. I'm meeting a friend,' I invent.

Sophie glances out at the rain. 'You will get wet.'

'I don't mind.'

'Your mother won't like it.'

'She'd let me. If she was here.' I cross my ringers behind my back.

Sophie shrugs.

★ ★ ★

I pull my hood over my head. The rain batters down, soaking my feet and legs. Water runs in rivers down the side of the road, gushing into gutters. I like the rain. It feels safe. I am hidden inside my hood, disguised. There are none of the summer crowds out. The river is deserted. Only gulls bob on the choppy surface, among the moored, empty boats.

The dinghy park is filled with sailing dinghies and rowing boats. Most of them turned upside-down or covered in tarpaulins. I wander through the puddles, my fingers trailing fibre-glass and plastic. At the end of the park, under a straggly hawthorn bush, is an old rowing boat. It has a pair of oars tucked under the seat. Rowlocks hang down, attached by frayed string. Water has collected in the bottom: a dirty puddle with dead flies, bits of leaf and the yellowed remains of hawthorn petals floating on the surface. It appears to be abandoned, or at least, hardly ever used. I walk around it, checking for holes. I take hold and pull. It's immovable. I bend my knees and yank with all my strength. It doesn't budge, just rocks towards me slightly, grating on the pebbly ground. I straighten up and look at the distance that needs to be covered to get the boat onto the river. My chest tightens. There's no way I can do this by myself.

'What are you doing?'

I swing round. It's only a boy. I look closer and recognise the plump boy from the quay. The one who lost the crab. His green anorak hood flops across his forehead. Water drips down cheeks, pink and plump as balloons. His pale eyes are spiky with black lashes.

'Nothing.' I offer him back the scowl he gave me the other day.

He looks at me with a level gaze. 'That your boat?'

'Maybe.'

'It's not, is it?' He looks cheerful. 'You nicking it?'

I stare at him. 'Maybe.'

'What for?' He takes a pear drop out of a paper bag and puts it in his mouth. It makes his cheeks bulge even more. He offers me the bag and I shake my head.

'I want to get to over there.' I pull my sleeves over my knuckles so that I can point out across the grey water to the distant shadow of the island.

He sucks noisily, squinting in the rain. 'What do you want to go there for? Looks creepy.'

I search his face for signs that he's making fun of me. His eyes don't flicker or slide away in that sly, tricky way I'm used to. He is solid in the rain, steady, interested. He's not one of the village kids, I remind myself. He doesn't know that he's supposed to laugh at me. I pull my shoulders back. 'I think my sister's there. I need to find her.' I wish I could explain better. 'Something has taken her.'

Now he'll laugh. But he nods, considering. 'What, like a monster or a murderer?'

'There's a Wild Man in the river. I think it's him.' I'm thrown by his attitude. 'I . . . I just know she's alive.' I shuffle wet feet. 'She's not drowned like everyone thinks.'

'Wild Man?' He raises his eyebrows.

I tilt my head towards the river. 'Hundreds of years ago a man got caught in fishing nets over there. He lived in the sea — still does. I've seen him.'

'Like a merman?' He crunches his sweet, splintering it between his teeth.

'Yes. But without a tail. He was covered in hair.'

'No clothes? Just hair?'

I nod.

He stares at the water. 'Wish I saw him.' He turns to me. 'And your sister,' he says, 'how long's she been missing?'

'Over three months.'

'But won't anyone take you across there,' he squints across at the distant bulk of the island, 'to get her?'

I shake my head. 'It's private. Owned by the

military. And nobody believes me.' I hunch my shoulders. 'I suppose it does sound stupid.'

'Doesn't to me.'

There's a figure approaching us through the rain. 'That's Joe,' he says. 'I live with him but he's not my brother. We're fostered.'

A thin boy in a clear plastic raincoat steps carefully around the puddles. I see that he couldn't possibly be this other boy's brother because he is African. He stands in front of us, thin and dark with black eyes and curly black hair that catches the rain in shining drops.

'Lunchtime,' the boy called Joe says. 'It's baked beans. You've got to come back.' I can't help staring at him. He is the colour of our dining-room table. He has large, snaggly teeth.

'Beans?' The plump boy is complaining, spreading his hands wide. 'Again?'

He shakes his head, muttering, 'Fish 'n' chips would be more like it. We're at the bleedin' seaside aren't we?'

He's stomping away from me, the other boy trotting beside him.

'Where are you staying?' I call after them.

'Caravan park,' the plump boy says over his shoulder.

I watch the two of them making their way between boats and puddles, thinking of the nursery rhyme about Jack Sprat and his wife. The plump boy stumbles into a puddle and I hear his distant swearing, the black boy's laughter.

I remember after they've gone that I never asked his name. *'Merde!'* I say aloud into the rain. I am drenched and there is no sign of it stopping. The water looked different against Joe's skin, brighter. Alice Redgrove once said that my sister had a touch of the tar brush. I hit her on the nose. A trickle of blood had run out of one nostril. She'd burst into tears and I'd had to stand in the corner of the classroom. Eva's skin is dark, but not nearly as dark as Joe's. She stands out because we are a blonde family. Eva once asked why her skin was different from ours and why her hair was black. Mum explained that she had a Jewish Portuguese great-grandmother. Mum said that the great-great-grandmother had been beautiful and exotic with olive skin, and that these things often skipped generations. I wished that I had inherited some exotic colouring, and then perhaps I wouldn't burn in the sun and look anaemic. Granny told Mum that I should be taking cod liver oil, and Mum makes me swallow a spoonful every day.

I think about the rowing boat — the heavy wooden weight of it — puzzling over how I'm going to drag it down to the water alone. Even if I borrow a trailer, I still have to get the boat onto it. My hood has come down. There's no point in pulling it back up. I can't get much wetter. Strands of my hair are plastered over my forehead. I wander slowly, my feet sloshing through puddles. Eva needs me. I have to find a way to move the rowing boat. A mother duck crosses the road with three ducklings following her. I stand with my hands in my pockets, watching them disappear through a hedge. Amongst the bits of tissue and biscuit crumbs in the gritty bottom of one pocket is the smooth curve of a fossilised shark's tooth. Once, prehistoric sharks swam over this land. They left their teeth behind, brown and shiny, scattered across the coastline, dug into the mud. Joanna was lying when she said that a shark had eaten Eva. I know she was. Man-eating sharks don't live in the North Sea. Not anymore.

As I approach our house, the front door opens and someone slips out, his head bowed against the rain. I have already unlatched the garden gate, my hand resting on the sign that says Holt House. It's too late to avoid him. I walk up the garden path. Straggly plants brush sodden tendrils and leaves against my legs. My heart jumps when I see that it's Robert Smith. We meet halfway on the path.

'Must be nice having Mummy and Daddy all to yourself,' he says with a wink. I don't know whether he is joking. 'You haven't seen me, right? I wasn't here.' His voice is harder. He pauses, and taps his nose. 'Not a word, not if you know what's good for you.' His face is livid with spots. He has mean eyes that are too close together. He doesn't move. I step off the path onto the drenched flowerbed to get past him. Thorns catch in my jeans.

Inside, the dog starts to bark. I can hear him scrabbling at the kitchen door. He must be shut in. Sophie has a foot on the first step of the stairs. She looks as though she's in a better mood. She puts up a hand to pat her messy hair into place, pulling a strand from her flushed cheek. She winds it around her finger and laughs. 'You look . . . drowned.' She raises one eyebrow. 'Take a hot bath, no?'

I stand in the hallway watching her sway up the stairs. I shrug my drenched coat from my shoulders and kick off my boots. A puddle has formed on the floor around my feet. Silver is whining. 'Just a minute,' I call, peeling off my socks, my toes cold on the floor. Upstairs I hear a door slam and the sound of a radio, pop music drifting through the house.

10

I have the curse. These are the worst, most humiliating days. I had to ask him if he could go to the chemist for me when it first happened. He'd blushed, ducking his chin. He won't buy anything for me. Says he doesn't have the money and anyway, it might attract attention. So I have scraps of old towel and a bucket of seawater to wash them in. The folded-over scraps are scratchy and bulky, making it difficult to walk. This must have been what it was like for Victorian women.

My stomach aches. At home, Mum would give me one of her pills and a hot-water bottle. I imagine the sensation of her fingers on my forehead. I can almost inhale her perfume: grapefruit, green leaves, yellow flowers. My mother. Once she was a girl who lived in Egypt whose parents were blown up by a bomb. I can't imagine what it was like to have that happen to your parents, or to live in a white house with shuttered windows looking over a desert. From her bedroom window she saw camels and palm trees. I wish I'd known her then. I wish I could go back in time and ask her questions. I'd ask her why she lied to me.

There is no working lavatory. I squat by the outer pagoda wall to pee, wet splattering concrete and weeds. Anything else and I have to tell him so that we can walk to the wire fence.

It's safe to dig in the shingle on the other side. I scrape out a hollow in the stones, scooping pebbles and grit with my hands. We have bits of torn newspaper to use. I long for rolls of white loo paper. Funny, I never thought I'd be saying that. I can't have any real privacy. He always lingers somewhere close, alert for any sudden movement. Sometimes I think that I'm being punished for a reason: for being bad, for being ungrateful, for being dirty; or because I wasn't supposed to be born in the first place.

★ ★ ★

I am so bored. I would kill for a novel, or even better, my sketchbook. I wish for the thick pages between my fingers, the soft flip they make as I turn them. When it was warm enough, my favourite place for drawing was on the swing that Dad rigged up for us under the chestnut tree in the garden with rope and a piece of old boat seat. Granny Gale found me there, secateurs grasped in hands huge in gardening gloves. 'Your diary?' she'd asked. I shook my head, showed her what I was doing. 'Ah, a different kind of diary,' she'd said, nodding and looking over my shoulder. 'You have a talent for observation.'

I'd smiled, thinking of how I'd draw her neat figure, with the battered straw hat and the scarf trailing across her narrow shoulders.

'Oscar Wilde once had one of his characters say that she never travelled without her diary,' she'd said, 'because one should always have something sensational to read on the train.'

She'd winked. 'But you shouldn't be parted from your pencils. A true artist never stops working, you see.' She'd waved the secateurs. 'Take your talent with you everywhere, Eva. Don't leave it behind.'

I didn't understand what she meant at the time. I do now. Billy has a book called *The Prophet*. He turns thin pages slowly, licking his fingers, pausing to reread passages. I watch him now, hunched into the nest of old blankets that he sleeps in, the rain falling outside. He sucks in his bottom lip as he concentrates, like a child. Sometimes his eyebrows move up his forehead slowly, two caterpillars crawling over his skin as if in disbelief.

'What?' He's felt my stare.

I drop my gaze. 'Nothing.'

He closes the book. 'I suppose you're a bookworm. One of them read-half-the-library types.'

I shrug. 'My favourite thing to do is draw. But I like reading. I like stories.'

'I've never really understood the point,' he says. 'There are films, aren't there?'

'So why are you reading that?'

'It could be in here.' He taps the cover briefly. 'It'll be in code, so I have to read it slow and careful.'

'What do you mean?'

'The message I'm waiting for. The one about you. She might have hidden it in here somewhere.'

I gaze at the worn book in his hands and feel something shrivelling inside. He's mad. How do you speak to a mad person? How do you reason with them? He gets up and comes over to hand me the book. 'I've had enough for the day. You can read it for a bit, if you like.'

Reaching up to take it, I accidentally put some weight on my ankle and wince.

'Let me see.' He gestures towards my foot. 'Still troubling you?'

I roll up the bottoms of my jeans to show him. My skin is puffy and flushed, the ankle shapeless and heavy.

He touches me and I gasp. 'I'll get some more seawater.' He frowns. 'You should have said.'

He's locked the door behind him. I sit alone on the only chair with the book in my hands. I flick through pages, my eyes skimming swarms of black letters. I am so hungry for stories, for anything that will take me away from this empty room. But this isn't a novel, it's a bit like poetry and there are pictures. I'm surprised. It doesn't seem to fit with Billy's personality. He doesn't seem the type to enjoy poetry. His lips move when he reads, silently mouthing the words, as if he's struggling to understand.

He lugs the bucket in, water slopping over the sides. He places it at my feet, indicating that I put my ankle inside. The seawater is cold.

He tips his head at the book in my lap. 'A bloke gave it to me when I was in the cells — said I needed it more than him.'

Cells? I stare at him. This is the first time he's mentioned prison. I open my mouth, but I don't have the courage to ask him what his crime had been. 'Tell me about the dream,' I say instead.

'The one about me.'

He pulls at his beard. 'The dream . . . I don't know.' He frowns and looks away.

'Please,' I say quietly. 'I'm interested.'

He shoots me a suspicious look and I hold his gaze, unblinking. The sound of the waves and the wind washes between us. He nods, as if I've asked him another question. 'A voice spoke to me,' he says slowly. 'At the time I was in a bad place. Didn't know where to go, or what to do. She told me to come here to the island.' He tips his face towards the lofty heights of the pagoda. 'Soon as I saw it, I knew this was the right place. You can see all around. Good for protection. Got myself a fishing rod. I could survive off the land for a while. I heard the voice again a week later. She told me that I would find a girl and save her life.' He hunches his shoulders. 'There was darkness and rain. I was running, searching, looking for the girl I had to save. But they were here too.'

He looks at me with narrowed eyes. 'They've been following me for a long time. They're close. Always watching. So we have to be careful. We're protected here. As long as we do what the voice says.' His tongue slides out, wetting his lips, and he nods. 'I'm waiting to know what I have to do next. That's why we're not going anywhere. Not till she speaks.'

I don't know how to respond. I don't want to provoke him. So I say nothing, curling and uncurling my toes on the gritty plastic bottom of the bucket. His words repeat in my head. A pulse beats at my temple, tightening in a band around my forehead, a headache like the ones that Mum gets.

He's sitting cross-legged at my feet and he nods at the bucket. 'Let's have a look at it now.'

He takes hold of my wet leg and places my foot on his knee. The swelling has gone down a little. There's a mild throbbing deep inside the flesh. He puts his fingers over my thickened ankle. Shocked, I hold my breath. But his touch is feather-light, barely touching at all. Softly, his fingertips circle my swollen skin. I feel a buzz of sensation running through me. He's taken my foot in his other hand, and he begins to work his thumb and fingers around the edges of my foot and around each toe, pushing firmly into the crevices, massaging the joints and around the contours of each nail. My bones seem fragile inside his grasp. I'm rigid, staring at my bloated skin and blackened toenails. His hand is engraved with dirt, his nails battered and ragged. I am silent. I have an odd feeling in the pit of my stomach: a kind of unravelling.

I don't know what this means. I don't know why he's doing this. His touch makes me queasy. I am alert and wary, afraid of this intimacy growing into something else. I cross my arms over my chest, clamp my knees together. I will kill him if he tries anything. I will kill myself. Blood pounds in my head: a thick, dark storm. I'm aware that I'm gritting my teeth. The grating sound echoes deep inside me.

He lets go of my foot, dropping it like a picked-clean fish carcass back into the bucket of water. He's staring at me, his eyes glassy bright.

'The angel sounded beautiful.' His voice is hoarse. 'I wait every day to hear her again. It's like a pain here . . . ' He touches the scruffy navy jumper over the place where his heart beats. 'I know she'll come back.'

There's a fluttering over our heads, a scuffle of feathers, and we both look up sharply. A seagull has landed in the opening above us. I see the white of tail feathers and the shape of wings opening.

I imagine his angel, something huge and glowing, a creature with a massive wingspan that hovers over the island at night while we sleep. I give her burning eyes and a low, deep voice. Perhaps she weeps when she sees what her words have made him do. Maybe she looks down into the pagoda and watches us huddled on our filthy blankets, and realises that she has made a mistake. Speak to him again, I beg. Tell him to let me go. Tell him that was the purpose of saving me. But there is no angel.

He rolls my trouser leg down and unfolds himself, dusting at his own trousers ineffectually. He stares out at the still-falling rain and hunches his shoulders. 'I'm going outside for a moment,' he says. 'I'll be watching the door.'

Billy's footsteps fade away until there is only the insistent patter of rain and the distant thud and rattle of waves on the beach. I sit with my foot in the bucket, hunching forwards. I feel boneless, exhausted. Once scientists and soldiers crowded into this strange room to work; I wonder if their ghosts move around us, invisible, efficient, recording measurements and facts.

I slide my hands over my aching stomach and close my eyes. I have to get away from this place. I'll make another plan when my ankle is better, when I don't have the curse. I want to go home. I feel like Dorothy in *The Wizard of Oz*. But I don't have any red shoes. I focus hard, wishing myself home, and I'm spinning away from the pagoda, away from Billy, flying across the sea, across the river to our house where my spirit slips through the gap in my bedroom window.

I'm going to see Mum and Dad and Faith. I'll watch their faces light up with surprise when I appear in the living room. Silver will scent me first from his bed in the kitchen, his ears pricked, a low growl in his throat. I want to hold them all, smell them, feel them, but as I float down the stairs I begin to dissolve, bits of me scattering into nothingness. I can hear my family, but they are just around the corner, in the next room, out of sight.

11

Clara lies in the darkened bedroom, a damp cloth on her forehead. She's taken a couple of her pills. They haven't had any effect yet. Sharp light flickers at the edges of her vision. It hurts to open her eyes and so she keeps them shut. She is disappointed in herself. It's the first time she's been in bed during the day for weeks. It feels like a setback.

It's Saturday morning. Faith came into their room early with something curled in her hand. She'd opened her fingers to reveal a large black beetle, dead, and big as a cockroach. Clara had raised herself on her elbows, the morning light already too bright. A migraine scrabbled behind her eyes, something dragged from her dreams, a creature not unlike the thing that sat on Faith's palm: oily black, sharp-footed, scaly.

'Lovely, darling,' she'd murmured.

Max had redrawn the curtains, fetched her a cloth and a glass of water and taken Faith downstairs. She'd heard their cheerful voices fading away, the dog barking, and then peace. Just wood pigeons outside her window. Even their soft cooing is uncomfortable. She craves complete silence, complete darkness. She thinks of Faith's expression as she'd offered them the beetle to admire. Where had her youngest daughter's obsession come from? Since she was a toddler she's collected bones, strange-shaped pebbles and fossils, slipping them into her pockets, hoarding them in drawers. Faith shows no fear of anything wild. When they'd come across an adder at the side of the path, Clara and Eva had stepped back, instinctively wary, but Faith had leant over the snake. 'It won't hurt you,' she'd said with a trace of scorn, 'it's more frightened of us than we are of it. Isn't it beautiful?'

Clara hears the sudden whirr of a hairdryer in another room. Sophie. It still shocks her that Sophie is living with them. She forgets sometimes that she is in the house, starting when Sophie appears quietly behind her. It's odd to think that the girl is only a little older than Eva. She has the beauty of youth, just as Eva did, that rare bloom that lights up the skin from the inside. But unlike Eva, Sophie has a look of boredom on her features, a language in the slump of her shoulders and loose hands that says she's seen it all before. But then perhaps it's just as well that they have an au pair who is unfazed by any awkward silences or tensions. She seems to have fitted into the household surprisingly well, seamlessly really, and Clara is grateful for it, and guiltily grateful that Sophie slips away to her room when her duties are done. But she doesn't appear to be lonely, just independent. She must have made some friends in the village as she's out most evenings. Clara had worried that an au pair would be bored here, especially a girl from a city.

Clara stretches in the double bed. Her bones grow heavier, sinking into the mattress, into the languid treacly depths of the pills. Noises outside the window fade: the throaty coo of pigeons, the crack of a branch on the acacia tree, the flutter of downy wings. The room retreats. She remembers sunlight, an afternoon from last summer.

She stands by the flooded reservoir with her girls. Sky arches above them, blue and clear. Flat water ripples and shudders, blown by the wind. 'Look,' Faith is shouting. 'There's something under the water!'

The three of them crowd around, sandals sinking into the mud at the edge of the reservoir, shoulders knocking against shoulders, Eva shrieking as her foot slips, and they peer at the lip of water, trying to see through the shadowy movement below. Faith is right. There is something just under the waves; it looks like two horns nudging the line between water and air.

'It's a deer,' Eva says, her voice shaking.

Clara follows the shape of the horns, curving like stiffened seaweed, and understands that they are really nascent antlers. In a head that bobs slightly, tipping towards the surface, a pair of large eyes gazes upwards. The deer seems to be looking straight at her. Clara starts, a gasp catching in her throat. Of course it's dead. Sightless. It is standing upright, fur rippling gently. The creature must have got stuck, Clara realises, then drowned as the water rose. Its tiny, sharp feet caught deep in the mud.

Eva is down on her haunches. She turns, her mouth sagging. 'Poor thing,' she whispers.

Faith nods. 'Horrible.' But she is staring with fascination at the deer, unblinking, enthralled.

Clara struggles out of the memory, opening her eyes into the dark room. She'd forgotten about finding the drowned deer. An afternoon of flat heat, the tail end of the holidays, after an August storm. She thinks of Eva with her hand pressed over her mouth. The three of them had stood together in silence, as if at the opening of a grave, before they'd turned and walked away, subdued, into the altered afternoon.

Clara blinks away the memory, snatching the cloth from her forehead. The coolness has leached from it, the damp fabric filled with her body heat. She lets it fall to the floor in a soggy heap. She turns over with a groan, pressing her face into the pillow. Forces herself to empty her mind. Feels a tumbling into nothingness. At last she can sleep.

★　★　★

There is breathing next to her, the breathing of a baby: that soft snuffling, the lift and fall of tiny lungs. Clara knows without looking that it is Eva, curled in blankets, swaddled tightly, her tiny face scrunched shut. Clara is filled with complete happiness. Her baby sleeps beside her. Nothing is more beautiful, nothing more perfect. There is the creak and whine of a door opening. A slice of light cuts across her face. She opens her eyes and squints into a yellow glare. The rustling of robes alerts her to somebody else in the room, fumbling movement, figures bending at the borders of sight. Clara forces her head off the pillow. Above her, they are lifting Eva out of the cot. There are two of them. Black cowls over their heads, the flutter of loose sleeves, thin white hands around her child. Eva begins to cry, a staggering, hiccupping protest.

'You're not fit,' one of the figures says in a low voice. 'Not a fit mother.'

Clara is trying to struggle out of bed to stop them taking Eva, but she is chained up, heavy and weak, her limbs bound tightly. She can't move, can't call out. No, she tries to scream. Don't take my baby.

'It's for the best,' the voice says. 'She'll be better off without you.'

'She has a new mother,' another voice whispers. 'A new family.'

The door shuts.

12

I found a dead stag beetle behind the cellar door. Normally I find them in the log pile by the shed. It has red antlers so I know it's male. In the Middle Ages they thought stag beetles did the work of the devil. Mum seemed to think so too when I showed it to her. She screwed up her face at the black armour and pincers. She didn't get up this morning. She's stayed in bed with one of her migraines, her bedroom door closed.

I'm tiptoeing along the landing because I don't want to bother her. I know where to step to avoid each creaking floorboard. My bare feet make no sound on the worn carpet. Sophie's door is open. I peer into the room, seeing Sophie brushing her hair in front of the mirror, her head tipped to one side. The brush travels up and down, pulling through a shining curtain. Some of her hair flies out in crackling strands. I catch the gleam of pinky gold around her neck before I understand. She is wearing Eva's pearls. She catches sight of me in the reflection and her hand goes to the necklace, curling it inside her fingers.

I meet her stare in the mirror. She doesn't blink or look embarrassed. I'm the first to turn away. I walk on, my heart hammering inside my ribcage. I don't know what to do. I pause outside Mum's door, listening. I can hear nothing but a rush of silence, the faintest trace of breathing. I bite my lip, my hand resting on the curve of the doorknob. I imagine Mum raising her head from the pillow, blinking through the gloom at me, her voice hushed and tense. I let go and hurry down the back stairs into the kitchen.

I'm relieved to see Dad standing by the sink eating a piece of toast and listening to the radio.

'Hello, Shrimp,' he says through a mouthful of Marmite toast. 'Want some breakfast?'

I shake my head.

'Not hungry?' He swallows. His fingers are shiny with butter. 'I'm going to watch the Olympic opening ceremony later on the telly. I expect the president will do the honours . . . that man loves the limelight.' He looks at me. 'You do know who the President of the United States is, don't you, Faith?'

I shrug.

He rolls his eyes. 'Ronald . . . ' he starts to say, but then looks at me properly. 'What's up?'

'It's Sophie,' I say, rubbing my left foot against the back of my other ankle. 'I think she's wearing Eva's pearls.'

He frowns.

I balance on my right leg. 'You know, the ones she got from aunt whatsherface.'

His smile fades and I feel guilty because I remember that that is how he looks nowadays and that I've altered his mood.

'Are you sure?' He scratches the back of his neck. 'Because that's a serious accusation, Faith.'

I nod, feeling sick. 'I saw her with them.'

He sighs and glances up briefly at the ceiling and I know he's thinking of Mum, asleep in a darkened room with a cold cloth over her forehead. He wipes his mouth and says, 'Right then.' His shoulders slump. 'I suppose I'd better go and have a word.'

I don't know what to do, alone in the kitchen. The rain has gone and the sun is flat white above the trees. Wood pigeons coo in the oak trees at the end of the garden. I imagine the river, sparkling, full of fluttering sails, holiday voices and people setting out to have picnics. I hate to think of Sophie wearing the pearls — even though we never met the aunt that gave them to Eva, even though Eva said the pearls weren't her style and hasn't worn them for years. It doesn't matter. The necklace belongs to her. I lean against the sink looking at the roses just outside the window, creamy petals falling open. There are bees hovering. The low buzzing is a friendly sound. I am alert to any noises above me: raised voices or shouting. What will Dad say? Maybe he'll sack her. I hope so.

Dad's footsteps are heavy behind me.

'You must have made a mistake, Faith,' he says, shaking his head. 'She's not wearing the necklace.' He crosses to the sink but he doesn't look at me. He scrapes his toast crumbs off his plate and then puts it in the sink. 'She's cleaning the bathroom.'

I put a fingernail in my mouth and bite it, tearing a strip off. I want to put my hand on his shirtsleeve, feel the strong twist of his arm underneath. I want him to stop talking and hug me, forget about the pearls.

'She was upset and I don't blame her.' He

111

turns to me, looking disappointed. 'Actually, she was very understanding in the circumstances, said anyone can make a mistake.' His face softens. 'We should be kind, darling. Sophie is alone here, remember, in a strange country. Think how you'd feel.'

I open my mouth to protest, remembering the bruise on her neck, Robert Smith leaving our house with a smirk on his face. I want to tell Dad that I don't trust Sophie. She was wearing the necklace. I know she was. But I don't want to upset him any more.

'Look, I know it's hard at the moment, but I need you to be grown up for me.' He puts out his hand and draws me close. I lean into the bulk of his chest, smelling a trace of washing powder, his spicy aftershave. 'You know how Mum is — we don't want to put more strain on her, do we?' I shake my head, rubbing my cheek against his shirt.

★ ★ ★

The caravan park is on the outskirts of the village. After the rain, the air is complicated. I can smell scents pooling in water, petals and leaves, rotting things, fox pee evaporating into the thick light. Mist clings and separates as I walk slowly through the heat, up the lane past the castle and the Robinsons' farm, brushing away flies and mosquitoes with swipes of my hands. I have to pass Joanna's bungalow on the way and I hear her voice in the garden, laughing with another child. They are on the swing in the front. I catch a glimpse of red dress flying up, the kick of feet in white sandals. I hurry past, head down.

There are about twenty caravans in the field, cars parked next to them, and a cluster of tents in the far corner. A dog is tied up outside the nearest van. It barks steadily. It's an Alsatian with a long, shaggy coat. I hold out my hand towards it in the way that Eva taught me. Let them smell you first, she said.

'You must be hot,' I murmur. His damp black nose touches my fingers and he wags his tail.

'You messing with my dog?' A thin woman with a sharp nose, a cigarette jammed in her mouth, leans out of the caravan door.

I jump and shake my head.

'You want to be careful.' She narrows her eyes, showing thin blue skin on her lids. 'He eats girls like you for breakfast.'

I step back quickly, my hand falling to my side.

She laughs, a rasping sound, and waves her fingers, smoke trailing. 'I'm only kidding, love. Soft as anything, he is.'

Encouraged, I ask her if she knows which caravan Joe lives in. She purses her lips and shrugs. 'Not on first-name terms with anyone; only got here the other day.'

'Joe is African,' I explain.

'Oh, the little coloured boy. Yes,' she nods towards the other side of the park, 'I've seen him. Think they're in the big brown van with the green estate car next to it.'

The caravan is parked out of the shade. The

sides and roof blaze. There is a black plastic bucket outside the open door. I lean over to look inside. The bucket is half-full of water and two large crabs lie motionless at the bottom. I nudge the bucket to see if they're alive. One of them moves its claws inside the swell of movement.

'Hello.' Joe stands beside me. His skin gleams.

'You're not supposed to keep them,' I tell him. 'They'll die. You're supposed to let them go after you've caught them.'

'Don't belong to you though, do they?' Joe says, his mouth folding into a line.

'She thinks everything belongs to her.' The plump boy steps out of the caravan. 'Crabs. Boats.' He winks at me. He has a burnt nose. Skin peels in shrivelled layers.

'It's like a rule,' I say. 'An unwritten rule.'

'Don't like rules, do we Joe?'

Joe smiles broadly.

A man's voice calls out from inside the caravan, and then a head appears in the doorway. A large, bald man sweating dark patches stands in his shirtsleeves. He's holding a fat baby in his arms. There are mermaids tattooed on his bristling forearms. 'Come and watch Carol for me,' he says to the two boys. 'I need to get down to the village shop. Look sharp, Fred.'

The man looks at me curiously and gives a small nod of greeting, but he's already handing the baby to Fred, who grasps her with both arms, holding her so that she faces outwards, her creased legs dangling down. She smiles at me, showing gums with two teeth pushing through. 'This is Carol,' Fred tells me.

114

'Hello, Carol.' I touch one of her curling pink fingers. 'I'm Faith.'

The inside of their caravan is unbearably hot. It feels sealed up. A fat bluebottle blunders against a grubby window. The place is packed with things. A tiny fold-out table is piled with plates and cups, jars of ketchup, a bag of apples and cartons of tea. There are folded towelling nappies, board games, crabbing lines, children's clothes and toys spilling over every surface.

I look around for a space in which to sit and give up. Fred jiggles Carol on his hip. He stands at an angle, jutting his hip out to make balancing a baby easier. It is obvious that he's an old hand at it. 'Sandra's at the castle with Penny, our foster sister,' he explains mysteriously. 'That was Les. Our foster dad.'

The last caravan I was in belonged to Granny. It had rose-patterned curtains at the windows, jasmine oil wafting from the folds. Her bed was covered in a faded ciderdown, mended with neat stitches, and she had jars of homemade jam on the shelves labelled in her writing.

Carol has begun to sob and Fred bounces her up and down, throwing her so high that her cheeks wobble. Her eyes widen. She looks surprised and then scared and then surprised again. But she stops crying.

A sharp knock on the outside of the window makes us all turn quickly. I catch a spreading leer, a flash of red hair. Joanna. I let out a gasp. There is the sound of giggling. Fred and Joe and I crowd into the caravan doorway to see two girls running off. The other one is Ellie Dawkins.

115

Joanna pauses to ask over her shoulder, 'Do your new friends know that you're mental, Faith Gale?' She runs on and stops again, pointing at Fred, laughing, 'Is that your boyfriend?'

'What's he called?' Ellie calls out. 'Fatty?'

'No,' Joanna shouts. 'Look, *that's* her boyfriend — the black one!'

Joe pushes past me and is down the steps and onto the grass. He's running fast, legs flashing behind him, and the girls scream, terrified and delighted. He stoops and picks up a stone, lets it fly with a firm twist of arm. The stone hits Ellie's ankle and we hear her yelp.

'Friends of yours, are they?' Fred hands me the baby and I find that she is heavy and warm in my arms. She tangles some of my hair in her fat, sticky fist.

'Sandra's taking me and Joe to see *Indiana Jones* tomorrow,' he says. 'I'll ask her if you can come too.' He shrugs. 'If you like.'

I lay my cheek against Carol's head, breathing in an unfamiliar baby smell. Under her hair, thin and sparse as an old lady's, she has brown scabs on her scalp. She gets hold of my wrist and pulls it to her so that she can suction her lips around the cold circle of my watch. She is surprisingly strong. I feel the slip of saliva on my skin and remember Eva. How she made me promise not to tell Mum and Dad about her boyfriend. Her wet palm pressed against mine.

13

I have that fraction of time when I wake in the morning, just before I remember where I am, when I feel normal. When, for a second, I think that I'm in my own bed at home: sketches and paintings are tacked up on the walls, clean brushes waiting in an old jam jar. On the floor, among a mess of discarded tights and shoes and sliding piles of books, Silver sprawls, his nose twitching as he sleeps. Downstairs, Mum is clattering around in the kitchen. Then the horror rushes in. I feel the deadness of it in my stomach, a cold, dead weight of pain, as if I've swallowed stones.

I read a novel once about an African slave in England. She ate dirt because she wanted to die. I wonder what would happen if I crammed my mouth full of shingle, choking it down. But I don't want to die. I want to see Mum and Dad and Faith again. I want to feel Marco's lips on mine. My ankle hurts. The swelling isn't so bad, but I'm walking with a limp. It aches at night and if I slip on uneven pebbles hot spikes shoot through the bone.

Billy has begun to keep a closer watch. He's tying my hands again when we go fishing, even though I hobble to make it over the shingle. He's right if he thinks I'm planning to escape. I have an idea. I'm going to push him into the pit. It is the most simple and logical solution. Only the plan is flawed because he rarely stands anywhere near it, and never with his back to me. He's not stupid. Also, although I am tall for a girl, he is taller and broader, and I'm at a disadvantage with my ankle.

If I had a run up, maybe I could do it. He warned me ages ago to never come up behind him. 'Don't surprise me, girl. Soldiers don't like surprises,' he'd said, and his thumb rubbed the hilt of his knife.

Hard to believe that he was a soldier. He'd be a disgrace to any army with his straggly beard and rancid clothes. He has no pride in his looks. Not like Marco. I can't bear to think what I look like. I'm glad there is no mirror here. My scalp itches all the time. The skin on my hands is dull with filth, my nails broken. I must smell. Sometimes I catch a whiff of myself: a pungent, thick scent, like an animal. My teeth are furry and I have ulcers that I can't stop probing with my tongue. I dream about my teeth falling out.

I'm a couple of miles from home, but I may as well be the other side of the world. When aeroplanes pass high in the sky, leaving vapour trails, I wonder if any of the passengers can see me, a speck on the ground. I don't exist in the outside world. I suppose I'm a memory. Sometimes I'm afraid that I died in the accident and really I'm a ghost. Billy is a ghost too. We exist in a limbo with the invisible scientists and soldiers waiting for something that never happens.

Each day Billy and I follow the same dull routine. It's all arranged around finding food

— picking it or killing it — and then the eating and drinking and expelling waste. At least Billy has his book to read, although it makes him angry. He shakes his head, repeats sentences aloud. It's better when he reads his letters. He keeps them folded in an old tin. He smiles when he looks at them, smoothing his fingers over the scrawled inky writing. He must have re-read the same ones over and over again.

We walk around the island and depending on his mood, he'll either bind my hands tightly behind my back, or he'll leave them free and just attach the rope to my waist. We stoop to pick wild sea peas, pulling them from under their purple flowers, and I've shown Billy how to eat samphire; he can't be a local because I had to show him how you can tear the green flesh away from spiky stalks with your teeth. 'You cook it in boiling water,' I explained. 'It's a bit like asparagus. But you can eat it raw too.' I think he thought I was trying to poison him; he watched me chewing with suspicion, before licking a plant with a cautious tongue.

If the seals are there on the point, lazing in the sun, it makes me remember the last time Faith and I came to the island. I miss her, even her annoying habit of collecting disgusting bits of bone and dead things, the way she used to hang around in my room, touching stuff, fiddling with my jewellery. I think about her hair, its ridiculous texture, soft and floppy against her scalp; I ache for the feel of it under my fingers, for the sight of her skinny limbs, knobbled at the knee and elbow, and her skin that mottles blue in cold weather like the veins in Dad's cheese.

I dressed Faith up as a goth once. We spent a Saturday afternoon transforming her with dark lipstick and black eyeliner. She sat on the edge of my bed with her hands clasped in her lap, tipping her head back and closing her eyes obediently. I backcombed her hair until it stood up in a white halo, the texture sticky with hairspray and thick as candyfloss. She laughed at herself in the mirror, tipping her head from side to side to see the tower of hair wobble. But dressed in one of my long black skirts with necklaces piled on, she really looked the part. I was startled. 'You're so lucky. Your skin and hair are perfect,' I told her. 'You look like a vampire. A beautiful one,' I added quickly, feeling a quick twist of envy. I would never look like that.

The island has a spirit. I felt it when Faith and I came over for our brief visits; but now I know it's true. The sound of wind in the gorse bushes and the movement of waves on the shore are like a creature shifting and breathing beneath me. The concrete huts and the pagodas are a malignant growth on its back. The hard surfaces and sharp corners, decaying remnants of atomic experiments, are things to be endured until time destroys them. The island is waiting. Eventually the buildings will crumble and fall, turning to dust. Grass and weeds will push up through the concrete road, breaking it into slabs, bindweed crawling along barbed wire, choking the rusting rolls. It's already happening.

There is a sense of being watched. Not just by Billy. He's right: something is watching us both.

120

I feel it as a darkness lingering just out of sight, in the shadows of empty buildings, behind broken glass.

We keep away from the side of the island that faces the mainland. There are too many yachts coming out of the mouth of the river, and a chance that someone on board will see us. On the other side of the island there is nothing to see but a fathomless distance of light and air and water. When ocean liners creep along the horizon they could be space ships coming from a foreign planet. Occasionally a boat will appear offshore when we're on the beach, and Billy pulls me down flat on the stones, lying over me, crushing me, until they've gone. More fishermen came at night. Billy heard them before I did. He tied me up, stuffed a gag in my mouth so that I struggled for air. He padlocked the door, crouching by it with his knife in his hand, muttering that if he had a rifle he'd soon get rid of them. He seems anxious. I catch him looking at me with a strange expression and my heart jumps.

The days are hot and long. But the summer won't last for ever. I am afraid of the autumn. I don't know how we'll survive when it gets cold. There will be less food for scavenging too. We'll starve to death. I have to get away. I have to go home.

* * *

'Billy, can I have some water?' I ask quietly. 'I mean clean water, to wash in?'

We are sitting by the fire on the beach after

121

another meal of cod. My fingers stink of fish all the time. Fragments of fish skin are caught deep under my nails, embedded in dirt.

It is dark. The sea draws slow breaths, raking pebbles across the shoreline. The moon glows mustard, low in the sky. Hunched over, Billy doesn't respond. I stare into bright embers. My tongue pokes at the bits of food trapped between my teeth. 'Please,' I let myself beg, 'I'm so dirty. I can't bear it. My skin has sores. They're not healing.' I know I'm pushing him; but I feel desperate enough to risk making him angry. The fire spits. Sparks flare and die. I catch a glimpse of movement above my head and look up to see a shooting star, its disintegrating tail of silver light.

He scratches his head vigorously, nails making scraping sounds. I wonder if he has head lice.

'Fresh water's too valuable to waste on washing,' he tells me gruffly.

'I can't go on like this,' my voice breaks. 'I need a proper wash. I'll get ill if I don't. I won't drink so much.' I take a deep breath. 'Please.'

He sighs. 'Maybe,' he says. 'I'll think about it. Maybe tomorrow.'

* * *

He puts me in the pit the next morning. When he comes back he's filled the big plastic water containers and acquired a thin bar of yellow soap.

'You can have one bucket of water,' he says, 'and that's it. No more.'

He sets me up behind the gorse bushes. I have the bucket, soap in my hand and a scratchy towel. The anticipation of feeling the slip of fresh water makes me grin, my lips cracking as they stretch. Billy is sitting on the pebbles about ten feet off, his back to me. He'll be listening out for sounds on the shingle. I can't move without alerting him. The stones give me away.

I kneel and scoop water into my hands, a clear cold puddle leaking between my fingers. Leaning over the bucket, I splash my face, gasping, rubbing all over and then lather up, bubbles blooming. I taste the sourness of soap, getting the sting of it in my eyes. It feels good.

I glance at Billy to check that he's still got his back to me and peel off my shirt and bra. I soap and rinse around my neck, under my arms. Trickles of water run down my skin, itching me. I can see the paler tracks they make through the grime.

My nipples harden under my hands. I remember how Marco's fingers brushed against my breasts, his intake of breath as he felt the form of them. One night, after coming out of the club, on our way to Lucy's house, our ears ringing from the thunder of bass, he paused to kiss me outside the Odeon. His tongue began to push harder, deeper. My heart contracted like a fist, warmth swelling between my legs so that I tilted my pelvis, pushing my groin into him. Our mouths were wet and wide, opened into each other. But Marco broke away with an exclamation.

Robert smirked from the shadows. There had

123

been a grinning pack of boys outside the kebab shop. They called out, whistling and shouting obscenities. Marco's mouth tightened. He walked away fast and I had to run to keep up.

'Twats,' he muttered. 'Can't wait to get away from this bloody place.'

I was silent, scurrying after him, hurt that he wanted to leave me and ashamed that I knew them. I had to stop myself clinging to his hand.

A week later I heard a moped behind me. Robert pulled over, his flaming face leering out of his visor. 'What you going out with a poof for?'

I glared at him, silent.

'He is though, in't he? Wears make-up like a girl.'

'You don't know anything about it,' I retorted. 'He's a musician. An artist. I wouldn't expect you to understand.'

'They're all words for pansy. Bet he hasn't fucked you, has he?'

I walked on, my face a mask.

I heard him laugh. 'You need a real man,' he called. 'And you know where you can find me.'

'In your dreams!' I shouted after him, gripping my hands into fists. I wanted to smash his slimy face in. His moped revved with a scream, moving away quickly down the road towards the village green. Light bounced off his helmet. If I could have thrown straight, I would have hurled a stone at it.

I remember the longing for a weapon to throw; wanting to hear the impact it would have

124

made, to see Robert's body hitting the tarmac, the wheels of his moped spinning uselessly as the machine slid across the road in the dust.

Trembling, I strip off the rest of my clothes and wash harder, pushing the soap between my legs, scrubbing. I leave red marks, my skin stinging. I have to get clean. There are only a few inches of scummy water left in the bottom of the bucket. I hold it over my head and tip, letting the remains of the water wash over me, dripping around my face and through my hair.

Wrapped in the threadbare towel, I look up. Billy is watching me, mouth drooping inside his beard. He seems as shocked as me. I don't know how long he's been there. We make eye contact for a moment and his face closes, becomes furtive. He drops his gaze.

I am furious and afraid. 'You said you wouldn't look.'

He reddens under his hair, shaking his head. 'I didn't see anything.'

I stand, wet and shivering in the wind. An unspoken promise dangles between us, broken. I feel vulnerable and tired. I can't face putting my dirty clothes on. Slowly, I reach for my trousers, balancing on one foot, tugging them on. Billy has turned his back again. His shoulders are hunched.

'Tell me when you're dressed,' he says in a subdued voice. 'I've been thinking. You can have a wash every week. It's only fair.'

The triumph of this falls flat. I close my eyes; I can't let myself imagine the weeks stretching ahead, the fumbling washes in a bucket, eking out the soap. I swallow and force myself to acknowledge him.

'Thanks.' I hear the sound of myself, thin and empty.

14

Sandra's gold earrings clash with her lemon-yellow fringe. From the back seat of the car I see into the rough, thick texture of her hair, dark roots pushing up underneath. We're driving into Ipswich in their green estate car with the radio blaring, Joe and I sliding about on the wide back seat, concertinaing into each other at every corner. Sandra's bony fingers tap out a beat on the steering wheel. Fred has to hold the aerial out of the window to get any reception. Sometimes the music squawks into static crackles and a fuzzy noise crashes against our ears and then Sandra yells, 'Hold it higher, Fred.'

Mum wanted to meet Sandra before she let me go with them. I was worried about what she'd say when she saw the untidy caravan. But she accepted a cup of tea and stood with Carol in her arms, cooing. Penny was there, playing with dolls on the floor. At five years old, she was too young to come with us. Her hair was pulled into tight pigtails. I looked at the stretch of scalp at her parting, wondering if it was painful. I fidgeted, twiddling the buttons on my cardigan, shuffling my feet in and out of my slingback sandals. I was afraid that Mum wouldn't like Sandra, would stop me from going to see the film. I was certain that she would disapprove of Sandra's lime-green ripped sweatshirt and black mini-skirt. I began to breathe when they laughed together. Sandra threw back her head, opening her mouth wide, showing fillings and a glint of gold at the back. Mum said how kind it was to take me with them. She pressed some coins into Sandra's hand. 'For the ticket,' she said. 'And ice-creams for everyone.'

We sit in the front row. When the interval comes on, the ice-cream lady stands in the aisle with her tray round her neck, and Fred and I queue for tubs of strawberry and chocolate, Mum's money in my fist. I imagine Granny tut-tutting, telling me it's immoral to be in a dark cinema while the sun blazes outside. The film makes me think about what it is to be brave, to keep going on a quest, never giving up.

Walking into the afternoon, the sunlight is like a slap. There are cars on the road, engines purring, and the sound of a siren in the distance. Shoppers pass us with bags dangling from their hands. The world seems too big and noisy. Thinking of Indiana eating chilled monkey brains brings a funny, watery taste into my mouth, especially after chocolate ice-cream. The mad priests and their human sacrifices make me afraid for Eva, of what might be happening to her. Fred and Joe run along the dusty pavement, leaping onto low walls and pretending to lasso each other. An old man with a lumpy face like porridge shakes his walking stick at them.

I have a brilliant idea. The boys can help me move the boat into the water. I bounce on my toes, eager to ask them. Sandra shouts at Fred and Joe to shut up and come and walk properly, but I can tell that she doesn't really mean it. The boys ignore her. 'Boys,' she twitches with a spasm of laughter, 'rascals aren't they? You should come to tea soon.' She stretches her sinewy arm towards me. 'Come in the next couple of days. We're off home soon. Shame, but Les has got to get back to work.'

Her fingers are papery on my skin, long nails red as a letterbox. My heart beats faster. Fred hadn't said anything about leaving.

* * *

As I wave goodbye to Sandra and the boys, watching their car driving away, I think of a letterbox: the place for posting messages. I wish I knew how to get a message to my sister, to tell her that I am coming. Black smoke spurts from the hanging exhaust pipe as the car disappears around the bend.

Inside the hall, I know that something is wrong. The air is tight and sharp. And then I hear their voices. Mum and Dad, arguing again.

'You're wrong . . . we need to think of Faith, what she needs.' Dad's voice comes from the kitchen. 'She doesn't want to grow up in a place where everyone knows that her sister drowned. People gossiping. She needs a fresh start. And she can't swim, Clara. Think about it.'

'Stop trying to make this about her.' Mum's voice is high-pitched. 'This is about you. You want to move because you can't stand seeing the sea anymore. It makes you feel guilty . . . '

'God damn it, Clara, what do you think

. . . that I don't know that?' Dad's voice has dropped to a low growl. 'You're never going to forgive me, are you?' Almost a whisper.

Silence. I move towards the stairs as quietly as I can. My hand on the banister. Dad wants us to move out of Holt House? This is our home. We can't ever move. We can't leave Eva behind.

One foot moves after another, trying to avoid the creaking joists. In my head 'Over the Rainbow' is turned up to full volume, filling the spaces between my ears with Judy Garland's voice. I imagine Granny joining in. We're all singing it now — the three of us, linking arms, skipping along a path lit up in rainbow shades. Judy Garland is smiling, gazing at me with spaniel eyes: *Somewhere over the rainbow, way up high*. But I can't stop myself from hearing the sounds that come from downstairs, words forcing themselves through the song.

'Sorry,' Mum says, 'I'm sorry. I'm trying to stop being angry. I really am. But, Max, we can't sell the house. I just feel odd about it. As if we're . . . deserting her or something. It's only been months. What if they find her body?'

'That's not going to happen now.'

'And what could we tell Faith? She really thinks her sister is going to come home. I don't blame her. Sometimes the only way I can manage is to let myself believe that too . . . I let myself think that she's away somewhere . . . that she'll walk through the front door again, run up to her bedroom like she always did, shouting for the dog, putting some God-awful row on the radio . . .'

There is a sob then. A muffled exclamation and the sounds that two bodies make when they come together, a slide of fabric, the whoosh of air as it escapes, compressed between skin and skin. I hold my breath, imagining the hug. Then a door slams and I hear Dad swearing, his feet on the kitchen floor. Mum must have left him there alone.

My rainbow path has dissolved beneath my feet. Judy Garland and Granny slip away, their fingers trailing through mine. I reach the top of the stairs, shoulders tensed. Eva is dead to them. I don't understand how they can let her go so easily. Dad could borrow a boat to sail across to the island. She's there now. She needs us. As I turn onto the landing I almost collide with Sophie standing in the shadows.

15

London, 1963

Clara rang from a pay phone on the landing of a terraced house somewhere in Birmingham. 'Jim has just sacked me.' She sounded almost jubilant. 'I don't blame him one bit. The run's over. They can advertise for someone else.'

'What are you going to do now?' he asked.

'I don't know . . .'

'Come home,' he said, impulsively, without a plan in his head, just the longing to see her again. They'd written to each other several times a week. He'd travelled miles to see her perform at weekends, taken her out during the day, walking unknown streets, sitting in Birmingham's coffee houses and restaurants, sheltering from the cold.

A hesitation. The crackle of static on the line and he caught the blurred sound of a stranger's voice in the distance. 'But Max, the thing is . . . I don't know where that is,' Clara answered quietly.

Her money was running out. The beeps started up: loud, insistent. 'With me, of course,' he shouted before the line went dead. 'Come and stay with me . . . stay as long as you like.'

★　★　★

He met her from the train. She only had two suitcases. 'Is this crazy?' she asked. 'Are we completely mad?' She was standing under the station clock with a painting of an exotic garden clutched under her arm. A rather mediocre watercolour, he thought, catching a glimpse of patchy colours and the uncertain outlines of trees, a blob of yellow to indicate a desert sun. But she explained that it was a picture of her childhood garden in Egypt, painted by her mother, and when they got home he hung it over the mantelpiece in the living room, taking down the framed reproduction Edward Hopper.

One of the suitcases seemed to be filled with books. In the days that followed, she collected more books, bringing them back from second-hand shops and libraries, so that they sat in piles on the floor next to the bed and the sofa. She put her things in the spare room, but from the first night she'd been sleeping in his bed. 'You've lured me into this,' she said, 'and now here we are, living in sin.'

'Do you mind?'

She buried her face in his chest. 'I'm happy. The happiest I've ever been.'

She talked about retraining to be a secretary and went through the telephone directory underlining numbers. 'I want to pay my way,' she said. 'I'll pay rent — contribute to the mortgage.' She'd inherited some money when she was twenty-one, she explained, but said she didn't want to fritter it away on daily living. 'It's the last thing I have of my parents'. I want to buy something real with it.'

Her parents had been killed in Egypt when she was ten. They'd gone to a Christmas Eve party at the Windsor Hotel in Cairo, leaving Clara at home with the nanny. She remembered them saying goodbye: her mother, beautiful in a dress of lavender silk with long white gloves fastened up to her elbows, a necklace glittering around her neck, her father stooping to kiss Clara, his face scratchy against hers. She'd inhaled cigar tobacco, starch and a trace of something musky. He'd called her 'Bear', put his large hand on her head. But she'd ducked away from his touch, refusing to turn and wave, because they were sending her to boarding school after the holidays, and she didn't want to go.

The bomb had been planted by the Muslim Brotherhood. There had been a spate of bombings in the city: soldiers had been killed, a horse, and two officials. Her parents had died instantly as they left the party, with Hanif, their driver, at the wheel, his fingers on the ignition.

'Everything about England was grey and damp,' she told Max. 'I was lonely and homesick. I missed my parents. I missed the flame tree in our garden. I longed for the warmth of its scarlet flowers, the way I used to hold up my hand to catch red reflections on my skin.'

When Max came home after work, he held his breath, hardly able to believe that Clara would be there. He entered the flat to smell cinders, charcoal: essence of burning. Clara even ruined macaroni cheese. He forked tasteless clumps of greasy pasta into his mouth and forced a smile. 'Delicious.'

'Liar!' She threw a bit of burnt cheese at him.

Max thought that it might help if she read a recipe book instead of a novel while she was cooking. But she laughed when he pointed this out, and Max didn't care — his mother had taught him to cook, so he'd often roll his sleeves up when he got back and throw a stew together while Clara sat on the kitchen table, sipping wine and talking to him. Who needed food when there were fresh flowers spilling out of a vase, and music playing on the record player? She asked if she should be looking for a flat, but he said not unless she felt uncomfortable with the situation. He wanted her to stay. When his friends came over for a drink and a game of poker, she poured them beers and joined in with the ironic jokes about fast women and cowboys. He met a couple of her actor friends, listened to the gossip, watched her pick up their effusive gestures and breathy mannerisms. They went to see *Lawrence of Arabia* at the Odeon and Clara teased him all the way home about how much he looked like Peter O'Toole.

By the time the nuclear weapons protestors arrived in London in April, the hard-packed snows had melted, leaving the streets naked and gritty, the roads blasted full of lethal potholes, and Clara had started her secretarial training. On the morning of the fifteenth, she didn't go to the course and instead went with two friends from drama school to join the marchers in Trafalgar Square, with her CND badge pinned to her jacket.

He got the phone call that afternoon. He'd

run out of the office, shouting a hurried explanation to the receptionist as he went, tugging his jacket on. He took a taxi to St Thomas' hospital and, after being directed by several nurses, down corridors and up flights of stairs, he found her sitting on a chair behind a green curtain, a patch of gauze over her forehead.

'It turned nasty,' she said, her voice small. 'I got separated from the others. There was fighting. Someone pushed me. I fell. I can't remember much more . . . '

He heard on the news that there had been organised troublemakers there. He blamed himself. He should have known. Max took her home and put her to bed, brought her cups of hot chocolate and grapes, sat with her until she fell asleep.

The next morning when he came to collect her breakfast tray, she was propped up against the pillows reading; she'd managed to drink her tea and eat a piece of toast and marmalade. He stooped to take the tray from her. 'Had enough?'

'Thanks.' She smiled up at him, putting the book down over her knees. 'I'm feeling much better. The headache has gone.'

He nodded at the spread pages. 'Any good?' It was the new John Fowles. It had a picture of a butterfly on the cover. He turned his head sideways to try and read the title.

She twitched her nose. 'Yes and no. It's great writing. But it's depressing as hell.'

'So I can distract you, then?'

'Please.' She gestured for him to sit next to her.

'Well,' he paused, remaining standing with the tray in his hands, 'I was wondering what you thought about getting married.' He cleared his throat. 'I know it means not being a sinner anymore, but I thought if you didn't mind, I'd like to make our relationship official.'

She glanced away from him at the book on her knees and fiddled with it for a few moments, fingering the pages. He noticed that the bandage above her left eye looked grey in the sunshine, fraying around the edges. His mouth lost moisture. It was too soon to ask. He'd got it wrong. At the hospital, when he'd been at the desk, trying to find out where she was, he'd wanted to ask for his wife. He'd desperately wanted them to understand the importance of their relationship.

'I know it's sudden,' he rushed his words, 'but I love you. I've never been more certain . . . we can have a long engagement if you like . . . '

'The thing is,' she interrupted him, 'I've always wanted children. Lots of children. We've never talked about it. And, well, you need to know that.'

She lay back against the pillow, her face oddly settled, mouth closed. Her eyes were clear and direct. He could see that she was serious.

'Of course,' he said, relief filling him. 'Children. Yes. I'd like that. So,' he gripped the edges of the tray tighter, 'is that a yes?'

Later, when he was lying in bed with her, her head heavy on his shoulder, he asked casually, 'How many were you thinking?'

She laughed. 'I used to want about ten. But

now I'd settle for three or four.' She moved her chin, settling more comfortably. 'Four sounds about right.'

'I see.' He was careful not to brush up against the wound where black stitches puckered her skin. 'We'd better get on with the wedding then.' He kept his voice grave, teasing her. 'Let me see.' He nodded. 'If we start with one every two years, we'll have a whole tribe before we know it.'

★   ★   ★

They had a summer wedding. She wore a white linen mini-dress; it swung heavily against her thighs, weighed down with clusters of fabric daisies sewn onto the hem. Grace Gale came, a few other relations on his side, work colleagues and friends. Some of the acting lot turned up. After the register had been signed, she and Max stood on the steps looking down on the King's Road. It was hot, and she was glad of her cool dress. Confetti fell around them in fluttering pastels and one of Max's poker-playing friends pointed a camera. 'Smile!' he shouted, crouching at the foot of the steps looking up at them.

She went to the doctor in November, running home, her breath trailing plumes behind her as she pushed her way through shoppers, not looking at the glittering shop windows, ready for Christmas. She remembered how as a child at school she'd sketched children: an imaginary line-up of children that she would have when she was grown up. There had always been one set of twins, and there would be a clever child with glasses and freckles and another who was slightly chubby. And then there would be the baby, plump and smiling, holding out its arms to her. Underneath each child she'd written his or her name, their age and characteristics. *Beth, 5, likes dancing and sucks her thumb. Tommy, 9, good at cricket and clever at maths.*

She'd hidden her drawings when anyone looked over her shoulder, lowering her head towards the desk, her arm curled around the paper protectively. At night, lying in her narrow bed in a room full of sleeping girls, she'd told herself that one day she would be old enough to leave school and get married. And then she would have a husband and lots of children. They would all love her; and she would be safe. She'd fallen asleep reciting their names.

★　★　★

'Hello?' she called breathlessly from the hall, unwrapping her scarf, dropping her bag on the floor. Max didn't reply, or even turn to look at her as she came in. He was glued to the television. Clara wondered what he was watching as she leant against him, kissing the top of his head, her eyes on the flickering screen. 'What is it?'

He pulled her onto his lap. 'Kennedy's been assassinated. God. It's unbelievable. The end of an era.' He shook his head wearily. 'Nothing good can come of this.'

She felt the shock of his announcement. Pressing her belly, Clara remained silent. She couldn't tell him her news, not under such a momentous shadow. She watched the screen, as jerky newsreel showed Jackie Kennedy, immaculate in gloves and pill-box hat, waving to the crowds next to her handsome husband: the glamorous couple bright under the Dallas sun. What followed was hard to understand, it was so quick: the confusion of bodyguards jumping from the bumper, the car turning a corner, its silver grill grinning like a shark; the slump of the president, Jackie bending towards him. And then the second shot, the splatter of what appeared to be light, but what she realised, a second later, was the ricochet of bone shards and spurting fluid. Jackie clambering across the boot of the car, her body sinuous, writhing low, like an animal.

Clara remembered how her father had rested his hand on her hair before he'd left for the party. 'Goodnight, Bear.' During countless sleepless nights, she'd tried to recall the weight of his fingers across her scalp. She'd learnt not to think of her parents in that explosion, blocking out the force of it, blowing the car into twisted metal and shattered glass. She'd concentrated instead on remembering the glow of the flame tree, the clarity of crimson reflections falling across her skin, a different kind of red, tender and kind.

The school library had been a refuge. She'd hidden behind book stacks, away from the shouts from the hockey pitch and all the giggling conversations that excluded her. She'd lost herself in the private activity of sketching imaginary people, a new family to love. She'd willed those paper children to take life, understanding only vaguely that they needed to grow inside her, like seeds blossoming into flowers.

She put her arms around Max's neck, inhaling his familiar smell, feeling his hands on her waist, fingers long and strong as her father's had been. And she swallowed her words, holding back the moment when she would tell him that they had begun their tribe.

16

Max slides the tray into the oven, apple slices layered in a haphazard jumble. He doesn't do neat, by-the-book baking. He makes a mess, splatters the kitchen in liquid mix, apple peelings on the floor. But his food always tastes good. Faith is up in her bedroom. He looks at his watch. The pie will be ready to eat in about half an hour.

Clara comes in from the garden, leaving the door open. The early-evening sun illuminates her, catches wisps of hair, turning them into a halo. He absorbs the blur of insect wings, songbirds' voices. There is a streak of earth on Clara's forehead. She goes to the sink to wash her hands. 'Smells good,' she says, under the rush of water.

He moves towards her, close enough to inhale fresh air, the raw tang of green shoots on her skin, and puts out his hand to wipe away the earthy smudge. She flinches. A tiny impulse of distrust. He tightens his mouth and lowers his hand. 'You have some mud or something . . . ' He gestures. Turns away. 'I'm making apple pie,' he says. 'Won't be long.'

He's made a salad, laid the table. Sophie has taken the evening off. Max is glad. Although she can cook basic meals, they are tasteless and bland. Food cooked without love is like food without salt, his mother told him more than once. If he can get home from the office early enough he is happy to make supper. He's struggling to think of other, more useful things he can do for Clara and Faith.

'You missed an exciting race today,' he tells Clara. 'Zola Budd running barefoot. She tripped the American girl, Decker. Crowd were booing her. Poor kid. She finished seventh in the end.'

Clara makes a noncommittal noise in her throat, taking a towel from the oven rail to dry her hands. Max frowns. She hasn't shown any interest in the Olympics. But he can't think of anything else to say. Once he would have asked her if she'd made a start on the children's book about the Wild Man she'd told him she wanted to write. Once they would have slipped into idle, pleasurable small talk, the kind that's punctuated with old jokes and fuelled by familiarity. None of that is possible anymore. The door opens and Faith comes in.

'Just in time, Shrimp,' he begins, relieved. But he stops when he sees the look on her face.

'I have to talk to you.' Faith stands fiddling with her cuffs, pulling them down over her spindly fingers. She looks at the floor, wrapping one leg behind the other.

'What is it?' Clara asks, dropping the towel on a chair.

'You're wrong about Eva.' Faith puts her chin in the air. 'She's not dead. She's on the island and we need to go and get her.'

Not this again. Max glances at Clara. But she keeps her face turned from him. He swallows, searching for the right words, but Clara is already speaking.

'We've talked about this before, darling. I know it's hard for you to accept, but . . . '

'It doesn't seem hard for *you* to accept!' she blurts out, her cheeks stinging. 'Dad and you, you just seem to think it's OK to believe that she's gone.'

'Oh.' Clara's voice is small. 'That's not fair.'

'It's not fair that we leave Eva on the island — leave her there with something bad.' She glares at them both. 'Why can't we just get a boat and go and look for her?'

'Mum's right. The island was searched,' Max explains. 'The coastguard looked along the whole of the coastline, including the island. They do this all the time. They know how to find people. There were several searches and there was a helicopter. She wasn't there, Faith.'

'But they could have missed her. People make mistakes, don't they?'

Max stares at her; he feels hollowed out, afraid. Faith is rigid, trembling. She curls her hands into fists under the saggy sleeves. The thought of getting a boat and sailing to the island makes him feel as though he's falling. The swell of the sea, the feeling of a boat moving under him has become part of his nightmares.

'The coastguard explained to us that she has been lost out at sea. It happens.' He pushes the words out, watching Faith's face harden. 'People.' He pauses. 'Bodies. They're never found.'

'Faith,' Clara says gently. 'You know that the

144

Wild Man isn't real, don't you? He's made up. A myth. A legend.'

'I hate you.' Faith bangs her heel against the cabinet behind her. 'I hate you both.'

She runs from the room, her head down. Clara makes a move to follow her, but Max reaches out an arm. 'Leave her.'

Clara stands watching as Faith slams the door behind her. She grimaces. 'God, she just won't let this crazy idea go. Perhaps, I don't know, perhaps we should do what she wants . . . ' Clara begins to pace around the kitchen table, her lips trembling, fingers flexing. 'If we take her to the island then we can prove it's not true.'

For a moment he wonders if he could do it. There are friends he could borrow a boat from. He blinks, remembering the howl of the wind, waves rearing and the sky suddenly black. He rubs his forehead, touches the scar on his head where he had eight stitches. He frowns into the blank of his memory. The moment he lost his daughter. There are snatches of colour: the orange of his lifejacket, the red of the coast-guard's rescue boat, a man's grey face when Max cried out, 'My daughter?'

'No,' he tells Clara. 'It would just get her hopes up and then she'd have to cope with being wrong. Can you imagine her disappointment? The coastguard told us we couldn't even expect . . . ' he lowers his voice, 'a body to wash up at this point.' He stands close to Clara, appealing to her with open hands. 'Faith has to trust us to know best. Maybe it's better for her to be angry with us. Maybe being angry with us helps her cope, a kind of — I don't know — a distraction from the hurt.'

Clara wraps her arms around herself. 'I hate this. I hate this not-knowing. If only they'd found her body. It would actually be better.' She huddles further into herself, hunching her shoulders. 'I want to see her, to be able to say goodbye . . . I need it . . . what do they call it? Closure.' She gives a brief, dry laugh.

Max goes to her, puts out a hand to touch her shoulder. She keeps herself tightly wrapped. 'That storm, Clara,' he says quietly. 'It was the worst I've ever been out in. There's no way she could have survived.'

'Not without a lifejacket,' Clara says in a dull voice.

'No,' he echoes. 'Not without a lifejacket.'

She shakes her head, avoiding his eyes. He sees her skin flush, colour rising across her throat onto her jaw, staining her cheeks. Don't say it, he begs her silently.

'I'll never understand,' she says, looking up at him. 'I'll never understand why she wasn't wearing it.'

Max grips his hands into balls, nails biting flesh. He wants to hit something. He wants to smash his fist into his head, to shake his memory free, remember what happened that day. When they'd shown him Eva's lifejacket he had staggered backwards, his knees giving way, because he knew what it meant: her certain death, and his stupidity, his guilt. His never-ending guilt.

He sniffs. The kitchen is filled with the stench

146

of burning, the caustic scent of scorched food. He opens the oven — clouds of black smoke make him cough, his eyes stinging as he slides the ruined remains of the apple pie out. When he turns, Clara has left the room.

17

Billy's knuckles are flayed to pieces. There are clots of dried blood crusting over raw edges, the wounds dark and sticky against his tanned skin. He punches the wall at night. The noise enters my dreams, bringing violence, hammers and fighting, until I wake with a start, understanding that the noise is real, his fists slamming into the pagoda. I put my hands over my ears, trying to block out the sound of bone on concrete, his breath coming hard and grunts of pain.

Neither of us speaks of it in the morning.

He handed me a brown paper bag yesterday, smoothing out the creases, and then reached into his pocket for a stub of pencil. 'Here,' he said. 'I know it isn't much, but you could do a bit of drawing if you like.'

Holding the pencil, I felt excited, the shape of it familiar in my grasp. I sat outside the pagoda, resting the paper on my knees, and drew the outlines of the gorse bushes and a seagull hovering overhead. My fingers were stiff. I was out of practice. Billy lay on the pebbles nearby, having a smoke. He pointed upwards with the tip of his rollie to the sign over my head that read 'Prohibited Area — Photography and Sketching Forbidden', took a drag, winking at me. Afterwards he crouched beside my knee.

'That's good,' he said. 'I like pictures of real things. You've got the look in that bird's eye

— evil things, gulls. Scavengers.' I smelt the nicotine on his breath. On the back of the bag I attempted to draw a portrait of Faith. I tried to capture the fine lines of her bones, the questioning look on her face, her mouth about to smile.

'My sister,' I said, when he looked over my shoulder. He just made a noise with his teeth. I have never spent so much time with one person and said so little. He'll never let me go if I don't make him see me as myself, as Eva. I want to hear him say my name. I'm beginning to forget the sound of it.

* * *

'Eva,' Marco said, elongating the sound as he drew the swirling shapes of my name on his arm with his finger. He traced each letter carefully. E.V.A. 'What do you think?' he asked. 'It could go just here . . . ' He tapped his left forearm, the skin pale, speckled with black hairs. 'I've been thinking of getting another tattoo.'

My heart jumped. I reached out to rub my thumb over his skin, feeling the grain of his flesh, uncertain if he was teasing or not. 'Hmmm, I think it would look good.' I nodded seriously, as if considering it carefully. 'Not too many letters. Lucky for you I have a short name. Less pain.'

He laughed then.

He took me home to meet his parents. They were folk singers, a singing duo with guitars and a tambourine. His dad had a drooping moustache. He smiled at me, top lip hidden

149

under a fringe of hair, showing stained teeth. Marco's mum patted her dark bun with a white streak running through it, silver bangles clattering around slender wrists. They told me to call them Pete and Paula, offered me a glass of red wine and invited me to supper.

They made their own bread, yeasty brown bricks that Paula sliced into thick doorsteps. There was a yoghurt maker in the airing cupboard and weird things in their fridge: soya milk, packets of wheatgerm. 'The bud of the glug glug cabbage,' Marco said, spooning a slippery piece of palm heart into my mouth.

He led me upstairs to his bedroom. It was painted dark purple and covered in posters. His guitar was propped on a stand in the corner. Music sheets covered with scribbled notes and lyrics were scattered on a table with a pile of dog-eared *NME* magazines. We lay down on his bed with the curtains closed and he played me music on his stereo. He cocked his head to one side, eyes closed, stroking my stomach in circles, his fingers loose against my skin as if they were acting out an impulse that was separate from him. '"Temple of Love" is one of the most important records of our time,' he told me quietly. 'Listen to the lyrics. Bloody brilliant.'

From deep in my belly I felt the beginnings of a loud gurgle, and clenched my stomach muscles, holding my breath against my body's treachery.

'Yeah. Amazing,' I managed.

Dust motes shimmered in the streetlight that slipped between the curtains. My skin crawled with feeling, desire flickering through my limbs like tiny flames.

'My parents like you,' he said later, casually, as he walked me to the bus stop.

I sat on the bus and smiled to myself, staring out over dusty hedges at endless fields, ponderous cows whisking skimpy tails, and thought about Paula and Pete. They seemed to think that I should be planning a trek to Nepal, a pilgrimage to India or a year out in the Australian bush. Sitting at their scratched pine table, they told me about the adventures they'd had while travelling in America in a Winnebago with Marco as a baby strapped in his carry-cot, interrupting each other and laughing. The stories made me laugh too, but at the same time I was filled with a lurching vertigo, as if I was standing at the top of a tall building, the world spread before me.

As the bus swayed around corners, I imagined being in London with Marco; his favourite place was Camden, with its cafés and stalls near the dank canal. You could find silver earrings shaped like skulls, buy Jamaican jerk chicken, spicy and hot from a barbecue. He'd talked about the bands he'd seen in pubs, waving his hands as he'd explained his passion for the new sounds. No wonder he couldn't wait to get back to the city. I wouldn't be an oddity there, I thought. In the city I wouldn't be the girl who was too dark, too tall and too loud. The girl with the wrong kind of hair. There would be thousands of people of all shapes and sizes and colours. My mind stalled at imagining the sheer weight of humanity all in one place. I knew that Dad and Mum had started out married life in a flat in Hammersmith and I wondered what had made them move to Suffolk, to live in a backward village on the edge of a marsh.

★   ★   ★

I gesture towards Billy's knuckles. 'You should give them a wash. Have you got anything to make a dressing?'

He stares at me and then down at his hands as if he'd never noticed the sting of raw flesh, bloody lumps, tendrils of skin peeling away. He frowns and shakes his head. 'It's nothing.'

Have it your own way, I think. Get blood poisoning then, and I'll escape and leave you here. He's chopping vegetables: carrots and courgettes. They are going into a pan to be cooked into a tasteless soup without salt or pepper. It's the broth we live off, in between occasional rabbits and fish. His hands move steadily, the knife fast and sure in his fingers.

'I was just beginning to teach myself to cook curries when I was at home,' I tell him. 'Never really taken much interest in cooking before, but my boyfriend likes Indian food, so I thought I'd try and make it.'

At the word boyfriend, he pauses for a second before slicing neatly into a carrot.

'It takes the whole day,' I continue, 'so many herbs and spices need chopping and mixing: cumin, coriander and turmeric. I wouldn't want to be a woman in India — you'd spend your whole time cooking.' I'm aware of rambling; but he seems to be listening to me and so I keep talking. 'It's delicious when it's finished though.' I inhale, almost able to smell the tang of a curry sauce, creamy and golden, bubbling as I stir it, my mouth watering. 'It's different from the Indian food you get in restaurants. There's only one Indian restaurant and that's in Ipswich. I went with my parents for my last birthday. Everything was oily.'

He grunts impassively. Takes the pan of vegetables and water carefully and lowers it onto the Primus stove. The stove is a new acquisition. It means we can have more cooked food, as there's no danger of betraying ourselves with cooking smoke. It is battered and rusted. I wonder where he found it. He strikes a match with a quick flick of his wrist.

'What about you?' I prompt. 'What kind of food do you like?'

He shrugs. 'Don't care much what it is. Just fuel to me.'

'Did your mother like to cook though?' I persist, my heart beating fast, aware of crossing a line.

He is silent, staring into the hiss of orange and blue under the pan.

'My . . . mother,' he repeats slowly, imitating my voice. 'She did well just to get a meal on the table.'

'Mine can't cook for toffee.' I feel tears pressing in behind my words.

He rubs his chin with the palm of his hand. I can hear the scritch and scratch of beard against skin.

'What are we doing here?' I ask in a rush, my voice wobbling, and I feel sick, knowing that I'm risking his rage. But the relief of honesty, of asking real questions is taking over, pushing the fear away. 'I don't understand. What do you want from me? We can't stay here for ever.'

He unfolds his long body and paces the pagoda, backwards and forwards, backwards and forwards. Then his shoulders tense and he lunges forward to slam his fist into the wall. I jump, hugging myself tightly. Dust crumbles, sprinkles the ground with a dry patter. 'Don't ask questions — it's not right.' His voice is a low growl. 'I told you before. I don't want to hurt you.' The cut on his knuckles oozes fresh blood.

'You don't know anything about me.' I'm trembling. 'You've taken me away from my life. My family probably think I'm dead and you don't care.'

He rubs his face roughly. 'It doesn't matter — what you were before — that's over.' He looks at me. There's a streak of red smeared across his cheek. 'I'm keeping you safe. All right? That's all you need to know.'

'But couldn't you at least get a message to my family, let them know I'm alive?' I bite my lip. I've been planning to ask him this for ages, thinking of ways to persuade him, and now it's come out wrong.

He looks at me as if I'm the mad one. 'We can't take those kinds of risks. You need to stay here. With me.'

'But I want to go home.' I begin to cry silently, rubbing my face with my hands. I don't care if he thinks I'm weak. 'Please. Just let me go.'

He walks up and down with quick, agitated steps. 'Things have taken away my life. I'm not the same as I was. I'm not crying about it, am I?'

'What things? What changed you?' I lower my voice, looking up at him.

I'm breathless, waiting for his answer. His words have begun something, opened a small crack. I want to hear more, to know more. I will him to speak. But he jolts as if I've stung him. Squatting on his haunches, he ignores me, prodding the vegetables with the knife. His hair falls over his face. 'You don't know anything.' His voice is cold.

I slump onto my hip, exhausted from my efforts, and press my hand over my aching forehead, touching hot, sticky skin. We are silent, listening to the hissing Primus and the bubbling water.

18

Mum has taken the dog for a walk. It's her new habit. She wakes early and has breakfast before us. Then she's off, the dog running before her down the lane to the marshes, tail wagging, nose to the ground, following smells. And Mum paces behind, shoulders back, striding out as if she has somewhere important to go. She can be gone for hours. She's always vague about where she's been. 'Oh, just along the sea wall,' she'll say. 'Trekked around the village, through the alder woods, you know.'

She's tanned from being out in the sea air and sunshine. Her hair is longer, straggly down her back. She comes home bringing scents of earth and sap. Before, she always had perfume on her skin, the papery aroma of books, and in the winter she smelt of wood smoke from sitting so close to the fire. Now, instead of curling up with a novel, she drums her fingers on surfaces, shifts her weight from one hip to the other. I've seen her in Eva's bedroom. She stays there for ages, just standing and staring out of the window towards the sea.

When she is in the same room as Dad they are too nice to each other. It's not normal. They act as if the other one is made of porcelain, like one of Granny's ornaments. I think it would be better if they shouted. But Mum hates raised voices, says that arguments give her migraines.

Dad is hunched over his coffee in the kitchen, his tie skewed around his neck. He's reading the newspaper, sighing and blowing air out from between pursed lips.

'Terrible thing, this miners' strike,' he says to nobody in particular, folding the floppy paper with a shake, his hand smoothing down the creases. 'Poor buggers. It's dragging on for ever.'

I am eating a bowl of cornflakes with strawberries sliced on top. Sophie is drying up, polishing each cup and plate carefully before placing it on the shelf. She crosses the kitchen with swinging hips and asks Dad if he'd like more coffee.

He nods. 'Thanks.'

The light sliding in through the window shines on the threads of grey in his hair. There are lots of lines at the corners of his eyes stretching out in a fan. He is thinner, deep gouges running from his nose to his mouth like a ventriloquist's dummy. He turns the pages of the newspaper, shaking his head. I crunch through a spoonful of cornflakes and try and think of something funny or clever to say to him. I don't know anything about the miners' strike. I've seen footage of it: hordes of angry men shouting at a van driving slowly through them. They banged on the sides of it with their fists, chanting. It looked frightening. But it was happening far away and we didn't know any miners, so I'd turned away from the TV, bored, and gone to my room to finish my book.

Sophie leans over Dad, pouring a stream of

steaming liquid into his cup from her cafetière. As she straightens, her hand touches his shoulder lightly, moves across his shirt, fingers curving around the shape of his muscles.

I remember Jack stroking Granny's cheek. 'You're never too old to fall in love.'

Dad doesn't seem to notice her fingers on his shoulder. My heart is hammering at my ribcage and I have a sense of panic, of not being able to pull enough air into my lungs. I choke on a strawberry and spit it out; milk slops over my bowl and spills in pale drops on the wood.

Dad looks at me, his eyebrows raised. 'Better get a cloth.'

Before I can move, Sophie is at the table beside me, nimble fingers wiping at the splatters, taking the bowl away. He puts down his newspaper, and tugs up his cuff to see his watch. 'Have to go.' He blows me a kiss and stands up, reaching behind him for his jacket hanging on the chair.

Sophie has it ready for him. She helps him slide his arms into the sleeves, smiling at Dad. 'Have a good day, Mr Gale.' Her accent means she can't pronounce the 'h'.

'Max, please.' He smiles back. 'I keep asking you to call me Max.'

I frown. Sophie doesn't always do what Mum asks her to, but whenever Dad is in the kitchen, it seems that Sophie is there too, cleaning and cooking and glancing at him from under her hair. And he makes such an effort to be nice to her. I don't understand why he tries so hard. He doesn't need to. Sophie can look after herself.

158

I trail after him to the door and watch him climb into the car, shutting the door with a clunk, leaning forwards to turn the key. He rolls down the window, glancing at the cloudless sky with sailor's eyes. 'Going to be another hot one.' The engine starts. He gives a brief wave. I wonder how badly he misses being out on the river and the sea. He used to run his hands over a boat as if it was alive, speaking to it as if it was a creature that could be settled by the tone of his voice. He bought an abandoned dinghy once with the words H.M.S. Fuck Off scratched into the fibreglass. The sailing club had sold it off cheaply because of the graffiti. Dad said he bought it because he liked to see the people at the yacht club gasp. But I know that he believed it needed loving. That's another thing about Dad; Mum says he can't resist lame dogs.

He looks different now that he's not sailing: he has faded and drooped. The red in his cheeks has gone. He doesn't look as tall as he used to.

I lean against the doorframe watching the car disappear up the road, humming. *Love is the strongest thing, the oldest yet the latest thing . . .*

★ ★ ★

From the outside the nursing home looked like a forbidding stately home, grey stone stretching up to meet turrets and gables. Inside it smelt of public lavatories and boiled food. I held my breath as I followed Granny and Jack down long corridors. The linoleum floor was sticky underfoot. There were handrails all along the wall, the paintwork smudged from ancient fingers.

A smiling lady in a bright-green dress came forward to take Granny's hand. 'Nice of you to come again, dear. They loved it last week.'

'This is my granddaughter, Faith.' Granny gestured for me to come forward and the woman patted my hair. 'Ahh, bless.'

I wriggled away, scowling, but the woman didn't notice — she'd opened a door to a large room. Heat hit me like a blast from an oven. Chairs had been placed in a wide semi-circle and in each chair a wizened person drooped, spine caving inwards, or slumped forward, some leaning on metal walkers, some on the arms of their chairs. I saw skin wrinkled as waterlogged paper, trembling hands, glazed eyes staring blankly in our direction. I took an uncertain step backwards, but Jack placed a hand on my shoulder. 'Steady lass. Give 'em one of your hundred-dollar smiles.'

Granny led me around the group, bending down, smiling and touching. 'Hello, Keith, brought my granddaughter along to join in.'

A grey man lifted his head slowly and winked. 'Nice to see a young face.'

Jack was placing the stylus on a record player in the corner. As he straightened, music came wafting into the room. The sounds of strings swept through the old people, heads began to bend and nod, shadows trembled, the dusty aspidistra plant in the corner lifted its leaves. Keith wiped his pale, watery eyes. 'My Mavis liked this one.'

Granny and Jack were dancing a foxtrot in the centre of the circle. I hummed and tapped my fingers against my thigh. Some of the old people

160

smiled and watched. Some were asleep with their chins tucked into sagging chests, saliva wetting their lips. Granny broke away at the end of the song and held out her hand to Keith. 'Care for a waltz?'

As Keith rose slowly from his chair and shuffled towards Granny, Jack was bowing to me. 'Madam?'

I remembered the steps. One, two, three. One, two, three. Jack's strong arms holding me up.

★   ★   ★

The kitchen is dim and shadowy after the brightness of the morning. I blink at the threshold. Sophie is shoving cereal packets back in the cupboard. She slams the fridge door as she spins away, looking at her watch.

'You like my Dad, don't you?'

Heat rushes to my cheeks. I didn't mean to say it. It came out before I could stop the words. She pauses for a moment and blows through her lips making a puffing sound. She nods and shrugs her shoulders. 'Of course,' she says. 'Why not?'

'You like him better than me, I mean.' I look at her steadily. 'Better than Mum.'

She comes close, puts her finger under my chin to tilt my face towards her. 'I don't have a father.' Her voice is low and soft. 'At my home there was no one. No one to take care of me.' I feel the curve of her nail pressing into my skin. 'You are jealous . . . *Pourquoi?*' She gives a short laugh and releases me, turning away as if I bore her. 'You have everything.'

19

London, 1966

Clara crouched over the lavatory, gasping at the contractions that pulled a band tight around her pelvis, crushing her. She knew these cramping pains. She'd had them before. She felt the hopeless gush of liquid between her legs, looked down at the slick of viscous fluid on her skin, the blood and water of birth coming too soon. She put her hands there for a moment, as if she could hold it back. She had to get to the phone, call Max at the office, call the hospital. She was crying in gulping sobs, the pain worse as she staggered up from the lavatory, fell to her knees and crawled into the hall. The carpet would be ruined. She didn't care.

★ ★ ★

They called it recurrent miscarriage: four late miscarriages one after another. Nothing wrong with her though, the doctor said cheerfully; it just happens like that for some people. You're young; you can try again. When you're ready.

She didn't feel young anymore. When she looked in the mirror, her face was like an old woman's. Tired lines around her drooping mouth, the faint scar on her forehead standing out, white against her grey skin. She couldn't recognise herself. Grief had etched lines onto Max's face, but he could smile at a joke. Look inside a pram. He'd even held a friend's baby in his arms.

She couldn't bear to see pregnant women, couldn't stand the sight of other people's children. It made her desperate, afraid, overwhelmed by jealousy, a clawing howl coming from the pit of her.

★   ★   ★

Back from hospital, in bed at home in the flat, her stomach was sore, her breasts already softer, smaller. The sounds of the street brushed against the closed windows; she picked out traffic, the voices of passers-by, whooping sirens in the distance, but the world seemed removed: a vague noise on the periphery of her consciousness. The life inside her had gone.

With all her pregnancies, she'd sensed a change in her body almost immediately. She'd described the feeling to Max as being like a ripe fruit, full and exultant. During the first pregnancy, she'd rejoiced in her thickening waist, her swelling belly and breasts. After the miscarriage, she'd been wary in her next pregnancy, afraid, walking with her hands clasped around her stomach as if she could hold her baby inside with the pressure of her hands. But scared as she was, she'd still dared to hope. The third one had hung on the longest. She'd just begun to give up on ever getting pregnant again when she'd been granted another chance.

The cruelty of losing that baby too had changed everything.

Max put his head around the door. 'Anything I can get you, darling? Tea?'

She shook her head. He was afraid of her grief. He didn't know what to do, what to say. He found relief in action: buying her bunches of roses, filling hot-water bottles, fetching drinks, presenting her with meals on trays, laid out with the best silver. She felt unsettled by their lack of communication, the sliding away of understanding, of connection. But nothing mattered except her inability to have a baby. She yearned for the feel of her child in her arms, longed for it every second of every day. At night she woke up crying. She couldn't think about going back to work, couldn't talk to anyone. She couldn't even read. Print blurred and she found that she'd been reading the same sentence over and over again, not understanding.

She stopped caring about washing her hair or choosing her clothes. It was too much effort to clean the flat, even drying a plate an impossible chore. Max employed a cleaning lady who came in twice a week and made Clara cups of hot, sweet tea in between scrubbing tiles in the bathroom or dragging the Hoover up and down the hallway. Wincing at the banging noises coming from the skirting boards, Clara wondered why it was that tea was seen as a miraculous cure for sorrow.

It was Max's mother, up for a visit from Suffolk to help out, who suggested adoption. 'You want a baby,' she nodded her head at them, typically forthright and practical, 'and there are plenty of unwanted babies who need parents. There are homes overflowing with them if you believe what the papers say.'

The atmosphere of the room tightened. Max glanced at his mother, a warning in his eyes, and frowned. 'I think . . . ' He looked over at Clara uncertainly. 'I think Clara wants her own . . . our own . . . '

They both looked at Clara. She shifted on the sofa. Her head was pounding. She seemed to have a headache every afternoon: a hammer working away inside her skull, smashing into the pulpy flesh behind her eyes.

'Adopting?' She licked parched lips. 'But how . . . isn't it difficult?' She swallowed.

'Maybe we should talk about it later,' Max suggested softly, leaning across to touch her hand. 'We need time to think it over . . . '

'But it would be ours if its mother gave it up,' she snatched her hand away, sitting up straight, 'wouldn't it?' Clara stared at him, her eyes bright. 'It would be my baby. From the moment I held it.'

* * *

Charlie Anderson was a junior partner in the firm. He and Max played squash together on Tuesday nights. Charlie was slender-boned with a head of thick ash-blond hair that would have spilled into curls if it hadn't been cropped short; he hardly had a sign of stubble on his smooth face. He made up for his boyish looks by wearing

165

immaculate dark suits, a serious expression and a pair of horn-rimmed glasses that Max suspected were fake.

'Drink?' Charlie asked, hair damp from the shower. It was their habit to have a swift pint in the local pub after a match, but Max didn't like to leave Clara alone for too long. His mother had stayed on for weeks to keep Clara company, but she'd caught the train home that morning, longing to get back to Suffolk and her garden.

'Go on,' Charlie said, when Max expressed his doubts, 'got something I'd like to run by you. Won't take long.'

Sitting in a corner booth, Max nodded, 'Cheers,' wincing at the first bitter sip. Before them a display of framed photographs of men with moustaches: long and drooping, thick and bristly ones, and the elaborately curled variety. The pub was famous for its eclectic collection of memorabilia.

'So,' Charlie wiped froth from his top lip, 'I've heard that you and your wife are looking to adopt.'

Max, startled, nodded cautiously.

'News travels.' Charlie shrugged apologetically.

'We've been looking into it, yes,' Max said. 'There are long queues at all the agencies we've tried. But we'll keep at it, we'll — '

'The thing is,' Charles interrupted, 'my sister has gone and got herself pregnant and the old man hasn't taken it too kindly. She's only eighteen. She won't say who the father is. She's in a home just outside London — you know, one

166

of those unmarried mothers' places. She's miserable. I've been to visit her a couple of times. The nuns are worse than prison wardens. It's pretty grim.'

Max's beer stood untouched in front of him. He leant forward, his heart quickening.

'She doesn't want just anyone to have her baby. She says if she could only know a bit about who was going to have it, know that it was going to a good home, somewhere educated and kind, then she'd feel less terrible about having to give it up.' Charlie looked up at the picture of Corgis hanging above Max's head. 'She's awfully pretty, Suky, and she's blonde, like me and you. Do you see what I'm getting at here . . . ?'

'How far gone is the . . . um . . . '

'Seven months,' Charlie told him. 'Due in April.'

'Who would we need to see?' Max frowned, trying to suppress his excitement. 'I mean, how does this work?'

Charlie smiled. 'A donation is all it takes, apparently, made out to the home. The nuns like cash best.' He raised his glass to Max. 'No queues, my friend. And no questions.'

* * *

The nuns didn't encourage visitors. One hour on Sundays was the rule. Max followed Charlie up a dark staircase and along a landing that smelt of disinfectant. Charlie was visiting his sister secretly; their parents had forbidden any mention of her name at home; friends and neighbours had been told that she'd gone abroad to work.

167

She was sitting on her narrow bed in an otherwise empty dormitory, cross-legged on her rumpled bed, a needle in her hands, bent over a fall of blue fabric. In the folds, Max made out a gold dragon, and watched as the girl's fingers sent the thread in and out of the cloth, spilling amber and red flames onto the fabric. A baby's blanket. She didn't look up. Charlie coughed. 'Su, this is the man I told you about.'

She was creamy-skinned with pale-blonde hair falling into her eyes. Her enormous belly pressed against her green dress, pulling her cardigan apart so that the two halves held together by one straining button. He noticed that there were flights of embroidered bumblebees and bright butterflies darting in and out of the line of buttons and around her cuffs, and guessed that they were her handiwork too. Her gaze was level, and he had the feeling that she was taking the measure of him, assessing him. He pulled in his stomach, squared his shoulders.

'You'll have to excuse me. Can't get out of bed today.' She raised her eyebrows. 'Orders to rest.' She grimaced. 'Orders come straight from God here, so no disobeying.'

She uncrossed her legs, stretching them out, wriggling her stockinged toes. Max saw that her ankles were huge, distorted by some watery swelling under the surface.

'Like an elephant's, aren't they?' She looked at him from under her lashes. 'I'm let off laundry duties for a couple of days. So I'm not complaining.'

Max glanced away quickly, clearing his throat.

'So you're here to buy my baby?'

Max started, his mouth falling open; but Charlie was already by the bed, bending over his sister. 'For God's sake, Su. Come on, you know this is the best choice we . . . you have.' He dropped his hand onto her shoulder. 'She's just upset. She doesn't mean it.'

Suky nodded. 'Sorry,' she whispered, bowing her head. 'The thing is, since . . . this,' she touches her stomach, 'I don't have any choices. Not anymore. And it's hard . . . it's really hard.' She gave him that look again, a challenge hidden in it. 'My brother says you and your wife want a child of your own.' She took a deep breath. 'I can't keep mine. We're not allowed to feed our babies or even take them out of the nursery. I hear them screaming. The other mothers, I mean,' she swallows, 'when their babies get taken. I have nightmares about it. I don't want my baby given away to a stranger.' Her face crumpled and she let out a sob. She pushed a fist into one eye, and Max thought that she looked like a child herself. 'Sorry. Thumping headache. I'm not really myself today.' She took another shuddering breath. 'I feel like my baby is being punished, and it's not fair on her. It's me that's in a state of 'mortal sin'.' She grimaced and held up her fingers to indicate speech marks hanging in the air. Her mouth began working soundlessly, her face reddening, fighting tears.

'Shhh . . . don't cry, darling.' Charlie was at her side, his arms around her, nuzzling the top of her head. Suky blinked at him, her lashes wet, and he leaned forwards, pressing his lips over her trembling mouth. Max felt shock flaring, quick and cold in his gut. He averted his gaze, staring out of the window with rigid shoulders.

When she looked up, she'd composed her face, wiped away the tears. 'Can't your wife have children?'

Max rubbed his nose and shifted his weight onto the other foot. 'She's had miscarriages,' he said abruptly. 'We don't want to go through that anymore.' He paused, remembering. 'Did you say 'her'?'

She nodded, a small smile escaping. 'I'm having a girl.'

'Suky has strong instincts about things, don't you?' Charlie rolled his eyes. 'Thinks of herself as a bit of a psychic.'

Ignoring her brother, Suky focused on Max. 'I want you to have her. I can make that choice, can't I?' She put a hand to her stomach protectively and immediately her eyes widened; she patted her belly. 'I just felt a kick. That must be a good sign.' She bent her neck and unclasped a necklace, handing it to Max.

Surprised, his fingers curled around the necklace. Water pearls. They felt warm from her skin, softly moulded nuggets, gleaming pinkish-gold in the weak light.

'For my daughter. To remember me by. And . . . ' She frowned. 'Afterwards. I want to have the chance to visit her sometimes, I don't know, as an aunt or something. I won't interfere,' her voice wavered, 'but I want to know what she's like. Otherwise, I don't think I can bear it . . . '

170

'You can sort all that out afterwards, old girl.' Charlie patted her shoulder. 'Let's get this bit sorted first.'

Suky looked at Max. 'You'll love her for me, won't you?' She lay back, her face pinched, hands folded limply across her bump. The embroidery slipping onto the bed.

Charlie smoothed the hair from her forehead. Leaning close, he whispered low so that Max could hardly hear, 'Of course he will. I told you I'd arrange everything. It's going to be fine, Su.'

There was a knock on the door. A nun put her head around it. 'Time's up.' She gave the three of them a suspicious stare.

Max thought of Clara at home in the flat, listless and distracted. She'd bitten her lip so often that it was bruised, sore skin smudging dark against her pallor. He couldn't remember the last time she'd smiled.

20

'Take her with you, will you?' Sandra gives Penny a small shove on her shoulders so that she totters towards us.

Fred shrugs and holds out his hand. 'Come on then, you. No lip, mind.'

Sandra is painting her toenails, her long thin legs hanging down from the caravan steps. She has her hair twisted around spiky curlers. Carol is asleep in a pushchair, shiny skin flushed with heat, her fat face folded into her neck, pouchy mouth dribbling. She is snoring gently, her fingers clenching and unclenching in her lap. I am reminded of the old people in the home.

'Thanks, love.' Sandra pauses with a tiny brush between her fingers. Her toes are splayed out, bits of cotton wool stuffed between them; the nails gleam fuchsia-pink. 'It'll give me a break before the baby wakes up.'

Penny stumbles next to Fred, her knees scuffed grey. She gives me a grin. Her pigtails stick up from her scalp, stiff as horns. As we enter the village, people glance in our direction. Some even turn to stare. Joe drags his feet along the pavement and scowls. I have enough change in my jeans pocket to buy two popsicles from the village shop. 'For you and Penny,' I say, pressing the coins into Joe's palm. 'We'll wait here.' I give Fred a warning look when he opens his mouth to protest.

As soon as the others have disappeared inside the shop, the bell clanging behind them, I turn to Fred and explain.

'So,' he says, in his slow way, 'you want me to help you move that boat into the water . . . the one I saw you with?'

'Yes.' I glance back at the shop. 'Don't tell anyone.'

'You're really going to nick it then?' He grins.

'Just borrowing it, to go to the island. I'll give it back.'

'Want me to come too? Me and Joe?'

I open my eyes wide. 'Would you?'

He nods, rolling his shoulders.

I breathe a sigh. It feels good to know that I won't be alone. I can't admit to being scared of the river to Fred, but he doesn't seem to be frightened of anything, so he's bound to make me feel braver.

The others are back, licking melting tubes. Penny is already covered in drips, a slippery mess over her hands and lips. Even her sandals have splatters of green.

Joe looks at Fred with one eyebrow raised. 'So, what's up?'

'Tell you later,' Fred says, leaning forward to take some of Joe's purple popsicle.

'Oi!' Joe snatches it back.

We wander down to the dinghy park, sitting on an upturned boat to look out at the comings and goings on the water. Fred stretches his legs in front of him and I see that his thighs are scorched with red stripes. From the river comes the snap of sails in the wind, the clinking of masts and seagulls crying overhead. The sailors are bright in orange and yellow lifejackets and I think of Eva's jacket, found floating alone on the empty sea.

The island looks paler in this light, bleached out. I wish I had the power to dive into the water like a seal, swimming under the waves and landing with flippers on the shore. Then I would become a selkie and rescue my sister.

Joanna and Ellie are on the quay, crab nets in their hands. They catch sight of us and nudge each other, pointing in our direction. I swallow hard, shoving my hands into my pockets, looking away, willing them to leave us alone, hoping Fred won't notice. It is embarrassing to be someone who is disliked.

Penny has squatted on the stony ground and is playing a complicated and private game using things she's found: a twist of blue rope, a fluted shell and a broken crab claw. Above her head, Fred explains the plan to Joe, who looks excited. We go over to the boat and test its weight, attempting to lift it between us. Locking our fingers under the solid wooden edge, together we raise it several inches from the ground. The dirty water in the bottom rocks and swishes from side to side, rowlocks dangling loosely on their bits of string, tapping at the planks.

'Know how to row, do you?' Fred indicates the oars with wobbling chin.

'Of course,' I say.

'Fred and me, we've never been in a boat before.' Joe's eyes shine, and I realise that it's an adventure to them. A sharp pang makes me catch my breath. This is serious. My sister's life is at stake. I nearly say the words out loud but I swallow them. I need their help — that's all that matters. The fact that Fred has volunteered to go across the river with me is like a gift, something I hadn't looked for, whole and shiny and unexpected.

I catch sight of a familiar figure, brown hair swinging across her shoulders. Sophie is on the quay, talking to Joanna. Joanna points again and Sophie turns to follow the direction of her finger.

'My au pair is coming.' I flush as I say the words, knowing the others don't belong to a world where you have such a thing. 'Better go. We should move the boat early.' I keep an eye on Sophie as she gets nearer. 'Tomorrow,' I hiss. 'First thing, before people are up.'

Sophie steps over the anchor chains and ropes with care.

'Your mother ask me to fetch you.' She wipes imaginary dirt from her trousers, and gives Fred, Joe and Penny a warning look. 'You can't play anymore. Come.' She beckons to me. '*Vite.*'

We walk back to the house in silence. She's been shopping for Mum and I can see a loaf of bread, a fat green lettuce and half a dozen eggs poking out of her straw basket. When she stops by the front door, leaning to slip the key into the lock, shiny plastic bangles rattle around her wrist. They are exactly the same as the ones on Eva's dressing table. There's no point in mentioning it to Dad. He would repeat that she is alone and far from home and we must be kind. Only I'm afraid that she wants more than a wristful of plastic bangles, more than the pearls even. She wants my father. I can't tell Mum or Dad. It sounds mad, and they have enough to worry about. They wouldn't listen anyway; losing Eva has made my parents deaf and blind.

21

I was nervous because Marco was coming to see me for the first time. His bus was due at the village square in an hour. I'd already spent ages trying to decide what to wear. Piles of clothes littered the floor. I'd just settled on my purple mohair jumper when Faith barged in. She began to dance, knocking her knees together, flapping her hands in and out, toes and heels twisting. She kicked her legs up, hands making circles in the air. 'Look, Eva,' she said, 'look at this.'

She bounced onto my bed, sitting cross-legged, gabbling so fast that she tripped over her words, telling me that she'd danced in an old people's home. Jack was teaching her the Charleston; 'I'm going to do another performance.' She rolled onto her stomach. 'This time on my own,' she nodded, 'a solo.'

I paused in the middle of colouring in my eyelids, wondering if glittery purple was too much for daylight, and glanced at her in the mirror. Her cheeks were flushed. I grunted, rubbing off the purple, thinking I must be mad to meet Marco right under Mum's nose. My head was full of trying to imagine him in familiar places and thinking up excuses in case I was spotted. I couldn't take in enough air. Faith's chatter pecked at me like a swarm of hungry sparrows. I glanced at my watch. I didn't want to tell her about Marco. I knew she'd want to see him.

'Will you get out of my room?' I turned in exasperation, hands on my hips. 'I don't want to hear about some poxy dance that's sixty years out of date. I have other things to do.'

She tightened her lips, trying to control their tremble, her eyes suddenly bright. She went without another word. I heard her footsteps on the stairs.

Silver, lying on my bedroom floor, put up his head and looked at me with his yellow gaze. 'It's not my fault she can't make friends,' I muttered, and the dog tucked his nose under his paw.

I'd found her crying once. Hidden under her eiderdown in the middle of the day. 'The kids in my class laugh at me,' Faith had said, her beetroot face smeary. 'Nobody likes me. They make fun of my warts.'

'It's because they're inbreds,' I'd told her. 'It's better in Ipswich. There are different kinds of people. Sixth-form college is OK.'

'But that's years and years away. I'm stuck here,' she'd screwed up her eyes, 'with the inbreds.'

I'd smiled as if it was a joke. I should have told her that I'd suffered too, explained how I'd been teased at school for being different. For being too tall, and having darker skin than everyone else. I hated my springy black ringlets. I'd even tried to iron them. My hair just sizzled at the ends, and the point of the iron clipped my chin. It left a triangle scar. I'd shut the door on that part of my life, moved on. Meeting Marco had set me free. I felt like I belonged with him, with people like him.

178

I got to the bus stop early, loitering near the wooden shelter, listening for the sound of the diesel engine. Faith's teacher went past on a bicycle; I pretended that I hadn't seen her. People came and went out of the post office. Two women with brown paper shopping bags in their arms paused outside to chat. I stared into the window of the antique shop, gazing at a round table and an ugly blue vase as if I was interested in buying them. How weird, I was thinking, that out of the three shops in the village, one sold something as useless as antiques.

The bus pulled up, the door opening with a hiss. I watched as five people got off slowly, pulling hats down, fastening coats, the last one a young woman with a toddler in her arms. Marco appeared, dark glasses on, his legs slender in black drainpipes, pausing at the top of the steps. We stood and stared at each other until the bus driver leaned over. 'You getting off, or what?' Marco winked at me over his glasses, jumping down. He looked fragile in the morning light. He wasn't wearing anything but a thin jacket, a crucifix dangling over his grey T-shirt. He sneezed. It was a chilly spring day and I was bundled up in a winter coat. I pulled the coat open at my neck, flicking my hair back from my face, licking my lips. 'Hi,' I said, aiming for a relaxed drawl, but it came out as a kind of squeak.

I hurried him away from the bus shelter. I didn't want him to see my name scratched into the wood, rude things scrawled in green paint. When he tried to hold my hand, I pulled away.

'Not yet,' I hissed. He took no notice, tickling me until, in the end, he'd been impossible to resist. I let him grab me close, hooking his arm around my neck. 'What's your hurry?' he asked. 'We've got all afternoon.'

Tucked under his armpit, I smelt spicy aftershave and stale nicotine, the chemical scent of hair gel. I looked down at our feet striding in unison, feeling the rub of his hipbone against my own, and a rebellious thrill rushed through me, excitement prickling my skin. We sauntered down the lane that went past the castle, him talking about his new guitar and me glancing around for snoops that might report back to my parents.

The path along the seawall is too narrow for more than one, but with our hips stuck together, his arm tight around my shoulder, we managed. I sneaked looks from under my hair. The weather had blasted his skin, turning it bluish. His cold had rimmed his nostrils with red, and he had a spot on his temple. I considered him lovely. His heavily lidded eyes gave him a sleepy, languid look. I got butterflies in my stomach every time he turned that look on me.

I stopped and took a roll of paper out of my inside coat pocket. It was slightly bent. 'For you.' I handed it to him, watching him unroll it, my throat tightening. 'It's not very good . . . '

He was looking at my picture. 'You did this for me?'

I nodded. I'd used black pen, drawing Dracula playing a guitar, a whole host of strange winged animals crowding into the background. Every part of the paper was covered with delicate lines. It had taken me ages. 'Cool.' He rolled it up carefully and put it in his jacket pocket.

We continued along the muddy path and our shoes grew heavier and heavier with cloying earth. He slipped and I braced myself to take his weight.

'This place,' he gestured to the river and the sea beyond, 'shit, it's bleak.' He inclined his head towards the island. 'What's that out there? Looks like factory chimneys. Is it an island?'

I nodded. 'Ministry of Defence.'

He sneezed again. Turned up the collar of his jacket. 'Think I'll always be a city boy. Give me some pollution, I can breathe more easily.'

I smiled as if I knew what he meant. It was true that I longed to escape the village, to get away from small-town minds, go to London and be free. But this was my home. I felt torn.

Something moved in the corner of my vision, a blur of kingfisher colour. I looked round sharply, fearing the worst: Robert and his mates back to laugh at us. I stared hard at the reeds at the foot of the bank, watching a slight tremor, the rustle of stems. A white swan raised its head above the line of the rushes.

'Is it true,' Marco pointed at it, 'they can break a man's arm?'

'Only if you do something stupid to annoy them,' I answered, giving the swan and the rushes one last keen stare.

We walked on into the wind, Marco complaining about a new single by The Cure: 'Shame, but they've sold out, you know. Since

181

'The Love Cats' they've really got commercial.'

'Who's your favourite band then — the most gothic of the gothic?'

He sighed. 'I still can't believe Bauhaus have broken up — 'Bela Lugosi's Dead' is one of the all-time great tracks.'

He stopped and turned, dipping his face abruptly to kiss me. His lips, at first dry against mine, became wet as his tongue moved in soft circles. I smelt the gluey taste of his germs, but it didn't stop my stomach caving in with wanting, the feeling of melting creeping into my legs, making them hollow. I dug my fingertips into the sinews of his arms.

There was a sound, a snorting gasping noise, not animal. A human. We broke apart, scanning the undergrowth with quick, jittery glances. It came again, smothered, and I recognised it as laughter. There were cows moving slowly on the horizon. The swan, calm and curved, moved at a sedate pace along the stream. Then I saw the shine of blonde hair, the blue of a familiar jumper, her shoulder poking out from behind an alder tree.

'Faith Gale,' I called out. 'I can see you. You'd better go home now, or there'll be trouble.'

I glanced up at Marco apologetically, but he was smiling, in relief or amusement I couldn't tell.

★　★　★

Billy is mending his fishing line. He bends over it in concentration. I am feeling frustrated, bored.

182

'Music,' I say, 'you must like music. What do you listen to?'

'Nothing.' He shrugs. 'I don't think about it.'

'Really? I thought all 'young people' liked music. Isn't it our expression, our way to tell the world who we are, what we think?'

'I don't want some pop star to speak for me, tell me what to think. Don't need music here, do you? Not with the sea and the wind.' He glances up at me. 'I like silence.'

'So you've never listened to any bands?'

'Genesis,' he mumbles. 'I've listened to them.'

'God, Phil Collins!' I snort, covering my mouth with a hand. 'Aren't they a bit old?'

'Laugh all you like. Pop stars don't know anything worth hearing. Think you're clever, do you, girl?' He raises his eyebrows. 'What bands do you listen to then?'

'Eva,' I say quickly, my heart beating faster, 'remember? My name is Eva.'

He runs the fishing wire through his fingers, testing it, and looks up at me, frowning. He bows his head again, examining the line in his hand. 'Eva,' he repeats quietly.

I am filled with a tingling sense of something like pleasure.

And my body softens with relief. He looks at me and I flush, dropping my gaze.

'I listen to Bowie sometimes,' I say. 'He's classic. Siouxsie and the Banshees. New Order. Sisters of Mercy.' I talk quickly, reeling off bands that I remember Marco talking about, playing to me, placing the stylus carefully, drawing breath as the first chord sounds. I hope Billy doesn't notice the shake in my voice. I'm trying to cover it up. I clasp my knees with my hands.

Outside, waves sweep onto the pebbly shore, rattling stones, swilling foam and rubbish up onto the shoreline. Gulls swoop and moan in white circles as usual. But everything is different, because he has used my name.

22

The phone call came at three in the morning.
Max answered, stumbling into the cold living room,
half-asleep, to hear Charlie's muffled, shocked
voice. Suky had gone into premature labour.
Something had gone wrong. She'd been transferred
to hospital in a coma, but the baby was safe.

Max went alone to the Mission. He felt that
until he had the child in his arms, he couldn't
trust that they wouldn't be disappointed again.
He knew that Clara couldn't bear that. The nun
that picked the baby out of the cot and handed it
over was motherly-looking, plump and lined, but
her small eyes were impenetrable as olive stones.
He wrote his name in a book called 'Register of
Removals'. It felt oddly furtive. The creature was
tiny, an exhausted, angry red face swaddled in
scratchy grey blankets. He remembered the soft
fabric in Suky's hands, the blanket she'd been
embroidering for her child. 'Is there another
blanket, Sister?' he asked the nun. 'A blue one,
with dragons?' The woman shook her head with
an impatient frown, opening the door, standing
aside to let him leave.

As Max placed the baby in the carrycot on the
back seat and drove home, he was scared,
overwhelmed by sudden responsibility, disorien-
tated by the abrupt switch into the world of

parenting. He didn't feel like a parent. The baby was an alien creature. It screamed all the way, not soothed by the engine, or the motion of the car.

Clara opened the front door, her face tense with anxiety. He lifted the child from the carrycot, terrified that he was going to drop it, and placed it in her arms. There was a distinct smell of fetid, soiled nappies. But Clara softened, her face shining bright. 'What is it?'

'A girl,' Max said.

* * *

Suky died without coming out of the coma. She never saw her daughter. Max's memory of the girl in the dormitory — fingers holding a needle, embroidery in her lap and swollen ankles up on the bed — faded. Although sometimes he woke at night, and lying in the darkness he would suddenly recall the look on her face as she'd handed him the necklace.

* * *

The baby that Max had placed in her arms wasn't the plump, cherubic creature of Clara's imagination. There'd been no blonde curls or blue eyes gazing up at her. Eva was oddly skinny, her premature body covered with flaking skin. Black hair stood up in a thick, inky thatch; a scrunched face refused to look at the world.

With her toothless mouth hinged open as wide as it would go, the baby spread her wrinkled

186

fingers and screamed. At the blast of anguish, Clara's breasts tingled. She put her hands over them in surprise. She slipped her finger into the child's mouth, feeling a gummy suction pulling at her. Immediately Eva spat the finger out in despair, yelling again even harder. 'Well,' Clara told her. 'You know what you want, don't you?'

Clara's fears of being an inadequate mother disappeared. Instinct took over. Eva took over. She'd howled night after night, sicking up her formula milk and contorting her tiny body in colicky spasms. There was so much to do that there was no time to think. Eva needed her, and that was enough. As days passed and familiarity grew, Eva began to respond to Clara, to echo her facial expressions, to relax at her touch.

Feeding Eva her bottle, Clara found herself gazing into a deep frown of concentration, milk bubbles collecting at blistered lips, eyes screwed tightly shut, and knew that this small being was a survivor. The spirit of the person she was going to grow into radiated from her, so that sometimes Clara glimpsed inside the unformed face the child that Eva would become, and layered beyond that her teenager and adult selves staring back. 'You're going to be all right.' Clara squeezed the wriggling toes gently. 'I somehow think you're going to have us both twisted around your little finger. And then the whole world.'

It didn't matter that Eva hadn't heard Clara's voice in the womb. It didn't even matter that Clara had never met Suky, had no idea who Eva's real father was. Because now Clara understood: all babies are strangers from a watery, distant planet. They come trailing secret dreams behind them, the alchemy of their characters forming with their first gasp of air.

Mother and daughter learnt about each other through days of windy colic, inexpertly fastened nappies, long afternoon naps and sleepless nights. It wasn't easy, but there was never a moment that Clara regretted their decision to adopt. One evening she saw a piece on the news about a mother cat adopting a baby squirrel and it made her realise that the drive to be a mother went beyond reason: the need to love and nurture a creature that needed you was stronger than blood ties, stronger even than the boundaries of species.

Eva was with her constantly, night and day, clinging to her, her lolling head tucked into her shoulder as she was carried around the flat with Clara singing softly. All the love that Clara had been unable to give to the four lost babies was funnelled into this small daughter. So much love that she thought it would burst out of her like a river. Eva had a Moses basket next to the bed, but in the bleary hours of early-morning feeds, Clara didn't put her back, so that Eva slept between her new parents, her limbs flung open in trust.

When Max suggested a fresh start, a move to Suffolk so that they could be near his mother, close to the river and the sea, Clara agreed. She'd become a recluse after the last miscarriage, depressed and unable to leave the flat, seeing no one, even her old theatre friends.

Because of that it had been possible to present Eva to the world as their baby, telling friends that Clara hadn't wanted to let anyone know that she was pregnant; and everyone who knew their history was sympathetic, not wanting to ask questions, only relieved that there was a happy ending after all. Max was embarrassed about the lie. But although he would have felt more comfortable telling people the truth, he remembered the nun bundling Eva into his arms, and the way she'd slipped the envelope of cash into a pocket hidden in the folds of her habit. It had left him with a bad taste in his mouth, an uneasy feeling in his gut. Better to put it behind them and move on, he'd thought. He found a house deep in the countryside and neglected to leave a forwarding address at the London flat.

When they'd arrived in Suffolk, the hedges had been thick with white flowers, different shades of green sprouting from trees and ground. Max had shown her the house, looking excited but anxious. 'It's not too big, is it?' he'd asked. 'You won't feel isolated, will you?'

Feeling her way into motherhood, lost inside the warmth of baby skin, breathing only Eva's milky breath, living in the slate depths of her eyes, Clara hardly noticed the landscape. The house had been perfect: a stone fortress against the rest of the world — a place where they would be safe.

23

I have the stub of Billy's pencil left. My most precious possession. I've been drawing over the walls of the pagoda between wires and pipes. There are pictures of seals, a boat in a storm. I've drawn Billy fishing and a close-up of my wrists bound with rope. There's an illustration of me washed up on the beach, with Billy crouched above. I'm drawing a rabbit in a trap at the moment. These are my cave paintings. I wonder if anyone will find them in months or years to come and follow the story with their finger, understanding what happened to me.

Billy stands with his hands on his hips watching me. 'I'm not that ugly,' he complains.

'Yes,' I say, not taking my eyes from my drawing, 'you are.'

'You've made me look like a bloody Yeti,' he says matter-of-factly. 'I'm going to do something useful. Check the real traps.'

I nod, continuing to draw, leaning close to the wall, inhaling musty brick. I sit back on my haunches, squinting at my drawing. I've got the dimensions wrong.

'Let's hope I find one like that for our supper,' he says, leaning over my shoulder. He breathes through his mouth, examining the picture. The tickle of his beard rubs the tip of my ear.

I listen to the sound of metal scraping in the padlock. He'll be gone for a while. There are several traps, all made with wire and nails, placed under the gorse bushes and close to the fence where rabbits build their warrens.

It's not often I have the pagoda to myself. I put the pencil away, tucking it carefully into the deepest part of my pocket. Unfolding myself from the floor, I walk around the edges of the pit, staring around me impatiently, as if there might be an opening that I've missed. The interior of the pagoda gapes above me; it must be twenty feet high or more, although I'm uncertain about anything to do with measurements and numbers. The only possible way to climb up is a rusted pull-down ladder fixed high on the wall. I drag the chair over and stand on it. But balancing on my toes, straining to reach as high as I can, my fingertips don't even graze the bottom rung.

Billy has left his coat dumped in the corner. If there's an empty paper bag or scrap of paper inside it, I could scribble out a note, hide it in one of the plastic bottles and somehow leave it hidden in the shingle the next time we go to the beach. I kneel beside the coat and search the pockets, but there are no bits of paper, just the tin that he keeps his letters in. It's old and rusted, a cigar tin with gold lettering peeling away. I click open the lid, releasing a rich brown tobacco smell. Pale blue letters are packed close inside. I pick one up, fingering creases worn thin and fragile with constant folding and unfolding.

My eyes slide across sentences, devouring words . . . 'the fellas in your brick sound like good lads. You watch their backs and they'll

191

watch yours . . . here's a quid for Mr Chuggy
. . . heard about the bomb on the radio . . . thank
god you weren't in the pub . . . sorry for your
loss, lad. Reckon we don't know how hard it is.
Only numbers on the telly while people are
eating their tea. It's you lads that see the blood
and gore.'

The same slanted writing covers every sheet. I
check the signatures. 'Gramps.' I like the way
Billy's grandfather writes. He seems kind. And
he doesn't appear to be talking to someone who
is mad or evil. Billy was telling the truth: he was
a soldier, and he fought in Northern Ireland. It
sounds like a normal soldier's life. There is
nothing about prison. Some of the letters aren't
completely covered with writing. There are
tempting blank spaces that I could use for a
note, but there's no way I could take one without
him noticing. He re-reads them constantly.

The sound of pebbles clattering makes me
start. Quickly, I refold the letters, swearing as my
shaking fingers accidentally rip one of them.
Trying to remember the order the letters went
in, I slip them on top of each other, snapping the
lid into place. Then shove the tin back into his
coat pocket, dropping the coat on the floor
where he left it.

As the key turns in the lock, I'm sinking onto
my blanket, folding my legs under me. My heart
is thundering. I compose my face, breathing
through my nose.

Billy glances at me suspiciously. 'Not drawing?
What have you been doing?'

'Oh, filing my nails, chatting to friends,

reading a magazine . . . you know,' I force a smile, 'the usual.'

A rabbit dangles from his hand; he throws it over and it lands with a sickening slump next to me.

'Sort it out,' he says, 'we'll have it for supper.'

'I need the knife.' I keep my voice neutral.

He stares at me. I suppress a shudder, rolling my shoulders casually. 'Can't do it without.'

He pads over holding out the knife. My fingers are clammy as they close around the handle. Billy crouches on the other side of the room. He rolls a cigarette with steady, purposeful movements, never taking his eyes from me. He's testing me, I think. I must pass the test to make him trust me. I need to encourage him to take more risks, let down his guard more.

With an intake of breath, I stick the blade into the fur, tugging to rip it open, making a split so that I can find the soft, warm belly. A curve of taut, purple skin appears and I swallow, not wanting to puncture it. I've watched Billy do this countless times. I know what to do. I try not to think, averting my gaze, as I push the blade through. 'Not as expert as you.' Words snag in my throat, my fingers slippery with blood.

He takes a long drag of his cigarette, watching me. 'You'll slice your fingers off if you don't look what you're doing.'

'Where did you . . . where were you sent,' I pant with each tug ' . . . when you were a soldier?'

He lets out a stream of smoke. 'Northern Ireland. Bogside.'

193

'Oh.' I look down at the mess I am making. 'Must have been hard, all those bombs and things . . . ' I grimace at resisting skin. Creamy fat lapping my fingers, stained fur sticking to my skin.

'It was boring most of the time.' He clamps the cigarette tightly between his lips, scratches his scalp. 'Except for the riots. They were fun. Firing rubber bullets into the scum. Yeah,' he smiles, 'that was good.'

He catches my expression. 'That was what they wanted us to think, to feel — the army, the government. It was a war. Only they wouldn't call it that. There was a bigger plan, you see. We were all being corrupted, like maggots in a carcass.' He shakes his head. 'You can't imagine what it's like . . . to be hated. Women and kids too. *Brits out* graffitied all over. You never knew what wall was wired to explode, what passing car would fire at you. They chucked fridges out of top-floor balconies on us.' He picks a strand of tobacco from his lip, frowning. 'And there we were, trying to fight back with one arm tied behind our backs.' He hawks phlegm from his throat and spits loudly.

'So why?' I look away, feeling nauseous, the ripe smell of warm flesh in my nostrils. 'I mean . . . what's that got to do with me . . . why I'm here . . . '

'Because . . . because of her.'

'The voice?' I lean forwards, my hands on the damp pelt. 'The one in your dream?'

'No.' He shakes his head. 'Yes.' He frowns. 'I mean the other one. I mean her.' His eyes glaze.

His face has gone slack.

I open my mouth but he gets up abruptly, dropping his cigarette under a twist of foot. He stands over me. 'Hand me back the knife. You're making a pig's ear of it.' He holds out his hand, fingers curled and ready. 'Enough talk now.'

I tighten my grip on the knife and think for a second of lunging forward, stabbing him in the leg. Severing an artery. There must be an artery somewhere inside the bone and muscle. I am hazy about the workings of the human body. Faith would know. But I can't anyway. I'm a coward. The thought of it makes me faint. I can hardly skin the rabbit.

I thought I was a fighter. But I'm not. I am useless. My little sister would be better at this than me. My legs are jelly-weak as I hand the knife over. He picks up the half-skinned rabbit, sucking in through his teeth and shaking his head.

I know better than to press him when his mood darkens, but I need to who know 'she' is. Maybe she's a girlfriend? If I can find out then perhaps I can reason with him, get him to understand that he's making a mistake. Whoever she is, I'm not her.

24

By six months Eva had grown fat and smiley, with sturdy brown limbs that looked so tender and inviting that Clara could almost sink her teeth into them. Eva's thatch of hair had fallen out to be replaced by glossy curls. She still refused to sleep at night, writhing in her cot and clinging to Clara's hand. Clara would lie on the floor, holding the small hand through the bars of the cot, waiting patiently for her breathing to change.

By then Clara and Max had moved to Suffolk. They were exhausted from the efforts of packing up the flat, settling into Holt House, unpacking endless boxes, painting walls and hacking through the overgrown garden. Max was also stressed from starting up an office of his own, his only employee a nearsighted secretary. And of course they were both sleep-deprived. In the dark winter evenings they often gave in to the temptation to drink a glass of wine, slumped at the kitchen table, fingers curled around glasses, exchanging details of their days in between yawns, with Eva at last settled for a few hours.

'I've been sorting out papers in the study,' Clara said one evening. 'Our marriage certificate. Eva's birth certificate. Don't we have some papers somewhere to do with the adoption?'

Max frowned. Rubbed his finger along the edge of his glass. 'No,' he admitted slowly. 'We don't have anything in writing because we didn't go through an agency.' He blinks. 'It was unofficial.'

'What do you mean?' Clara paused, the taste of Chablis souring on her tongue. The kitchen pulled shadows into corners. Wind rattled the old windows.

'Clara, you know all this; I told you. That's how it happened so quickly. Why Eva was so young when we got her.' He shifts on his chair. 'I paid them a donation. That's what they called it.' He frowned, pulling his ear. 'I signed a book. Put my name and address next to Suky's name. It was like hundreds — I don't know, thousands — of other unofficial adoptions. There are no legal documents.'

'But how can we prove she belongs to us?' Clara sat back in her chair, her eyes wide. 'We should have papers, shouldn't we?' She leaned forward. 'Make them up,' she hissed, her heart racing. She pushed her glass away. 'You're a solicitor. Fake them.'

'I can't.' Max shook his head. 'I can't do that. I'm not a criminal, Clara.'

'What if that girl's family wants Eva back?' The possibility screams inside her like a siren. She has to stop herself from shouting. 'What then?'

Max set his mouth in a line. 'They won't.' He tries to take her hand, but she pulls it into her lap. 'Look, I've thought about this already. It was them that put her in that place, for God's sake.

197

Locked her away. Charles said that they told everyone she'd moved abroad. They were ashamed of her.' He raked his fingers through his hair. 'Why would they want her child — the baby they were forcing her to give away?'

'Forcing?' Clara tensed her jaw. 'I thought you said she wanted us to have the baby?'

Max cleared his throat. 'She did. She wanted her child to go to a good home. But . . . she didn't have a choice. I got the feeling that a lot of the girls there wanted to keep their babies. It was a production line, Clara.' He glanced at her, then down at the table. 'Babies being given away for money. Nuns taking cheques, handing babies to strangers. It was wrong. But we were desperate. Then Suky died. That sealed it for me, because I'd made her a promise. I promised her we'd love her child.'

When Max had first told Clara that he'd found a baby to adopt, Clara's aching body had softened, the rigid craters of herself relaxing and expanding with relief. She was going to be a mother. She'd heard the tremble in Max's voice as he'd told her the facts. But the only details that Clara had fastened on were that she'd be able to hold her new baby when it was a few weeks old.

Clara wishes she'd listened more carefully. She has a new fear. The fear that Suky's family might one day arrive on their doorstep to claim Eva as their own. She returned to the subject several times over the months, asking Max to forge the paperwork. But every time he shook his head. When pressed, Max told her wearily that he'd

198

made an oral agreement in good faith with Suky and Charles. He had signed the register of removals. They had Eva's birth certificate. He kept repeating these facts as if they were enough.

★ ★ ★

Winter in Suffolk had been an endurance test. The house creaked, tiles slid loose under the onslaught of winds, the roof leaked; Clara couldn't seem to get warm however many clothes she wore. When the river banks flooded, the garden became a bog, water seeping under the kitchen door. The marshes were sludge-grey under a bleak canvas sky. There were wild storms that turned the sea black, sweeping inland flattening trees, slamming doors and knocking fences over. Eva had a cough and a chest infection that dragged on and on. Clara crouched over the cot at night, her coat heaped on her shoulders, shivering in the dark, terrified that Eva's hacking cough would stop her breathing.

The relief of March came. Buds began to open, sticky hearts unclenching. There was new colour on the ground, sea lavender blooming in purple patches. As the month went on, daffodils and crocuses grew in bright clusters in the garden, catkins feathering the willow tree. Clara woke on 30th March, Eva's first birthday, and looked out of the window towards the sea. The sun was a silver circle, carrying the ghost of winter in it, a memory of mist and ice. 'At last,' she thought, 'things will be different now. Better.'

Eva had just learnt to walk. The narrow, dank

path close to the house was a soft place to fall, and full of interesting things to examine: earwigs and the slow gleam of slugs and spiders' webs wrapped in pale tunnels through a dense tangle of bramble and nettles. Clara walked behind, arms out to catch her if she fell, watching Eva noticing a curl of bindweed or the movement of light on a leaf, her fat fingers reaching for each new object, wide-eyed.

'Let's go home.' Clara picked her up, holding her squirming body close. 'After your nap there's birthday cake for tea, sweetheart. Daddy made it. You've never tasted chocolate before.'

On the walk back to the house, Eva sighed, moving her thumb into her mouth, her head drooping onto Clara's shoulder. Clara's arms ached from holding the slack body, her child growing heavier against her with every step.

★　★　★

There was a car she didn't recognise parked outside the house, a shiny grey BMW. Clara felt a tightening inside her chest. She had the urge not to go in, but to turn on her heel, walk away quickly down to the sea, with Eva tucked inside her coat.

As she opened the door, Max met her in the hallway. 'Darling,' he touched Eva's lolling foot, 'we have a surprise visitor. Suky's brother.' His voice was thin, but loud enough for someone in the sitting room to hear it.

Clara widened her eyes. 'How did he find us?' she mouthed.

'The phone book, probably.' His voice dropped, his face suddenly slack. 'M.J. Gale Solicitors and Co.'

She shook her head. 'I don't want him to see her,' she whispered urgently. 'Max, what if he's come to take her?'

Max was pale under his tan but he put his hand on her shoulder, giving it a reassuring squeeze. 'We mustn't panic. I'm sure he's just come to visit her. It's understandable. His sister's child.'

Clara held the heavy bulk of Eva's sleeping body closer. 'Well, it's her nap time. I'm going to put her down.' She frowned. 'If he's come to see Eva, he'll have to wait for her to wake up.'

Grace was in the hall putting her coat on. She'd come over for birthday tea; she patted Clara's arm. 'I won't stay. I'll leave you to it. Don't want to get in the way.' She glanced into Eva's sleeping face and back at Clara. 'Chin up. I'll be in the cottage if you need me.'

'Don't go . . . ' Clara held onto her thin hand. 'Grace, I'm frightened.'

'She's your daughter. Remember that.' And she was gone, the door closing softly after her.

Upstairs, Clara laid Eva's limp body in her cot, tucking a blanket around her, smoothing back the damp curls from her forehead. Eva's eyelids flickered and her thumb slid from her mouth, leaving a trail of saliva. 'My daughter,' Clara repeated softly. A smell of baking wafted from the kitchen, filling the house with a damp, sugary scent. Clara spent a moment in the bathroom, dabbing her lips with colour, combing

201

her hair. She straightened her jumper, flattened her hands over her hips. She stared at her pale face in the mirror. What does he want? She turned away. Her palms were sweating. She wiped them over her skirt.

In the living room, a man was rising from a chair. His blond hair receded from a high, pink forehead. He looked at her with interest; his eyes, she noticed, were biscuity, almost colourless.

'Charles Anderson,' Max was saying, 'this is my wife, Clara.'

'You'd better call me Uncle Charlie.' The man smiled and came forwards. 'Where's the child?'

'Eva,' Clara said. 'She's sleeping.' Clara sat opposite him, folding her feet under her, her hands clasped in her lap. 'She usually sleeps for about an hour or so.'

Charles looked over her shoulder sharply, as if Eva might be secreted behind the sofa. He shrugged. 'So, she's a healthy baby is she?' He smiled. 'All her fingers and toes?'

Clara glared at him. 'She's very healthy, thank you.'

As he sipped his tea, he took furtive glances around the room. Clara wondered what he thought, what impressions he was getting. They'd only just finished unpacking boxes. Books were arranged in tottering piles on the floor. Clara's mother's painting hung over the mantelpiece. Clara knew that it wasn't a particularly good example of a watercolour. She wanted to explain that her mother had painted it, and was at the same time angry with herself for caring what he thought. She tried to hide the distrust she felt, lowering her eyes. Charles kept up a steady stream of polite talk, telling them that he'd been made a partner at work and recently got married.

'What made you want to see Eva now?' Clara heard her voice, the choke in it. She dipped her head and took a gulp of tepid tea.

Charles put his head on one side as if considering. 'I promised my sister I'd keep an eye on her daughter. It was the last thing I said to her,' he opened his hands, 'after all, the child is family. I'm only sorry it's taken me this long. But it was hard at first . . . losing Suky.' He crossed his legs. 'You don't mind, do you?' he asked. 'I take it you've told Eva that she's adopted.'

Max was beginning to talk but Clara cut through him, 'No, of course we haven't told her.' She stared at Charles, her chin lifting. 'She's too little. She won't understand.'

A wail came from upstairs. All three of them looked towards the ceiling and Charles put down his cup expectantly. 'Ah, awake already. Perhaps she can sense her uncle's here.' He gave Clara a satisfied grin.

She got up silently and went to the door, her feet heavy.

As she re-entered the room with Eva yawning in her arms, Charles jumped up, and Clara stopped, her body poised for flight, her heart racing. Charles came forwards, and Clara tightened her grip on Eva. But he faltered, tripping over the rug, and his expression drooped into bewilderment. 'This is Suky's child?'

Clara nodded warily, putting her nose into Eva's dark hair, smelling the milky scent of her.

'I don't understand.' Charlie frowned. 'Has there been a mistake? I was expecting a child that looked . . . that wasn't . . . '

'Her colouring?' Max said.

'I thought she'd look like . . . like Suky.'

'Yes, we were surprised at first.' Max stood next to Clara, looking into Eva's face. 'But genes are strange things aren't they?'

★ ★ ★

Charles didn't stay for long. The conversation became more stilted. Charles told them that his father had died recently and that he'd inherited the family home. 'A ruin of a house, needs plenty of restoration work.' His hands shook as he raised his cup to his lips. He stole glances at Eva, but he didn't ask to hold her. Sensing an atmosphere, she behaved badly, throwing her beaker on the floor and crying when she wasn't allowed a second piece of cake.

As they stood in the doorway waving goodbye, Max leant close and said, 'Don't think we'll be seeing him again.'

'He just can't get away fast enough, can he?' Clara hugged Eva close. 'Anyone would think she has horns on her head.'

Eva turned her chocolatey face upwards and grinned.

'He'd come to take her,' Clara said.

'No,' Max began to protest.

'Yes,' she contradicted, 'I knew it from the moment I saw his car. You heard him. They've just inherited some stately pile.' She hugged Eva close. 'He's married. He has money. He's in a position to take Eva back.' She was trembling.

Max frowned. 'Well, if that was his plan, he's changed it now. She obviously wasn't what he'd expected.'

'I don't know why he was so certain that Eva would be blonde. I hope he doesn't get over the shock of it. What did he think? That he could just take her away from us? I'll never give her up,' Clara said, turning to go into the house. 'She's our child. He'd have to take her over my dead body. Papers or no papers.'

'Dead bodies plural,' Max said, slipping his hand into hers.

25

The dinghy yard is empty. I lean against the rowing boat. A low mist swallows my legs so that I shiver, feeling damp and cold. The river has shrunk, leaving sloppy banks of mud stretching down to the water. Seagulls appear out of the pale like small ghosts, rising from the water on outspread wings. I've forgotten to check the tide. It's going out, pulling back towards the sea. Low tide will make it harder to get the boat into the water. But we'll manage, I tell myself. There is a concrete slipway, even if it's slimy with green.

I'd escaped before anyone else woke up, taking the remains of a joint of lamb out of the fridge to give Silver to keep him quiet. He couldn't believe his luck. Mum won't be happy when she finds out. Leaning against the wooden side, I listen hard for approaching footsteps. Maybe they won't come after all. There is no wind to set masks clanking, no wave swell to move the water onto the shore. It is strangely silent, the river dark under a layer of shifting white.

I look at my watch. They're late. I give the boat a tug, straining at the shoulders. It's heavy as a boulder. I'll never move it on my own. I hear a crunch of footsteps, the murmur of voices. Fred and Joe appear beside me, like pantomime wizards materialising out of stage smoke, Fred chewing on a bread crust.

'Couldn't get out of the caravan without

Sandra knowing.' He swallows his mouthful and yawns. 'We had to tell her we were meeting you in the end. She just told us to be quiet so as not to wake the baby.'

'Right. Well, now you're here let's get on with it.'

Fred chews a last mouthful, licking stray crumbs from his lips. 'Not much of a breakfast.' He takes hold of the boat. 'Joe, you grab the other side.' He nods. 'Faith, lift the end.'

'The stern,' I mutter.

We stagger across the dinghy yard, tripping over anchor chains and ropes, the boat swaying between us. Joe groans. He drops his side and shakes his fingers, wincing. 'Weighs a ton. How is it going to float?'

Reaching the concrete slipway, we slither on slimy seaweed, staggering to keep our balance. The boat seems to get heavier, bashing into my knees. I curl my aching fingers tighter. Water laps around my ankles. As it touches the river, the boat changes character, becomes frisky and playful. It bobs and pulls, the tide catching at it, plucking it away from me. Fred and Joe stand at the brink, looking uncertain.

'You sure you know how to do this?' Joe asks, shivering.

I'm up to my knees in freezing water. I frown at him. 'Just get in, will you?'

Joe clambers in first. Fred follows, attempting to swing his leg over the side. He holds on with both arms, scrabbling to get his leg high enough, clinging on for a moment before he falls back with a heavy splash. Hopping up and down, he keeps trying, swearing and rolling his eyes, making a joke out of it, but he's out of breath, hands and knees scraped red. His shorts are soaked up to his waist. Joe tries to help, pulling at Fred's arms, grabbing a handful of jacket and tugging so that Fred flounders, half in and half out of the boat.

'Careful! You'll tear it . . . ' Fred gasps, collapsing over the side into the bottom, rubbing scraped shins.

Climbing in after him, I manage to push off with one foot, sending the boat out into the river. I pick up the oars and set them in the rowlocks. Looking over my shoulder I realise that the island is invisible. Mist hangs across wider stretches of the river. I think I can make out the dark contours of a pagoda like a strange fortress from a dream. Setting my shoulders, I begin to row towards the mouth of the river, dipping the blades, trying to find a rhythm. It's not as easy as I imagined; with a rattle and a bump, the oars keep slipping out of the rowlocks. When the boat catches the mid-stream current, I hardly need to use oars at all.

Fred's gone the colour of cheese. He grasps the sides of the boat with clenched fingers. 'Why are we going so fast?'

'We're moving with the tide,' I explain, 'don't worry.' But I hear the emptiness of my words.

Moored yachts loom out of the white, towering over us. The boat hits something beneath the waterline; there is a dull thud and a slight veer to the left. Joe gasps and peers over the side, craning to see. 'It's a man's head!' He turns to us with round eyes. 'In the water. We ran over him!'

The memory of the Wild Man's face comes to me, the blurred features taking certain shape in my mind. I imagine him now, a gash on his forehead, sinking back inside seaweed hair and inky blood. Feeling sick, I drop the oars and make myself look. There's a round shape receding behind us. It's bobbing low in the water. I catch the shine of a smooth surface.

'It's a buoy.' I'm almost laughing with relief.

'But that's just as bad!' Fred exclaims. 'Is he all right?' He leans over to look into the mist and the boat tips abruptly to one side.

'No.' I hold the sides of the boat and try to explain. 'Not that kind of boy.'

The two of them turn to me, puzzled. And Joe lets out a yelp. 'My feet are soaking.'

He's right. I realise that several inches of river water swills in the bottom of the boat. We'd emptied it before wc set off. 'Are there any bailers?' I gaze around the interior, hoping for a tin can, an old cup, anything we can use to scoop with. But there is nothing, and the water is rising fast. I look behind me. I can hardly see land. We're in a rotten boat. None of us are wearing lifejackets. I clench my teeth, trying to ignore my scrabbling panic, but I can't ignore the sense of failure dropping hard and heavy through my insides. We'll have to go back.

'We're letting in water.' I begin to flail the oars, attempting to turn the boat.

'Sinking!' Joe jumps to his feet. The boat judders and lurches from side to side, and I let go of the oars to grab his wrist. 'You'll have us over!' I tug at him, feeling the jab of his bone. 'Sit down!'

One of the oars, already out of its rowlock, slips sideways. Fred lunges forwards, hands reaching for it. The oar rolls overboard.

'Bugger!' Fred throws himself against the side, leaning as far as he can, fingers reaching for the oar, which is being carried away on the tide. He flails his arms, attempting to reach further, his fingers batting waves. The boat tips at a dangerous angle.

'Stop it Fred!' I clutch my seat.

Joe starts forward as if to grab Fred, but the extra weight causes a sudden violent tilt. The edge of the boat kisses water. Like a sack of kittens, Fred slithers overboard. I watch the arc of his heels in the softening air. There is a deep splash and silence. The boat, swinging back with the lurch of a fairground ride, makes Joe lose his balance. Out of the corner of my eyes I see the wooden seat catch at his knees, sending him crashing onto his shoulders.

I'm staring at the waves, searching the water. It seems thick as a grey carpet. Impossible to see through. I pray for Fred to surface and there he is, his head bobbing up like a cork, eyes wide and blank, spitting river. He splutters, trying to call out, his hands scrabbling. He chokes and coughs as water washes into his gaping mouth. Before I can shout, he's going down again. I see the swirl of his hair, a bubble of sodden jacket.

Joe is still sprawled in the bottom of the boat. 'Get up! Help me,' I hiss at him, grabbing the remaining oar, but he just keeps lying there. I'm thrusting the oar in Fred's direction, prodding the water. When Fred breaks the surface I shout for him to grab it. His head tips back, mouth sagging. He looks tired. 'Come on!' I urge. 'You can do it.'

He reaches out, his hand moving slowly. He touches wood and slips away. I can hear myself panting. I think I'm crying. The fear in Fred's face turns his mouth into a snarl, wipes colour from his eyes. He can hardly keep afloat. I'm thrusting the oar further out. Behind me, Joe has set up a low moaning.

'Try again!' I yell.

Fred makes another effort, a last surge, and manages to touch the oar. I watch his fingers curl and grip, feeling the tug. I'm exultant for a split second before I realise that Fred's weight is pulling me in. I brace myself, slamming my knees against the wood, leaning back. He keeps swallowing water, his head slipping under the surface. I'm not sure how much longer I can hold on when I hear the sound of a motorboat.

* * *

Ted the quay master appears beside us. He cuts his engine and leans over to hook Fred in with one strong, gnarled hand, bundling him into his boat. He's tossing a rope over to me, indicating that I should tie the boats together. I fumble with the knots, ashamed, relieved.

'What do you lot think you're doing?' he growls, starting the engine again. 'Out here with no lifejackets in the mist.'

Crouching in the bottom with Joe, I don't answer. Joe's lips are pale, his breath coming in ragged gasps. One of his shoulders doesn't look right. It sticks out at a weird angle and his arm is sort of just hanging, like a broken doll's.

'Joe?'

His eyelids flicker and he looks at me without any recognition. His eyes slide back, showing wet whites and broken red. The sound of the gulls is like laughter above me. I daren't move him. He lies where he fell, water sloshing around his ears. I glance behind at the island emerging out of the evaporating mist, pagodas rising into the sky.

Strands of damp hair twist around my face like wet ribbons. Holding Joe's thin hand in my own I tell him over and over that everything will be all right, but I'm not sure if he understands. His freezing fingers are dead in mine. His eyes flutter open, staring at me, bright with pain. Fred is coughing. I hear the chatter of his teeth as he sits, hunched in the other boat. With Ted's engine puttering and the smell of petrol in my nostrils, I set my face to the mainland. I can't look back.

26

A soft tug at my scalp wakes me. I'm confused. It feels as though fingers are threading through my hair. I blink. It is hardly daylight. Billy looms just above me, crouched low, his face so close to mine that I breathe the stink of his unwashed teeth. Shock pins me down. His touch trails across the rise of my cheekbone, fingertips crawling along the angle of my chin and into my neck. I swallow and shiver, shaking my head mutely, wanting to pull away, but I can't move.

'You look like her,' he says in a distant voice. 'Except your skin. The colour of your skin.'

I twist my arms across my body, wrapping them tightly, trying to fold myself inside the blanket. But there is nowhere to hide. This is what I've been frightened of since that first morning, waking to find him staring at me, just his eyes visible over the scarf; and when I caught him looking while I was washing in the bucket, his mouth gaping inside his beard.

I am strangely calm. I glance down at the knife hanging from his belt, checking that it's there in the greasy sheath. I will kill him or he will kill me. But I won't let him rape me.

His touch moves back to my hair. Stroking through the length of it, his fingers snag on tangles and knots. I lie very still, my heart hammering against my ribs while I curl my hands into fists, clenching them into packed balls

213

to smash into his face. He circles my neck with the broad span of his fingers as if he's measuring the circumference. The expression on his face is far away, thoughtful. He holds me for a moment, his hands resting quietly against my skin; thumbs on the jump of my vein. He closes his eyes, mouth trembling.

I feel hollow. Weak. 'Don't,' I say, my voice breaking. 'Don't.'

Billy lets go with a startled jerk, staring at me as if I'm the one who's done something wrong. He backs away, shuffling from his knees onto his feet, spinning around to crouch in the corner, pulling his arms over his head, protecting himself, or blocking out a sound.

I put my hand to my neck in confusion. He didn't hurt me. But the sensation of his fingers lingers.

'What . . . do you think you're doing . . . ' I begin to ask in a broken voice, catching my breath, struggling onto my elbows to look at him.

He doesn't answer, reaching to pick something up. He comes across with the coil of rope in his hands and I know that he's going to put me in the pit. 'Stand up.' He doesn't look at me. His face is grim and closed. I smell sweat on him. Rank. Bitter. I am trembling, waiting for him to fasten the rope. But when I glance down at the opening of the dark mouth, I can't stand the thought of it. My bladder aches. I need to pee. I plant my feet, shaking my head, pulling away from him. He takes the knife from his belt, holding it up with trembling fingers. The blade glints. 'Don't be stupid.' His left eye twitches. He yanks the rope tight around my waist. 'You'll be safe there.'

The pit swallows me as he lowers me into shadows, the rope straining around my waist. Standing on the bottom, I watch as the frayed end jerks out of sight. I breathe deeply, tasting stale air, pushing away a tangle of panic. I want to scream; instead I whisper, 'Billy. Don't leave me.' There is nothing but the sound of his feet on concrete and a door shutting. The wind makes a soft whistling noise through the pillars high under the roof. The sea sighs in the distance. And I hear a scuffle and thud and know it's the sound of his fists against stone.

I yank down my jeans, squatting in the furthest corner to release the liquid pressure inside. Hot urine splashes my bare feet. I crawl away from the wet, finding a patch of pale morning light to settle in, hugging my knees and listening to the sounds of muted violence, remembering him touching my face, his expression as he said: 'the colour of your skin'.

* * *

My first boyfriend, Philip, was a farmer's boy, the year above me at school. He was fifteen and I was fourteen. He'd asked if I'd come home for tea, meet his parents.

Autumn. There were leaves gathering in drifts, speared against the spiky hedges. Fields swept up to the skyline, newly ploughed, the earth dark and raw, soft as an underbelly. We walked hand in hand through the farmyard, smelling dung and the milky heat of cows. The beasts were penned in, a shuffling crowd of piebald hides, turning wary eyes to watch us. Philip grasped the top of the pen and jumped up to stand on the middle rail. He had a stick in his hand; he leant over and brought the stick down hard on the nearest bony bottom. The cow let out a low cry and shuffled into the herd, bumping against the rest of them in panic. A long stream of shit hit the dirty floor behind her, steam rising.

I put my hand over my mouth. 'You hurt her.'

He laughed. 'Only a cow.' Jumping down from the rail he pressed his lips against mine, so that I felt the roughness of chapped skin, the point of his tongue. 'If you're going to be a farmer's wife you can't be soppy about animals.'

Inside, his mother waited by a table laid with a blue cloth, a brown teapot and jug. There were scones and a Victoria sponge. His father came in wearing overalls, his hands pink from scrubbing.

Philip lost his jaunty manner in their company, sat meekly with his eyes down, chewing on a scone, pale crumbs dropping into his lap.

'So Eva,' Mrs Green asked me, 'where are your family from, originally?'

I sipped the treacly tea, considering. 'London,' I said. 'Before I was born.'

'Not from round here, then,' Mrs Green persisted.

Philip and his father helped themselves to slices of cake, bit into the jammy middle, chewing noisily, their eyes glazed.

216

'Well,' I shot a glance at Philip, but he ignored me, 'my granny is from here. Grace Gale. My dad grew up here.'

Mrs Green nodded, but didn't look impressed. She sniffed. 'I know Grace Gale.'

I knew there was an answer lacking, one I was expected to provide. Mrs Green was waiting for it. I thought about my mother talking about her father, the consulate, her childhood abroad. 'My mum's family lived in Egypt,' I said eventually.

'Egypt?' Mrs Green raised her eyebrows and gave her husband a meaningful look. 'I see,' she said.

The clock on the wall ticked. There was the sound of chewing. A tabby cat walked across the kitchen with her tail in the air.

'More tea?' There was something triumphant in her manner as she poured the arc of shining liquid into my cup. Mr Green wiped his mouth with his napkin, leaving it scrunched on the table. Pushing back his chair with a noisy scrape of wood against floor, he left the room.

The next morning at school, when I went to find Philip at break, he moved away from me, setting his shoulders stiffly. He avoided looking at me, keeping his back turned, laughing loudly at something another boy said. I felt the cold draught of a door shutting in my face.

* * *

I didn't want to be like the cows — helpless, penned in — but that's how it felt in our village. It was suffocating. I was trapped by the look in

217

people's eyes: the look that said I was different, that I didn't fit in. Mum and Dad are so protective. They always have been. They're like a double act, with Mum making me feel guilty every time she gets a migraine, and Dad trying to stop me growing up. Sometimes he'd actually hand me a tissue to wipe lipstick off my mouth. Stand with his hands on his hips waiting for me to do it.

In Ipswich there are clubs where you can dance until morning. In the darkness, inside the music, there is space and time. Boys with hot mouths, their lips opening on mine, made me feel wanted. I liked it when they pressed their hips against me, so close that their belt buckles pinched. They asked me to go outside with them, begging me in thick, urgent tones above the music, their voices vibrating against my ear. But I never did.

'Eva Gale, you make me laugh. What are you waiting for?' Lucy asked. 'Saving yourself for Prince Charming?' She thought I was old-fashioned, a bit of a prude. But I wanted someone to look at me the way that Dad looked at Mum. Lucy's parents were divorced. Her mum didn't care what she did. Staying overnight with her gave me an alibi. We got the bus into the town centre without fail every Friday and Saturday night, our lips slick with gloss and our skirts hitched up.

The man on the door stamped my hand. The dark, shabby interior was dense with cigarette smoke and expectation and bodies. Swaying to the music, a glass of rum and Coke in my hand,

I was invisible and desirable all at the same time. Blurred faces appeared out of the gloom, asking me to dance, wanting to be close: village boys and townies, punks and the posh boys from the private school in town. None of them princes, only frogs. But then Marco walked into a gothic night at the club on the market hill, and everything changed.

27

Mum and Dad are angry with me.

'You knew it was wrong . . . ' Dad's voice broke, 'stupid.' He dropped his face into his hands. 'You'll spend the rest of the day in your room to think about it.'

I'd wanted his attention for so long and now that I had it, he couldn't even look at me. I saw that his shoulders were shaking. I'd made him remember Eva and the storm. Mum was pale and dark-eyed. She led me upstairs by the hand, and stood by the door.

'Dad is right, Faith. You must think about what you've done.' She wrinkled the skin on her forehead. 'And when you are ready, we'll go to apologise to those poor children,' she sighed. 'And Sandra.'

An ambulance came to the quay to take Fred and Joe away. Medics wrapped them in blankets. A crowd gathered to watch. The mist had gone, the sun breaking up in dazzling brilliance on the morning river. Among the strangers, I caught a glimpse of Ellie Dawkins' smirking face. I looked away from people staring, pointing, the whispers starting.

Fred seemed to be trying to smile at me before they shut the doors, but his teeth were chattering too much for his mouth to work properly. Joe's eyes were closed and he was a funny colour. His dark skin had gone grey, as if he'd smeared ashes over his face.

The whole of my class will hear about it. I count on my fingers. I only have days left until the end of the holidays, just days between now and the moment I have to walk into the classroom again. Fred and Joe are my friends. I can't think about the fact that they might have been killed because of me. Drowned. I only wanted to get to the island. I hadn't thought of anything else. Perhaps they won't like me anymore. I put the edge of my hand in my mouth and bite hard. Pain leaps to the surface, a sharpness that connects my skin and my teeth. It makes me feel better. When I let go I have a set of indentations in my skin, a crooked red pattern.

I can hear Mum and Dad murmuring downstairs. I expect they are discussing me. I lie on the floor, pressing my ear against the carpet and listen hard, trying to make out words. But nothing is clear. Lying on the carpet, I start to sing: *it was only a paper moon, hanging over a cardboard sky* — there is a crash below me as if something has been dropped — *but it wouldn't be make-believe if you believed in me.*

Granny and Jack holding each other, hand against hand, his arm around her waist. They bob and dip and spin away from me. I want to follow them. I want to run after Granny and explain what happened, and she will tell me that I am right to try and find a way back to the island. She'll lean close, so that I see the web of lines around her mouth as she whispers *your sister is alive and she's depending on you.*

Lying here I can look under my bed. There is a

thick layer of dust. Clumps of it gather, charcoal-grey, fusty, sticking in the corners. It doesn't look as if Sophie ever cleans under the beds, even though I heard Mum asking her to. I reach under to slide out my box of treasures, dipping my hand inside to pull out a bone. It is pockmarked and stained with green. I think it's the fibula of a sheep or a deer. It's about the length of my forearm and I can circle it with my thumb and first finger. It's not weird to collect bones. I like thinking about how things work, especially living things. How complicated and clever bodies are. Bones are beautiful. I found this one buried in mud on the banks of the stream.

I wonder if your sister's skeleton is floating around . . . Joanna's voice is in my head and it won't go away. I start to hum, but I can still hear her . . . *or if it's broken apart* . . . Shut up. Shut up. The bone feels cold. I drop it back in the box.

I get up and go to the window to look at the island, putting my hand flat on the glass in greeting. 'Eva,' I whisper, 'are you there?'

There is movement below. A shape leaning against the house, two heads together. I stare as the heads pull apart, and I see that it's Sophie and Robert Smith. He's laughing, his hand reaching out to touch her, fumbling under her shirt. She wriggles closer. Suddenly he tilts his face up and I catch the shine of his eyes.

Holding my breath, I step away from the window, out of sight.

28

It is one of those last, lingering summer days that burn with the intensity of a bonfire. On the mainland the farmers will be harvesting. I imagine dust rising behind combine harvesters, the corn cut and baled. A landscape should change with the seasons, shifting into autumn. Here it's the same day after day: speckled pebbles, the stubborn green of gorse, brown waves churning relentlessly. Only the sky changes, making colours soften into dullness or brighten in sunlight.

Billy and I are eating raw carrots and beans in the pagoda. Lunch. I long for bread, for slices of brown bread and butter, the chewy crust giving way to the airy inside, a nutty flavour, yeasty and satisfying. I bite down on earth, crunching on it, bits of grit sticking to my tongue. The string from the bean pod catches in my teeth.

The thick concrete walls of the pagoda are always cold to touch, making it cool inside whatever the weather. There are no windows to let in the light, just the gaps at the roof, giving glimpses of blue.

'I'd never been in one of these places before,' I tell Billy, my tongue fishing for scraps of carrot.

'This is where they developed Britain's first atomic weapon,' he says, leaning against the wall. 'Blue Danube it was called. Tested it here too.'

'You know a lot about it,' I venture cautiously.

'My grandfather told me things. See the way it's built?' He gestures to the lofty roof with the pillars holding it up. 'Built for containment you see. Prepped for high-yield blow-outs. The roof is designed to fall inwards if there's an explosion.'

I look at the space above and think that this is a good place for containing other things, with no way out except the door that he keeps padlocked.

'Where is your grandfather?' I ask.

He frowns. 'Gone. Like the rest of them.'

'You mean dead? Your parents too?'

He lets his hands fall to his sides. 'Good as dead anyhow.'

He squints through the dim air. We listen to the birds crying, the sound of the sea breathing in the distance. 'We should get out of here, go over to the ocean,' he says, 'get a bit of sun.'

Wordlessly, I hold out my hands for him. He pauses for a moment, as if considering, before he takes a length of rope and binds my wrists, wrapping the rope a couple of times, finishing with a skilful knot.

* * *

The sea crashes onto the shore, swollen waves and white foam. I take a quick look up the beach. It's my hope that someone might do what Faith and I used to and steal over to visit the place for an illicit swim, sail across to trespass for the thrill of it. But the long line of shingle is empty. Light shimmers across the baking pebbles.

Billy stops and bends to pick something up.

He holds it out to show me; a small egg sits in his palm. He stoops and closes his fingers around another speckled shell. 'We can have them for supper.'

Far above us a black-and-white bird circles. I look up, lowering my lashes against the glare. 'It's a tern,' I say. 'They nest in the shingle.' The bird drops and skims past Billy's head with an angry scream.

'Too late now,' he laughs into the sky triumphantly. 'Shouldn't leave 'em lying around.'

He tucks the eggs into his pocket. We'll eat them later, hard-boiled in seawater and peeled while they are still too hot to touch, hunger clenching in our bellies. I remember the morning I found the chick in the egg. I made such a fuss. It's hard to believe I'm the same person as that teenager in her school uniform living her comfortable, protected life.

We sit on a ridge of warm stones, looking out towards the horizon. Billy rolls a skinny cigarette and puts it between his lips, ducks to light it.

'You must have been with people all the time in the army. Teamwork and stuff.' I hunch my shoulders, my bound wrists resting in front of me. 'Aren't you lonely here?'

'Why would I be?' He takes a deep drag and lets the smoke drift out of the corner of his mouth. 'Loneliness is in the mind. It's a weakness.'

'People need people,' I say. 'It's the way we're made.'

He shakes his head. Greasy tendrils slide over his shoulders. 'People hurt people. It's safer alone. Safer not to trust anyone.'

'What about me?' I turn my head, squinting into the light, the edges of him flickering and blurring. 'Do you trust me?'

'No.' He sits up straighter, hugging his knees. 'You don't understand. Not yet.'

I swallow. 'You're right. I don't.' I push away my anger. I need to go for a swim, take out my frustration on the force of water. I nod at the waves. 'Can I go in?'

He glances at the sea and then at me.

'It's all right,' I tell him, 'I can't get very far. Not with the current.'

He undoes the knot slowly and I rub my wrists. We are close. He kneels before me, the rope spilling from his hands. I stare at him in silence and he looks back, unblinking. I'd never noticed before that his eyes have flecks of yellow around the pupil like sunrays. I look away first. 'Right,' I stand up, 'I'm going in.'

I know he's sitting behind me, cross-legged and impassive. He'll be staring as I struggle out of my jeans and shirt. I am aware of my old, dirty underwear, my exposed skin. I limp down the slope, pebbles sliding under me, the pinch of them under my soles. The water is cold, even in this weather, and I gasp for a moment on the edge, before throwing myself into an oncoming wave.

The sea closes over my head, swirling and grainy. Opening my eyes under water, I look up towards the surface; afternoon light filters through in shafts of brilliance, turning the sea transparent and green. I remember how I swam here while Faith waited on the beach. As I break the surface, I see her there, pale face and pale hair, anxiously watching for me, drawing her knees under her chin.

Instead of my sister, Billy narrows his eyes. I am sick of him, sick of the tangle of his hair, his unblinking scrutiny of me.

I face the sea, feeling the urge to swim away from the shore, to keep going into the restless mass of ocean. I imagine the colder depths, the startled shoals of fish parting for me, floating jellyfish brushing my skin and Faith's creatures — mermaids and selkies and The Wild Man himself — turning their gaze towards my thrashing limbs. I think of myself out there, treading dark water, as an ocean liner bears down on me, my waving hand invisible to the sailors on deck.

Startled by the sound of breathing, I turn sharply to find Billy standing up to his waist in water behind me. He's taken off his shirt and his chest is ferociously white. The curve of each rib is a hooped line; his collarbone juts out like a shelf from his shoulders. He looks like a prisoner rather than a jailer. He clamps the stub of cigarette between yellowing teeth, puts his hands into the water, bending with a shiver to splash his chest. He hasn't taken his trousers off. Their dark shapes billow through grey-brown strands.

He's watching a sailing boat. I consider trying to attract their attention, but he's right behind me and it's too far away to see us. Billy's fingers close around my arm. 'Time to get out.' His breathing sounds odd, fast and jerky, as if he's been running. 'Now.' He tugs me sharply.

We stagger out of the sea up the shingle incline; he's holding me close to him, gripping my arm. I taste salt in my mouth. He stoops, gathering my clothes and his shirt in one quick movement, bundling them under his other arm. 'Hurry.' He marches me away from the exposure of the beach, heading inland.

'There's no one . . . ' I gasp.

Despite his emaciated frame, I feel the strength of his muscles, the sinewy force of him. He looks behind us. 'They're coming.'

'No,' I protest, 'the boat's far away.'

He shakes his head impatiently. My feet are bare and I wince at sharp stones and thorns under the gorse bushes. He holds my wrist tightly and pulls me with him, his long strides covering the ground quickly. My ankle hurts. He doesn't slow down, even though I'm limping properly, gasping in pain and dragging behind him. We step over trailing razor wire, the sea at our backs. Keeping to the old concrete road, he hurries me past the empty huts with their broken windows and clustering shadows, glancing over his shoulder as he tugs me on towards the pagoda.

Billy has locked us in. Before he got the padlock out, he'd spent about twenty minutes crouching by the door, peering around the corner. He'd still been breathing strangely, swearing under his breath, muttering to himself. Now he's in his corner, reading the book. I can feel his frustration. He curls his beard around his finger, pulling at it, repeating words. He's nodding his head, rocking himself, the low intonation of his voice reminding me of prayers rising in an empty church.

I shiver, tucking myself into the blanket. The sea has left my skin chilled, crusted with salt. My hipbones stick up, pointy as sticks under my fingers. It's as if I'm melting away, losing myself. And I want my body back. The curves and fullness of me. I want to be held, to be loved. I want Marco to be here, lying above me. I try to imagine his warm breath in my mouth, his hands on my face. 'I love you,' I whisper into the air. But he isn't there. I can't find him.

There were things I felt about Marco that I couldn't tell anyone — not Faith or Mum or even Lucy — feelings I had when Marco and I were alone together, and how, on his bed, he'd fumbled through my clothes to lick my nipples, raising his head to look at me with half-closed eyes. 'Is this all right?' And me nodding, yes, more please, because I'd never felt anything like it before. He'd slipped his fingers inside my knickers, pushing into the tight inside of me, setting up a rhythm until the rising pressure made me call his name. I'd clung to him, feeling embarrassed and grateful and surprised. 'God, I want to sleep with you, Eva,' he'd gasped into my hair. 'You're driving me mad.'

Billy has stopped humming. Memories drain away and I'm alert, because Billy has got his tin of letters on his lap. He's leafing through them. I hold my breath. He's taken one of them out, unfolding it and holding it up to the light. It's the one with the rip. He fingers the torn edges

229

and I can see his shoulders stiffen. Quietly I push myself backwards, muscles tensing as I angle my body away.

He staggers to his feet and out of the corner of my eye I see him curl his hand into a fist; he starts to slam clenched knuckles into the wall, but then pulls back sharply. He rakes his hand through his hair instead. Now he's looking around him wildly, grabbing at the Primus stove, dragging the containers of water into a group, bundling up his blankets. He spins on his heels, staring at me. 'They know we're here.' His left eye twitches and flutters. There's sweat on his forehead. He stares at the locked door, taking out his knife. 'They're coming for us.'

'No,' I whisper. 'No. It wasn't . . . them.'

'What?' He glares at me, distracted, hair flopping into his eyes.

'It was me,' I say quietly. 'It was me that read the letters. I didn't mean to tear it. I'm sorry.'

He tightens his fingers around the knife. 'You?' He shakes his head.

'I'm sorry.' I pull my knees to my chest, shrinking as he strides over.

He stands over me, clutching the tin in one hand and the knife in the other. Abruptly, he drops to my level, pushing his face into mine, his mouth opening wide. 'Tell me!' He's shouting, spit flying, and the knife is at my cheek. He looks frightened and angry and blank all at the same time.

I flinch away from the blade, closing my eyes. 'What?' My voice is a squeak. The sharp edge presses against me, a rim of cold steel. I imagine

230

it slicing me open, how easy it would be for him, like skinning a rabbit. My heart is thundering.

He hisses, 'Are you a spy?'

'No.' I push the word out, afraid to move.

And then the bite of the blade is gone. I open my eyes.

'Tell me why then.' He's kneeling before me, rubbing his face with quick agitated movements.

'I wanted to know more about you ... ' Tentatively, I touch my skin where the steel pushed against it. 'I didn't mean any harm.' I swallow. 'I just wanted to know something about your life. You never tell me.'

He looks puzzled; slowly he straightens up, sliding the knife back into the sheath on his belt. 'What did you find out?'

'That you have a grandfather. Someone who loves you.'

He presses scabby, broken knuckles to his lips and turns away from me. We are both silent, breathing heavily. I'm trembling all over, and I clasp my fingers tightly to stop them shaking.

'I don't know where he is,' he says quietly. 'He's gone.'

'I'm sorry ... '

'He lived in the village.' His voice is rough. 'It was the thought of him that kept me going. Sleeping in ditches, stealing from bins. Gramps would know what to do, I thought. If I could just get to him. He'd explain everything.' Billy gasps. 'I knocked on the door. Nothing. Looked through the window. Rooms were empty.'

Billy gets up and walks to the other side of the pagoda, his arm slung across his face. 'He didn't leave a message for me. I couldn't ask the neighbours. I couldn't draw attention. I just had to go. Keep running.'

'He lived in the village?' A sudden sense of urgency makes me lean towards him. 'What was his name, your grandfather?'

'Jack Train,' he says quietly. He leans against the wall, his forehead against concrete.

My hand flies to my mouth. 'But I knew him.' I blink at Billy through the gloom of the pagoda, remembering the white-haired man stepping out of Granny's garden shed, how he'd taken my hand in his. 'He was a friend of my Granny's. More than a friend . . . ' I see his palm on the small of her back, her smile over his shoulder.

'Gramps?' He's staring at me, his mouth gaping.

'That makes us, I don't know, almost related or something.' I shake my head. The connection between us is tangible. His grandfather loved my granny. It seems incredible and yet I realise now that he'd told me several times that his grandfather was a local. For some reason it had never occurred to me to find out if I knew him. And now that I do know who he is, I can see echoes of Jack in Billy: the jut of his nose, his height. And in Billy's voice the fainter trace of Jack's accent.

'Where is he?' His eyes shine.

'Billy,' I say gently. 'He had a stroke. He died just a few weeks after my granny.'

Billy looks as though I've struck him. He drops his head in his hands and shuffles away. I want to pull him to me, hold his thin shoulders, feeling the knots of his spine under my cheek. I stay where I am on the ground. 'I'm sorry,' I whisper. 'They made each other happy.'

I watch him walk to the other side of the pagoda. Night is falling outside. Long fingers of darkness fold him inside them. The wind catches at the edge of the concrete sills, hissing. There is the rustle of Billy sitting in his corner. I curl up on my blanket like a foetus. My lip is bleeding. I must have bitten it. I can still feel the edge of the knife — the bright sting of it. The smallest extra pressure and it would have sliced through my skin. I think of Granny and Jack in the allotment, wonder at their shock if they could see their grandchildren now, see us here in this place together. But something else edges into my thoughts, a blossoming of hope. Because now Billy knows that I'm connected to his grandfather, perhaps that knowledge, and the memory of Jack, will be the key to my freedom. Perhaps now he will let me go.

29

Max gives Sophie a lift into town once a week on his way to work, so that she can attend college. Sophie sits beside him in the passenger seat. She smells of a perfume that he's not accustomed to, can't seem to get used to: musky, powdery, with heavy floral undertones. Lilies, he realised the first time he'd smelt it, recognising the deep, lush aroma. He's used to the light lemony fragrance that Clara uses. This is overpowering — heady, sensuous. He rolls down his window, smiles at her briefly, apologetically.

'How are you getting on, Sophie?' Max addresses his question to the windscreen. Country lanes are dangerous at this time of year, the banks so overgrown with tangled brambles and weeds that it's impossible to see what's around the corner. 'College OK?'

He catches her Gallic shrug from the corner of his eyes. 'It is OK,' she says in her smooth voice. Since she's been with them, the hot days have turned her skin bronze. Eva became darker in the summer, the reflective glare from the water intensifying her tan.

Max slows down and pulls over onto a verge to let a lorry pass. Huge wheels turn a foot from the car. The farmers are harvesting and the air is dense with gritty dust, the nights full of the growl of machinery in the fields. He rolls the window back up quickly to prevent the car being filled with fumes and bits of straw.

'Your older daughter,' Sophie says. 'How many years had she?'

He starts, a flush flooding his face. 'Eva?' He swallows. 'She was seventeen.'

'A big difference then,' she mused, 'between her and her sister, no?'

'Yes.' Max's fingers grip the gear stick as he changes down into third. 'I suppose so.'

He remembers the moment Clara told him that she was pregnant with Faith. The joy that surged through him. 'Maybe the fact that we didn't plan this, didn't try, maybe that will make it different.' Clara had been shaking. 'But I'm so frightened,' she'd whispered.

His job had been to soothe her, reassure her. Max was frightened too, but he couldn't let her know. His instinct was to wrap her up in cotton wool and banish her to bed for nine months. Instead, his mother had stepped in. She was living in the garden by then, in her caravan. So she was there every day to walk Eva to and from the village primary school, to cook and look after them all. It helped keep him sane when he was stuck in the office, to know that Clara wasn't alone.

'Was she beautiful?' Sophie's insisting voice brings him back to the moment and he finds himself imagining his daughter's face, her dark eyes blazing at the slightest provocation, her large mouth opening when she smiled to show the gap between her front teeth.

He nods. It's been a long time since anyone talked to him about Eva. And nobody has asked him questions like this since the accident. After the initial shock, he is glad to have this self-contained French girl talk to him about his daughter, grateful that she doesn't tighten with embarrassment and change the subject.

'I am an only child,' she sighs. 'In my apartment, it is only me and my mother. And sometimes her . . . men friends.'

Max clears his throat, uncertain of how to respond. They're on a bigger road now, and there are other cars to negotiate. They've reached the outskirts of Ipswich and there are roundabouts and junctions. In his peripheral vision, he sees her sweep her hair behind her ears.

'Faith misses her sister,' he says. 'They were close, despite the age gap.'

'She has you.' Sophie sits up straighter. 'Faith is lucky to have a good father.'

Max slows the car, halting at a set of red traffic lights. Uninspiring rows of uniform houses line the road. He remembers Faith after her escapade in the boat. She'd been quietly defiant, completely unrepentant, and yet she must have been shaken up badly by the incident. He'd been too hard on her. She'd frightened him. She couldn't even swim properly, damn it. He turns to Sophie and she holds his look. He glances away.

'I don't know that I'm such a good father.' He is aware that his tone is bluff, but he needs to keep his voice steady. 'Not at the moment.'

'Oh, I think, yes.' She has a slight lisp. 'You are a kind man.' And he feels the touch of her fingers on his forearm. She presses down, a small pressure. Skin against skin. Clara and Max have not touched for so long. At the shock of someone else's fingers, all the hairs on his arm rise.

There is a polite beep from behind. The lights have changed to green. His feet work the pedals, hands clumsy on the wheel.

He drops her outside the civic college. He sees it through her eyes: an ugly building, a square block of concrete, clumsy and tatty. Kids in dull clothes drift past. He notices several of them dressed as if for a Halloween party in flowing black with white-painted faces. He feels sure that Paris has nothing as hideous as this. In the months before she drowned, Eva had also taken to wearing dreary layers of black clothing: skirts that dragged at her ankles, strange fingerless gloves and jumpers with trailing threads. She'd stomped around in a pair of big, heavy-soled boots. He couldn't understand it. She'd laughed and called him old-fashioned when he'd told her they looked as though they belonged to a construction worker on a building site.

He's about to say goodbye, give Sophie a brisk wave of his hand, to take back some formality, a notion that he is the employer and she the au pair. But she's already leaning forwards, enveloping him in the heady scent of lilies. She brushes both his cheeks with her own. He hadn't shaved that morning and her fine hair slides across, catching in his bristles.

'Thank you,' she smiles. She has very small, white teeth, he notices, like a child's.

Max watches her walk away, her bag slung over her shoulder. She is less than two years older than Eva. But she seems much older. There is something knowing about her; you'd almost call it an inscrutability, a control at any rate that Eva had not had time to acquire. And he reminds himself that Sophie has grown up in Paris, a capital city, whereas his daughters are country children. He and Clara had wanted that innocence for them. They'd wanted to keep the girls safe, protected from city life.

Max drives to the office feeling unsettled. He winds down the window fully to try and cool the hot car, clear the heavy air. He's stuck behind a bus and it pumps diesel fumes. The smell makes him nauseous. Sophie's perfume remains around him; he can taste it on his tongue, sour and cloying. It occurs to him that Sophie is the same age as Suky was. He struggles to remember Suky's face and instead he sees the embroidery in her hands, delicate stitches threading through folds of fabric, the work held on her lap under the bulge of her stomach.

His legs are sticking uncomfortably to the wool of his suit trousers. His collar feels too tight around his neck, as if it's strangling him. Clara hadn't thought much of the clothes he had to wear to the office. 'My clients expect me to wear a suit,' he'd protested, as she'd giggled at the sight of him done up in a pinstripe suit in a heatwave.

She'd shaken her head. 'Men are such impractical creatures.'

She'd been looking cool and sexy in a mini-dress. It was years ago, when mini-skirts were causing newspaper headlines. She'd even worn one to get married in. A white smock with big fabric daisies around the hem, and her hair cut like a pixie's around her ears. 'If you bend over, you'll flash your knickers to the world,' he'd whispered to her at the registry office.

'Who says I'm wearing any?' she'd replied, dipping her head demurely into the bouquet of real daisies that she was carrying.

They'd begun their marriage thinking that love was all they needed to carry them through a life together. Those bleak years of having one miscarriage after another had almost destroyed them, yet they'd survived it, the love holding on. But the grief of Eva's drowning hasn't brought them together; it's pushed them apart, forced them into separate places. He is determined that this isn't the end. Moving house is the only answer, he thinks. It will give them a chance to begin again. It has to.

30

Mum and I stand at Joe's bedside. He looks very small in the hospital bed, tucked in under a fold of white sheet and a blue blanket. His legs make straight, neat lines under the blue. The bed is raised, supporting him at a reclining angle. It has metal bars, a bit like a cot. There's a heavy plaster cast on his left arm. Sandra and Fred are sitting on chairs on the other side of the bed. Sandra looks at us with a stern face.

It's a children's ward, so the walls are painted in primary yellow and green. Plastic sheep dangle from the ceiling and there are cardboard Disney characters on the walls. Scrawly pictures drawn by kids are tacked up on a notice board behind the nurse's desk among the thank-you cards. Pluto's long face grins down at me from behind Joe's bed. Mum reaches into her bag and pulls out the presents we bought on our way to the hospital. She offers Joe a foil-wrapped box of chocolates and a paper bag full of dusty purple grapes. He reaches for the chocolates with his good hand.

'You can't open 'em, you narna. Give 'em to me.' Fred stretches across to take the box, ripping off the outer cellophane with loud crackling noises.

'How are you, Joe?' Mum asks. Her hand trembles against mine.

'Lucky to be alive in the circumstances.'

Sandra's voice is hard. She blinks and raises her chin. 'He's as you find him. It's a complicated fracture, the doctor says.'

'Yes.' Mum's voice is quiet. 'Faith has something to say, don't you, Faith?'

Sandra looks at me, her mouth pushing out, as if her tongue presses at the inside of her lips. Her red nails tap on her handbag making a cross clicking noise. Joe stares up at the ceiling. He's pretending we're not here. I swallow and blink and turn my feet inwards, standing on the edges of my shoes. Fred has his head down, rustling inside the chocolate box, and Sandra turns to him and snaps, 'Not now, Fred.' She takes the box away and puts it on Joe's bedside cabinet, shaking her head.

'I'm sorry,' I say in a whispering voice.

Hunched low in his chair, Fred winks at me. I remember his surprised face surfacing through the waves, grey water closing over his head, his hand opening and closing. And I am sorry. Sorry that I took them with me. Sorry that I hadn't thought about lifejackets. Sorry that the boat was rotten. Most of all, I'm sorry that I never managed to get to the island to find Eva.

Sandra gives a small toss of her head. She takes a tissue out of her bag and blows her nose loudly. 'Oh, for God's sake, let's all have a chocolate and forget all about it.' She gives Fred a light push on his shoulder. 'Get up, treasure, and let Mrs Gale have your chair.'

Mum and Sandra sit together on the plastic chairs and begin to talk in low voices, their heads together. Mum touches Sandra's hand gently.

241

Sandra crosses one leg over the other and says she wishes she could have a fag.

Fred leans over and puts a chocolate straight into Joe's mouth. 'Butterscotch,' he tells him, 'your favourite.'

He offers me the box, but I shake my head, pulling my cardigan down over my hands. He looks at me. 'Don't worry. Sandra's just mad cos Les has gone back to work, so she's left here on her own.'

'How long till he gets out of hospital?'

'Couple of days, they said.'

'It was an adventure though,' Joe says, sucking the sticky sweetness off his teeth. 'Best bit of the holidays.'

$$\star \quad \star \quad \star$$

In the car on the way home Mum is quiet, frowning through the windscreen. 'Dad and I have been talking,' she says, slowing down at a junction, looking left and right but not at me. 'We've been talking about selling the house. We think it's time to move.'

My heart starts to beat very fast. 'We can't — '

'Hear me out, love,' she cuts across me. 'We think that it would be best for all of us, for us as a family, to move away from the area. A clean start.'

'But Eva — '

'We'll never forget Eva — she's in our hearts, she's part of us — but she's not coming back, Faith.'

I try to stay calm. 'No. That's what you think.

You don't know that.'

Mum takes her hand off the steering wheel and squeezes my knee. 'I wish she was on the island, Faith. I wish there were such things as miracles and magical creatures.' Her voice tightens. 'More than anything in the world, I want Eva to be alive. But you have to understand that it's not real.'

Through the muddle of her words, music starts up in my head: Ella's voice insisting, *But it wouldn't be make believe, if you believed in me.* Or is it Granny that's singing to me? I hum the next line.

'What?' Mum shoots me a glance.

'Nothing.' I fold my arms tightly. 'I won't leave.' I imagine, for a second, camping out under the oak tree, under a tarpaulin, homeless.

'It'll take some time to get used to the idea. I was against it at first too,' she's saying in a soothing voice. 'But after the whole rowing-boat fiasco . . . well, I had to reconsider. Dad is right, Faith. It would be kinder. To all of us.'

'When?' I ask tightly.

'We'll put the house on the market in the next week or so,' she glances at my face and adds quickly, 'but I should think it'll take a while to find a buyer. It won't be an easy house to sell.'

Summer is slipping away. I can see a few yellow leaves on the trees, imagine the smell of wood smoke in the air. Term is about to start. I think of scratched wooden desks, the stink of rubber and sweat in the changing rooms. The bell for break, a rabble of children's voices, all of us trapped, running round and round the square

243

of tarmac that teachers call a playground. And I still haven't managed to get to the island. I feel panicky, as if something is chasing me — a creature with wings spread wide.

Mum is talking to me again: 'Don't, Faith. Leave your warts alone or they'll never go.'

I look down and realise that I've been scratching, digging my fingernails under the lumps. I fold my hands up into fists, ball them in my lap, and stare out of the window at the blur of passing landscape.

★ ★ ★

Dad is glued to the television. Mum is in the bath. I can hear music coming from Sophie's room. They all think I've gone to bed. But I'm not asleep. Every night I practise holding my breath so that I'll have more chance of saving myself if I fall in when I go to the island.

Sitting cross-legged in the middle of my patchwork eiderdown, Granny's old one, I close my eyes and suck up as much air as I can, holding the air prisoner behind my lips.

My lungs are pressed shut. I can hear my heart banging inside my ribs. I don't like it. It makes me panic. It reminds me of being under water, like the time we capsized. There's a bubbling inside, as if liquid is boiling and snapping through me like an ocean. A dull thundering starts up in my brain. Everything hurts. My eyes are going to pop out. I'm desperate to open my mouth. I clench my lips tighter, and snatch a glance at the clock on my bedside table. But I've already forgotten what time it was when I began. Lights flash on and off. When I close my eyes, sticky blobs of colour crawl across my inside eyelids. I feel dizzy and sick. I open my mouth to gasp air, big shuddering breaths, one after the other, my chest heaving.

Falling sideways, I do nothing but breathe. Air is delicious. I catch a waft of rose oil, the comfort of Granny rising from the worn eiderdown. When I begin to feel normal again, I'm angry. I pinch the skin on my arm, twisting till it burns. I'm useless. I must keep practising. It's the only way to get better. Dad was always telling me and Eva that success is ten per cent inspiration, ninety per cent perspiration. But not breathing feels like suffocation. I'm not sure if I can do it again. Not yet anyway. I reach out my hand to switch off the light, slipping my legs under the covers and pulling the pillow under my head. Lying on my back, looking into the darkness, I wonder if I'm a coward. I wish that I was as strong as Eva, but my sister has inherited the brave genes, leaving me the little withered ones that make me afraid.

31

Billy hasn't mentioned Jack and Granny again. Nothing has changed. I am still a prisoner and I don't know why. If anything, Billy is being even more careful about locking us in at night, even more diligent about tying my hands whenever we're out of the pagoda, which is less and less.

The hours pass slowly. Small things have to entertain me. He passes me a bruised apple and I take it gratefully. Eating it will fill in some time. His knuckles are a mess of broken skin and weeping flesh. They look as though they might be infected. I wince and look away, and can't stop myself blurting, 'Why do you do that?'

He frowns and turns his back on me as if I've offended him. It seems as though he's gone into one of his silent moods. He can keep it up for hours. I bring the apple closer to my lips, my mouth filling with saliva in anticipation, but he's contemplating me, chewing his lip and scowling. He jabs a finger. 'Reckon you've got a whole heap of things you could do with your life if you wanted it. Privileged, aren't you, with your books and painting?'

I stare at him, my mouth slack. He glares and our eyes hold each other's. Nervously I shuffle back until I'm pressed against the cold wall.

He waves his hand. 'Not many choices — not where I come from. Nobody was an artist there. If I'd stayed at home it would have been the end.

Trapped. Not just the tunnels. I mean the drudge of it: each day the same, sucking the life out.'

I slide down into a sitting position. My lips are dry and I curl my tongue, wetting the lizard texture of them. He's not looking at me anymore. He's staring at the walls and his eyes are bright in the mask of his face.

'There were only two choices. Go down the pits or join up. I always wanted to be a soldier.' Then he asks quietly, slyly, 'What do you think soldiers are for?'

I grip the apple's fat, waxy contours, uncertain if it's a rhetorical question or a trick. After a moment, he says, 'Trained to kill, aren't they? For king and country and all that.'

I nod, drawing my knees up tighter into my hungry belly. I don't understand why he's telling me this, but I don't like where it seems to be headed.

'Thought it was fuckin' brilliant when I got my tour of duty in Northern Ireland. I'd been a squaddie for two years and I knew the weight of a rifle in my hands, the pull against my shoulder when I squeezed the trigger. You kept your gun closer than a girl, looked after it better too.' He tilts his chin. 'I was a good soldier. Even after a beasting, I just set me lips and picked it all up, started over. It's all in the mind, see.' He taps his forehead. 'That's the trick. Never giving up. It's about endurance.'

He pulls at the straggling hair of his beard. Flecks of spittle show white in the corner of his mouth. He paces backwards and forwards, takes a glance to see my face. 'Operation Banner. Mean anything to you?'

I frown, puzzled.

'Hunger strikers. Bobby Sands dying in his shit-smeared cell. Got everyone wound up.' He wipes his mouth with the back of his hand. 'That was the buzz in the barracks. We hadn't been told anything from high up. I knew what nasty fuckers the IRA were though. The thought of killing one made my pulse race. It was what I'd been training for.' He stares at me.

I nod.

'Northern Ireland was different from what I expected. Felt like a lie from the moment I got there. Didn't like being cooped up in the sangars. Felt like a fuckin' sitting duck. Places stank. Some of the men pissed in them. Going out on patrol was best. With my rifle in my hands, all of me on red-alert, I could hear better, see more clearly. I was sharp. Had all the right instincts.'

'Why did you leave?' I watch him pacing the pagoda. 'What happened?'

He ignores me. His eyes are glazed again, as if he's sleep-walking. 'On the streets there's this smell of burning peat. You're a ghost: nobody looks at you. Not straight on.'

I press the apple to my lips. Its scent reminds me of early autumn mornings, wet grass and wood smoke. Helping Dad in the garden, sweeping leaves into mounds, Faith throwing handfuls of them at me, wet shapes fluttering down, burnished and gleaming.

'First riot I was in, you wouldn't believe the

noise: banging dustbin lids, referee's whistles. A mob roars like the sea. One woman spat in my face.' He's looking at me again, pacing up and down. 'A bottle hit Napper,' he shakes his head, 'broken glass, blood everywhere, him on his knees, clutching at his eyes, screaming. There's me hauling him towards the truck, and I look up, right at this kid who couldn't have been more than ten, lad with freckles. The kid hurls a brick at me, hard as he can.' He screws the heel of his hand into an eye. 'They hated us. All of 'em. But I'd never felt anything like it before, an excitement, felt it knocking at me ribs.' He pats his chest. 'It's like a drug, you see. That feeling. An addiction.' He squats on the floor next to me so that our knees are touching. 'Army is full of people who are like me. Like I used to be. Lads who have no choice, who want to be told what to do. Easy targets for brainwashing.'

His left eye flickers, his mouth sagging inside stained hair. He looks exhausted.

'But your hands . . . ' I remind him cautiously.

He glances down at his knuckles and spreads his fingers wide with a look of surprise. He stares, contemplating the shape of his hands as if he's admiring them. 'Just a scratch.'

★ ★ ★

The evenings are drawing in. Shadows are longer; the sun seems lower in the sky. In the early hours a mist comes creeping, different from a summer mist; this one has the promise of frost in it. I don't need a watch to tell the time. I can

249

see it in the sky and in the way the light falls. It's September. The change in weather has given me a sore throat, a scratchy tickle like sharp fingers working inside the texture of my flesh.

Life is distilled here. There is only the movement of the sea and the sun coming up and setting again. Those rhythms inhabit me; I feel the measure of them inside my pulse, my breathing. I thought I knew this place when Faith and I used to steal across on the boat. I thought it was barren then, devoid of life. How could I have been so blind? Tiny white flowers push up between pebbles. Tall yellow grasses move like a wheat field, whispering in the wind. I've seen small brown voles, a stoat once. Rabbits scatter, darting into their burrows, running blind with panic in the wrong direction. I saw a fox yesterday. It crept under the gorse bushes, belly low to the ground, rust coat shining in the light. When it sensed me it froze, turning its mask towards me. I remembered the dead fox that Faith and I found, the carcass writhing with maggots. There is nothing left of it now. Not even a bone.

Billy isn't asleep. He's sitting in the doorway, his legs in the corridor, smoking. I can see the curl of smoke, his bowed head. He turns, looking towards my corner. Moonlight catches the planes of his face, turns his eyes into empty sockets.

'You asleep?' he asks me.

'No.'

He throws his cigarette butt away. I watch the spit of red. 'I keep praying for her to come back.' His voice is tight and I see his head in silhouette

250

drop forward into his hands.

I raise myself onto my knees, hearing them creak. The floor is hard and cold. 'Who do you mean?' I ask quietly.

His tone is flat, expressionless. 'The voice.'

'What are you going to do?' I wish I could see his face properly. I can't judge his mood without a visual guide. He hasn't tied me tonight, so I walk cautiously through the darkness, feeling my way around the pit, stepping across milky stripes of moonlight.

'I don't know,' he says, hesitating over his words. 'I've done what she asked. I need to know what comes next. She must be testing me.'

I'm standing close to him, my heart knocking so loudly at my ribs that the thud of it feels audible. I take a deep breath. 'Perhaps it's over,' I say softly. 'Perhaps . . . perhaps now it's time to let me go. There isn't anything else she wants you to do.'

Billy is very still. I clear my throat. 'It's what Jack would have wanted too, I think — '

Billy has uncurled in one fluid movement. He's standing in the doorway with his legs spread, widening to fill the frame. 'Don't tell me what Gramps would have wanted.' He shakes his head and grabs my arm, holds it tight. 'You don't know.'

I swallow. 'I'm sorry. You're right. But, please, just let me go. I'll never tell anyone.' My voice falters. 'Never.'

'No,' he says, thick and low. 'It's not time.'

I can smell him, the prickle of sweat and fear, the unwashed stench of his skin and greasy hair, the bitter tang of cigarette smoke. I lick my lips, trying to pull away, but he holds on, fingers wrapping tightly, and there is a tremor in his body, a shake. He gives me a push. 'I never said you could get up. Go back to your corner. Lie down.'

He stoops above me, binding my hands. 'You're trying to trick me,' he mutters, yanking the rope tighter. 'Is it them? Did they get to you?'

'No,' I tell him. My throat closing. 'No.'

'If you don't shut up I'll gag you.'

'Please don't.' A cough grates in my chest.

His mouth is set in a line as he ties the knot at my wrists. 'I'm doing this for you.' He sounds disappointed as he stoops over my legs to bind my ankles. 'For you, Eva.'

I am passive, unresisting. He pulls at the rope until it bites. I thought things were changing. After finding out about Jack and Granny, after his rant about the army, I hoped it signalled a change, that he'd begun to open up to me, begun to trust me. The rope is too tight around my wrists. I can't get comfortable. Lying on my back I stare into the lofty heights of the roof, watching the movement of clouds through the opening, narrow slices of open sky caught between the concrete bulk of the building and the heavy roof. The tickle is in my throat again and I cough. My chest feels bruised, as if I've fallen down a flight of stairs.

32

As she hurries out of the library after work, her mind busy with plans to call into the supermarket and pick up a packet of pasta, some milk perhaps, and dog food, mustn't forget dog food, Clara stumbles into someone. There's a jolt. She feels a frail arm against her ribs, an elbow jabbing her side. The folds of a black habit flutter across her. A cross swings on a chain, silver in the light. The collision is over in a few seconds. Clara steps back. A tiny, stooped nun smiles with ancient, washed-out eyes, nodding forgiveness.

Clara stands on the pavement apologising, staring after her, watching as the elderly nun crosses the street. She appears gently purposeful in her floating robes, diminutive, harmless. Clara breathes fast, air sticking in her chest. Her lungs don't work properly. It makes her feel dizzy, as if she might faint. She puts a hand against the library wall, 1960s breezeblocks grazing her palm.

She keeps having the same dream. She and Suky blur at the edges, blending into one person, lying in bed in the darkness, with her newborn baby beside her. And always there are nuns bending over the cot, picking Eva up with spiky fingers, carrying her away. Sometimes, at unexpected moments during the day, Clara hears Suky singing to her drowned daughter, or her voice telling Clara: *You've lost my baby.*

Clara can't contradict the ghost. The voice in her head. Eva has been lost and it is their fault. Max and Clara. Eva was entrusted to them. Trusted them. Believed they were her parents. Max had always wanted to tell Eva that she was adopted. He'd argued with Clara after Faith was born, but Clara had gestured towards the baby suckling noisily in her arms. Couldn't he see that having Faith made it more impossible? How could they tell Eva without making her feel rejected? As far as Clara was concerned, Eva *was* her child; she felt that belonging in her bones, in the fibre of her being.

As Faith grew up, Clara and Max spotted characteristics and features in her that reminded them of each other, of their parents. They were careful not to mention it in front of the girls. Strangers considered the girls, acknowledging how different their colouring was, and Clara would smile and hold her breath until invariably someone pointed out some imagined family likeness. 'Their eyes are the same shape,' or 'You can see those cheekbones came from the same gene pool.' People saw what they wanted. And always, Eva's height connected her to Max: one blond and one dark, the two of them heading towards the river with loping strides. Clara had mourned the loss of the small toddler who'd followed her from room to room. Eva was no longer her constant sticky-fingered companion, but a leggy child that craved independence, looking past her mother to the excitement of her father and the sea. But even as she'd missed her,

Clara had been glad that Max and Eva shared a passion. She'd trusted him to take care of her.

When Clara arrives home, her arms full of shopping, she doesn't mention the nun to Max. She hasn't told him about her recurring dream. She guesses that he must have his own unspoken nightmares. Anyway, they've stopped talking about anything except the necessary, the everyday. She can't seem to do anything about it. There's a voice inside her screaming, but her lips won't make the shapes to let it out. As if she is paralysed.

She calls goodnight from the threshold of his study door. He turns and gives her the hesitant smile she's come to dread: lips folded over guilt and resentment, unhappy eyes that beg her for something she can't give. She mounts the stairs, her hand heavy on the banister. She knows that when she falls asleep she'll see the face of a dead woman, Suky coming to her to share a grief that nobody else understands.

* * *

While Max sleeps fitfully at his desk, files pressing a ridge into his cheek, he dreams that Clara comes downstairs to find him. He thinks he feels the light touch of her fingers on the back of his head, tracing the raised line of his scar. When he wakes, he's alone.

Upstairs, he opens the door to their bedroom quietly. Clara is in a deep sleep, sprawled across the bed on her front with her arms flung out. It's a warm night and the window is open. He blinks

255

in the darkness, using the trickle of moonlight filtering between the curtains to see. Clara's night-dress has rucked up underneath her, showing the smooth slope of her lower back, the rise of her buttocks. He sits on the bed and puts his hand towards her. Even without touching her, he can feel heat rising from her skin, soft and intimate. Leaning close, he inhales her sleeping breath. She moans faintly and turns her head and he stands up quickly, his heart beating.

★ ★ ★

Max wakes to the sound of wood pigeons. He can hear wind in the trees, and a sound of waves in the distance, the pull and push of water on a shore: air in and out of lungs. He hates that sound. It used to mean home to him; it used to mean freedom. Now he can't look at the water beyond the sea wall without thinking about Eva. If he could change places with her he would. He wishes every day that it had been him that was lost and her that was found. His brain is trying to recover something that he knows is there. He can almost touch it — the thing that will tell him how it happened, how his daughter died.

He has part of a memory: Eva standing by the cabin. He'd been at the tiller, wrestling with it, trying to keep the boat steady, waves washing over the side. She's there before him, her chin raised. Sometimes she's wearing a lifejacket. Sometimes she isn't. Trying to find the images is like looking for a scattered jigsaw puzzle, the pieces buried in sand. He can only see fragments and he can't make a whole picture with any of them.

He knows without turning his head that Clara has left the bed. There will be a twist of sheet, an indentation in her pillow, a faint smell of her lingering on the cotton. On the mornings that she doesn't go to the library, she gets up before him, goes straight out on one of her long dog walks, or disappears into the garden to weed and plant, kneeling on a piece of plastic, his mother's old gardening hat on her head. Since Grace died, Clara has taken over the gardening; she says it's all a bit haphazard, that she doesn't really know what she's doing, but to her surprise, she's found that she likes delving about in the earth, watching seeds becoming plants.

He misses his wife. He longs for Clara's touch. She used to have a way of touching his face, removing the anxieties of the day as her fingers brushed across his forehead. He has a sudden memory of her underneath him, pressed hip to hip, her arms holding him tightly. He groans, moving his head from side to side, hearing it creak, the sinews in his neck tight as piano wires.

At least she has agreed to put the house on the market. 'Thank God,' he says to the ceiling. 'Thank God.'

He plans to move the family to Cambridge. An old friend has an office there, has asked him to join them several times before. He must make the phone call, set up a meeting. Faith can have a different life. He hopes that the children there will be more understanding of his dreamy youngest child. He's seen her walk past the village kids with her face set. He knows she doesn't have any real friends here.

Saturday. He sighs at the thought of the empty day stretching ahead. No more Olympics to distract him. It had been almost cathartic to watch those athletes, their struggle, their faith in themselves and the moment. He'd cried sometimes, watching them pass the finishing line, heads flung back. How he dreads the weekends. Work defines him now. It's the only thing that he can do. He's taken on too many clients, but he needs to be busy. No time to think about anything else. He and Eva used to sail at weekends. Sometimes they'd all go off as a family in the Cornish Shrimper, take a hamper and swimming things and drop anchor off the coast somewhere, all of them eating sandwiches and crisps on board, playing a game of cards. Eva leaping into the freezing water for a swim, persuading him and Clara to join her. This time of year he and Eva would be getting their last sails in before putting the boats away for the winter.

He pulls on a dressing gown and stumbles down the corridor yawning, thinking that he'll have a bath. Everything seems to ache. His back, shoulders and knees creak like an old man's. He's aware of the changes in his body since he stopped sailing. The muscles in his shoulders and arms have softened and weakened. His skin has lost colour, become dull and ashy. There is never enough air in his lungs. He feels tired all the time.

As he gets to the bathroom, reaching out to

push at the slightly open door, he hears music. The sound swells louder, familiar, haunting. It's a pop song that Eva used to listen to. His heart beats faster. The door swings wide, releasing the song on a cloud of steamy heat. A girl emerges. She has wet hair lying in tangles over her shoulders like a mermaid. Tanned skin glistens; her breasts are covered in a green sheath that she holds around her.

She laughs, apologising, wrapping the green a little tighter. She is holding a small transistor radio, the pop song muffled now by the folds of her towel. She presses the off button with a creased finger.

'I forgot to lock the door,' she smiles at him.

'Sophie,' he says. His heart slows. They are lucky to have her, he thinks, smiling an apology of his own. She's a friendly girl, and a hard worker too.

He shuts the door and leans over to turn the taps; there's a squelch of soggy fabric between his toes. He looks down at the sopping bath mat and wonders why Sophie was using this bathroom. It's supposed to belong to him and Clara. The other bathroom, the children's bathroom at the end of the corridor, is for her use. And yet, what's the point of silly rules? What does it matter which bathroom she uses? Perhaps she prefers the shower in this one. Eva used to complain that the one in their bathroom was always broken, only a dribble of water coming through.

'How am I supposed to wash my hair?' she'd complain. 'Why have you got the best shower in

259

the house? You don't even have hair.'

That wasn't strictly true, of course. Max runs his hands across his scalp, combing through the roots of curls; he's not sure if he's imagining it, but his hair seems thinner; it feels brittle between his fingers. He drops his hands. Eva had tight curls that fell in ringlets around her face. Sophie has lovely hair too, a curtain of it. What colour would you call that particular gleaming brown? Chestnut, he thinks, like the ones that fall from the tree at the bottom of the garden, spiked cases splitting to let the gleam of nut push through.

Disappointingly, his bath water is lukewarm. The hot water has run out. The empty tank groans above his head, clanking in the attic among the cobwebs and spiders. He lies in the white oblong and thinks that it fits him like a grave, narrow and straight. He soaps himself half-heartedly under his arms, swishing the cloth around his body. His limbs feel numb, dead. It's been so long since he felt the pull of the jib in his hands, braced his legs against the curved side of a boat, felt the strength of the wind against him.

There is a quiet knock at the door and Max starts, water slopping sideways.

'Would you like coffee, Max?' a muffled voice asks. 'I'm making some now.'

At first he mistakes it for Clara. Then he recognises the softness of the accent, the polite tones. It's the first time Sophie has used his Christian name; she wouldn't do it before, although he kept asking her to.

He moves his hands over his groin as an instinct. It seems wrong to be naked with only

260

the width of a plank of wood between him and her. He imagines her cheek resting against the grain of it. 'Yes please,' he answers, clearing his throat, 'be down soon.'

He thinks he hears the door handle turning and scrabbles out of the bath in a panic, almost slipping in the puddle of water on the floor. When he opens the door, a towel knotted around his waist, there is no one there.

33

Mum has already gone off for a walk. I saw her through my bedroom window this morning heading towards the sea with Silver running in circles around her. Dad is in bed. He sleeps in at the weekends. He never used to. He used to be the first one up in the morning whatever day it was.

A boy from the local estate agents came yesterday and banged in a For Sale notice on a wooden post by the garden gate. He had floppy hair falling into his eyes and he was wearing a suit that looked as though it belonged to some-one older and bigger than him. When he caught me watching him out of the window, he pushed up his sleeves and grinned, holding the hammer over his shoulder.

At least if we sell the house I can move to a different school. Going back was just as bad as I thought it would be. I'd sat on my own at break while Joanna and Ellie whispered about me with their friends. The thought of Monday morning scoops out a hollow in my tummy. Sophie is in the kitchen spooning coffee into the cafetière. Her wet hair drips like a slimy tail down her back, making a spreading damp patch in the red of her dressing gown. As she pads around the kitchen the silk clings and opens around her legs. She ignores me, peeling an orange as she waits for the kettle to boil. The sharpness of the orange makes me feel hungry. Strips of peel fall in spirals from her neat fingers. She puts a whole segment into her mouth, chewing. Her tongue slips out, catching a dribble of juice, and she dabs at her lips with a napkin.

'Can I have some toast?' I ask.

She shakes her head. 'You can make it yourself, no?'

She pours two cups of coffee and leaves the room, a cup in each hand.

★   ★   ★

The caravan site is half-empty. There are patches of yellowed grass and ruts of earth where caravans and cars used to stand. An abandoned deckchair is on its side and there's a deflated beach ball sagging in the grass. Bins overflow with rubbish. The lady with the Alsatian is still here. She nods at me as I walk past and her dog pulls towards me on his chain, wagging his tail. 'He hasn't forgotten you,' she calls, tapping her cigarette onto the ground. I wonder if she knows about Joe being in hospital and it being my fault.

Sandra opens the door.

'Is Fred here?' I ask, looking down at her pale pink legwarmers and her fluffy slippers with hearts all over them. 'Can he come and play?' Behind her I can see Carol shrieking and banging her beaker on her highchair.

Sandra scrunches up her forehead. 'No, sorry pet.' She raises her hands and lets them fall. 'He's still got a nasty cough.'

Carol's beaker lands on the floor, the top

spinning off. A mess of purple liquid splatters across the floor, spreading in puddles and drops. Sandra lets out a sigh of annoyance. 'She's playing up big-time today.'

'Please.' I stand, shifting my weight from one foot to the other, hoping she'll change her mind.

'I'm not promising anything.' She raises thin shoulders under her pink housecoat. 'Maybe another day, before we leave. I'll think about it.' Then she shuts the door in my face.

As I walk away I hear a rattling noise and turn to see Fred's face behind the caravan window. He squashes his nose, spreading it flat against the glass. Inside the misty circle of his breath, his nostrils are two black holes. Stepping back, he gives me a thumbs-up. Then he's gone. I watch the square of smeared glass for a moment but he doesn't reappear.

I drag my feet, walking without thinking. I don't know where to go. I've got no plans — nothing to do. I can hear the sound of children's voices coming from the rec. I hurry in the opposite direction, away from their shrieking and laughter, past the castle and down to the river. On the sea wall, the wind has got up, blowing cooler air in from the ocean. There are only a couple of boats with their sails up. Most are moored, masts clanking in the breeze.

The island sits out of reach, bleak and empty. I stare at it, my eyes watering in the wind. However hard I strain to focus, it's too far away to see anything properly. I have a sudden doubt: what if Eva isn't there after all? What if I'm wrong? I push the thought away, staring harder at the island. From here, the empty buildings aren't visible, just the tops of the pagodas sticking up, dark blocks against the sky. The part of the island that I can see is a pebbly expanse with clumps of low greenery. Distance smudges details, like the pastel drawings Eva used to do, smearing outlines with her fingers, blending one colour with another. I wonder if the seals are on the point, scenting the air with their cat's noses, eyes brimming with tears.

It's high tide. Water laps at the foot of the sea wall. The broad expanse of river is rough with small waves, whipped up by the wind. I don't know how I'm going to get across. The stretch of sea that lies beyond the river's mouth is even more terrifying. Thinking of Fred's cheerful face, his thumbs-up sign through the grubby window, I swallow, scuffing my heels in soft muddy ground. I won't cry, even though the back of my throat is tight and hot. Funny how knowing them has made me feel worse. Before I met Fred and Joe, I'd got used to being lonely.

'I can't do it,' I tell the water. 'I can't find her on my own.'

'Remember the Charleston,' Granny's voice says in my ear. 'How brave you were, dancing in front of all those people? You did it on your own, Faith.'

When Jack showed me the steps, he told me, 'Give it the old razzle dazzle.' He'd put a finger under my chin. 'Head up. Big smile. Make it up if you forget. They'll never know; not if you do it with a smile.'

I'd been nervous, my heart racing, palms

sweaty. I'd wanted to run away from the circle of faces peering at me from their armchairs. Some had been expectant, some blank. One or two had been asleep, mouths sagging, arms crossed over hollow chests.

I can see Jack standing in the hot, stuffy room, Granny just behind, watching me, willing me on. I'd tried to ignore the funny smell, not just boiled cabbage and bleach, but the smell of old people.

I like old people's hands, veins pressing up through the surface, thin as paper and mottled with sun-spots. You can see the tendons and tiny bones, as if the inside is coming through the outside. It gives me a calm feeling to think of the lifetime their hands have spent loving people, hugging children, soothing fevered brows, making food, sweeping away dirt. But when Jack held out his hand to me there in the room, I'd hesitated.

He beckoned impatiently. 'Come on Faith. No time to lose.'

I close my eyes and feel his fingers clasping me, warm skin, rough and thickened with time. He lets go as the music starts and I'm on my own. I move my feet, tapping out the rhythm. I open my eyes, blinking into the sunlight, remembering that once I'd started dancing, it had felt like flying. It felt as though I could do anything.

A gull swoops low across the river, snatches at the water and rises, a fish dangling from its beak. I start to walk fast with my arms moving by my sides, head down, thinking about how to get onto the island. Even if I could get a dinghy into the river, I don't know how to rig it, and anyway, I'd be too afraid to sail it on my own. I know that fishermen sometimes go over, but I can hardly ask them to take me when they're doing it illegally in the first place. Deep in my thoughts, I don't see the boy until I nearly tread on him. He's sitting in the grass on the side of the path, long legs bent under his chin, staring at the river.

He looks up, as startled as me, his face pale and thin under a dark cap. He's dressed in black. His hair rises, slick and shiny, in a wave from his forehead. He doesn't look as though he belongs here by the river. He looks as though he should be on *Top of the Pops*. We recognise each other at the same time and he uncurls his body, staggering onto his feet, brushing mud from his jacket.

He stares into my face, and I realise that he can't recall my name. But I know his. 'Marco,' I say. 'It's me. Faith. Eva's sister.'

He nods. 'Thought it was you.'

'What are you doing?'

He screws up his mouth, looks at me sideways, embarrassed.

'Have you come because this is . . . where she drowned?' I look at the water.

'Yeah,' he says. 'Stupid, but I thought I'd kinda feel closer to her here.'

'She's alive,' I say in a rush. I can't help it.

He raises black eyebrows at me.

'She's not dead. I know she's not. I think she's out there somewhere.' I nod in the direction of the island. 'She didn't drown. Something took her.' I bite my lip.

He stares at the island and frowns as if considering. 'Nah,' he says slowly, 'I'd know if she wasn't dead. Have a feeling about it. And I don't.'

Disappointment drops through me heavily, making me feel unbalanced. He's like Mum and Dad. I don't understand. If he loves her, he should have the same feelings as me. Shouldn't he? He should know that something isn't right, that she hasn't drowned. It's like a pressure in my heart.

'Isn't there some military shit over there?' he's asking. 'Bombs and things?'

'They tested atomic bombs. It's still out of bounds. Private land.' I lean closer to him, lowering my voice even though there is nobody else around. 'Me and Eva used to go there.' I touch his arm. 'She's there now.'

He shakes his head. 'If she was, someone would know,' he says. 'The coastguard would have found her body. Anybody living there would starve, wouldn't they? And what about fresh water?' He looks at my face. 'Don't get your hopes up, kid.'

I open my mouth but he's already speaking. 'I came to say goodbye to her, really. I'm going away.' He twiddles the silver ring in his ear lobe. 'I've moved out of my parents' back to London. Staying on a friend's floor for now. I'm in a band and we're doing some gigs around the country. I'm off in the van. Got to meet the others in Ipswich tonight.'

'Tonight?' I rub my nose. 'Well, I'm going to go to the island,' I tell him. 'I'm going to look for her.'

'It won't be dangerous with all those bombs?' He frowns.

I cross my fingers behind my back. 'No. They're only on one half of it.' I don't mention selkies or the Wild Man. I can't trust him not to be like other people.

'I don't get why you think Eva's there. But it's kind of cool that you do.' He gazes across at the island with narrowed eyes. He doesn't believe she's there. He just wants to, which is a different thing.

I frown. 'I can't explain.'

'Well,' he takes a pen out of his jacket, 'can I give you my parents' address, in case there's any news?'

We don't have any paper so he asks for my arm and I push up my sleeve, scrunching it as high as it will go. The pen slides across my skin in a ticklish whisper. He has to hold my wrist and turn my arm around to fit the whole address in. We both look at the dense scribble covering my forearm. 'They'll know how to reach me. I don't have a phone yet,' he says, 'or a permanent address.'

He blinks, his mouth turning down. 'Just before she was lost, she was supposed to . . . meet me. We had a plan. She was going to catch the last bus into Ipswich. But she didn't. I waited but she never turned up. I never heard from her. That was strange. Not like her.' He adjusts his cap above his quiff, clearing his throat. 'I can't get her out of my head. I've written a song about her.'

'Oh.' I'm not surprised. I think that anyone

who could write a song or a poem would write one about Eva.

'I'll play it to you one day.' He tips his head on one side. 'Funny, you know you don't look anything like her.' He looks disappointed.

It feels like an insult, even though I know it isn't. I raise my chin. 'Some people think I do.'

He holds up his hand in a stiff salute. I watch him walk away, thin and dark. He hunches his shoulders, narrow-hipped in his black trousers.

A man in a canoe glides past on the river. The canoe cuts through the water almost silently, the man working the oar expertly, dipping it from one side to the other. He must be going against the tide, but he's travelling fast, water slapping at the side of the boat, the pointed prow breaking a path through the current like a sword.

When I look back at Marco he's already become a tiny marionette figure, disappearing into the greens and blues of the fields, marching out of sight. I look down at my arm, at the slightly smudged letters staining my skin.

34

Today we woke to a birdless sky, heavy with cloud. A fierce rain has been falling since daybreak. It beats down on the shingle. Billy and I huddle inside the pagoda, damp and shivering. The roof keeps us dry, although sometimes water finds a way in through the gaps between the pillars, a sudden splatter of wet down my neck.

I pull the blanket tightly round my shoulders. The tickle in my throat has gone, but now it's swollen inside and it hurts to swallow; my head is heavy and thick. I sneeze, wincing as the shock pounds inside my brain.

Billy glances at me and then disappears outside for a couple of minutes and comes back with dripping hair and rain-darkened stones in his arms. He places them in a ring on the floor of the entrance, drags over a couple of branches and a piece of driftwood that he piled in the corner a couple of days ago, breaks them across his thighs and piles them carefully into a wigwam shape. But when he strikes a match, only the outer grains of bark catch. I watch as beads of gold flare, dying almost instantly. However much Billy rearranges the position of the branches or gets down on his belly to blow, the rest of the wood refuses to burn. 'We need kindling,' he mutters, squatting on his haunches and staring into the rain, chewing the inside of his mouth.

A minute later, I hear the sound of ripping.

He's got the book in his hands, tearing it up, shredding pages of *The Prophet*, breaking the spine with a brutal twisting.

'Don't,' I whisper. I can't bear to see anyone destroying a book. Then I understand. Small flames feed hungrily on the screwed up pages. I watch lines of print blur and darken in the heat. Flames eat holes inside the poems. Branches glow hot and begin to burn. There is a pop and sparks burst. I shuffle closer to the warmth, grateful and tired. Even my bones ache. I sneeze again and drop my forehead onto my knees, closing sore eyes.

'Wish I had some whisky,' I murmur, remembering how Dad would always suggest a dram of whisky as a cure-all. The smell of it made me recoil. But the peaty taste, mixed with lemon and hot water, sweetened with honey, was what I craved when I'd had flu. Dad would hand me the glass with great ceremony, nodding approvingly. 'That'll have you feeling better in no time.'

'Yeah,' Billy says, 'I could do with a drop of the hard stuff right now. Keep out the cold. On check-point duty, half the men we stopped fell out of their cars pissed. Jesus, their breath alone could knock you out. The Irish drank more than me dad. Got some good bottles off 'em though.'

The smoke from the fire is bitter. I cough, swallowing, trying to suppress the pain in my throat. 'Sounds like they weren't so bad then.'

He stares into the flames. He is silent for a few moments and then he gives me a tight little smile. 'There wasn't any love lost. It was them and us. I was off-duty when a bomb went off in a pub. They needed help to get the bodies out. Starlight was already there — the medics — but there weren't enough to go round. People sitting on the pavement.' He reaches into his pocket and pulls out his papers, takes a few strands of tobacco and rolls a cigarette. 'You could smell the cordite, burning flesh.' He licks the paper, rubbing it together between his fingers. 'Inside the rubble I saw bits of body, scraps of clothing, odd shoes, a pair of smashed glasses. I remember picking them up. The metal was hot.'

He lights his rollie with a stick from the fire. Takes a deep drag. 'I found Chalky there, one of the blokes from my brick, sitting on the ground. Blood on his face. He didn't recognise me at first. I got him up on his feet, helped him outside. Suddenly he clutches my shoulders: 'Am I going home?' he says, sobbing like a kid. 'I want to go home.' So I told him he was and he seemed calmer then.' Billy pokes the fire, throws on a piece of driftwood. 'I started to go off, get a medic over to him, and that's when I heard the whistling noise. A soft little thwack. I turned round and Chalky gave me a look, kind of surprised, his mouth opening like he was going to speak. He crumpled, hit the ground, and I saw the hole in his chest.'

'What'd happened?'

'Sniper.'

'I'm sorry,' I say. 'He was your friend.'

'More than a friend,' he says, examining the end of his rollie. 'Just four of us in a brick, you see. Done our training together, lived together,

273

fought next to each other.'

I shiver, feeling cold and hot. I want to lie down; my body weighs too much for my spine, which is boneless, a slippery thread. I droop, slumping over to rest my cheek on the cold, damp floor. The wind and the sea make lonely noises, and I wonder if I'll get really ill and die here. I think of the German soldiers, their forgotten bones buried under the shingle. I feel sick. I close my eyes, trying to push away images of the destroyed pub, the broken glasses in Billy's hands. Billy leans over me.

'You need to drink,' he says. 'You can have my water. Here.' He measures out some water into a tin cup, places it inside the curl of my hand. I close my fingers around the sides of the cup, but I'm too tired to lift it, too tired to sit up.

★ ★ ★

The Bell is thick with cigarette smoke; the juke box drops another disc, Lionel Richie's honeyed voice singing 'Hello'. Marco shakes his head. 'Can't stay here much longer with this noise.' He looks pained. 'Maybe we should go back to my place. Listen to some real music.'

I shift closer to him, wanting to feel the angles of his body against mine. He looks elegant in his long black coat, like a cross between a highwayman and Dracula. He puts his arm around me and I lean into him. I'm wearing my new dress. I found it in the Oxfam shop in town; black netting swishes around my legs. I've lined my eyes in kohl, drawn the outline of my lips in

274

dark red. Goths *want* to look different. They exist on the edges of society, flaunting their costumes: night-people, flamboyantly other. It's easy for me to feel at home in their world.

Marco dips his head to kiss me. The noise of the pub turns around us: glasses clinking, the blur and chatter of voices, Lionel's lingering vocals. We break apart, breathless, and I laugh. Nobody even glances at us. We're invisible. The locals here have seen plenty of the art-school crowd come and go, goths, a few punks with safety pins in their noses. These older locals are implacable, timeless, sipping at their beer, ignoring the rest of the world.

'They wouldn't blink if you dropped a bomb on the place,' Marco says. 'Stuck in a time warp.'

'It doesn't seem to bother them.'

'Nothing bothers them,' he sighs, 'that's the problem.'

A boy in a checked shirt stands by the juke box. He stares at the play list and makes his selection, jabbing at the button with a stubby finger. Daryl Hall and John Oates begin to play and Marco puts his glass down. 'Let's get out of here,' he says.

We're in the street. It's cold. The air is wet with drizzle. I turn up the collar of my thin jacket. The only part of me that feels warm is my hand wrapped in Marco's fingers. We walk quickly, the wind at our backs. It's only about fifteen minutes to his parents' house. I love going there. When we're in his room, there's no banging on the door asking what we're up to. Music is always playing, and his mother might come, bangles clattering, to stand at the foot of the stairs: 'Let me know if you guys want something to eat.' His father shouting from the sitting room, 'There's a bottle of wine open if you want it.'

We have a routine now. Squatting on the floor of his bedroom, Marco will pull out a single, placing it on the turnstile with hushed reverence. His room is dim and warm, the light shaded in red. We'll lie on his bed and as the track begins to play, he'll kiss me. I hold his fingers tighter at the thought. Anticipation crackles through me like electricity, making tiny hairs rise, prickling across my skin. We walk quickly through the fine drizzle. He squeezes my hand back. I've decided that I'm going to sleep with him. I love him. I'll tell him soon. Maybe tonight.

There is a group of boys walking towards us. I can tell from their loose strides and loud voices that they're drunk. They are pushing each other at the shoulder, beer cans in their fists. Bursts of laughter reach us. I begin to slow down, realising that the street is empty apart from the approaching boys and us.

'What's this then?' Robert Smith looms out of the tangle of faces, pressing close to us. His breath stinks. 'Pretty boy out for a walk.' He stares at me with distaste. 'Fuck. What do you think you look like? A bloody witch.' He opens his arms wide, beckoning his mates, inviting their approval. 'Fancy dress tonight. Look at this, fellas. Romantic, eh?'

The others laugh obediently, coming closer, faces split into leering grins.

Marco pulls me to his side. 'OK,' he says, 'you've had your fun, reached the extent of your wit. We're moving on.'

We begin to walk past them, but Robert lurches in front, blocking our way. 'What did you say?'

'Can't you understand English?' A vein at Marco's temple pulses. 'Didn't think so.'

'Fuckin' poof.' Robert narrows his eyes. 'You don't talk to me like that.'

'Watch my lips,' Marco says.

'Just let us go,' I say, but no sound comes out; my heart is beating so hard it feels as though it's hammering out of my ribs.

Robert smiles; he turns and hands his beer can with elaborate care to someone behind him. He rolls up his sleeves slowly, methodically, and clenches his right fist. With one lunging movement, he steps forward to take a swing at Marco. Marco drops my hand, ducking so that Robert misses, but the momentum carries Robert on so that he stumbles past, half-falling. Another boy catches him, sets him on his feet.

Robert staggers back to us, his face a twist of rage. There's wet on his chin — beer or spit — as he shouts, 'Hold him.' Several of the others grab Marco's shoulders, clenching their fingers tightly on his black jacket, pinioning his arms. Two of them jostle him on either side, trapping him between them.

'Stop it!' I start forwards, my palms beating at Robert, my fingers reaching for his face; but he shoves me hard, so that I stumble back, arms flailing to stop myself from going down, net skirts catching in my heels.

Robert takes his time; he gobs on the ground before pulling his shoulder back, taking aim. There's nowhere for Marco to go, and he turns his head trying to avoid Robert's fist. The punch lands on the edge of his cheek. I hear the impact of bone on bone. A spurt of blood flies out of Marco's mouth; his neck makes a cracking sound and I scream.

There's a warning shout behind us. The boys let go of Marco, and they run, laughing, their uneven footsteps echoing in the street; Robert looks back, his mouth twitching angrily. 'I haven't finished with you yet,' he shouts.

Marco is breathing hard, wiping blood from his lips; he puts his hand up to test his jaw tentatively. And a man and a woman come up. 'You all right, son?' the man asks, puffing and out of breath. 'Bastards, I could see what they were up to.'

Marco nods, feeling the damage to his jaw.

'Want us to call the cops?' The woman looks into my face, and in the glow from the streetlight I can see that she's frightened and kind. She has lipstick on her front teeth.

Marco is still panting. He gives a mute shake of his head. 'No, don't worry,' I tell her. The couple dither around us for a few more moments, and the woman pats my shoulder anxiously. 'Thank you,' Marco says, trying to steady his voice, 'we're all right now.' The two of them disappear into the black, shiny night, her arm in his. The woman's shoes make a clicking noise on the wet pavement.

Marco holds a trembling hand to his face. 'Think I might have broken a tooth.'

'You idiot,' I tell him. 'What were you thinking?'

'I don't know. I wasn't, I suppose.' He puts a finger inside his mouth and prods gingerly.

I let out a sob. A streetlight above us blinks. The rain comes down harder and there's a grumble of thunder rolling over our heads.

'Come here.' He puts his arms around me, pulls me into his chest. 'It's over now.' Our hearts pound against each other. And we stand in the damp night, reflections of lights in puddles at our feet, my face against his wet jacket, smelling wool and tobacco.

★ ★ ★

'Eva,' a voice says. 'Drink this.'

Water trickles into my flaming throat. I cough and swallow. 'Marco,' I whisper. But there is no answer. I can feel fabric at my chin and press my face into it, trying to find him behind it, the thump of his heart beneath my cheek. I push my fingers into empty folds, and tears start, blurring the shadowy air.

★ ★ ★

I wake inside my blanket, limbs stiff and sore. It's dark. My throat is hot and tight. Looking up I can make out stars caught in rectangles of blue. I move my head to the side, licking my lips.

'Here,' a voice says and someone lifts my head,

279

supporting me, and I taste liquid at my lips, let it enter my mouth, moving over my tongue. Fingers stroke my forehead. I open my mouth, wanting to say 'thank you,' but there are only strange grating sounds.

'I didn't know you were so brave,' I tell Marco.

And he looks at me and smiles. 'Not really,' he says, 'stupid probably. Like you said.'

I lean forward and kiss the bruise on his jaw, moving my tongue over the flowering of purple.

35

Clara is in the kitchen standing at the sink. She's staring out of the window at the rain. Max wonders if she's heard him come in. She doesn't move. She remains absorbed in the blur of falling water outside the glass. He waits for a moment, taking in the uncombed streaky hair, her thin shoulders, square inside the dark denim shirt. She stands on one hip like a dancer, the other leg thrust at an angle, toe and hip turned out. The pose reminds him of something, and then he remembers: the sculpture of one of Degas' little ballerinas that he saw in an exhibition in London with Eva years ago.

Max moves towards Clara, until he's standing just behind her. He's struck by the familiar scent of her perfume. The underneath smell of skin. He wants to bury his nose in the tangles of her hair. He puts his hands on her shoulders, feeling their fragility. As if she would break. She jumps at the pressure of his touch and he feels her muscles tensing, bones lifting against him. Slowly, he turns her until they face each other.

They stare at each other gravely. His heart stutters and he can hardly breathe. He closes his eyes and dips his face, searching for her mouth with his own. He wants her so much. But she twists from under his hands.

She looks at the floor. 'I'm sorry,' she says in a small, polite voice. 'But I just can't.'

'It's OK,' Max attempts, his voice croaking.

'No, no it's not OK,' she bursts out, tearful, hands balling into fists. 'I can't go on like this. I feel stuck. I can't let go of anything. And I'm angry with you. I'm still angry.'

'What can I do?' His shoulders sag. It's hopeless. The distance between them seems insurmountable.

'If you could just remember what happened,' she says, rubbing her eyes. 'I don't understand how you lost her. I can't believe you let her sail without a lifejacket.'

'Clara, we've been over this.' Max looks out at the rainy garden. 'I don't remember. Maybe it wasn't done up properly . . . I just don't know.'

'You were supposed to look after her — you were supposed to keep her safe.' She shakes her head, her cheeks wet. Her voice breaks. 'And I miss her. I miss her so much.'

He pulls her to him, wrapping his arms around her. She endures his embrace, her spine straight, unrelenting.

'I miss you too,' he whispers into her hair.

'I know,' she says, lifting her head away from his chest.

He lets her go and her hands flutter to her face. 'Somehow we have to carry on,' she says in a tired voice, and he notices how dull her eyes are, how her cheekbones jut out over deeper hollows. 'The estate agent rang.' She turns her back on him, beginning to clear the draining board, piling plates into a cupboard, picking up a pan. 'Someone's coming to see the house tomorrow,' she says over the clattering of metal.

Max has to get away. He doesn't really make a decision. He finds himself walking the path to the sea wall. His legs are shaky. It's still raining, but he hardly notices the water soaking his clothes, sliding across his skin.

He trudges through the marshes, watching a heron standing on one leg by a dead tree. When he reaches the sea wall, he clambers the slippery bank, inhaling the tang of briny air. He hasn't been here since that day. He can hear the familiar clink of masts on moored boats, the cry of gulls, wind in the grass. Rain on water. He looks down into the pock-marked river, and it seems impossible that the accident has happened, impossible that Eva drowned.

He doesn't blame Clara for her feelings — for her rejection of him. She's right. He has failed. From the moment he saw Clara on that stage, fumbling over her lines, he was filled with the desire to look after her. Her vulnerability frightens him at times; he can't understand how someone so intelligent doubts herself as she does; but somehow it gives her a humility that makes her more beautiful. He sees an echo of something similar in Faith.

Eva was different. Even as a baby. He loved the passion in her, though it led to fights and arguments. Eva storming out of rooms, slamming doors. 'Why can't I stay out till twelve?' she'd demand. 'Other people do. This is the 1980s, Dad!' He fought her because he knew he was right. He remembered Suky, her childish face above her bloated body. Her folded hands had looked helpless, resigned, placed neatly across the top of her pregnant belly, like someone already dead.

It strikes him that he has no idea what Suky was really like. Since Clara's refusal to tell Eva that she was adopted, it had seemed crucial to push thoughts of Eva's birth parents from his mind. Max frowns into the wind, recalling the short time that he spent in the dormitory. He understands now how brave Suky was to give up her baby, to endure time in the 'home' that had seemed more like a prison. He remembers her certainty that she was having a girl. The pearls lying in his hand, warm from her neck.

'Love her for me,' she'd said, looking up at him from her bed, weighed down by her swollen legs and heavy belly. So much trust. And he has squandered it. He closes his eyes, tipping his face to the sky, feeling the lick of the wind on his skin, the tongue of the rain. The sounds, smells and textures of this place will always be home. Despite everything.

Eva loved the sea as much as he did; she'd been brought up by it, knew the sounds and habits of it. Max had taught her how to sail and the skill of listening to the ocean, watching the sky, understanding the movement of a boat on water. But perhaps there were sailors somewhere in her bloodline. Eva was made up of fragments of strangers. He wonders if cutting her away from all that had been a kind of criminal act. He shakes his head. It wasn't until they'd had Faith that he had understood the importance of inheritance, the way a child holds elements of other people inside them. Every day he sees the contours of his mother rising in Faith's narrow face. He turns his back on the river and the island, walks away from the sea, inland, back to the house. The rain has stopped.

At the edge of the marsh, he notices knots of green blackberries inside a hedge of brambles and ragged nettles; they shine with moisture. On closer inspection, he sees that there are clusters of ripe ones too. He picks a large, dark clot of fruit. Brushing away a tendril of cobweb, he bites into it, letting the succulent sweetness burst on his tongue. Almost immediately a bitter taste makes him grimace; he spits it out into his palm and looks at the splattered mess of purple. There's a maggot at the centre, pale and twisting. His stomach churns, bile rising in his throat as he wipes his hands on some dock leaves, and then on his trousers.

As he enters the hall, kicking off his muddy shoes, shaking the wet out of his hair like a dog, he can taste the horror of the maggot, its gritty flesh between his teeth. Sophie appears from the living room.

'Have you seen my wife?'

'She's in her bedroom.' Sophie comes closer to him. She looks concerned. 'You are sad. No?'

Max leans back, forcing a smile. 'A little. Maybe.'

'I'm sorry,' she takes another step towards him, 'is there anything you would like?'

'No.' He clears his throat. 'No. Thank you, Sophie.'

'You are always alone.'

Of course she would notice the atmosphere in the house, hear the arguments. Max is embarrassed. It's not fair on her. He takes a deep breath. 'Things are a little difficult at the moment. It's nothing for you to worry about.'

She shakes her head. 'I want to make you happy.'

Max shuffles backwards and finds that he's up against the banisters, wooden spindles pressing into his spine. He's not sure what she means. It must be the difficulties of another language. He trips over his discarded boots. She puts a hand on his chest. 'Wet,' she murmurs, 'you are wet.'

She moves close enough to lean against him, her heart suddenly beating over his ribs; he is momentarily winded by the shock of her breasts squashed against him. He can see the sweep of her lashes, the pores on her nose. A strand of hair has caught in the moisture of her lips and without thinking he pulls it free. Sophie looks up at him and something in her expression, some need or expectation, makes him push her away. She stumbles a little and he clears his throat, makes a show of bending to pick up his muddy boots, loud, hearty words spilling from his mouth: 'Terrible summer I'm afraid. Rain drives you mad, doesn't it?' He puts his boots in the cupboard, talking over his shoulder. 'It doesn't usually rain like this. It must be the wettest summer we've had for years.'

Sophie gives him a cool look, arching her eyebrows. She walks up the stairs without looking back.

Max groans; he feels like a fool. He searches for memories of things he'd inadvertently done to encourage Sophie, things he'd said that might have created the situation. Or did he imagine it? Was she really inviting him to kiss her? Now he's not so sure. He's never been good at establishing distances between himself and people; he's always been uncomfortable with formality. He has the same problem at work. His clients are more friends than clients. They feel that they can pop in without appointments. Many of them don't pay his bills. He knows that he's good at the legal side of his job. He's not so good at maintaining boundaries. He must be more careful.

36

I put the lid down on the lavatory as quietly as I can and climb onto it. Squatting on the slippery plastic with my back against the cistern, I prepare to wait. Outside the cubicle, I can hear another pupil washing their hands. There's a splatter of water and then a shuffle of footsteps and a door closing. It stinks in here. I wrinkle my nose, trying not to inhale. I look at the scribbles of graffiti: Becky loves John. Mrs How is a Big Fat Cow.

Beyond the girls' loos is the noise of break-time. It washes through the little frosted window high up in the wall: a chatter of voices, the shouts and screams of the playground. When the bell goes and everyone is banging down their desk lids and scrambling to leave the room I drag my feet, stopping to do up my shoelaces, pausing to blow my nose, trying to take as long as possible to leave the safety of the classroom. 'Come along, Faith,' Mr Barlow said today, 'if you don't hurry up you'll miss playtime.' He'd stood by the door, holding it open for me.

I've tried hanging around with the quiet kids, Emily and Lou, but they look at me with sad faces and whisper that I'm bad luck and they're sorry but they don't want to play with me. I don't blame them. It doesn't matter where I go, Joanna and Ellie always find me. In some gritty corner, or behind the bike-shed, they'll start: 'Where's your boyfriend then?'

'Oh, she put him in hospital,' Ellie smirks, 'didn't you know? She's dangerous.'

'And careless,' Joanna laughs. 'Got rid of her only friends by nearly drowning them. And that's after she already went and lost her sister.' Joanna puts out a finger and pokes me. 'What have you got to say for yourself?' She comes close enough for me to smell what she had for breakfast. 'Cat got your tongue?'

Some more people came to look around the house yesterday. They walked into all the rooms. I trailed after them, spying. 'Lovely light in here.' 'But we'll need to change the carpets of course.' 'What would we do with the garden?' I crouched behind the doors, hating them. If we move I won't have to see Joanna or Ellie ever again. If we move I'll never find Eva. The two thoughts smash together in my head. Nothing makes sense. I grip my wrist, pushing two fingers inside the tiny dip where my pulse ticks and suddenly I'm listening to the beat of my blood, thinking how the artery twists around tendons and muscles like tree roots. And I feel a bit better.

I hear the sound of the door swinging open, more footsteps. I let go of my pulse. The cubicle door rattles; someone is trying the handle. I watch the silver bolt moving up and down in the lock. Go away, I'm whispering, go away, go away.

'Faith Gale, are you in there?'

It's Joanna's voice. I draw my feet in closer, wrap my arms around my knees tightly and close my eyes. The cistern is cold against my back.

'She's here.' Ellie's triumphant voice. 'Sat on the toilet.'

I open my eyes to see Ellie's face; she's pressed herself sideways under the cubicle door, smirking up at me, her eyes bright. 'What you doing? Got the runs or something?'

I look down at her. She looks odd. Her face only just fits sideways in the gap between the cubicle door and the floor. She seems to be missing the rest of her body. Her head is a detached, freckled football. In one quick movement, I'm off the seat. My knee flexes, leg kicking out. My toe makes contact with Ellie's nose: it feels soft and then hard.

She screams, her mouth opening so wide that I see her tonsils, red in the back of her throat. The face disappears. Now there is angry pounding on the door, the sound of Ellie making gurgling noises. There will be blood. Noses bleed a lot. There are so many blood vessels. I stand with my hand clamped over my mouth, half-laughing and half-crying. 'You're dead!' Their voices shout. 'You're dead. After school. We're gonna get you.' The whole cubicle rattles. A loo roll from the next cubicle flies over, unravelling in a white streamer. There is the sound of the bell and after a few moments their footsteps on the floor and the swing of the door closing.

I stand with my back against the cubicle door, humming: *if I didn't care more than words can say, if I didn't care would I feel this way?*

Jack and Granny are sitting on the bench outside Granny's garden shed in her allotment. It is dusk. They sit very close, their shoulders

290

touching. The Ink Spots are playing on the radio. The sound crackles into the evening air, a harmony of gentle voices, and there is the smell of mint and lavender.

37

Max has never worked harder. He ends up taking paperwork home every evening. And yet each case seems so utterly meaningless, so pointless. As a small-town solicitor, all his clients are known personally to him. He passes them in the street daily, waits behind them at the bank and at the checkout queue at the supermarket. They tell him things about their personal lives. Like a doctor or a priest, he is considered safe and neutral. The fact that he sits in an office with his framed law certificates behind him is mortifying. It's him that feels like a criminal.

But at last, after months of lethargy, things are changing. He spoke to his lawyer friend, John, at the Cambridge firm and John was delighted by the idea that Max was at last considering joining them. Max has yet to tell his clients that he's abandoning them and shutting up the business.

The estate agents have brought a few prospective buyers around to look at the house. There is no offer yet, but apparently someone is coming back for a second view. Max can't let himself think too hard about leaving. Holt House has a sense of stoic kindness, a weather-beaten grace that Max loves. Sometimes he finds himself touching the walls, stroking doorframes as if the wood and stone have absorbed a pulse, as if memories breathe voices into the air: the lives of his children, their childhoods imprinted into the fabric of the place. He can see Eva flouncing away up the stairs, her angry tread echoing through the floorboards, Faith staggering around the kitchen, clutching at the table legs as she learned to walk. He will always be grateful to Clara for putting her inheritance into it.

At some point, he and Clara will need to drive over to Cambridge and look at property, consider schools for Faith. Perhaps they should rent first, take their time to find the right home. He and Clara must sit down and talk it through.

They haven't talked for a long time. The way she is now reminds him of how she was when she was going through the miscarriages. Except she won't take the drugs she'd been treated with then, says she'd rather feel the pain properly this time.

★ ★ ★

He drives home through country lanes, seeing that some of the fields have been ploughed already, turning them into dark squares. The trees overhanging the road are peppered with yellow leaves. Soon the sides of the road will be covered in the slime of rotten leaves and there will be drifts of them in the garden; he will have to start to sweep them up at weekends, raking piles to make into a bonfire. It was a job that Faith and Eva had loved to do with him, the task degenerating into a battle with leaves flying everywhere and Eva chasing a screaming Faith around the garden.

At home, Clara is in the kitchen unpacking bags of shopping. She's got her head in the fridge. She peers around the white door when she hears him come in and looks at him with a neutral expression. 'Haven't started supper yet.' She picks up a packet of meat and puts it onto a shelf. 'Not sure where Sophie is. I said she could have the evening off because she's been cleaning to get the house ready for the second view. They're coming tomorrow.'

Max is relieved that Sophie is out. He's found it awkward being around her since that odd, disconcerting moment between them in the hall. Sophie maintains a hurt and dignified silence around him. He has tried to reassure her with his manner and friendly tone that whatever happened, it's all forgotten and put behind them.

Silver gets up off the floor to greet him. The dog pushes his nose into Max's hand, wagging his long tail so that it bangs against the table, whips across Max's knees. He leans down to pat Silver's lean side, pulls his silky ears.

'Where's Faith?'

'In her room. Doing homework.' Clara bends down and picks up a tin of tomatoes. 'Year five seems to mean she has something to do most nights.'

As he mounts the stairs, he slides his tie out of his collar, pulls his shirt undone at the neck, snapping off a button by mistake with fumbling fingers. It rolls away down the steps behind him, a tiny white wheel. In the bathroom, he splashes his face with cold water, dabbing his eyes dry with a towel. He looks at himself in the mirror.

He hopes that this second view will lead to an offer on the house. He'll take almost any price they care to name. The three of them must make a new start. It's the only way that they'll have any chance of moving forwards.

'Forgive me,' he says quietly, seeing Eva's face shining back at him out of the mirror. 'Forgive me my love, but we have to try, we have to try and go on living without you.' He sees that Eva's mouth is dark with plum lipstick and reaches out his thumb to smudge it away. The mirror is a cold shock on his skin. God, he misses her so much. The pain of it is physical. He breathes deeply, steadying himself, and turns away from the glass.

38

Fingers move at my neck. Cold air creeps over my skin. I think of ice cubes, snow in the garden, the white crunch of it under my feet. Only I'm not out in the snow, I'm burning up on a beach, baking under a fiery sun. Huge birds swoop across the sun, their wings casting shadows over me, making me shiver. I look up into the curve of beaks, the glitter of yellow eyes. Vultures. They are waiting for me to die, waiting to rip into my flesh, pull me apart. They will toss my bones into the sand. I put my arms across my face and cry out.

Someone untangles my arms. Fingers push the hair back from my forehead. There is water at my mouth. It drips into my parched throat. I'm so thirsty. 'Mum?' My lips move but there's no sound in the desert.

'You look like her, you see,' a voice says, 'same hair, same lips. Different colouring. That's all.'

Marco stroked my skin with slender fingers, giving me goose pimples. He told me that I was beautiful. He said he noticed me the minute that he walked into the club. He had to have a drink to pluck up the courage to come over and talk to me. Imagine that. He looked so cool. I never thought that he'd be interested in me: a boy like him.

Marco is holding my cheeks in his hands; he places his lips over mine. I open my eyes and I'm looking into the face of a stranger. A man with a

296

beard stares back, his open mouth wet inside a tangle of hair. No, I'm shouting. No. But he's kissing me again. And it's strange because I like it. Billy. His name comes back to me and I want to laugh. This is all wrong, I want to say. I love Marco, not you. But I can't speak because his mouth is on mine, soft, insisting. He's holding me tightly, as tightly as I want to be held, and now his mouth is pressed at my ear. It's all right, Eva, he murmurs, I'll look after you. I'll always look after you.

I'm floating above the pagoda, looking down on the island and the ring of sea, the waves blinking white and dark against the pebbles. There are stars all around me. Enormous and bright. I am free, light as air, and I know I've been here before, inside this flight, this letting-go. A man's voice is speaking again. It sounds as if someone is fiddling with the volume control. The words rush towards me and then fade away, pulling me back to the heaviness of earth.

There is a floor under me, hard and cold. 'I saved you like she told me to . . . ' the man's voice says, 'only thing is, I think now it's you that's saving me.' I recognise the voice. I find a name. Billy. I whimper, my fingers clutching at something rough across my chest. I hold onto it. It's a lifeline. I think Dad has thrown me a lifeline and now he will pull me to safety. The boat rocks wildly above me, the bow rearing up high on the crest of a gigantic wave. I hold my breath, knowing that it must crash back down into the trough, and that it will smash me under it, drowning me.

39

Clara puts the receiver down in the cradle with a click. It was the estate agent. His client has made an offer. It's not far off the asking price and Clara has told them that they'll take it. Max will agree of course. She feels out of balance; it's happened quicker than she thought it would. The house is so remote; she couldn't imagine anyone else wanting to live here. But apparently the new owners intend to use it as a country retreat, a weekend house. She wonders how Max will feel now that the move is really happening. Max has loved this house since childhood, walking past it as a boy on the way to the river with a fishing rod in his hand.

Clara goes into Eva's bedroom. She sits on the bed and picks up Eva's old teddy, holding its lopsided, balding head to her chin. She smells dry sawdust through the patchy fur. All of this will have to be packed away. She imagines the boxes stacked up and ready to be loaded into the removal lorry. But she can't imagine living anywhere else. What will they do with Eva's things? They can't throw them away. She supposes that she'll ask Faith what she would like to keep — the water pearls, of course. Clara will choose some things for herself, and give the rest of it to charity. It hurts to think of giving away clothes that hold the fading smell of Eva.

Clara remembers getting out of the car on the

day they arrived from London. Max had been flushed with excitement and nerves. He'd bought Holt House without her. She had been too busy and preoccupied with Eva to house-hunt. She'd stayed in the flat, making up formula milk and staring into the twitching, mewing face of her baby.

Eva was in Clara's arms that day, swaddled in a shawl, carried carefully against her chest. The house was pale stone, much bigger than she'd imagined. A Georgian front attached to an older, rambling back. She'd walked in through the front door and up the central staircase with the beautiful, turned spindles and curving banisters. The back staircase leading to the kitchen had been straight and steep, and she'd worried about Eva, imagining her as a toddler, slipping and falling on the sharp stairs, landing on the flagged floor of the kitchen.

Eva had never fallen down the stairs. No one had, except Max once, when he'd tripped and banged his head on the low lintel of the kitchen door. She'd worried so much about the children. And now the worst that she could imagine has happened and she feels numb and unable to worry anymore. Yet Faith is still here, and needs looking after, needs her parents to be parents. Clara puts the teddy down, arranging its wobbly head carefully against the pillow.

The house is crammed with seventeen years of their lives. She'd better make a start on the enormous task of sorting through it. There are a couple of old boxes in the garage, bin bags under the sink. Clara pushes herself off the bed, rolls up her sleeves.

When Max gets home he finds Sophie in the kitchen ironing. There is the smell of clean laundry and damp cotton. The iron hisses as she runs it across one of his shirts. She looks up briefly, observing him without any obvious feeling. She returns to the shirt, banging the iron down, pressing it hard across the white collar. He backs out, feeling, again, that he is somehow in the wrong.

Clara is on her knees in their bedroom. The dog is lying on the floor nearby. His tail moves against the floor in acknowledgement. Clara has piles of clothes on the floor. She's emptied boxes from the attic on the bed. He sees ancient files, photo albums, an old plastic dolls' house, and a sack of baby clothes. She looks up, distracted and dishevelled.

'They've made an offer,' she says, pushing hair from her forehead. 'Only three thousand under. I've told them we'll take it. I've made a start. Sorting things out. For the move.'

Max looks at the dolls' house, remembers the birthday that they gave it to Eva, her face as she'd torn away the wrapping paper. He'd stayed up until the early hours of the morning putting it together, bruising his thumb, and losing screws under the kitchen table as he'd struggled to follow the incomprehensible instructions spread out before him.

'Well,' he says, trying to keep his voice steady. 'So it's really happening. I'll help you with . . . ' he gestures towards the piles of things, 'with all this.'

'There's a surveyor coming tomorrow.' Clara throws a handful of papers into a plastic refuse sack. Her voice is strained. Tearful.

'Clara,' he says. 'Let's leave it for now. Come and have a glass of wine. We can do some clearing at the weekend. Get Sophie to help.'

Clara shakes her head. 'It has to be done. There's so much . . . I don't know how we've collected so much . . . stuff.'

Max sits heavily among the objects on the bed; he strokes the dusty roof of the dolls' house, feeling an aching sorrow in his gut. He can't bear the thought of throwing this away — or anything else. It seems to be marking the end of their life with Eva. But it was his idea to move. It was his need that had forced the decision. Now he feels nothing but doubt and loss and a dragging weight of grief and exhaustion.

40

He says he thought I was going to die. I don't remember much. Strange dreams. Vultures. A desert. I know he looked after me, fed me sips of water and chicken soup. I imagine that he stole a scrawny hen from some farmer's yard, wrung its neck and stuffed it into a sack. There are feathers on the floor near the pit: a soft scattering of russets, curls of white.

When I was ill nothing existed outside the edge of my skin. What went on here in the pagoda was like a vague dream, and the dream world became my reality. I remember fragments from that landscape; brightly coloured moments, odd, out of kilter things, like seeing everything through the prism of a fairground mirror.

Billy strolls over to me, puts his hand in his pocket and pulls out an orange, presenting it to me on his open palm like a magician. I peel it slowly, inhaling the bitter tang of the peel, the sweetness of the juice. It is strange to be awake, sitting up, back to the simple existence of waking life. There are so many hard edges and the daylight hurts my eyes. He watches me separate it into segments. My fingers are unsteady.

'Here.' I offer him one.

He shakes his head.

I let the fruit burst slowly on my tongue, working the flesh between my teeth, nibbling the spongy pith, sucking the pips before spitting them out. I have learnt to concentrate on one thing at a time. I can make the eating of an orange last for ages, savouring every single part of the fruit.

I cough. Remnants of my illness hide in my body; I feel them as a catch in my breathing, soreness in my muscles. There is sunshine through the door and I want the warmth of it on my face, heat seeping into my aching bones. 'Can I sit outside?'

He finds me a spot against the sloping concrete wall of the pagoda, facing the ocean side of the island so that I'm out of the wind. He doesn't tie my wrists. I look at the familiar deserted huts, the old concrete road, the drooping razor wire and the straggly line of gorse bushes. Beyond the rise of the shingle is the sea. I can hear it raking against the pebbles. He puts my blanket around my shoulders, tucking it in almost tenderly with clumsy fingers. He sits beside me, legs bent, and takes a last deep drag of his rollic, grinding the stub under his heel. 'Thought I was losing you.' He shakes his head.

I fiddle with the frayed edges of the blanket. 'Then why didn't you take me to the hospital?'

He squints. 'I was near to it a couple of times.'

I'm not sure if I believe him. 'And now . . . ' I begin.

'I saved your life,' he says. 'Again.'

'I wouldn't have been ill though, if I'd been at home.'

He shrugs. 'Maybe.'

There's a hole in his trousers and I can see a patch of pale grimy skin, a sprouting of hair.

'Who is the girl that looks like me?' I turn to him. 'You talked about her again, when I was ill.'

At first I don't think he heard me. He picks up a stone and plays with it, rubbing the surface with his fingers, rolling it across his leg. 'Her name was Marie O'Connor,' he says eventually. 'A schoolgirl. Lived with her family in Belfast. She had four brothers.'

'What happened to her?'

'She's dead.'

'I'm sorry. How . . . how did she die?'

'I killed her.'

My spine is rigid. I hold the blanket tighter around me as if it could offer protection. I'm struggling to pull air into my lungs. I can't look at him. I stare straight ahead and I hear him swallow, the gulp of his Adam's apple. He shudders, as if he's cold out here under the sun.

'It was a routine night VCP,' he says in a distant voice. 'But then we got a tip-off that someone big was coming through. We were to stop them and take them straight to the Ray.' His hand closes around the stone. 'Every driver was a suspect.' He stares into the middle distance, his eyes widening as if he can see something lurking there. 'And then this one car, it wasn't stopping. It was making straight for the barrier, headlights blinding me. It veered across the road, mounted the pavement. Coming towards me.' He swallows. 'I took my rifle. Very calm. I took aim and fired. Windscreen shattered. I fired off a couple of rounds. The car smashed into a telegraph pole. Head-on collision.'

He's still holding the stone. I see his scarred

knuckles whiten, tendons tight as he squeezes tightly. He hurls it away. It lands with a muted rattle. A speckled gull swoops down and up on a flap of broad wings.

'I approached the car,' he says, 'opened the door. Driver dead. Slumped across the wheel. He was only a kid.' His voice is thick. 'Then I looked in the back, aiming my torch at their faces. Two more boys. And a girl. A girl lying across the seat, slumped to the side.' He takes a ragged breath. 'She'd got this pale skin and curly black hair like that girl in the fairy tale. Her eyes were open, looking right at me. Very blue eyes. The torchlight made them shine. But she'd got a hole in her head.' He taps the centre of his forehead. 'Just here.'

'But you thought . . . '

'Doesn't matter what I thought. They weren't IRA. They were kids out on a joy-ride. Stupid. Stupid.' He strikes himself hard on the temples with the heel of his palm. 'She was seventeen.'

'What happened then?'

'I was arrested. Taken back to England for my trial.' His head falls forwards, and all I can see is the slide of his matted hair. He wraps his arms around his legs, burying his face against his knees. 'I'd killed three people. I was a murderer. But I was hustled out of the country, taken to a military court over here. They acquitted me, then wanted to send me straight back to Ireland. Another tour of duty. I couldn't do it.' His voice hardens. 'They meant for me to kill those kids. It was a conspiracy. Why would they have told me the IRA were coming through?' He's talking to his knees, to the ground. 'They thought I'd be their creature after that.' His shoulders tremble. 'I killed her. Jesus. I fucking killed her.'

I move my hand, thinking of touching him. But I can't. Slumped next to me with his bones sticking through his jumper, he seems vulnerable in a way he never has before. And I feel a shift in our relationship, a change in him.

He sits up, wiping his face with the back of his hand. 'You're the only person I've talked to about it,' he says.

'Billy,' I try pitching my voice, aiming for a reasonable tone. 'It was a mistake. You didn't mean it. Look, we can't hide here forever. Maybe it's time to leave,' I say quietly. 'Take me to the mainland and I'll never tell anyone what happened. I'll never speak about you.'

He sits up straight, staring over the shingle towards the sea. He's chewing the inside of his lip, working his mouth silently inside all that hair. 'It's not over yet. I can't do it, Eva. I can't let you go.' He sounds almost sorry.

I think about the girl in the car. We're nearly the same age. And we're linked through Billy. A boy we should never have had contact with if things had been just a little different. I wonder what led her to get into the car that night. Perhaps it was her boyfriend at the wheel and she'd been persuaded or bullied to come along for the ride, or perhaps she did it for love. It makes me dizzy to think of all the decisions that have been made by people over the years that have led me here to the island, to be trapped with him. I can feel a hot prickling under my lids.

'She's here with us,' he says, putting his hands over his eyes. 'The angel. I have to wait for her voice. She's very close. I know it.'

My chest rattles with the effort of breathing. My limbs feel weak, hollowed out. I clench my fists. Tilting my face to the sun, feeling its warmth, I think of Mum and Dad and Faith. I can't find their faces anymore. I'm losing them. They've become vague shapes flickering at the edges of my memory.

41

I don't leave by the school gates. Joanna and Ellie will be hanging around, waiting for me. I slip out of the back, across the playground. After the last person has collected their bike I climb onto the bike-shed, grazing my knees as I haul myself up. There's a ploughed field behind the school. Brown earth shines in freshly turned furrows. It seems like a long drop, further than I thought. I hang my feet over the edge and reach for the fence that runs across the back of the school grounds. It's made of wire and I test my weight on it, clinging onto the edge of the bike-shed roof. Then I close my eyes and jump.

It's soft underfoot, but the ground comes up with a jolt. My knees smack into my cheek. Eyes watering, I roll sideways, dirt in my mouth and ears, hands and knees wet and sticky, plastered with clay soil. I crouch for a moment, breathing hard. I'm half-hidden by the hedge. When I can stand up, I make my way around the edge of the field, going at a trot, bent over to stay under cover of the spiky hedge.

There are only three caravans left on the site. The woman with the Alsatian has gone. The bins are no longer overflowing, but the broken deck chair is lying on its side in the overgrown grass. The stripy seat lolls like a tongue.

I knock loudly on the door of the boy's caravan. There's no answer but I can hear crying.

308

I take a guess that it's Penny that's making the noise. I rap my knuckles again and this time it opens. Fred looks at me, grinning, with a jam sandwich in his hand. 'What have you done to your cheek?' he asks. 'You're in a state.'

Sandra stops telling Penny off and straightens. 'Hello Faith,' she says. She glances to her left. 'Look who's back from hospital.'

Joe is sitting at the fold-out table next to Penny. A bandage makes a sling around his neck. His cast isn't white anymore. It's smudged with scribbled messages and names. He can use his hand though, because he's twiddling a Rubik's Cube with it.

'He's the only person I know who can do the blasted thing,' Sandra says.

Joe looks embarrassed and nods at me, pushing the cube away. Sandra is in the middle of feeding Carol in her high chair, and getting Penny to eat her fish fingers. Joe and Fred have finished their tea, but Penny's bottom lip sticks out and she looks at me tearfully, her food congealing and uneaten. Sandra has a streak of ketchup on her chin and a blonde wedge hangs over one eye. 'We're off tomorrow,' she tells me, brushing her hair back, leaving crumbs in the bleached strands.

She won't let the boys come down to the river with me. She folds her arms and says, 'No further than the castle, or else.' She shakes her head when Penny asks to come with us, which makes Penny's quivering mouth open wider. Her pigtails, tied at the ends with pink bobbles, wobble like a pair of deely-bobbers as she yells.

Sandra sets her face and pushes a slab of fish finger onto a fork. 'Here, Madam.' She prods the fork towards Penny's resisting lips. 'You're not going anywhere until you finish your tea.'

'Quick,' says Fred, grabbing my hand, 'before she changes her mind.'

We're walking through the caravan site, Joe lagging a little behind. Fred's fingers are hot and sticky with jam. He doesn't seem to notice that he's got his fingers entwined with mine. He's chewing his last mouthful of sandwich. I glance around, not wanting to be seen by anyone from school.

'What are you holding hands for?' Joe asks.

I feel my face flush and tug my fingers away, wiping them on the back of my school skirt. I stop to pull up my socks, crouching over my bent leg, using it as an excuse to hide my flaming cheeks.

'Are you glad to be going home then?' I ask, not looking at them.

'Don't want to go back to school much,' Fred says, 'but it's all right. Be nice to see me mates.'

Jealousy twists inside. I hadn't thought that he'd have other friends besides me. Feeling stupid, I keep my eyes on the ground and make a gargling noise in my throat.

Joe asks if I want to write on his plaster. He pulls the grubby bandage back so that I can read the scribbles of black and green and red. Fred suggests that I write my address on it. It occurs to me that we may not be living at Holt House for much longer and I feel like crying. I find a pen in my school bag and write my name in a space near his elbow. I underline Faith Gale and draw a smiley face next to it. He'll have the cast cut off his arm soon. He says they'll use an electric saw. I imagine the sharp bite of steel teeth, a whirring noise and the plaster falling away in two halves. Inside Joe's arm will be wasted away, weak as a baby bird. A nurse will throw the plaster remains into the bin. The lid closing on a jumble of sliced-up plaster with the scribbled messages: my name and address lost and forgotten.

'Give us something to write on and I'll leave you our telephone number,' Fred is saying. 'We'll probably be back next summer.'

I watch him inscribe the number on the first page of my maths book and I feel better. He props the book on his knee, bending close to the checked blue and white paper. His tongue protrudes from the side of his mouth. And I remember that I have Marco's address written down at home. Now I can add Fred and Joe's number to it.

At the castle, we run up to the flat roof. 'You can see the island from here.' I point across the marshes and river.

'Do you still think your sister's there?' Fred is panting. He wipes a drip off his nose on the back of his hand.

I nod. 'But I don't know for how much longer.' It's a thought that sprouts inside my head like a fungus. What if she's taken off the island before I get there? What if I miss her and it's too late?

'What do you think she's been eating all this time?' Fred wrinkles his forehead.

I stare at him. 'Maybe the Wild Man catches her fish.'

The boys look at their feet. Joe says, 'You've got to rescue her.'

'I know.' I watch a flight of swans flying over the allotments. 'I've got another plan.'

'Sandra won't let us help though.' Fred sounds sorry.

'It's OK. I can do it on my own.'

He touches my shoulder.

Joe starts for the door. 'Come on. We don't have long.'

We run down the stairs, our feet slamming into the worn stone, bruising our shoulders against narrow curved walls. Even though it's the wrong time of year and the hill is damp and muddy in places, the worn grass offering less bounce, Fred and I roll down the hill. Joe stands at the top whooping encouragement. I open my eyes to see the flicker of light and dark as I turn over and over, my hip hitting a hard lump, my hands grabbing at clumps of grass. Fred and I land in a heap at the bottom, laughing. He has mud on his clothes. Sandra won't be happy.

'I'll show you where my granny had her allotment,' I tell them, leading the way across the castle grounds to the old listing wooden fence and the patch of allotments. I can't see anyone working in any of the gardens. The tabby cat that I saw before is sitting on a bench cleaning her white stomach, back leg pointed in the air.

Joe is already clicking the latch on a gate. I

follow although I'm suddenly uncertain. Granny and Jack once said their allotments were their second homes. 'Mind the flowers. Don't stand in the beds,' I whisper.

We wander past canes holding up runner-bean plants, the heavy heads of globe artichokes, neat rows of spring onions and parsnips. A small, wizened apple tree is heavy with fruit. Rotten apples lie in the long grass, half-eaten by birds, brown and mushy. Fred stoops to pick one up and throws it at Joe. Joe lets out a shout and turns away, the apple spinning past his head. There's someone in the furthest allotment, an elderly lady with a headscarf on. She's bent over, pulling things out of the ground.

I hold up my hand. 'Be quiet a minute.' I want to distract Fred and Joe from chucking the apples, but also I've heard something strange: a low, rhythmical banging, and a kind of grunting noise like an animal in pain. I signal to the others to follow me and we edge slowly around the corner of the garden shed, stepping over a pile of plant pots, past a propped-up spade. A man has his back to us. I'm staring at a naked bottom, very white and round, his trousers baggy around his knees. He's pushing his hips in and out like a piston. There's a woman's leg raised around his hips, her arms hanging onto his neck. She's moving with the force of him, her head knocking against the shed, brown hair spilling across the wooden planks behind her.

She opens her eyes over his shoulder. Her mouth is wide and pulled down; her lids flutter as she fixes me in a familiar stare.

Fred grabs my arm, pulling me. The boys are laughing as they stumble away. We crash through a clump of rhubarb, ripping up leaves, crushing them under foot. I slip on spinach, knock cauliflower heads into the soil. It was Robert Smith with his trousers round his knees. I feel sick. I want to get rid of the image of his pale buttocks, his hips ramming against Sophie. She'll tell him that I saw, and I remember his sneering face in our garden, what he said to me then.

We stop under the shadow of the castle. There's no sign of them following us. 'Going at it like dogs,' Joe says, cradling his cast with his good hand.

'Yeah,' Fred is leaning over, hands on his knees, panting, 'in broad daylight too.'

I'm trembling. I look away, clearing my throat. 'It's disgusting.'

Fred gives my arm a shove. 'You country people. You're all alike.'

I aim a sharp kick at his ankle, but he jumps out of the way, laughing. He's surprisingly fast for a fat person, but I don't say it aloud.

'We've got to go.' Joe's looking at his watch, and he jerks his head at Fred.

I rub my nose, feeling awkward, my mouth dry.

'See you around.' Fred grabs my hand and gives it a shake. 'Next summer.' I feel his hot fingers wrapped around me. Then he's walking away, Joe by his side, waving.

The world seems empty without them. I curl my hands into balls, shoving them in my pockets, the feel of Fred's touch fading from my skin. I

314

forgot about my warts. Fred isn't the sort to care about things like that. Down on the seawall there is just one motorboat powering through the river, leaving a spreading trail of wake. Cormorants dive and surface, black heads sleek. I stand and look over to the island. I have failed. 'Eva,' I whisper aloud. But all I can hear is the roar of the powerboat, the noise of the engine fading into the distance.

As I'm walking home, picking my way from one tuft of grass to another, feet unsteady in the mud, I see the man in the canoe again. I watch him, admiring his slick movements with the paddle, the agile speed of his boat as it slips through grey water. Unlike the powerboat, the canoe is silent. The man is dressed in bright red, matching his boat. He makes a brilliant patch of colour that I follow easily, watching him paddle on towards the harbour and the quay.

42

Clara is trying to clear out Eva's bedroom. But she can't seem to actually put anything in the cardboard box she's brought up for the purpose. She keeps picking things up and sitting or standing with them in her hands. Nothing goes in the box. Everything in this room holds memories. She can't pack any of them away.

There's a novel by the bed, dog-eared, abandoned. A piece of paper sticks out. She hadn't noticed it before. Eva's bookmark. Clara picks up the book and flips it open to the marker, wanting to see what Eva had been reading, to smooth her fingers over the same page. She unfolds the bookmark. It's a letter. The untidy beginnings of a letter. And she sees, with a thud of shock, that it's addressed to her and Max. Clara holds the paper closer, reading the familiar writing. It's even more chaotic than usual, letters swirling into circles that come undone and trail away into dots and dashes.

Mum, Dad . . . But that's not who you are, is it . . . I don't know what to call you, how to say this...

You're not my real parents. Why didn't you tell me?

I think I've known all my life that something was wrong. Only I thought it Was me — ME that Was Wrong.

If he knows then who else? How can I face people ever again?

After last night, M won't want me anymore. Maybe he won't love me. You won't care. It's your fault. You don't even know that I have a boyfriend. I love him. You can't stop me, not anymore. I HATE you both.

The words fall through her, sliding and crashing into each other. Clara puts a hand over her heart, fingers pressing against a shooting pain. She doesn't understand. Someone told Eva about being adopted? She reads the lines again, seeing Eva crouched over the paper scribbling those words while her world became false, unrecognisable.

When did she write it? Clara stares at the scrappy letters, the creased paper. There is no date, no clue. The message trails away, the words breaking up, ending in a stain of ink. Clara gasps aloud. She hadn't thought that losing Eva could get any worse. A spike begins to stab behind her eyes; it strikes harder. She winces, ducks her head as if to ward off blows.

She stumbles from Eva's room, the letter in her hand, the light dimming and closing like a tunnel before her. She wants Max. He'll be home soon. He'll know what to do. She fumbles down the landing into her own bedroom, crawls onto the bed, pressing her face into the pillow, blotting out the day. And all she can see before her is Eva's face. Her drowning face falling away into darkness, mouth opening soundlessly, the look of a martyr on her, of someone betrayed.

* * *

317

Faith is at her desk in her bedroom. Max clears his throat as he enters, but she doesn't seem to hear him. Her room is filled with the lush voice of Ella Fitzgerald, an orchestra of strings swooping and crooning in the background. He sits on her bed. 'Doing your homework?'

She lifts her shoulders briefly.

He notices the dark shadow of a bruise. 'What have you done to your cheek?'

She puts a hand up to her face. 'Nothing. Must have bumped into my door. Can't remember.'

'Faith, I wanted to ask,' he clears his throat, 'how you're feeling now, about Eva? About . . . everything?'

Faith, hunched in her seat, hasn't moved, so he stands up and walks over to her. 'Of course you're still missing her. We all are. But are you a bit more . . . settled?'

Faith turns and gives him a stare and then looks down at the open book on her desk. 'I don't want to talk about it anymore, Dad.'

'Are you sure?'

She makes a noise in her throat, her eyes fixed on the work in front of her.

Max sighs; he rests a hand on her thin shoulder. 'If I thought it would do any good, any good at all, I'd go to the island. But I'm afraid it would make it worse.' He wishes that she would turn and look at him. He stares down at the top of her head. Faith is immobile beneath his touch, head bowed, as if she's waiting for him to leave. He squints at the open exercise book on her desk. Beneath the swing of her pale hair, the blue

318

and white checked paper seems to be filled with algebra workings-out. 'Doing your maths?'

'Trying to,' she says.

'Know where Mum is?'

She shakes her head. He leaves her to it, closing the door softly behind him. Ella is singing of springtime in Paris. Strange choice of music for a ten-year-old. He doesn't know how she can concentrate with it on in the background. Eva used to be exactly the same. Only her music had been louder, more insistent. He and Clara had spent evenings shouting up the stairs, telling her to turn it down.

As he enters their darkened bedroom, Clara pushes herself into a sitting position. She half-falls out of bed, lurching unsteadily towards him, a sob catching in her throat.

'Thank God you're here.' She is holding something towards him. Her hand is shaking. 'I found this,' she says in a low voice. 'It was tucked into her novel. By her bed.' She falters. 'It's a letter. From Eva. To us.'

His mouth is parched. He tugs back the curtains to let in some light. The writing in his hand pulls into focus. His heart begins to thud, his eyes skimming the scrawl of words. He has the flash of memory again. Eva looking down at him angrily.

'Nobody knew,' Clara is saying quietly, 'nobody except Charles. And your mother.'

Max makes an effort to think. The scribble of words repeats in his head. He remembers Charles looking at Eva with distaste on his face. 'Charles,' he says slowly. 'I don't understand.

319

But it has to be him.' He walks across the floor, his hand moving to the back of his head, touching the vulnerable place there. 'But if he got to her — why didn't she tell us? How long did she know?'

They stare at each other, their faces blank and tense. Max begins to pace around the bed, the letter grasped in his hand. 'Perhaps he changed his mind about staying out of her life.' He frowns. 'He must have seen her alone.'

'Yes. That must be it. He told her, didn't he? For spite.' Clara's eyes are huge; her face shrinks around them. 'I was afraid for so long that one day he'd come for her.' She puts her head in her hands. 'I worried all the time about that family taking her back. But he just wanted to destroy us. It was the sea that took her.'

'I can't believe she knew about the adoption and didn't say anything.'

He feels her stillness. 'She learnt how to keep secrets,' she says quietly. 'We taught her how.'

Max shakes his head. He says nothing. He can hardly remind Clara that for years he'd tried to persuade her to tell Eva the truth.

Clara flinches as if he'd spoken. She goes to the window, standing with her back to him, looking out at the river in the distance, the rise of the island just visible. She breathes in deeply. 'I thought it was the right thing, at the time. I didn't want her to feel different.'

He stands, hanging his head.

She leans forwards, pressing her forehead to the glass. When she speaks her breath mists the window. 'I was selfish.' He can hardly hear her. 'I

320

wanted Eva to be mine. It was for me. Not for her. I wouldn't let myself think about Suky. I just kept pushing the thought of her away. She was a child herself.' She stops, puts a hand to her mouth. 'Only a year older than Eva is now.' Her voice breaks. 'Oh God, Max, Eva died knowing that I lied to her.'

He goes to her, feeling too big in the room, too clumsy, not knowing if she wants him to touch her. He stands close, his hands hovering at his sides. 'Clara,' he whispers. She turns and presses her face against his chest, and he puts his arms around her, holding her. The relief of her body against him is almost unbearable. His knees sag. He drops his nose into her hair, smells the garden, smells her. The dog gets up, shaking himself noisily, and moves around them, his tail beating against their legs.

Clara's voice is muffled in his shirt. 'She was in love. We didn't even know. So much we didn't know about her. And now she's gone.'

Max holds Clara, stroking her hair. Out of the horror, he feels something warm and bright, because Clara is in his arms and she said the word 'we'. If they can share their grief, if they can see this through together, then there is still hope for them. He wraps himself around her tighter.

He sees Eva in her orange lifejacket, her face twisted with anger. He blinks, trying to remember. Something happened on the boat. Something bad. Before the accident. He sees the boat turning, a scrabble of limbs as it crashed over. Eva's hand stretched towards him. He struggles to pull the memory free, tug it into the glare of his conscious mind. There she is before him again, and she's dressed in black lace, her mouth dark with lipstick and she is soaked through, water pouring from her, and no lifejacket.

43

Above us stars glare down, white holes cut out of a dark paper sky. Billy has stuck his fishing rod deep into the shingle, used a bit of wood to prop it up, so that he can leave it and lie down next to me. We're on our backs, staring into the sky. The pebbles are warm from the day's heat. The night is still. No wind. I listen to the sound of waves moving lazily against the shore.

'I saw a shooting star,' I murmur sleepily. 'I know it's not really a star. Dad said it's dust and stuff from space. But I like the idea of a star falling.'

'Yeah,' he blows through his lips, 'people are always trying to get proof for things. But the world's not like that. You can't explain it.'

I raise myself on my elbows to look at him. 'I thought a soldier would be more, you know, on the side of practical things.'

'I am. I am practical.' He turns his head to look at me. 'But I know what I know. There's what we can see and what they want us to see. And then there's the truth. But we're not supposed to understand any of that.' He lowers his voice. 'They don't want us to know. They want us to be ignorant.'

I hesitate for a moment. 'So the voice . . . '

'A few years ago I would have laughed in your face if you'd told me that I would be listening to an angel. I'm not supposed to hear her. It's dangerous for them.'

'You mean the . . . things that are watching you — us — the bad things?' I glance behind me at the crouching shapes of the gorse. 'Do you know what they are? Who they are?'

'High-ups in the army. The government. In on it together.' He frowns. 'I don't know what the plan is. Not yet. But they're poisoning us with lies, with chemicals. Everything is a set-up. It's about power. Corruption.' He sits up abruptly. 'They're always watching me. Waiting for a slip-up. Waiting to take me over. But I'm cleverer than that. My army training, see. It comes in useful. They're not going to catch me out.'

He looks at the quivering line, and moves like a cat, springing to his feet, grabbing the rod, turning, reeling in, and I look past him at the waves, watching for the sudden spark of brilliance, how it fires through the dark mass, igniting a green lacing.

★ ★ ★

I've persuaded Billy to let me hang our blankets outside to air. I can't stand the stink of unwashed skin, fish and damp. They need boiling and disinfecting to clean them properly. I would like to make a bonfire of them, my clothes too, pile them in a heap and strike a match. I've beaten the blankets with a stick and flapped them around, and now they're draped over gorse bushes, caught on green prickles like offerings to the sun.

Billy sits on the shingle nearby, watching, a

half-smile on his face. He has the stub of a cigarette glued to the side of his mouth. 'Storm coming,' he says, squinting into the sky. He doesn't seem to notice the filth we live in, the state of our bodies. I pause, panting with my exertions. I haven't recovered completely. I still wheeze. At night it feels as though there's something heavy pressing on my chest.

Billy holds out the remains of his cigarette. 'Want a drag?'

I shake my head. It's the first time he's offered me a smoke. I'm thinking about how to tackle the inside of the pagoda. Get rid of the crumbling concrete pieces, thick dust and splatters of bird shit. I look around for something that I could use. In a few moments I've collected some withered sticks and a handful of long grasses, pleased with myself because I've made a kind of broom. Stooping, I bend my elbow and flick, sweeping in firm movements, but the sticks crumble and the ends of the grass splay uselessly. I straighten, resting my palm on my aching spine, frowning.

Billy has followed me inside. He shoves his hands in his pockets, lounging against the wall. His lips roll back as he laughs, showing his teeth. I wipe my forehead with the back of my hand. 'Yeah, well. At least I gave it a try.'

'Spring cleaning!' He loops his fingers next to his ear. 'In this place? You're crazy!' He wanders away, scratching his head. He's still laughing. I glimpse a strip of flesh between his trousers and jumper as he pushes his arms above his head in a slow yawn. He pauses on the edge of the pit, arching his back lazily. This is the moment, I understand with sudden clarity. This is my chance.

I run at him. Head down, shoulders hunched. My head crunches into his ribs, arms flailing around his waist. He lets out a cry of surprise, his body tensing. He has lurched forwards, his foot slipping at the edge of the pit. He teeters for a second and my feet scrabble on the floor, pushing against him as hard as I can. But I don't have the strength. He is all bone and muscle. He surges back, his weight falling into me. His arm is around my neck and I can't breathe. He swings me around, my feet leaving the ground, my jaw cracking under the pressure. He's shouting but I'm smothered inside folds of his clothes. I can't make out words.

He has me by the shoulders, holding me away from him at arm's length; I'm forced back, leaning over the pit. His fist clenches around my jumper, twisting tight. My feet feel the floor, trying to find the edge, pushing away from the void behind me. His face is closed. He's got me with one hand, his arm flexing with the effort. I tremble on the brink, moving my lips. 'No.'

His fingers open in slow motion. I seem to hang in space and time. Billy and I stare at each other, our faces full of surprise. Then I fall, light and air rushing past.

I hit the bottom and pain jolts, ricocheting through my spine. Flames lick hips, pelvis. All breath gone. I am winded and empty, limbs spread wide, one arm flung up behind my head. I'm too afraid to move. My legs are numb. I can't feel them.

Mum leans over me. *Eva, love, time to get up. You'll be late for school.* Dad is standing in the kitchen: *What time do you call this, Duchess?* Faith, smiling up at me from under a fall of pale hair. *My sister, the drama queen.*

★ ★ ★

When I open my eyes, I'm looking at an old beer bottle. It seems huge, magnified. The glass is cloudy, the label ripped and faded. Behind that I can see the office chair on its side like an old drunk; the stub of a missing leg sticks up, severed and raw. I smell damp and urine, rust and concrete. Slowly, I reach my hand down the length of each of my legs, carefully assessing the angles of my bones, pressing my skin to check for feeling. The numbness has become a fizz of pins and needles. I don't seem to have cracked anything. Inside my shoes, I ask my toes to perform a cautious wriggle. They obey me. I squint towards the rim of the pit. I can't see Billy.

I am not dead. But I may as well be. The home that I dream about every night is a lie. My family is a lie. I haven't looked in a mirror for months. If I saw my reflection now, I don't know that I would recognise myself. Everything I thought I knew has changed. I am not who I thought I was.

I don't want to remember. I don't want to.

★ ★ ★

Sitting in the Bell, Marco twisted his lager glass between his fingers. 'Don't go home. Stay tonight.' He put his hand on my thigh, his thumb rubbing. 'My parents will be fine about it.' But I knew that mine wouldn't be. I was already going to be late. I shook my head. 'Can't. You know I can't.'

He waited with me at the bus stop. We kissed under the shelter. A man muttered, 'Get a room,' and I pressed my face into Marco's shoulder to stop myself laughing, lips against the spring of his muscle.

'You've got to stop telling your parents you're with Lucy when you're out with me. They'll find out, you know,' he said. 'You're nearly old enough to do what you like. You won't need their permission for anything in a year.'

I made a face, embarrassed. 'They're a bit overprotective,' I mumbled.

'Tell them about me. You're a big girl now.' He cocked one eyebrow. 'Not ashamed of me, are you?'

* * *

The bus was overheated, nearly empty. It wound its slow way through country lanes and sleepy villages. I leant my head against the shuddering glass. I'd decided that Marco was right. I would tell them. I was suddenly confident that Mum and Dad would like him, despite his hair and his tattoo and being older than me. I loved him. That was the important bit. I loved him enough to sleep with him. Although of course, I wouldn't tell them that.

It was on the bus that I worked out a plan. It was really very simple. Staring at the black glass, I caught my reflection and grinned. All I had to do was slip out of the house after everyone had gone to bed and catch the late bus into Ipswich. I could be with him all night, as long as I was up at the crack of dawn. Marco was right. I was a big girl now and I was sick of Dad trying to stop me from growing up. The only problem might be Silver; if he heard me, I knew he'd start barking, his tail knocking against furniture and doors, waking the whole house. I was thinking about that as I walked home, about how to avoid disturbing the dog. We were studying *Romeo and Juliet* at school and I remembered the scene where they'd pretended that the thrush they heard was a nightingale because they couldn't bear to accept that their night together was over. That was how I felt about us: we were meant to be, and our love deserved a whole night spent in a bed, not some sordid fumbling in a back alley on a Friday evening.

The next day I phoned Marco to tell him the plan. I stumbled over my words, suddenly embarrassed. When he understood what I meant there was a silence. I twisted the cable around clammy fingers.

'Are you sure?' he asked. And then in a husky voice, 'I want you so much.'

'Yes.' My insides turned watery. I held tight to the receiver. 'I want to,' I whispered, glancing back at the empty hallway.

'I'll meet you at the bus station tonight,' he said. 'But Eva, then promise me to introduce me to your parents. I'll win them round.'

I laughed. 'What an ego.'

I climbed out of my bedroom window. I'd done it before. There is a drainpipe to cling to and a short drop onto the porch roof. From there it's an easy scramble to the grass. A big moon made the ground silvery. I took the back route, past the castle, thinking of Marco. I was wearing my best knickers, perfume behind my knees and elbows. The trees stood still. There was no wind. A whining noise behind me made me jump. I recognised the sound of a moped coming out of the darkness, and I put my head down, walking faster.

The beam from the headlight caught me. Small moths fluttered inside the white glare. I turned, shading my eyes. Robert took off his helmet, grinning. I kept on walking. He cruised beside me, the engine puttering. 'Where's pretty boy?'

I folded my shoulders. 'Go away, Robert.'

He stopped the moped, lurching forwards to grab my arm. 'Someone needs to teach you manners.' He shook me. 'What makes you think you're better than everyone else?'

I was shocked by his touch, my eyes sliding past looking for an escape. He wouldn't let go of my arm, fingers pinching. I tried to wriggle away, but he held me tighter, twisting my elbow, burning my skin. He pushed me into the dark grounds of the castle.

'I've got an interesting story to tell you,' he breathed, 'and you are going to listen to it, you snotty bitch.'

My heart staggered like broken wings. I swallowed, looking around for help. Panic flapped and scrabbled inside my ribs. We were alone. The shadows of the castle stretched long and straight over the moonlit grass. Beyond the grounds, I could see the jumbled shapes of the allotments, the shapes of bushes and plants and the outlines of sheds. An owl hooted from the copse of trees at the foot of the escarpment.

'My uncle works in the pub,' he said. 'Worked there for years. People tell publicans things, spill out their troubles over a pint or a shot.'

'It's late, Robert.' I tried to pull away. 'I've got to catch the bus. I'll miss it . . . '

He held up his finger and wagged it at me. 'Naughty, naughty. Mustn't interrupt. Hasn't anyone told you it's rude?' His face, close to mine, was all nostrils and teeth. 'As I was saying, there's my uncle minding his business behind the bar, and in comes this stranger. Posh bloke. And he's in a bit of a state. Orders a stiff drink. Tells my uncle he's just had a nasty shock. Seems he'd come a long way to see his sister's bastard brat. He'd wanted to do the right thing by the child — bring her up as his own. The sister was dead. So he'd come to take her home with him.' I waited, limp in Robert's grip, unable to move. 'Because guess what?' Robert asked, speaking slowly. 'The kid had been taken by a couple, and was living right here in our village. Wasn't that a coincidence, Eva?'

He smiled. 'See, this kid's real mum was a slut, got herself knocked up. Posh bloke already knew that. But turns out the brat had a touch of tar brush about her. Posh bloke said that couldn't be, because he knew who the father was. But that kid's got mixed blood, the poor sod kept saying. Bad blood.' Robert whistles and shakes his head. 'What do you think of that? This happened quite a few years ago. But the girl's still here, isn't she, Eva?'

I squirmed away, images from his story spooling behind my eyes. I could see the man at the bar: sweat shining his top lip, his fingers trembling against his glass. Robert jerked me close, mouth against my ear, his words vibrating, 'Next time you want to act high and mighty, remember you're nothing. A half-breed bastard.'

He let me go and I ran, stumbling towards the castle. The ground tipped and lurched. A sob caught in my throat, a stinging bubble, choking me. But he was coming at a run, heavy footsteps pounding. I gasped as he slammed into me. He swung me round, pushing his face against mine. His mouth opened: cold, clammy lips, tongue like an eel.

I hit out, flailing through darkness. Bone cracked against bone. I felt the give of his flesh, smacked into the angle of his elbow. He grabbed my wrists and held them by my sides. 'Not so fast.' He was leaning over me, forcing me back. I stumbled, fell, and he landed across me, pinning me down. 'I reckon you owe me for that story.' I smelt stale beer, something foul. He was scrabbling at his belt buckle. The metal stuck into me. 'I'm going to show you what a real man feels like.'

His hands ripped at my top, grabbing my

breasts, fingers digging at my skin. 'You know you want it. Your sort always does.' His mouth was at my neck. I tried to get away from the wet of his saliva, the edge of his teeth. The nub of his shoulder stuck into my face, shirt fabric filling my mouth. I tried to shout, feeling his other hand pulling at the button on my trousers, nails scratching. I twisted my head free, gulping air. No energy for words. He was too heavy, too strong. He'd got his fingers inside my trousers, ripping at the zip; his knee was between my legs, trying to force them apart. His tongue jabbed at my mouth. I opened wide, felt the slither between my lips and bit down, hard as I could. Flesh broke like raw fish between my teeth. He roared and started back, his hand clasped over his mouth. Rolling sideways, I managed to scramble to my feet, yanking at my trousers, running blind through the night.

Sliding through the gap in the fence into an allotment, heart thundering, I jumped a flowerbed. Feet thrashed through roses, thorns catching at my skin. I heard Robert behind me. But he didn't know the layout of the allotments like I did. I ducked into what used to be Jack's garden and dropped to my knees, crawling on my belly, canes of runner beans shielding me. I waited, cheek against the gravel, trying to be silent while Robert stamped past on the other side of the vegetable bed. When I couldn't hear him anymore I got to my feet, getting off the crackle of small stones to wade through plants, tubers and leaves rustling, stalks snapping beneath me, feeling my way to Granny's old shed. It was padlocked. I bent down, scrabbling in the dark, telling myself that the new owners wouldn't keep the key in the same place. Stupid. But my fingers fumbled over a large rock, poking beneath it. Something slimy. A slug? Then a small cold shape. Robert's voice came from the next allotment, calling my name.

I stabbed the key towards the centre of the lock. I couldn't see what I was doing. The key clicked into place. I stumbled inside, crouching in the darkest corner, pulling a sack across me. I heard Robert outside the shed, breathing hard. He swore under his breath. The shed smelt of soil and metal. I could taste his blood in my mouth.

I hid under rough, musty sacking, cobwebs in my face, hardly breathing. I waited, hunched over, kneeling in the same position until my limbs seized up with cramp. But I didn't dare move. My ears strained for sounds. Hours later I heard a frenzy of scraping coming from the bottom of the door. I went icy, stiff with fear. The scratching started up again. Choking with panic, I tried to decipher it: a key in a lock? A knife blade? And I began to breathe, understanding that it was the sound of busy teeth and claws. A rat probably. But still I was too frightened to push the suffocating sacking from me and stretch my burning legs. Eventually light began to mist the panes of the window above me. I could hear birds singing. Peering out, the interior of the shed developed contours and depth, shapes becoming themselves: shelves piled with plant pots, trowels hanging from the wall, an old pair of gloves sticking out of a bucket. It was only then that I dared push open the door. I went as quickly as I could through the wet grass, forcing my aching limbs to jog down the lane, all the time listening for a moped's engine.

I let myself into the sleeping house, crept up the stairs, managing to get into my bedroom without waking the dog. I struggled to strip off my clothes, wiping my fingers, not wanting to have the smell of Robert on me. Crawling naked under my covers, I think I must have passed out.

When I woke, my stomach churned, memories skidding into my head. I wanted to believe it had been a nightmare. But I could feel Robert's tongue, the trickle of his blood in my mouth. I brushed my teeth while I ran myself a hot bath, locking myself in the bathroom. I felt dirty. There were scratches across my stomach, thumbprint bruises on my arms. I lay in the water and cried. I looked at my body, skin the colour of tea, and I knew that Robert hadn't been lying. All the things that I'd felt all my life, but not understood, came rushing in. It was as if someone had untied a blindfold and slipped it from my eyes. Things I'd only sensed with my fingertips were suddenly revealed, towering over me.

Mum knocked on the door. 'Eva?' I crossed my arms over my chest, holding my breath. The lock rattled. She called. 'Do you want breakfast? I'm cooking eggs and bacon for the others.' Clearing my throat, I told her that I was fine. Not hungry. I tried to sound normal, leaning forward to run the tap to disguise the shake in my voice. There was no hot water left. Scum floated on the surface, leaving a tidemark. I noticed bits of hair and grey stuff like foam. I was nothing. Worse than nothing. Robert's hands and tongue and words squirmed inside me. As I hauled myself out of the bath, I remembered that Dad and I were supposed to be sailing that day: our first sail since the winter lay-off. But he wasn't my dad. Robert said they'd taken me. Taken. My brain stuttered around the word, unable to make sense of it.

I stayed in my bedroom until it was time to go down to the river, my mind racing, full of anger and pain and plans to run away. I grabbed a pen and began to scribble a letter to Mum and Dad. The people who said they were Mum and Dad. I wrote what came into my head without thinking, words to leave behind — to explain but most of all to punish. I couldn't finish it. I began to cry, sobbing until my eyes were gluey. Then I stuck my face under the cold tap, slipped the letter in my novel, got dressed in my sailing clothes and met Dad down on the quay because I didn't know what else to do. I felt pathetic, afraid, all my rage balled up inside me like a fist that couldn't punch free.

He'd been rigging up. The sky was dark, clouds rolling in. The water was agitated, angry little waves slapping at the boat, restless wind in the sails. 'Bit blowy,' Dad said. 'You still up for it?' I'd nodded, not able to look at him. 'Do your lifejacket up, Eva,' he said.

I couldn't understand how he hadn't seen the change on my face. I wanted him to ask me what

336

was wrong. I wanted him to hold me and explain and make it all right. Questions cracked and clashed in my head, piling up like a log-jam. On the boat I went through the motions, pulling ropes, nodding when Dad said anything, avoiding eye contact. As we got past the island and out to sea we realised that the weather was blowing a real storm. The waves were big and the sky had darkened to black. 'Better get the sails down,' Dad yelled. 'I'll start the engine.' The boat was rolling by then, waves washing over the side. I struggled to undo the cleats, wild canvas flapping out of my arms. I wasn't frightened. I was too angry. I held onto the mast, my hands slipping on the wet, looking down at him couched by the engine. 'I know,' I told him, my words rushing out, ripped away by the wind. He'd frowned, cupping his ear. 'I know about you and Mum,' I shouted. 'I know that you're not my real parents. You lied to me.'

Through a tangle of hair blowing across my face, I saw shock rearrange his features. He was sitting at the stern. He couldn't move because the waves were crashing against us, the boat struggling through the peaks and troughs. His hand was clamped hard around the tiller. 'We're going in,' he'd shouted. 'I can't talk now. We'll talk about it on land.'

'I don't want to talk about it,' I yelled. 'I hate you.'

I staggered across the deck, clinging to the mast, to the wire, flinging myself towards the cabin. The deck reared under my feet. I thought I could hear Dad shouting my name. I would run away, I thought. I'd run to Marco. But then I realised that he didn't know what had happened. He must have waited at the bus stop, watching passengers getting off, one by one. He would have walked home alone, hands thrust in pockets, thinking that I'd changed my mind, thinking that I'd stood him up. I stopped in the middle of the tilting deck, my hands flailing to steady myself. Out of the corner of my eyes, I caught a wall of water rising.

★ ★ ★

Billy hasn't come back. There's no answer when I call. I can hear wind across the pebbles, rain falling hard. Above the pagoda roof comes the low rumble of thunder. A sudden crack of lightning shakes the walls of the pit. He's gone for good this time. There's a flutter of feathers high above me, and a rustling as if some huge creature is settling in the rafters of the pagoda. Night comes slowly, trickling shadows into the pit. Soon I can't see my hand in front of my face. I remember the stench of Robert's breath in my mouth, my lips caught in his teeth. I curl up in darkness, wrapping my arms around my knees and wonder how long it takes to die of thirst.

44

'Wake up, love.' Mum raps on the door. She comes in, opening my blind, letting in grey morning light. 'Horrible day, I'm afraid. Did you hear the thunder last night?'

From my pillow, I watch her looking through the glass. Squalls of water hit the panes. She leans over me. 'Come on sleepy head,' she pulls at my covers, 'you'll be late for school.'

I slip my feet out of my nest of sheets and blankets, sitting for a moment on the edge of the bed, yawning. I had nightmares again. I can't remember what they were. Only the feelings remain, dark and frightening. I rub my eyes. Mum strokes my head briefly, ruffling my tangles, calling over her shoulder, 'Don't go back to sleep!' as she shuts the door behind her.

Then I notice my hands. There are no warts on my fingers. Every single one has disappeared. I touch my skin in wonder, feeling it smooth, as if it has always been like that, as if I dreamed the warts. I spread my fingers wide to study them again. There are no bumps, or scars or marks of any kind. I walk over to the window, my fingers held up, staring at them from every angle. It's like magic. My hands look like everybody else's.

I eat breakfast alone. Dad has already left for work. Sophie hasn't come down yet. Mum is busy at the sink, washing my porridge pan. I have to force myself to swallow the thick

339

gloopiness of the oats. What are Fred and Joe eating for breakfast? Their kitchen will be as small and cosy as the caravan. I expect Sandra will be cross and flustered, and that Penny or Carol, or both, will be crying.

It is quiet in our kitchen. The clock ticks on the wall, rain pattering against the glass. I push my bowl away, half-eaten. Mum leans against the sink sipping a cup of tea. 'My warts have gone,' I tell her.

'Oh Faith,' she comes over, 'look at that! Didn't I tell you they'd go all on their own one day!'

As Mum examines my hands, I remember that I dreamt about Eva again. She was reaching out to me, breaking the surface then sinking away. I'd tried to tell her that I was coming. Shouting out through murky water that she had to hold on. But she'd been shaking her head, as if she was telling me that I was too late.

★ ★ ★

Puddles leak into puddles, our garden path and the lane slick with water. My school shoes and socks are already soaked. I pull my hood over my head, adjust my satchel, and in case Mum is watching from the window, begin to walk in the direction of school. But after a moment I double back and hurry past the house, following the track that leads across the field to the seawall and the quay.

Ted's figure appears through a blur of water. He's trudging through the rain in the opposite direction, a shiny figure in oilskins. I freeze, heart beating. But he ducks into his hut without seeming to notice me. In the dinghy park, I push my satchel under an upturned rowing boat and pick up the canoe at one end, grasping it tightly, testing its weight. It's slippery and awkward, heavier than I thought. Little by little, I drag it across the ground, scraping over anchor chains and gravel, closer to the slipway. A woman walks past with a dog. I pause, but she ignores me. The paddle is wedged inside and I pull it out as I steady the canoe in the river.

The boat rocks wildly from side to side as I ease myself slowly into the low seat, tucking my legs inside the fibreglass shell. I stab at the riverbed with the end of the paddle to steady it. Clouds of mud swirl towards the pitted surface. I swallow, thinking that I could still change my mind; drag the canoe back into the dinghy park, find my bag and go to school.

One careful push with the oar and I'm floating away. Too late now. Each movement I make sends the canoe tipping and my heart lurches. I try to remember the way the man in red used the paddle, the swing of his shoulders as he'd dipped the oar in at one side and then the other. He'd kept very still, only his arms moving, like a wind-up toy. I try to do the same. The canoe begins to move in the right direction. Water dribbles down the paddle and up my sleeve, waves splashing over the side. A lot of water is getting in, and I remember that the canoeist had a tarpaulin cover around his middle, stretched to cover the opening. But there is no tarpaulin. I paddle on, hot from my exertions, my school skirt clinging to my mottled legs.

I feel the bite of the tide and struggle to dig the paddle deeper, wrenching against the force of the current. A large seagull settles on the water close to me. I don't dare look behind to see how far I've come, but up ahead is the line of water where the river meets the sea, and beyond that is the island.

I pass moored yachts with empty creaking decks and rolled sails. I feel very small in the canoe; the boats tower high above. A man pops out from a cabin and stares at me with his hands on his hips. I ignore him. Something surfaces in front of the prow and slides out of sight under the waves. I freeze for a moment, paddle in mid-air. A face appears, close enough for me to see a cat-like nose and liquid eyes. The seal dives again. There is a flick of tail. I almost feel its body twisting below the canoe, the invisible roll of its movement. I hold my breath, waiting for it to reappear. I think I've lost it then the dark head comes up further off, turns to look at me and disappears.

It's a message from Eva. Setting my shoulders, I grip the paddle with sore hands. I'm almost there. I work the oar, finding my rhythm, heading for the island. I can pick out details on the shore now: colours of pebbles becoming clearer, outlines of bushes and shrubs revealing shapes of leaves. I glance up, looking for the pagodas. I'm passing the point, leaving the river and entering the sea. There are proper waves here and as they hit, the canoe rocks, salty water drenching me.

I hear the roar of the powerboat. The white boat comes out of the rain fast. From my angle all I can see is the underbelly of the pointed bow. I can't see who is driving it. And I know they can't see me. The boat appears to be coming straight at me, like an arrow. I have no time to get out of the way. No time to shout.

45

Billy's voice breaks the silence. 'Eva.'

I must be imagining it. My throat is aching with thirst. My tongue sticks to the roof of my mouth.

'Eva.'

I lick my lips and turn my head slowly, blinking in the early-morning light. I'm alive. The bottle gleams by my face. A shadow falls across me. I sense movement against the side of the pit. Raising myself onto my elbows, I turn my head to see a rope dangling. I heave myself into a sitting position, my head throbbing. Billy is leaning over, staring down at me, his face red and distorted by the angle. He gestures towards the rope. 'Grab it.'

It's difficult to stagger onto my feet: every bone aches, every muscle pulls, tight as a corkscrew. Hobbling over to the rope, I try to tie it around my middle, but my hands fumble, fingers numb and useless, and I whimper in frustration. Billy shouts down instructions and eventually I manage. I cling to the rope, slumping against it. My feet leave the ground and I'm heaved up in unsteady lurches, clamped around the straining fibre, the rope biting into my waist. I scrabble with my knees and feet against the concrete, and the rope turns, creaking, so that I flail from side to side. I can hear him above me grunting with effort.

When I appear above the edge, he reaches out with one hand to grasp my jumper. He has to drag me out of the pit; I have no strength to help him. I sprawl across the cold ground at the edge of the drop, the rope coiled under me. The first things I see are the dead withered grasses of my sweeping sticks. Billy sinks down next to me, pulling me across his lap, breathing heavily.

'I'm sorry,' he's saying, his voice thick. 'I'm so sorry.'

He's wet. His clothes are soaking. Water dribbles onto my face, dripping from his hair. He has his arms around me and I can't speak. Shaking my head I curl up in his arms. 'I thought you'd left me,' I manage to say.

He rocks me against him. The stink of him is comforting, familiar. 'Are you hurt?' he asks. I shake my head again.

'You were lying so still,' he says, 'Eva, I thought I'd killed you.'

'I wanted to die,' I tell him.

He hands me a bottle of water and I drink it greedily, letting it spill across my chin. 'I never meant to let go,' he says. 'I don't know what happened. I went blank.'

I'm too exhausted to move. We stay where we are, Billy sitting with me sprawled on his lap. He slumps over me. 'You're all I've got,' he murmurs and he touches my cheek. I listen to the sound of the waves and rain outside and the rasp of his breathing.

'I don't know who I've got,' I say. 'Just before the accident, I found out that my real mother is dead. Mum and Dad didn't tell me. They let me think that they're my real parents. All this time.'

He is silent. I hear his stomach rumble, the rub of his parchment lips, and I think he didn't hear me; then he asks, 'Were they cruel?'

'No!' I'm shocked, sitting up.

'So they loved you, looked after you?'

'Yes,' I admit. 'But they should have told me . . . '

'Why?' He narrows his eyes. 'Maybe they had their reasons.'

'But I don't know who my real parents are . . . '

'Real parents?' He shakes his head. 'They're your real parents — the ones who took care of you. The rest is just biology.'

After a while he says, 'How did you find out?'

I tell him about Robert and what happened that night. I didn't think that I'd be able to speak of it to anyone. I don't recount it very well. I talk without thinking or shaping anything or even trying to make sense. It just is. As I tell him about it, he tightens his arms around me until he's gripping me hard, his chin pressing against my head, and his breathing changes, becomes louder, but he doesn't say anything. He listens without interrupting until I've finished.

Then Billy gets up, unfolding his body stiffly. He shakes his head, and he frowns into his beard. 'Maybe I didn't understand,' he says, tapping his fingers against his forehead. 'I got it wrong. I wasn't there when I was supposed to be.'

He's walking up and down the pagoda, marching like he must have done in the army, and he's muttering angrily to himself. I don't know what he's talking about. My chest hurts and I'm tired. He must have remembered to fetch in the blankets from outside before it rained. I crawl onto them, pulling one of them over me. I can smell the honeyed yellow of gorse flowers. I close my eyes, shifting on the hard floor to find a patch on my side that isn't sore. He lies down behind me and I'm grateful for the warmth of him close against my back. His heart thuds against my spine. He holds me, one arm heavy across my waist. 'You're going to be someone,' he says, his voice muffled against me. The vibrations of his voice passing into my bones. 'You'll be a painter. Like you want to be. An artist. Don't forget. It's important.'

After a while, he moves away, standing up. My back feels cold without him. He leans down. 'I'm going to check the traps,' he says. 'You must be starving.'

I watch him leave the pagoda, seeing the rain falling in sheets outside through the openings at the top. I can hear it on the pebbles. I remember that I heard the rain last night as I lay in the pit, and how the sound of it had seemed lonely and strangely human.

46

The powerboat cuts past in a streak of white. Its wake crashes towards me. The canoe flips upside-down in a quick twist. I'm in the river, water shooting up my nose and into my mouth.

A roaring noise. I'm falling through inky darkness. Gritty clouds swirl around me. I begin to flail with my arms and legs. I can see light above, the paler world of sky and air. But I can't reach it.

A dark shadow slides across the light: a pointed nose. The canoe. I stretch up towards it, break the surface, my lungs igniting. I fill them with oxygen. Waves slap my face, wash over my head. Rain beats down. In the distance boats bob, a flutter of faraway sails, a sliver of land. And then I'm sinking again. I'm too heavy. The water wants me, pulls me under with wet hands. I can't see anything. But I feel things flitting around me: fins and scales, the brush of wings, a sweep of tail.

Something closes around my arm. Fingers tight on my skin. I am being pulled towards the light. It grows brighter and brighter until it bursts open. I find the cold relief of air in my lungs. I am coughing. There is an arm around my neck, solid and unyielding: I struggle and the arm tightens so that I can't breathe. I let myself go limp and my legs float up behind me.

My mouth slips under water and I swallow

and cough. Panicking, I push my hand through water and grasp a soft handful of liquid earth and round shapes of stones. I kick my legs and they strike ground too. I am half-crawling now. The arm is still around my neck. When it lets go I'm on my hands and knees in the shallows, cold water lapping at me.

I look up. A man crouches over me. He is panting, dripping with water. I can't see his face; he's covered in dark, thick hair. The skin that I glimpse between the hair is waxy and bluish. A tangle of beard moves. He's speaking, but I can't understand him. I remember that they cut out his tongue. He reaches waterlogged fingers to me.

47

Clara is sick of the rain. She turns away from the sight of it at the window, but she can't get away from the noise: the battering, claustrophobic sound. It feels as though it wants to take over the house, washing away human and man-made things, dragging them back to the ocean. This part of the country is under sea-level; walls can only buy time, hold back the ocean for a little while longer. It is useless, she thinks, useless to fight it. Water is insidious, powerful, corrupting.

She puts the radio on as a distraction, fiddling with the dial to find a channel that she wants to listen to. She switches through programmes, unable to settle on anything. Wincing at a sudden blast of static, she turns it off. Clara makes herself another cup of tea and leaves it to go cold on the side while she tidies the kitchen, tripping over the dog, picking up breakfast debris, cleaning surfaces, brushing toast crumbs into the bin. She has just opened a letter from the estate agent. Apparently the surveyor's report hadn't been good. The prospective buyer has made a lower offer to take into consideration the fact that the roof needs serious work, and there is a damp problem in the cellar. 'Of course there's damp in the cellar,' Clara says aloud, 'we practically live in a marsh!' The cellar floods several times a year. Black mould furs the whitewashed walls, paint peeling away. Green slime creeps across the floor. They can't store anything down there.

Sophie hasn't come to help clear up. She must have overslept. Clara had been almost relieved when she didn't show up. But now she feels irritated. Sophie has overslept several times and often neglects to finish her jobs. She's not pulling her weight. Clara goes up the stairs, passing the few half-filled boxes strewn across the hall. She's not sure what she will say to Sophie, but something must be said.

Clara knocks on Sophie's door. She waits, her mouth dry. There is no answer. Clara knocks again and turns the handle. The bed is unmade, covers spilling out in a tangle. All the drawers hang open, sticking out at different angles. There are screwed up papers, old magazines and dirty plates on the floor. Clara walks over to push the drawers back into place and realises that they are empty. She goes to the wardrobe. Inside, naked hangers dangle in the gloom. There is one pair of muddy shoes abandoned in the corner.

Clara's heart is beating fast. She hurries onto the landing, checks the bathroom. A tap drips in the basin. She runs downstairs, looking into every room, calling Sophie's name. The house is filled only with the sound of rain. Clara walks back up the stairs slowly. She goes into Eva's room and sits on the bed, picks up the teddy and holds it tightly, hugging it to her belly.

Water runs down the windowpanes: a liquid glaze, twisting open, weaving shut. Clara stares at it, pressing her cheek against the toy's patchy head. Sophie has gone. Clara shakes her head.

351

Why would she sneak away in the night? If she'd wanted to leave, she only had to tell them. Clara gets up and paces the floor. She will have to call the agency. Explain what has happened. They must check that Sophie is safe. She feels a chill wash over her. She shivers, an unexplained panic starting up inside. Something is wrong. Eva's jewellery box is open. Clara pushes her fingers through the mess of broken earrings and cheap bracelets. The velvet pouch with the pearls inside is missing.

With shaking fingers, Clara stares around the bedroom; she begins to search through drawers and inside the wardrobe, realising that Eva's best woollen coat is no longer hanging in the wardrobe and neither is her battered leather jacket; a Lalique vase that she and Max bought for her in Paris has been taken from the mantelpiece. Clara thinks a mohair jumper has gone from the drawer. A purple one that Eva liked to wear with red trousers. Clara sits again, her legs giving beneath her. She feels nauseous.

She breathes deeply, trying to control the fury that is tearing through her insides. They are just things, she tells herself, just objects. None of them contained Eva — the essence and life of her — did they? Clara bites her lip, covers her face with her hands and moans. All this time Sophie had been a stranger in their home. They never knew her. Clara rubs her forehead, feeling the nagging pain of a migraine beginning. Everyone is a stranger. We can never know another person. Not really. People are full of contradictions. That's why we look for certainty, she thinks with sudden clarity, because we need to shore ourselves up against the terrible uncertainty of everything.

And what about Eva? When she found out about being adopted, it would have destroyed all certainty. Isn't she, Clara, worse than a thief? She stole Eva's past from her, her parentage. And she stole her security, her knowledge of herself.

She walks downstairs to the hall on hollow legs, gripping the banister as the steps blur and move beneath her. She will have to phone Max and tell him about Sophie. She'll have to call the agency, perhaps even the police. As she reaches the telephone it begins to ring. Surprised, Clara stands for a second, staring at it. She picks up the receiver cautiously.

'Hello,' says a voice she doesn't recognise. 'I'm calling from St Mark's Primary. Faith Gale wasn't at registration this morning and we haven't had a call from her parents. Is this Mrs Gale I'm speaking to?'

48

The Wild Man leads me across the island. I'm cold, shivering. He walks quickly without waiting and I have to run to keep up with him. My feet splash through puddles, slipping on mud. He's taking me towards the pagodas. We crunch through shingle, stepping over straggling wire onto the old concrete road. He hurries along, avoiding the craters filled with twisted metal, drifts of rubble and broken glass. He doesn't look behind. We pass deserted huts with empty windows and bits of old machinery left to rust in the grass. There is no sign of life anywhere. Not even a rabbit.

When we come to the first pagoda he stands back to let me go first. Rain slides down my face, falling from the end of my nose, trickling into my mouth. I hesitate and he gestures impatiently with his hand. Mesh doors hang open on broken hinges. I move, stumbling over the high doorstep to get into the building. There's a narrow corridor and I wait while he unlocks a door, pushes me ahead of him into a big room.

'Look what I dragged out of the sea,' he says as he comes in behind me, closing the door.

I blink in the gloom, shivering. A bundle of rags in the corner stirs and out of the lumpy shapes, a creature sits up slowly. It makes a strange noise — half-cry, half-sob — and holds out its arms towards me. 'Faith,' I hear it croak. 'Faith. Is that you?'

I feel as though I'm in a dream. But the child walking across the pagoda is real. She crouches before me, staring with round eyes, and I can see that she's drenched, hair and clothes water-darkened and dripping. She is shivering. I reach out with trembling fingers to touch her face. Her skin is cold. 'What are you doing here?' I can hardly speak.

She throws herself into my arms, the damp, dense weight of her nearly knocking me backwards. I'm buried in her neck, my lips on her salty skin. She smells of the sea, and under that, she smells of home. She pulls back to look at me. 'Eva.' She fingers my hair, pats my cheek. 'I knew you'd be here. I knew.'

I glance over at Billy. He's leaning against the wall staring at us and I can't see his face, can't guess what he's thinking.

'It's my sister,' I tell him. 'This is my sister.'

'He rescued me,' Faith says, her voice a low buzz against my ear. 'I fell in.'

'My God.' I clasp her to me; the wings of her shoulder blades push through her school blazer. 'She can't swim.' Icy strands of her hair get into my mouth. I rub along the bony ridge of her spine to try and warm her.

'What are we going to do?' I look at him over her shoulder, trying to see his expression.

He shrugs. 'I'll get the Primus going. Get something to eat.'

'You don't understand,' I say, 'they'll be looking for her.'

Faith is silent, hugging me tightly, her cheek pressed against my chest. 'You're thin,' she says. I move my hands across her head, stroking her tangled hair. Her body convulses in shudders, her teeth chattering behind blue lips, and I think it must be shock, or even hypothermia.

'Give me your blanket,' I tell him, 'she's so cold.'

After a moment, Billy stoops and gathers up his coat, comes over and squats by us. He drapes it around her, staring at Faith's white face. 'You came for her? Your sister.'

Faith nods.

'You knew she wasn't dead?' He touches Faith. 'You can see things, can't you?'

She shrinks away from him. I wrap his coat around her, the familiar musty stink of wool. 'But what are you going to do?' I look at Billy. 'Someone will have reported her missing by now. The police might have been called. The coastguard. There'll be a search.'

He's moved further away, standing at the other side of the pagoda. But he seems to be in a daze, mesmerised by Faith. Through spasms of shivering, she's begun to hum, her voice vibrating against my ribs. It's one of her old songs. Her comfort music. I murmur, 'It's all right, Shrimp. It's going to be OK.' I get up slowly, leaving her on the floor so that I can get closer to Billy.

She keeps humming, and I remember fairy lights flickering on green leaves. Lemon cake and foxtrots around vegetable beds. Jack and Granny holding each other close.

'Billy . . . ' I need him to understand, shake

him out of his dream. 'Somebody will come . . . '

He holds up a hand to silence me. 'I wasn't a coward, Eva.' He's alert again, and he takes hold of my arm, tugging me closer, staring into my face urgently. 'When they wanted to send me back after I killed her, after the trial, I would have been a target for the IRA. But that wasn't the reason I deserted. It wasn't about me being afraid.' He's squeezing me so tightly that it hurts. 'I couldn't let them use me again. You see that don't you?' His eyes are wide. I see myself caught inside his pupils, tadpole-like, staring back. 'Tell me you understand.'

I nod. He releases my arm, his shoulders slumping. 'You should go.' He tilts his head towards Faith. 'Take her. Go to the shore. They'll see you.'

'Come with us,' I say. 'You can get help. You can sort it out.'

He shakes his head. Faith has shuffled around the edge of the pit, his coat trailing behind her. She slips her hand into mine. Pulls at me. 'Eva. I don't like it here.'

Billy looks at me. 'Go.'

'No.' I bite my lip. 'Please. Come with us. You can't keep running.'

'It isn't finished yet,' he says, 'not for me.' He leans close. 'It's all right, Eva. I heard her.' He smiles. 'She came back. I was filled with her voice — more than a voice. It was like sunlight, water, something that gets into every corner. And I know what to do. She told me.'

When Faith and I step outside the rain has turned to a misty drizzle. There is the crash of waves, the shift of wind across pebbles. Terns cry overhead. It feels strange to be leaving him. As Faith and I walk along the concrete road hand in hand, I hear feet crunching through shingle, and my heart skips a beat. But he's not coming after us; he's walking in the other direction towards the opposite shore, to the open ocean. He trudges up the incline towards the gorse bushes, head down. He doesn't look back. 'Where is he going?' Faith asks me.

'To the sea,' I tell her.

'Oh, of course.' She turns to stare at him.

'Faith,' I squeeze her hand, look at her closely, 'we won't tell them about him. Not at first, anyway.'

I don't look over my shoulder at the square concrete block with the concrete pillars and strangely shaped roof. The image of it is imprinted on my mind. I won't be able to forget the smell: rust and earth and damp, the stink of the pit and its hollow loneliness. My drawings will stay there, shaping our story for anyone that wants to see. The last one an angel with spreading wings. At the shore, I shade my eyes, looking through the drizzle towards the cloudy mainland.

PART TWO

FOUND

49

When Clara opens the front door she finds her eldest daughter before her, wrapped in an old coat, her arm around her sister, smiling her wide, gap-toothed smile. The one that Clara gazes at in photographs, recalls in dreams, thinking she'll never see again. Eva coughs, straggly hair falling across her face, and Clara grasps the wood of the frame, knuckles whitening, as if trying to hold on to the fact itself. Her lost child is alive.

'Eva?' Her voice trembles.

Max appears from the hall. He makes one sound, the noise crushed in his chest, and Eva straightens, trying to smile at him, wiping her mouth with the back of her hand. To Clara, it seems that the air sings, webbing them together, pulling light around their family as they stand in the doorway, half in and half out of the house, staring at each other. A part of her brain tells her that she will remember this moment for ever, and the moment itself seems to slow and crystallise. It has stopped raining and the world is full of green scents and soft mist. Water glitters on leaves and grass, and inside the tangles in Eva's hair.

Faith clutches her sister's hand and grins with excitement. Clara is vaguely aware of Ted standing on the garden path. But all her attention is on her girls, pulling every detail into her hungry gaze. She and Max step forward at the same time, blundering against each other in the narrow doorway, elbows and shoulders colliding as they gather both their daughters between them. There are no words, just strangled sounds of surprise and relief escaping from throats. Clara rubs her mouth against the textures of her children, hugging them close, wanting to pack them inside her ribs, absorb them through her skin. Faith pushing up under her shoulder, Eva's cheek pressed next to her own, slick with tears.

*　*　*

Seeing Mum and Dad again, the pain on their faces, how can I be angry? I can't reach back beyond the time on the island to find my old self, my old reactions to their lie. I don't want to. Everything is different now. I missed them, longed for them every moment I'd been away. Mum is crying. We all are, laughing and crying, and we're hugging each other on the doorstep. I'm held inside a tangle of limbs and skin and kisses. Their smells and shapes are familiar and strange, less and more than I'd remembered. They look tired, Dad paler, more stooped than before, and Mum thinner, tanned and untidy. They keep hugging me close and then holding me at arm's length, fingers gripping my arms, staring at me as if I'm a precious, exotic bird that will fly away if they let go.

Inside the house, I can't take it all in. We go into the sitting room, which somehow seems smaller. Colours are overwhelming, vivid, insisting. Silver is going crazy, leaping at me, his eyes bright, tail beating in a frenzy of love. His claws scratch my legs. Then Faith is leading him away and I can hear his muffled barking from the kitchen. Mum drapes me in a blanket, wraps it tightly, and I smell the clean blue of our washing detergent. All around me, forgotten scents are making my nose itch. I'm inhaling coffee, carpet, perfume, dog. Dad fetches a bottle of brandy from the cabinet, sloshes it into glasses. I smell that too, rich and sharp at the back of my throat.

Ted has come in, and he's sitting in an armchair, holding up a hand to take a glass from Dad. He's talking, sipping his drink. 'A man from one of the moorings . . . young girl alone and heading towards the sea . . . red canoe.' Ted scratches his knee with blunt fingers. 'Checked the dinghy park . . . ' He winks at Faith. 'I'd glimpsed young trouble here in the rain earlier this morning playing truant . . . '

I'm trying to listen. The sounds are too loud. It's been a long time since I heard voices. Billy and I were silent a lot. He talked quietly. My world has been watery, wind-blown, wide. These words clatter inside my head.

'So I headed straight to the island. Had a hunch I'd find her,' he looks at me, 'but I hadn't expected the two of them. They'd been standing hand in hand, just as if they'd been waiting for me.'

I sit on the arm of the sofa. My legs too weak to hold me. Both Mum and Dad are asking me questions and I try to answer. My teeth won't stop chattering even though I don't feel cold. 'A man,' I manage. 'He found me. Saved my life

363

and then he wouldn't let me go.' I can't breathe. The air is suffocating. I pull the blanket away from my neck. 'He kept me in the pagoda . . .' Billy. My throat closes. A sob escapes, hard, fierce. More are swelling through me. And then Mum is holding me and crying too and telling me that I don't have to do this now. 'Later,' she's saying, 'take all the time you need. Hush.'

'I'm going to phone the police.' Dad's face hardens ; his mouth dips and wavers. 'They need to get over there.'

'Shall I run you a bath, darling?' Mum asks, patting my arm.

I nod. 'I'd like to see my room.'

'We kept it exactly as you left it.' Mum hugs me again, wincing. 'You're so thin,' she whispers. 'Are you hungry? What would you like?'

I am tired, drained. It feels odd, walking back into my old life. Objects are the same but I'm different, and so they are too. I need to be alone. I can hear Mum calling out to Faith, telling her to give me a moment. The door shuts behind me. I lean against it, looking around. The mirror on my dressing table shines, the glass flickering with reflections of the room. I hold my breath as I come closer and the frame fills: a human swimming towards me.

Above the pots of make-up, nail varnishes and jewellery, a wild girl looks back. A face full of bones, the cut of angles, skin stretched tight. Her eyes huge inside dark hollows. A filthy, matted tangle of hair flops across the girl's face, reaching down her back in twisted curls and dreadlocks. I blink and lean closer until my breath mists the reflection. I feel the cold of the glass touch my lips, sit back and put my hands to my face, running my fingers over the living warmth of nose and cheeks. It is my face, my eyes looking out of the mirror with the feral glitter of an animal's. I see Billy there. His features hover above my own, the lines and planes of his face touching mine like an echo.

50

I had to stay in hospital. They said I'd had pneumonia and was suffering from malnutrition. They stuck a drip in my arm. The hospital ward was loud with the clatter of voices. Sounds from the outside pressed at the windows: traffic, horns and sirens. Even at night there was an underlying hum, the machinery of the place ticking over: generators and engines. It hurt my ears. The sheets were clean. Their crisp edges felt raw against my newly scrubbed skin.

Reporters wanted to speak to me, but Dad wouldn't let them. The police came. I answered their questions about Billy. I thought that it would be better if they found him. Maybe they would help him; he could stop running. Everyone asked me if he'd hurt me: the police, the doctors, Dad. They had a particular look on their faces when they asked me. I shook my head. At night, as I listened to the nurses padding efficiently across the floor and their whispered exchanges, I wondered where Billy was and how long it would be before they caught up with him.

There was a manhunt the day I was found, locals joining the police in looking for Billy. Dad went too. I begged him not to. His mouth tightened. 'He needs to be found, Eva. What he's done is unforgiveable.' Dad's voice broke as he crushed me to him, the boom and swell of his heart hard against my ribs. 'I need to do this.' He looked at me, his eyes bright. 'I'll be back soon.'

Dad returned hours later, muddy, tired and dispirited. The hunt had been fruitless.

★ ★ ★

Today Mum and Dad are bringing me home from hospital, and it feels like one of the dreams I had on the island. As we walk up the garden path, I stare at the house. There's a glint of autumn sun on the windows. Nothing has changed: still the worn, pale texture of the brick and the twist of wisteria that grows over the front door, everything exactly as I'd imagined for all those months. Silver is barking. As soon as we open the door he throws himself at me, dinosaur paws on my chest, almost knocking me over. His mouth opens in a smile, his amber eyes looking into mine.

'Well,' Mum laughs. 'That's it. I'll be second best now that you're back.'

The house, which all my life has seemed cold and full of drafts, encloses me in safe, thick, windproof walls. It still amazes me that I turn a tap and there is fresh water to drink, hot water to wash in. My back aches from the softness of mattresses. I've been told to introduce different foods into my diet gradually because everything is too rich for my stomach. I am bewildered by the choices that are suddenly available to me, the demands they make. Sometimes I begin to panic and I have to close my eyes and imagine that I'm back on the island. I breathe deeply, remembering the sounds of the sea, wind on shingle, wings unfolding.

My bedroom is different from how I'd remembered: smaller, scruffier. More childish. I touch things, trailing my fingers across the crystal desert rose, trying on armfuls of bangles, fingering the clothes in my drawers. They don't seem to belong to me anymore. I hug my old teddy, standing at the window to look across the garden and the marshes towards the sea. The island is a dark mass, between sky and horizon. One day, probably when I'm very old or dead, the island will disappear. The pagoda will be swallowed by water, starfish clinging to the rusting pipes, shoals of fish flitting through the interior, fins brushing my cave-drawings, wearing away the story of Billy and me.

Faith knocks at the door. She comes in slowly, looking up under her pale hair, suddenly shy. I pat the bed and we sit cross-legged on the cover, grinning at each other. 'I can't believe you're really here,' she says.

'Well, get used to it,' I tell her. 'I'm not going anywhere again. Not for a long time.'

'Eva.' She stretches out a hand to touch me, her fingers a whisper against my skin. I bite my lip, thinking how odd, we share not a drop of blood. But we've grown up together, inhabit the same memories, love the same parents, and we love each other. It has to be enough. She is my sister. I'm sure they haven't told her about me. She would have said something. Faith can't hide things from me. I wonder if I should tell her. But I can't face it. Not yet. I reach out and give her a hug. 'You were very brave you know, coming to find me.' I press my mouth against the ticklish strands of her hair. 'I'll never forget it.'

'What about Marco?' She pulls back, looking at me earnestly. 'I've got his address.'

'Have you?' I'm surprised by the sound of his name. By Faith remembering him. I shake my head. 'It's over, Faith. I don't want to talk about it.'

She looks disappointed. 'But why is it over? He came to the river. He loves you.'

'Really? Well,' I force a smile, 'I'm not the same person. Just leave it, Faith. All right?'

'He'll know though,' she mutters. 'It's in the papers. So he'll know that you didn't drown. He'll know you're home.'

I push her off the bed, just like I would have done before. She sprawls on the floor, mouth open. And then she grins up at me.

'You need to take an interest in your own life.' I raise my eyebrows. 'What have you been doing with yourself all these months? Learnt any new waltzes or Charlestons?'

'Granny and Jack aren't here to teach me.' She scrunches her nose. 'Idiot.'

We're playing a game now, finding a shared way of being, remembering the rhythms of it. This is how we are together. It's like a dance.

'Ever heard of a thing called classes?' I put my hands on my hips. 'Ask Mum to enrol you in some. You're good, Faith. You have talent.'

Of course I do think about Marco. Faith is probably right. He'll read about me in the papers, or he'll hear it from someone else. There is a part of me that expects him to contact me.

Newspapers love stories like mine: kidnappings,

369

people coming back from the dead. Several of the papers have rung up offering money for my exclusive story. Dad told them to leave me alone, but in private he says that if I ever feel like telling my side of things and earning some cash for my future then we can talk about it, choose the right newspaper or even find a publishing deal. 'But not yet,' he says. 'Give yourself time to adjust. To be at home.' He's treating me like an adult at last. It feels good. But I still have to ask him what happened when I was a baby. How they became my parents. There's so much to deal with, too many tangled feelings.

The newspapers are full of Billy. My 'evil kidnapper'. There are photos of him in his uniform staring out of front pages. One article says that Billy had an impeccable career up until the moment of the shooting. Popular with his fellow soldiers, he'd acted 'out of character' during the tragic mistaken shooting of civilians at a check-point. He was found not guilty by a military court and had been deemed fit to return to duty in Northern Ireland. After that Billy had absconded from a local barracks and disappeared into thin air. Depending on the paper, he's 'deranged', 'a survival expert', 'a danger to society' or 'mentally scarred'. I stare at his photograph and see an ordinary young man, clean-shaven and smart in his uniform. He looks into the camera with a serious expression. Puzzled, I search for the Billy that I know inside the grainy print eyes staring back.

It's raining again. I lie in the comfort of my bed and listen to the sound of water drumming on glass. I imagine the creeks and mud pools in the marshes seeping full, and how the ground in the dark garden will be softened and turned to mud in the downpour. The sea is crashing against the shingle beaches of the island. I know that the walls of the pagoda are damp and chilled, shadows moving as birds settle inside the opening under the roof, looking for shelter.

Where is Billy? The island has been searched. The whole area is crawling with police. Sometimes I wonder if he attempted to cross the Channel in his boat and drowned. I tell myself it's more likely that he's disappeared into the woods or the marshes, sleeping rough, scavenging scraps, hunkering down in a new hiding place. Or perhaps he's got away from Suffolk and is heading north to where he came from. Maybe there'll be a friend or relative there that will offer him shelter. I twist the sheet in my fingers, unable to sleep.

There is a noise outside. It sounds like the clatter of a dustbin lid. I freeze under the blankets, ears straining to hear it again. I think I hear soft, stealthy movement. Feet on sodden ground. I get up and make my way across the moonlit floor to the window. I pull back the curtain and stare down into the pitchy depths of the garden. I can't see anything. My first thought is that it might be Billy and my heart leaps. But then I put my hand over my mouth because a certainty fills me: Robert Smith is down there. The thought makes me sick. I drop the curtain, stepping back from the window. I don't know what to do because even if he isn't in my garden knocking over dustbin lids, sooner or later I will see him, step-ping out from under the bus shelter, stopping beside me on his moped. He'll always be there, with his knowing eyes and his leer. And I don't think I can bear it.

51

They said that it wasn't the Wild Man that had taken Eva. It was someone called Billy. But I recognised him as soon as I saw him on the island: the face from the river, from my dreams, hundreds of years old. They'll never find him. He's not from this world. He's disappeared into the river again, dark and invisible as a seal.

The police asked Eva lots of questions about him, but they had to do it in hospital because she was ill. We all visited her there, bringing little treats for her to eat and sitting by her bedside. She seemed different: quieter, sadder. Her eyes watched everything, wary and alert. She reminded me of a deer in a forest clearing. Mum cried on the way home after the hospital visits, sobbing in the front seat, and Dad leaned across and put his hand on her knee. She and Dad had discussions behind closed doors at home.

*   *   *

I had some time off school. Then it was back to normal. I went through the gates into the playground on the first day with my satchel on my hip, keeping my head down like always. But straight away a crowd gathered around me. They wanted to know what had happened, all the details. I felt like a hero. People were nice to me. Teachers as well. I was treated as if I was important. Kids in my class wanted to sit next to me and talk to me, even the ones who usually ignored me. At lunch I was invited onto three different tables at the same time.

The only people who didn't come over were Joanna and Ellie. They stayed away, sulking in corners, shooting dark looks in my direction. At the end of the day I found them whispering together in the hallway. It looked as though Joanna had been crying. I stopped to ask her what was wrong.

'None of your business,' Joanna said, her eyes pink-rimmed.

'It's her cousin,' Ellie said, her arm around Joanna's shoulder. 'Her cousin has gone missing.'

'Who's her cousin?'

'You know,' Ellie whispered, 'Robert. Robert Smith. Nobody knows where he is.'

I frown. 'Maybe he went off with my au pair. She's gone too. And they were . . . going out together I think.'

'Don't be daft,' Joanna said. 'He'd never go off with her. He hates foreign food and that. And anyway, he disappeared last night when he was on his way to see a mate. They found his moped and helmet just abandoned on the side of the road. He loves that bike. He'd never leave it with the keys in it.'

'He'll come back,' Ellie said soothingly to Joanna. She turned to me and raised her eyebrows, gave a wink.

I remembered Robert standing over me on the wet garden path. Most of all I remembered his naked bottom, hair at the base of his spine like a tail.

★ ★ ★

After school I find Mum, Dad and Eva waiting for me in the kitchen. Dad has made a cake. I can smell cherries and the buttery scent of warm sponge. Mum is pacing around the table, riddling with her ring and her watch, clasping and unclasping her hands. Silver is in his basket; he twitches his tail when he sees me, thumping it against the flagstones.

Dad clears his throat loudly and motions for us to sit down. 'Mum and I have something to tell you. It's something we should have told both of you, a long time ago.'

Eva and I pull out chairs at one side of the table and Mum and Dad settle on the other. It's the four of us again, all together, just like I'd wanted it to be; but it feels wrong, stiff and formal like an old-fashioned painting. I'm frightened. I look up at Eva for support, but she doesn't take her eyes off a scratch on the table. Dad clears his throat.

'After we got married,' he says, 'Mum and I wanted to start a family. We wanted a baby very much. But it didn't happen. There were pregnancies. But . . . ' he glances across at Mum, 'we lost the babies.'

Mum blinks, looks at Eva and away. For a second I imagine Mum and Dad absent-mindedly leaving babies behind, in supermarkets, by the river, on a train. But then I know they mean that the babies are dead and I can't understand how that happened and I want to ask if they died in Mum's womb and why. Only Dad is already saying something else. 'Then I met a young woman called Suky who was unmarried and pregnant.' Dad rubs his nose. 'She wanted us to have her baby. That baby was Eva.'

'And she died?' Eva asks in a small voice. 'My mother?'

Dad nods. 'I'm sorry.'

Eva has balled her hands up on the table and she's digging her nails into her skin. 'So that girl, Suky. She was definitely my mother?' Eva frowns. 'My real mother?'

Dad coughs, as if he's choking on a cake crumb, except he isn't eating any. He leans across the table. 'Yes,' he says, 'Suky was your mother.' He reaches out to touch Eva's hands. 'She died soon after you were born.'

'It's my fault that we didn't tell you that you were adopted.' Mum is talking very fast. 'Dad wanted to tell you. But I felt you were my own.' Her voice jerks and wobbles. 'I didn't want you or anyone else to ever think you didn't belong to us, to our family.' Her nose is red and she struggles to get more words out. 'That . . . that we didn't love you exactly as we love your sister.'

Dad looks at me and Eva, his eyebrows pulling together. 'You can ask us anything you like.'

'Why didn't my mother want me?' Eva's voice seems to come from a long way off.

'Oh, darling.' Mum's eyes brim and spill over. 'She didn't want to give you away! I know she loved you.'

I shift on my chair, push my thumbs against the edge of the table.

Mum folds her hands under her chin, as if she's praying. 'But she was only a little older than you are now.' She's hunched over, looking straight at Eva. She doesn't seem to notice tears sliding down her cheeks. 'With no support, no family to look after her, she didn't have a choice.'

'Things were very different in the sixties,' Dad says. 'The place she was in, the home for unmarried mothers . . . ' He breaks off, frowning. 'It wasn't a kind place. Your mother and I have always felt lucky, but at the same time . . . I don't know, guilty I suppose, to have been given you.'

'Guilty?' Eva sits up straight. 'You did steal me then?'

Mum lets out a sound like air punched from a stomach. 'No! No, it was an adoption. Suky. Your mother. She agreed. And your uncle.'

'Things were not well-documented I'm afraid.' Dad hangs his head, his voice low. 'It's always been a fear, that someone from your mother's family could try and claim you.'

Eva stares at her hands again. 'Not now though,' she says slowly. 'I can live with who I want now, can't I?'

Dad nods. I notice that he has taken Mum's fingers in his. I stare at all three of them, examining the details of their faces. I can see things that I always knew but had never properly considered: Eva is everything I'm not — dark and beautiful and strong. We couldn't possibly be related by blood. She bends over the table, gazing at the little red marks she's dug into her hands. I'm afraid that she's going to get up and leave, go and find her other family. Even if her mother is dead, she'll have relations, uncles, cousins, grannies and grandpas maybe, people that don't have anything to do with me or Mum and Dad. I feel panicky at the thought. It makes Eva seem far away again. I want to say something to make her stay. My mind is blank and I can feel myself getting hotter and hotter.

'What did my mother look like?'

I sigh, air rushing out of my lungs. Eva hasn't jumped up and run away; she stays in her chair, elbows on the table, asking more questions that Mum and Dad don't seem to know how to answer. Dad says that Eva has an uncle in Berkshire, and that they can contact him, that he should be able to answer more questions about Suky. He nods at Eva. 'You've met him already, haven't you? Wasn't he the person who told you about the adoption?'

Eva swallows, and I feel her stiffen. 'No,' she says, 'no I never met him.'

'But then,' Dad frowns, 'who told you?'

'Someone in the village.' Eva shifts on her chair. 'That man, my uncle, I think he said something to the barman at the pub the day he came to see me. When I was a baby.'

'Village gossip.' Mum looks pale. 'Does everyone know?'

'It doesn't matter,' Dad says. 'We have nothing to be ashamed of. None of us do.'

Nobody is eating any of the cake. I sniff the sweetened air, my mouth watering. It's just a story, I realise. A story about Eva's beginnings, like something you'd find in a guidebook. A history. It isn't about today; it isn't about her real life with us, all those years we've been a family, growing up and arguing and doing things together, making memories.

'She's still my sister, isn't she?' I ask.

'Yes,' Mum says, wiping her eyes. 'Yes, of course she is.'

Eva turns. 'Do you want me to be?'

I nod, spitting on my hand and holding it out to her. She does the same. We clasp fingers, pressing wet palm against wet palm.

'One more thing,' Dad says. 'We have to decide if we sell the house or not.'

'Can we pull out now?' Mum looks surprised.

'Of course,' Dad says. 'It's our home. We can pay for the wretched surveyor. Reimburse their losses.'

We have a show of hands and all of us want to stay in Holt House. I can't imagine living somewhere else. I can't imagine not being able to hear the sea from my bedroom, see it from my window.

'Are you sure?' Mum asks Eva.

'This is home,' Eva says.

Dad cuts a huge slice of cake and puts it straight into his mouth, crumbs spilling across his chin, moist chunks of cherry falling onto the plate.

52

The ache inside is over. Clara sleeps soundly at night. She and Max roll into the same warm dip in the middle of the bed instead of clinging to the outer edges. They sleep pressed against each other, limbs entangled. There are no more dreams filled with the rustle of nun's habits, their thieving whispers and Eva's anguished cries.

Suky has gone. Clara is restored to herself; the boundaries of skin and self are intact and separate. Sometimes she thinks she sees the flutter of blonde hair at the edges of her vision, brightness in dark corners and shadows. When she is alone there is perhaps a faint echo remaining of a mother murmuring to her baby, half-songs and promises of love and protection.

Clara would like to be able to tell Eva about Suky. But she has no information, no facts, only the secret knowledge of her dreams. Max has suggested to Eva that they contact Charles. As her brother, he will have photograph albums, stories, perhaps a family tree to offer. But Eva seems reluctant to speak to Charles. 'Let her have time to think it through,' Max said. 'It's a lot to take on all at once. She's been through so much. And she's grown up, don't you think? She can make her own decisions.'

Clara watches Eva closely, looking for signs of trauma, the after-effects of her experience showing as damage. Eva is different. She is more considered, slower to anger, more self-reliant than she used to be. She doesn't seem frightened. She only gets angry when people say negative things about Billy. She is strangely protective of him. 'Must be Stockholm syndrome,' Max whispers, 'like Patty Hearst.' Clara thinks that this outcome has to be preferable to the alternatives. She refuses to think of what might have happened to Eva in that deserted concrete bunker. When she considers the young man who took Eva, Clara feels an odd sense of gratitude to him. He kept Eva safe. And in the end, he saved both her children's lives.

Eva's experience has given her a gravity, a weightedness. Her physical appearance is the opposite though and Clara is trying to put meat on her bones. She offers Eva regular meals, vitamins, hot drinks laced with fortifying powders. As she sits across a table from her girls, watching Eva and Faith together, being a family again, eating meals and talking, weaving moments out of simple everyday gestures, this seems to Clara to be what happiness is.

★ ★ ★

Max woke up with a memory of Eva clinging to the mast of the boat, wild water everywhere and her glaring down at him, spitting, 'I hate you.' The lifejacket orange and wet, tightly zipped, the belt knotted at her waist. He'd known it all along, his brain hiding that same memory from himself. The whole day is clear to him now, up

381

until the moment that the boat turned and something hit him on the back of the head. He recalls Eva's puffy eyes and sullen face. He should have asked her what was wrong, made her tell him. He'd wanted to get onto the water too much, was itching to have a sail, the first that year, and he hadn't heeded the warning signs: the darkening sky and restless waves. Worst of all he'd ignored Eva's strange expression, her silence.

Eva explained that Billy found her washed up on the beach. 'He saved my life,' she'd said. The man could have been a hero, Max thought; instead he'd thrown her lifejacket into the sea, holding her against her will in a damp, primitive place. Leaving her family to presume that she was dead. Billy was deliberately cruel. Wicked. Evil. Max repeats those words to himself.

Max's anger feels like a relief to him. After all these months of passive uncertainty, living with the corrupt, insinuating effects of guilt, the weight of his grief, he wants to take action — he wants to find Billy and punish him. He is a criminal. The police have let him slip through their fingers. Max reads every newspaper, frustrated when the articles about the kidnapping begin to dry up, replaced by more recent news. He keeps a box file full of clippings about Billy. He phones the local station daily, demanding to know what new information has come to light. He wanted to borrow a boat to go to the island, to see if he could find traces of the kidnapping himself, clues that will tell him where Billy is, but the island is out of bounds and Clara

382

begged him not to go. 'It will be upsetting. Disturbing. And you won't find anything the police haven't already uncovered.'

Eva comes into the study as he is re-reading an article about Billy's life before the army, the box file open on the table, a notepad full of his scribbles next to him. He hears her make a noise in her throat and looks up from the file, his hands curling into fists either side of the article.

'Stop it.' Eva bends forwards, snatching at the paper. His fingers grasp the edges automatically and there is a tearing; Eva stands flushed, holding a ripped section in her hand. 'What are you doing?' She screws the paper into a crumpled ball. 'Let it go. It's over. I'm home now — isn't that what matters?'

He rubs his forehead hard. 'Of course. Of course that's what matters.'

'So stop obsessing about Billy.'

Max flinches.

'You can't even hear his name, can you?'

Max runs his tongue over his teeth. 'I can't help it. It's how I feel — as a father. I want to kill him. When I think of you there . . . '

'No.' Eva slides into the chair next to him, flips his notepad closed, her hand spread across it.

'What kind of power did he have over you?' Max asks quietly. He struggles to control his voice. 'When you first came back to us, you were covered in bruises. Your back and hips black with them. And your ribs sticking out like a starving child . . . ' He feels a hard sob in his throat.

Eva places her fingers over his lips. They rest, light and cool, on his skin. 'I know what he did was . . . bad. But I'll never forgive you if you hurt him,' she says. 'You don't understand. Nobody does.' She swallows, sitting upright, looking away. 'It makes me feel alone.'

'I don't understand. You're right.' He bows his head. 'But I'll try to,' he promises her. 'And I'll try to let it go. For you.'

She isn't a child anymore, he realises. He reaches out to her, touching her newly cut hair. She doesn't move. He takes her chin in his hand and gently turns her head so that they're facing each other. Her eyes are bright, challenging.

'Did you hear me?' he asks quietly. 'I said I'd try.'

She nods and ducks her head to rest her cheek on his shoulder. Carefully, he puts his arms around her. He has to hold her differently now. The love is the same but rules and boundaries have changed. He remembers how she clung to him when she found the chick in the egg and knows that she'll never need him quite like that again. He shifts his position on the chair, accommodating the shape of her head, the strong line of her jaw.

53

Mum is unpacking some groceries from a brown paper bag. Milk. Bread. A bag of apples. She shakes her head. 'I've just heard something extraordinary.' She pauses and looks at me. 'Robert Smith is dead. It looks like he killed himself. They found him at the foot of the castle walls.'

Robert lies in long grass, his limbs contorted like a smashed puppet. His neck is broken, the spinal cord snapped. His eyes stare up at me, unseeing, filmed in dust. *Half-breed*, his dead lips whisper.

Billy. And the next thought that comes into my head is that he loves me that much. Enough to kill for me. I shut a door in my mind. The door to those thoughts. I must be a bad person. Robert is dead. I'm sorry. God. I'm sorry. I don't know whom I'm apologising to. I can't feel my feet. I stumble backwards into a chair, and my head slumps forwards, heavy in my hands. The room pitches and I close my eyes.

Mum is bending over me. Her voice comes from a distance. 'I'm sorry. How stupid to blurt it out like that.' She touches my shoulder. 'Darling. I would never have . . . I didn't think you knew him very well.'

I bite the inside of my lip, folding my hands together to stop them trembling. 'No.' I force my voice not to shake. 'It's just a bit of a shock. What happened?'

She's running the tap, filling a glass for me. She's talking, telling me that there's going to be an inquest. Apparently everyone in the village is gossiping about it. Some girl in Ipswich has gone to the police, claiming he raped her. Mum hands me the water and I take a sip; it trickles into my throat, cold and slightly earthy. She sighs, 'They're saying that it was probably fear or shame that made him do it — throw himself off like that.'

Robert wouldn't commit suicide. He wasn't the sort of person to feel shame. The police will work it out soon. I picture the struggle, shadows flickering across the dark roof, a hidden moon and Robert's desperate scrabbling against the ancient stone, the long drop below lurching towards him. Or perhaps he was already dead before he fell. His neck broken with a professional twist. I should feel something — guilt, sorrow.

Alone in my room, I stare out of the window at the garden, noticing the trees, alight with crimson, gold and orange leaves, blazing above shaded grass, the sun low over the horizon. I frown, concentrating, forcing myself to picture Robert, to find pity inside me. But what I feel is relief. He will never step out of the bus shelter with a smirk, or wait for me by the oak tree. He'll never touch me again. His eel tongue and searching fingers are done — they're cold flesh on a mortuary slab. Only the truth is that if I'd had to face up to Robert again, I think I would have handled it better now. I wish I could have told Billy that. I'm stronger because of him. Billy must have wanted to punish Robert as badly as

Dad wants to punish Billy. It's all mixed up in my head, making me feel crazy. When I told Billy about Robert, was I giving him a death sentence? I think so. Now I do. But I didn't know then. Did I?

It seems unreal. No court will let Billy go this time. I'm afraid for him. I stare into the mirror, but I don't see his face anymore. I'm returning to myself. I am clean, tamed, with my washed face, the knots and tangles of hair chopped out, so that it looks like it always used to, tight curls to my shoulders. The glitter in my eyes is less wolfish, less wild. It is a strange kind of loss.

'Eva?' Faith is standing by my door.

I nod and she comes in, throwing herself onto the bed to watch me. 'Are you putting on make-up?'

'No.' I turn and smile at her.

'Are you OK? You look sad.'

I get onto the bed with her, leaning against her slight shape. 'I am a bit sad. But it's hard to explain.' I take her hand and her fingers close around mine, squeezing. Her skin is smooth and warm against my own, and I look down in surprise. 'Your fingers?'

She smiles. 'The warts are gone. I just woke up one day. The day you came back. And they weren't there anymore.'

She leans over to pick up my sketchpad left open on the covers, and begins to leaf through it. It's filled with quick drawings made from memory in chalk and pencil. She stares down at the pagoda wreathed in mist; a clutch of tern's eggs in shingle. She turns the page and contemplates

Billy's face. She closes the book and puts it on the side-table.

'You miss the Wild Man.' She rests her hand on my leg for a moment.

'Billy?'

She nods.

'How do you know?'

'You were together for so long. Just the two of you. And now you don't see him anymore.'

I nod. 'Nobody else gets it.'

'You've been inside another world.' She begins to hum 'Moon River'. We lie down together, and I feel the vibration of her lungs, the song wavering around us, her frail voice only just holding the melody. She's inherited tone-deafness from Granny. I'm crying, silently, listening to my sister singing in the winter afternoon.

November 1984

I'm going to have to repeat a year at school, start again with my A-levels. After that I want to try out for art school. Billy told me I'd be an artist. He'd muttered it into the folds of my clothes, his lips moving against my back; but his voice had been urgent, as if it was essential to tell me there and then, as if he was running out of time. As if him telling me would make it happen.

★   ★   ★

In the kitchen, Dad is talking about buying a new boat in the spring. We can't decide whether we should get a Laser or a Firefly. Dad thinks that the Laser would be better for racing. Band Aid comes on the radio — 'Do They Know It's Christmas?' I turn it up.

My mouth is full of toast and honey when Silver leaps to his feet, hackles up, and begins his deep barking, howling like the Hound of the Baskervilles.

'Someone's at the door,' Dad says. 'Shall I get it?'

I swallow, wiping my mouth. 'No, don't worry.'

I shut the kitchen door behind me, locking Silver in with Dad. I hear muffled barking and Dad shouting 'Shut up!' as I open the front door.

I don't recognise him at first. His hair is light brown, longer. It has a curl to it. He is barefaced without dark eyeliner or powder. He's wearing an old denim jacket, ripped jeans with holes at the knees and a pair of trainers. He smiles. 'Hi. It's been a long time.'

I'm unable to move, except to clasp my hands over my mouth.

Marco puts his head on one side. 'Does that mean you're pleased to see me?' He opens his arms. I hesitate for a moment before stepping inside them. I smell clean clothes and a hint of aftershave. My shoulders are stiff. My front teeth bang against his collarbone.

'You don't look like a goth,' is all I can think of to say.

'And you're thinner.' He holds me at arm's length, looking at me. He hugs me close.

I clear my throat, pushing my hair out of my

eyes, stepping away from him. It feels disloyal to let him hold me, disloyal to Billy. After I've taken him inside and Silver has jumped around, smelling him, and Dad has shaken his hand and said, 'So you're 'M'?' with his eyebrows raised, I take Marco for a walk down to the river wall, because I'm jittery and nervous and I need to be alone with him.

It is grey and cloudy, the wind sweeping in from the sea, blowing gulls high overhead on outstretched wings. The trees are nearly all bare now. Black twig branches scratch the sky with dark fingers. I tuck my coat around me and we walk side by side, not touching. I'd imagined this moment so often in the pagoda, thinking of it as something beautiful, a happy ending, but now it feels awkward and strange.

'The thing about goth music,' he's saying, as if there has been no pause between the last time I saw him and this, 'is that there's no message in it. I'm into music that makes a difference now. Like this whole thing with Band Aid. Bob Geldof has shown that pop music can change things.'

'How did you know I was alive?' I ask, interrupting him. 'Did you read about me in the papers?'

'Sorry.' He shakes his head. 'I'm rambling aren't I? I'm nervous.' He cranes his head to see me. 'Your sister wrote to tell me. I didn't contact you immediately. I was away and I wanted to give you time, you know?' He tightens his grip on my arm. 'It's a big thing, what you've been through. God,' he spits, 'that bastard.'

'It's not that simple, Marco.'

Marco stops and looks at me, frowning. 'What do you mean?'

I turn my back on him, wrapping my arms around myself.

'Did he touch you?' Marco puts his hand on my shoulder. 'All those months together.' He gasps, 'God, what did he do?'

'No.' I shrug Marco's fingers away. 'He didn't touch me and I don't want to talk about it. I'm sick of people thinking they know when they don't.'

'OK,' he sighs, 'I'm sorry. But you can't blame me for thinking it. Don't be like this, Eva. You've been in my head. But after you didn't turn up, I thought you'd changed your mind. Gone off me.'

'Something happened to stop me getting on the bus.' I pause but he doesn't ask me what and I go on quickly. 'Look, it's not that I've changed my mind exactly.' I examine his face; his languid gaze meets my stare and nothing happens inside. No butterflies opening their wings. 'But I've changed, Marco. I'm different.'

'You mean it's over?' He picks at the frayed edges of his jacket.

'I think you've moved on too.' I look at him with eyebrows raised. 'Don't tell me that there haven't been other girls . . . '

'Well, yes, but,' he colours slightly, 'I thought you were . . . that you'd gone.'

'I'm not angry, Marco.' I put my hands in my pockets, hunching my shoulders against the wind. 'I don't blame you. I just think I need time, you know. Like you said, I've been through something big. I'm not ready for a relationship.'

He shrugs. 'Maybe it's just as well. I'm going to be travelling a lot now. With the band and everything.'

We stand together and I feel released. I touch his hand lightly. He's a stranger. We're looking over towards the island. He nods. 'I wrote you a song.'

'Thanks,' I reply, but I'm looking at the shape of the distant landmass, the inky sketches of the pagodas against the sky.

★ ★ ★

Marco left to catch the train back to London. He told me that his band had signed a deal with Island Records. 'Funny,' I said, thinking aloud.

'What?' He frowned, not getting it.

'Nothing.' I thought of Billy crouched over the fishing line, telling me we didn't need music when we had the sea and the wind. I still have his coat. Faith slipped it over my shoulders when we were in Ted's boat. It hangs in my wardrobe, fusty, smelling of him. The tin of letters is in the pocket, and I worry that he must be missing them.

Billy was right. Mum and Dad are my real parents. But I did have another mother, a birth mother, and she was only a little older than me. She died because of me. I try to imagine her long blonde hair and pale skin. Dad said that Suky had somehow known that she was having a girl. She'd been embroidering a blanket for me. He said that he remembered dragons, dragons blowing out flames, spreading wings across blue fabric. I won't contact my uncle. I know that he's the man that Robert had been talking about — the posh bloke with sweat on his lip, fingers trembling on a glass. Whatever he can tell me about my mother will only be his story of her. I'll never know the truth. And perhaps it's enough to believe that she loved me, even though she never saw me, never held me in her arms. There must be something of her in my features, in my voice or mannerisms. When I sign my name now, sometimes I draw a tiny dragon next to it, and it's like a sign between me and her.

54

Clara and Max are in bed together. It's the middle of the afternoon, but they have the house to themselves. Clara won't let him speak; she runs her tongue across his lips, slots her limbs into the spaces left by his, searching for the way they used to be. Her fingers feel for the familiar shallow dip at the base of his throat, hands working across his flesh as if she is sculpting him. She imagines the skeleton weight and density under his skin, the mystery of pale angles opening and closing. He cries out, and she presses her mouth into his neck.

Max rolls over and looks into Clara's face, smoothing the hair back from her forehead. She pulls him close, her arms around his shoulders. They lie, skin against skin, breathing together. Outside, the wind whistles through the bare chestnut tree, stirring the old swing into ghostly movement.

After a while, Clara asks, 'Are you sorry, that you didn't take the new job?'

He shakes his head. 'I would have felt bad about leaving my clients. I feel a loyalty to them. God knows why. None of them pay their bills on time.'

'Or ever.'

They laugh, and Clara rolls on top of him, holding his wrists. There is a struggle, Max pulling her towards him, Clara resisting, before she collapses and slides into the hollow of his shoulder, letting her cheek rest against his chest, breathing in the familiar, potent tang of sex.

'God, I missed you,' he says.

She murmurs an agreement and raises her head to look at him. 'Max,' she says slowly, 'do you think it's doing Eva some good going to see that therapist? She seems more settled somehow, more herself.'

He nods. 'It must be good for her to have someone neutral to talk to. A safe place.'

'I keep wondering . . . how do you think Faith knew about the island?'

Max makes a sound in his throat and she hears it echo inside his ribs, passing into her cheek as a tremor on her skin. 'I don't know.' He shifts his arm under her head. 'Instinct? Telepathy?' He stares at the ceiling, frowning. 'All I know is that I didn't listen to her, take her seriously. And I should have.'

'No. Don't do that,' Clara says quickly. 'Don't feel guilty. It sounded so far-fetched. We did what we thought best.' She rolls over to glance at her watch. 'I'll have to get up in a minute,' she says. 'Got to pick her up from her class.'

'I can get her.'

They both hear it. A distant boom, echoing out in waves, but it's big enough and loud enough to rattle the glass of the window. Clara sits up, her mouth open. Max swings his legs over the side of the bed and strides to the window, the curves and planes of his naked body vulnerable in the winter light.

'Jesus,' he says. 'There's smoke coming from

the island. I think one of those old landmines has detonated.'

With her heart beating fast, Clara scrambles out of bed to stand beside him. A plume of smoke rises from the hulk of the island, spreading black and acrid into the sky. Clara shivers. She reminds herself that she knows where both her girls are, and that they are safe. He slips an arm over her shoulder.

'If anyone was in the middle of that, there won't be much left I'm afraid,' Max says in a low voice.

Clara frowns. 'Maybe it's the military,' she suggests. 'They could be clearing the land.'

They stand in silence for a moment, Clara thinking about Eva, realising that it could have been her stepping onto the shingle with the bomb under it. She doesn't say anything. She is certain that Max is thinking the same thing.

The island is a silhouette against a pale smoke-stained sky. It will always look different to her now that she knows how it concealed her lost child from her. Those months apart from them, when she was held prisoner, have given Eva a new strength, something to fit inside her passion and give it shape. Clara remembers the tiny baby with clenched fists and a big howl. From the moment that Max placed her in her arms, Clara knew that Eva was a survivor. It is Faith that has surprised her with her determination and bravery. Faith's certainty that her sister was on the island is a mystery, something they'll never understand. But people are extraordinary, she thinks, unknowable, as islands are, half-hidden and full of shifting contours. 'I feel so lucky,' she murmurs. 'As if we've all been given a second chance.' And Max squeezes her hand.

They turn away from the window and the view of the island, moving around each other in the way they always have as they collect clothes and slip on shoes. They don't look back at the spreading clouds obscuring the outlines of the pagoda, smoke shapes rising heavily, lifting enormous wings into the sky.

AUTHOR NOTE

I've located this book in Suffolk and some of the places I mention, like Ipswich, are of course real. I've included the myth of The Wild Man of Orford, based on written evidence recorded in the 1100s. When writing about the castle in *Without You*, I was inspired by my childhood memories of Orford Castle. In order to create an island lying just off the Suffolk coast, I used the military history and geographical details of a fascinating spit of land known as Orford Ness. The Ness is a large area of shingle and sand, mudflat and salt marsh, that lies between the river and the North Sea. In 1913 the War Department created airfields there for the Experimental Flying Section. Since then it's been used for top-secret experiments on a range of weapons, with hulking 'pagodas' added in the 1950s to contain the blast from atomic weapons. Because the area was a bombing and rocket range, dangerous debris remains, including unexploded bombs. It is a bleakly beautiful place, with shingle, lichen and grasses making a backdrop to the rolls of rusting wire, crumbling concrete slabs and listing barns left behind by the military — and of course the distinctive and forbidding shapes of the pagodas themselves, visible from miles away. The spit, shrouded in secrecy for most of the twentieth century, was home to German prisoners of war, many of whom died of influenza and were buried in the local graveyard. The spit's contours are ever changing as sand and shingle shifts with the movement of water. Hares, foxes and rabbits run under a huge sweep of open sky. Each winter there are battering winds from the North Sea, and always the cry of the sea birds as they swoop restlessly over shingle and wave. Although I made use of much of this rich material to create the island in *Without You*, the island itself is fictional, as are the caravan site, the village and Holt House.

ACKNOWLEDGEMENTS

A huge thank you to the team at Little, Brown and Piatkus. I count myself very lucky to have Emma Beswetherick as my editor. Thank you so much, Emma, for your continued belief in me. It means more than I can say. Also thanks to Lucy Icke who held my hand through the process of publishing a first novel. And to Eve White, my agent, who has given me friendship, support and advice; and of course to Jack Ram for all his help.

I am grateful to Andrew Warren, late of the Royal Fusiliers, for giving me an insight into the army in Northern Ireland. The Fusiliers completed 37 tours of duty in N.I. — more than any other infantry regiment.

Thank you to Tony Booth for his sharing his in-depth knowledge of popular music with me, in particular the gothic movement.

Thank you Alex Sarginson for putting me right about sailing terminology and boats.

Thanks Kinnetia Isidore for advice about using French.

I am indebted to my first readers who, in some cases, read several drafts — thank you all so much for giving me your time and invaluable feedback: Alex Marengo, Sara Sarre, Karen Jones and Ana Sarginson; and to the post-MA writing group that workshopped sections of the book with me: Viv Graveson, Mary Chamberlain, Cecilia Ekback, Laura McClelland and Lauren Trimble.

Love and thanks to my family and friends, in particular Alex, Hannah and Olivia, Sam and Gabriel for being there.

These books were helpful in my research:

A Long War by Ken Wharton, Helion & Company Ltd (2010)

Love Child by Sue Elliott, Vermillion (2005)

The Baby Laundry for Unmarried Mothers by Angela Patrick with Lynne Barrett-Lee, Simon & Schuster (2012)

We do hope that you have enjoyed reading this large print book.

Did you know that all of our titles are available for purchase?

We publish a wide range of high quality large print books including:
Romances, Mysteries, Classics
General Fiction
Non Fiction and Westerns

Special interest titles available in large print are:
The Little Oxford Dictionary
Music Book
Song Book
Hymn Book
Service Book

Also available from us courtesy of Oxford University Press:
Young Readers' Dictionary
(large print edition)
Young Readers' Thesaurus
(large print edition)

For further information or a free brochure, please contact us at:
Ulverscroft Large Print Books Ltd.,
The Green, Bradgate Road, Anstey,
Leicester, LE7 7FU, England.
Tel: (00 44) 0116 236 4325
Fax: (00 44) 0116 234 0205

Other titles published by Ulverscroft:

THE TWINS

Saskia Sarginson

Isolte and Viola are twins. Inseparable as children, they've grown into very different adults. Isolte is a successful features writer for a fashion magazine with a photographer boyfriend and a flat in London, while Viola is desperately unhappy and struggling with a lifelong eating disorder. What happened all those years ago to set the twins on such different paths to adulthood? As both women start to unravel the escalating tragedies of a half-remembered summer, terrifying secrets from the past come rushing back — and threaten to overwhelm their adult lives . . .

THE BALLOONIST

James Long

Running from a troubled past, Lieutenant Willy Fraser, formerly of the Royal Flying Corps, has chosen the most dangerous job on the Western Front — a balloon observer hanging under a gasbag filled with explosive hydrogen, four thousand feet above the Ypres Salient, anchored by a slender cable. Swept across enemy lines after his balloon is damaged, Willy is hidden by Belgian farmers, whom he grows close to during his stay; with their aid, he manages to escape across the flooded delta at the English Channel and return to his duties. But once he's back in the air, spotting for artillery and under attack, Willy can only focus on his own survival — until he is forced to make an impossible decision that threatens the life of the woman he has come to love.